# DINGHAI FUSHENG RECORDS

**2**

CAROSHA

KARAKORUM/LONGCHENG

Yin Mountains

Huhebashige Peak

CHI LE CHUAN

PYONGYANG

CHANG'AN

XIANGYANG

Longzhong Mountain

MAI CITY

SHANGYU

Yangtze River

JIANGNAN

北

西

東

南

The DIVINE LAND

# DINGHAI FUSHENG RECORDS

## 2

WRITTEN BY

### 非天夜翔
### FEI TIAN YE XIANG
### (ARISE ZHANG)

COVER ILLUSTRATION BY

### XIAOCANG

INTERIOR ILLUSTRATIONS BY

### VIN

TRANSLATED BY

### MOON, ELESTREA, ZRYUU

Seven Seas

*Seven Seas Entertainment*

DINGHAI FUSHENG RECORDS (NOVEL) VOL. 2

Published originally under the title of 《定海浮生錄》 by 非天夜翔 Fei Tian Ye Xiang
Author© 2017 非天夜翔 (Fei Tian Ye Xiang)
This edition arranged with JS Agency
English Translation copyright ©2025 by Seven Seas Entertainment, Inc.
All rights reserved.

Cover by Xiaocang
Interior Illustrations by VIN

Seven Seas press and purchase enquiries can be sent
to Marketing Manager Lauren Hill at press@gomanga.com.
Information regarding the distribution and purchase of digital editions is available
from Digital Operations Manager CK Russell at digital@gomanga.com.

Seven Seas and the Seven Seas logo are trademarks of
Seven Seas Entertainment. All rights reserved.

Follow Seven Seas Entertainment online at
sevenseasentertainment.com.

TRANSLATION: moon, Elestrea, Zryuu
ADAPTATION: Max Machiavelli
LOGO DESIGN: H. Qi
COVER DESIGN: M. A. Lewife
INTERIOR DESIGN: Clay Gardner
INTERIOR LAYOUT: Karis Page
COPY EDITOR: Jack Hamm
PROOFREADER: H. Lou, Pengie
EDITOR: Harry Catlin
PREPRESS TECHNICIAN: Salvador Chan Jr., April Malig, Jules Valera
MANAGING EDITOR: Alyssa Scavetta
EDITOR-IN-CHIEF: Julie Davis
PUBLISHER: Lianne Sentar
VICE PRESIDENT: Adam Arnold
PRESIDENT: Jason DeAngelis

ISBN: 979-8-89373-414-0
Printed in Canada
First Printing: August 2025
10 9 8 7 6 5 4 3 2 1

# DINGHAI FUSHENG RECORDS

## 27

ON THE ENDLESS, barren plains outside of Tongguan County, some six thousand people were spending the night out in the open.

A gust of wind blew by. It was early summer, but the night still held a hint of spring chill; it went unnoticed by the people from the Sixteen Hu, though, who had already nodded off in the cradle of the surrounding rivers and distant mountains. Under the moonlight, those mountains cast a curtain of shadows over them all. The plains echoed with the howls of wolves, and the Big Dipper hung low in the night sky. The starry river above created a brilliantly shimmering backdrop to the summer night, like drops of light splattered across a black canvas.

On the ground, Chen Xing was lost in thought, bundled up in a blanket and staring into the campfire. Xiang Shu had been silent since they left Epang Palace. None of his subordinates dared to disturb him, Chen Xing, or Feng Qianjun. They left the three of them sitting quietly by themselves and started a bonfire under the lone tree in the wilderness. In doing so, they made it even less likely that anyone would try to cozy up to Xiang Shu.

Feng Qianjun lifted the cloth that covered the corpse, revealing the stooped body of his elder brother, Feng Qianyi. Feng Qianyi's legs had been amputated below the knee, and his years of using a wheelchair had weakened his lower limbs, giving him a childlike stature. On the banks of the Tong River, Feng Qianjun stacked up a pile of firewood and set fire to his brother's corpse.

As the fire blazed brightly and swallowed Feng Qianyi's body, another gust of wind blew past, catching the ashes and scattering them into the sky. Chen Xing noticed a faint wisp of light that rose with the ashes and flew toward that starry river above. Following his gaze, Xiang Shu saw a second expansive, dazzling band of light set against the brilliance of the galaxy above. It looked like a massive river flowing across the night sky.

"Do you see it?" Chen Xing asked. When Xiang Shu frowned slightly, he went on, "The divine veins. The final destination of all dao in the world. Laozi said that that which is spiritual, existing above the tangible, is called the dao. That which is tangible is called the vessel. All things that live in the human world will one day leave their vessels, their physical forms, and return to the Great Dao."

"Is that the Spiritual Qi of the Heavens and Earth?" Xiang Shu asked.

"No. The divine veins and earth veins are higher-level streams than spiritual qi."

Feng Qianjun returned to Chen Xing and Xiang Shu with the box he'd gathered his brother's ashes into and a small jade plaque. He wiped the plaque clean and turned it over, studying it under the light of the fire. A few words were carved on it: Great Han Exorcist Feng.

"The Xifeng Bank's largest stronghold was in Luoyang," he said. "When my dage took over the family business from our father, I was learning how to keep the accounts. From the time I was seven until the year I turned sixteen, I only saw my dage once every two to three years."

Still wrapped in his blanket, Chen Xing kept silent. He knew that this was the kind of situation where Feng Qianjun needed to talk to relieve the distress he was feeling.

"Back then," Feng Qianjun continued, "Luoyang was still under the Yan State established by the Murong clan."

The Xifeng Bank had established itself in Luoyang, a capital city of great renown, with the wealth to rival an entire nation. The bank maintained secret connections to the Jin State in the south, though, awaiting an opportunity to welcome the Jin army in to recover the country they'd lost. Later, Fu Jian sent people to conquer the Great Yan, and the city fell in the span of a single night. Every member of the imperial Murong clan was taken prisoner, and in the end, the clan surrendered to Fu Jian.

During this battle, Feng Qianyi had fled with his family. Unfortunately, it was a time of great turmoil. His family's soldiers died in battle, his wife was killed by enemy soldiers, and he lost both of his children. And to add insult to injury, a war chariot ran him over and crushed both of his legs.

When Feng Qianjun received this grievous news, he immediately headed north to find his older brother. It took several years, but he finally found Feng Qianyi in Chang'an. When they reunited, Feng Qianyi had not spoken much of the past; he'd dismissively told Feng Qianjun that such things simply had to be endured on the path to greatness. The Great Yan had fallen, so their new target was to be Fu Jian. They could also try to cozy up to the Murong clan, the scions of a fallen nation, and use them as necessary.

"I still remember the day I first met Qinghe," Feng Qianjun said, sounding dazed. "She and her younger brother, Murong Chong, had been confined deep in the palace. Gege sent me to deliver her some jewelry we'd bought. Murong Chong didn't like to talk, but Princess Qinghe was elated, and she asked me what my name was... She wanted to know if Luoyang's peonies had bloomed, and she had a lot of questions about the goings-on in the north."

Feng Qianjun came back to himself and forced a smile for Chen Xing. "After the demise of the Great Yan, I hadn't returned to Luoyang for three years, so I had to come up with some lies," he said. "When I went home and told Dage, he said, 'Luoyang, Guanzhong, Youzhou, Yongzhou—these places all belong to us Han. What right do the Xianbei people have to claim Luoyang as their home?'"

At this point in the conversation, Xiang Shu got up and left to give the two Han men some privacy.

Feng Qianjun smiled helplessly. "But it was a Han who destroyed the Great Yan's Murong clan. Under Fu Jian's orders, Wang Meng won the war and plunged the people of the four passes into misery. The Murong clan despises Wang Meng for taking a position as Fu Jian's official. Tianchi, do you hate them?"

Chen Xing thought of his father's death. He looked off into the distance at Xiang Shu, who was sitting on the ground, leaning on a piece of rock.

Slowly, he said, "Before he died, my father said that it doesn't matter if you're Hu or Han; we're all residents of the same vast Divine Land. When the Five Hu moved south, many people ended up dead or wounded, and many innocent people died in the war. But was that not also what happened during the Jin Dynasty's War of the Eight Princes? The aristocratic Han who fled south wanted revenge, but what about the soldiers and civilians who died during the mayhem of the Eight Princes? Who were they supposed to ask for a reason for their deaths?" He sighed. "Ultimately, the problem is war. War needs to end. And if we can't get to the root of this drought fiend chaos, there will be a massive outbreak, and neither the Hu nor the Han will be able to continue fighting. They'll all meet the same fate. Death."

Feng Qianjun was silent for a moment. He looked down at the Saber of Harmony and Life, hefting it in his hand. "Do you plan to head north with the Great Chanyu?"

"I don't know," said Chen Xing, worry bleeding into his voice. "Time's running out, but I still don't have a clue what caused the Silence of All Magic. At the very least, I have to find the lost mana in the next three years. After that, even if I washed my hands of all of it, there will still be other people out there who can fight the 'master' Feng Qianyi was talking about. We definitely aren't the only two exorcists left in this world. There must be others who inherited that legacy..."

Chen Xing had his first clue: the Dinghai Pearl. He still wasn't sure what the truth was, but the records stated that in the year following the Silence of All Magic, the Dinghai Pearl had still had a vast amount of power stored within it. It had to be related to the Silence of All Magic somehow.

Unfortunately, the world was vast. Where was he supposed to look for it?

"Leave investigating the drought fiends to me," said Feng Qianjun. "I'll set out first thing tomorrow morning."

"Where are you going?"

"I might sneak back into Chang'an. I could also make a trip to Luoyang or go searching for the tombs of the Eight Princes... In any case, I will investigate the people my dage worked with before he died and figure out how he obtained the secret to controlling resentment. You should focus on searching for your Dinghai Pearl."

"Feng-dage, this isn't something that should be rushed."

"I can basically control the Saber of Harmony and Life," Feng Qianjun added, musing aloud, "albeit in a different way."

It had been news to Chen Xing that an artifact once powered by the Spiritual Qi of the Heavens and Earth could also absorb resentment and be used that way. It was as if fate was saying that darkness should counter darkness. The thorns surrounding them, the black vines and withered tree yao, had been quite powerful; by calling upon the ancient art of harmony and life, Feng Qianjun had awoken the forests and led them to victory.

Using the saber this way had also transformed Feng Qianjun. He had become a dark exorcist. If he repeatedly drew resentment to himself to activate the Saber of Harmony and Life, it would take a great toll on his body. Chen Xing reminded Feng Qianjun of this again, but Feng Qianjun said, "Don't worry. If there's no resentment, I won't be able to call upon it."

That was true. To wield the Saber of Harmony and Life and summon those withered tree yao and bloodthirsty vines, Feng Qianjun had to be in a place where resentment was abundant. If he wasn't in a region where lots of people had died, he would have no way to activate the saber.

"Give me a bit more time," said Chen Xing. "Let me think this through."

Seeing that Chen Xing would not be convinced so readily, Feng Qianjun nodded and gestured for him to rest. Chen Xing wanted to just sleep under the tree, but Feng Qianjun nudged him and gestured to Xiang Shu. Taking his hint, Chen Xing went over to Xiang Shu.

Xiang Shu's eyes were shut, and he didn't say a word as Chen Xing approached. When a crow cawed hoarsely above them, however, he startled awake. Chen Xing watched curiously as Xiang Shu looked up with a hint of fear and panic in his eyes, but he quickly recovered his composure when he saw a flock of crows flying overhead.

"I have to go find the Dinghai Pearl," Chen Xing whispered, "but all the records we took out of the Yin Yang Mirror are gone."

"I know the place they mentioned," Xiang Shu said. "Come with me."

Chen Xing was taken aback. The map on the last page had had the word "lake" written on it. Chen Xing had come up with lots of guesses as to what that might refer to—maybe it was Yunmeng Lake? But that place only existed in legends, and no one knew its exact location. "Is it in the south?" he asked.

Xiang Shu didn't answer him at first. He moved aside a little to make space for Chen Xing. "Let's go back to Chi Le Chuan first," he said when Chen Xing joined him. "There are a lot of things that require the support of the tribes."

Chen Xing did some quick calculations. When he left Mount Hua, he'd still had four years left. Now, summer was dawning over the Divine Land, which meant he was down to three years; he was short on time. He just nodded, though, deciding not to hurry Xiang Shu.

Late that night, in the silence of the plains, Xiang Shu suddenly opened his eyes and looked out into the distance. Feng Qianjun had already gotten up from under the tree. With his older brother's ashes, he mounted his horse and wound around the periphery of their temporary campsite. When he saw Xiang Shu awake, he raised his hand in farewell.

Xiang Shu shut his eyes again, and Feng Qianjun slipped away into the darkness.

It was the zi hour, and Huanmo Palace was filled with a blood-red light. A heart the size of a house hung suspended in midair, slowly bobbing up and down. Countless blood vessels wound around that strange, immense heart, creating a web of veins that spread to all corners of the phantasmal palace. Thousands of blood vessels burrowed into the walls, where they drew resentment from the earth itself as nourishment. They converted the brilliant glow of the earth vein into an endless stream of purple-black energy, then injected that energy into the heart.

A masked scholar in a black robe walked slowly into the palace, carrying Princess Qinghe's corpse bridal-style. As the scholar approached, the heart itself spoke in a hoarse voice. "This mortal was resistant to my control."

"Feng Qianyi was too eager for revenge," the scholar replied, "and the wielder of the Heart Lamp broke his array. Our plans were disrupted."

"Foolishness!" The heart's voice was furious. "You have utterly wasted the elite demonic troops you were given!"

Placatingly, the scholar said, "Feng Qianyi has been burned to ash, so that can be considered his punishment. My lord, please, quell your rage. There will always be humans to use. There are still hundreds of thousands of nomads in the Ancient Chi Le Covenant, more than enough to fill this gap. But that Shulü Kong..." He fell silent for a moment. "The greatest warrior outside the pass... Even if he was chosen as the exorcist's protector, that does not explain his preposterous strength. Very strange. And why did the Heart Lamp choose him?"

"He is but a mortal. He has limits, no matter how strong he is. Why do you fear him?"

"My lord may not know this," the scholar said in a respectful tone, "but despite the limited number of people who live as part of the Chi Le Covenant, they remain a force that we must not underestimate. If they were easily overcome, we would not have gone to so much trouble. Capturing Shulü Kong and instrumentalizing him would save us a great deal of trouble."

"Do not concern yourself with that right now," came the hoarse voice of the heart. "How should the Ten Thousand Spirits Array be dealt with? After so many years lying in wait, it would be a pity to let all our efforts go to waste over this one accident. Counting Zhou Yi, the exorcist has already managed to kill two of your subordinates!"

"Now that Fu Jian has single-handedly ruined the Great Wall and banished Shulü Kong, Chang'an poses no immediate threat," said the scholar. "We are still hidden. Chen Xing has fled beyond the pass with Shulü Kong, so it will presumably be some time before he returns to the Central Plains. I shall send Zhou Zhen to deal with them and ensure they pose no further threat to our lord's resurrection. And of course, with the Silence of All Magic, only the Heart Lamp can cause any sort of a stir. Even if we left them be, they could not accomplish much. My lord..." The scholar set Princess Qinghe's body on the altar situated right below the massive heart. "Please grant this woman a new life. She is the crux of the Ten Thousand Spirits Array in Chang'an."

The heart let out a cold laugh. A congealed drop of blood trickled languidly down its membrane and landed with a soft plop on Princess Qinghe's corpse, which took on a reddish glow as resentment curled around it.

As summer gave way to fall, the Sixteen Hu, led by Xiang Shu, left the Great Wall behind and entered the sea of grass, which stretched for miles around them in all directions. Chen Xing had never seen such an extensive and majestic grassland, and he found this northern side of the Divine Land imposing to behold. With the sky arching far above them, the sprawling land before them, and flocks of birds circling overhead, it was a far cry from the prosperous cities within the pass.

On their journey north, more and more families had joined them. The Qiang and Di tribes had lived in Guanlong for a long time, but they hadn't received any preferential treatment; like the other tribes, they'd been sent out on expeditions with long, drawn-out battles, and they were taxed heavily if they requested reinforcements. After years of severe droughts, the people no longer had any way to make a living, and they had to give up the lands they farmed. They decided to follow the Great Chanyu north to seek a new means of supporting themselves.

By this point, the procession was made up of more than ten thousand people. It was a magnificent thing to behold. Xiang Shu and his troops procured some carriages and purchased all the necessities on the way. When they passed through the Great Wall, the Qin generals dared not try to stop them; they just opened the gates and let the procession through. As they left the Great Wall behind and entered the grasslands, eventually they formed a convoy headed toward the ends of the earth: Chi Le Chuan.

Chen Xing had asked Xiang Shu's entourage what kind of place Chi Le Chuan was, and they had told him that it was the northernmost region of the Divine Land—the last habitable region. North of it lay a vast tundra; endless snowfields buffeted by harsh winds and snowstorms. It was a barren wasteland. Very few people who ventured out there ever returned.

The major branches of the Five Hu who lived within the pass originated from areas like Mount Paektu, the Xing'an Mountains, and Xiliang. They formed the Ancient Chi Le Covenant at Chi Le Chuan. Chi Le Chuan was where the Xiongnu and Tiele peoples came from, and it was the shared homeland of all the peoples that the Han dubbed "Hu."

The landscape before Chen Xing was just like the lyrics in the song: *Chi Le Chuan, under the Yin Mountains; the sky is like an arched yurt covering the plain whole.*[1]

"The people living there are mainly nomads, and there are very few doctors," Xiang Shu said. "We should acquire some medicines of the Central Plains along the way to take back to Chi Le Chuan." Chen Xing wrote out a list of medications, which Xiang Shu's subordinates purchased.

Chen Xing had some spare time now, and he sat in the carriage and watched Xiang Shu write and draw on a piece of parchment. Feng Qianjun's sudden departure worried him, but a more urgent matter was at hand: finding the whereabouts of the Dinghai Pearl as soon as possible. Returning mana to the Divine Land would halve Chen Xing's heavy burden. He was confident that one day, not too far in the future, the ancient profession of the exorcists would recover enough to gather a tremendous force. Then they could fight the mastermind behind Feng Qianyi, and the drought fiends that mastermind had created.

For now, he just hoped that Fu Jian would rein in his resentment a little and lay off the large-scale massacres.

"I really have no clue where the lake mentioned in the books is," Chen Xing mused aloud.

Xiang Shu's fore and middle fingers were hooked gently around a stick of charcoal. The way he held a writing implement was different from how a Han would, but his slender fingers made it look elegant. On a piece of parchment paper, he sketched an outline of

---

1   This is an ancient folk song called the "Song of Chi Le" (敕勒歌).

meandering mountains and rivers. A terrain took form under his fingers.

"Oh!" Chen Xing exclaimed.

From the single glance he'd taken at it, Xiang Shu had managed to memorize the map on the last page of the ancient book in the Exorcism Department. Now he showed his recreation to Chen Xing. "Here?" he asked.

The map showed a lake that lay before three disconnected peaks, which rose into the clouds. The lakeside was generously studded with forests. What a strange topography; there were lakes on the plain and mountains by the lake. The map was annotated in the Tiele language.

"Yes, yes, yes!" Chen Xing felt like he had just obtained a great treasure. He took the map from Xiang Shu. "You actually remembered it all!"

"It's not Yunmeng Lake, and it's not in the south," Xiang Shu explained. "Legend has it that it's north of Chi Le Chuan—far, far north. Its Tiele name is Erchilun, and it's called Carosha in the Xiongnu language. The name refers to the place where the dragon fell to its death."

"You've been there?" Chen Xing asked, surprised.

"I saw it in a book an old man gave me when I was a kid."

Chen Xing looked down at the map, then up again at Xiang Shu, who had picked up a new piece of parchment as he thought back to what he saw on the book's second to last page. "You guys have books too? Where are your ancient records stored?"

"Why?" Xiang Shu asked coldly. "Are you Han the only ones worthy of reading and writing?"

That wasn't what Chen Xing had meant, and he quickly explained as much. He'd only wanted to take a look, thinking perhaps he could find clues in the place where the Chi Le Covenant stored their ancient texts.

The carriage forged ahead through the grasslands. Off in the distance, the vague outline of a mountain range shrouded in mist appeared on the horizon—the moment it came into view, everyone in the procession cheered. Chen Xing looked up. They rounded the hillside to find a great number of tents set up across the sweeping plain, against a backdrop of mountains and rivers. An end-of-summer wind began to blow, and Chen Xing felt as if a striking picture scroll was slowly unfurling before his eyes.

They had arrived in Chi Le Chuan.

The scene before him was stunning. Under the shadow of the Yin Mountains and in the gentle embrace of the Kundulun and Dahei Rivers, the grasslands stretched for thousands of miles, like a rug upon which nearly two hundred thousand herders made their living. Innumerable tents dotted the land, stretching from the hillside all the way to the foot of the mountains! At the start of autumn, almost all the nomads outside the pass migrated to the Yin Mountains, which were sacred to the Sixteen Hu, to worship the range with the Ancient Chi Le Covenant.

A child spotted the convoy from the bank of Kudulun River and shouted, "The Great Chanyu is back!"

A beautiful woman who had been washing clothes by the river stood up and started to sing in a resounding voice. The warriors in the convoy responded with a hearty song of their own. Xiang Shu remained seated in the open-air carriage, but he stowed the sheepskin parchment away. His long legs dangled off the edge of the carriage as he adjusted his posture, shifting so he was half lying down.

Thousands of galloping horses rushed out from the Ancient Chi Le Covenant, heading toward them, with several young men in the lead. The Xiongnu and Tiele peoples shouted loudly, but Xiang Shu ignored them. In an instant, the group of young men gathered around the convoy, all talking at once. Smiling and laughing, they hounded Xiang Shu with questions. Chen Xing listened blankly, unfamiliar with the languages they used, but from the looks on their faces, he guessed that they were badgering Xiang Shu about where he had been.

The corners of Xiang Shu's mouth curved up in a slight smile— a rare sight. Eventually, the rest of the convoy following behind the young men kicked up a fuss, so the young men turned back to help with unloading things and settling the caravan in.

One young man said something in the Xiongnu language, and, holding out a wooden rod, moved to enter the open-air carriage and strike Chen Xing. Chen Xing quickly dodged, frowning. He thought that the guy must have been saying something along the lines of "What, you even brought a Han back with you?"

"Get lost!" Xiang Shu finally said in the Tiele language. The young man burst out laughing and galloped away on his horse.

People kept trying to get close, as if to ask Xiang Shu for favors. When they did, Xiang Shu either didn't answer them or just acknowledged them with a lazy "mhm." In the end, the people who'd come to meet them led the Hu from the convoy away to settle them in. Those who'd joined the convoy to move north seemed as excited as if they'd found long-lost relatives. Evidently, they were experiencing the kind of comfort and freedom that came from returning home.

"Seems like they haven't been living very comfortably since they entered the pass," Chen Xing said. Compared to life in Chang'an City, where they had to follow Fu Jian's rules, study to become officials, and achieve official ranks, these Hu obviously preferred the freedom of life on the grassland. It was carved into their bones.

Xiang Shu didn't respond. More and more people left the convoy, until only the two of them remained. Their two carriages went on to the foot of the mountains east of the Ancient Covenant, into one of the valleys. There were very few people living there. When they saw Xiang Shu, they all cheered.

The carriage stopped right in front of the biggest tent. Xiang Shu jumped off the carriage, and a thought suddenly occurred to Chen Xing: Xiang Shu was the Great Chanyu and had long since reached a marriageable age. Did that mean he had a wife and children at home? But there were few people in the valley, and the royal tent in which Xiang Shu lived was very quiet. It stood at the foot of a mountain, where the source of a stream lay; the location was obviously venerated.

A lot of people came over to greet Xiang Shu. Xiang Shu replied to them in the Tiele language, and they dispersed. Chen Xing looked around curiously. "Is this your home?" he asked.

"I need to gather the elders for a meeting," said Xiang Shu. "Go do whatever you want." Then he said something to the other people, presumably asking them to help Chen Xing settle in.

Someone led a horse over. Xiang Shu mounted it easily and galloped out of the valley.

"Hey, wait!" protested Chen Xing. "I don't understand your language!"

After Xiang Shu left, a good number of young Tiele men approached Chen Xing and studied him curiously, then began to discuss something among themselves. The corners of Chen Xing's mouth twitched with frustration, but all he could do was nod politely.

Someone threw a wet cloth at him, and Chen Xing hurried to thank him. He used it to wipe his face, thinking, *So beyond the Great Wall, they receive guests by getting them to wash their faces.*

The crowd muttered a bit more, then burst out laughing. Someone pointed Chen Xing to the tent. "Okay," he said, "I'll go rest now. Please don't trouble yourselves."

Chen Xing lifted the flap and entered Xiang Shu's home. He saw a huge blue embroidered rug spread out on the floor and lots of other furnishings around the tent. Bedding, tableware, short tables—it had everything you could ask for. There were even screens that had been transported from the south, and a bookshelf in the corner filled with pictorial books and ancient texts of the various tribes. The lighting was excellent as well; there were snow-proof windows at the top of the tent, and the light that streamed through illuminated the inside brightly.

Its master had been away from home for so long, however, that everything was covered in dust.

The young Tiele man brought a bucket of water inside. He pointed at the table, then patted Chen Xing's shoulder. "Start now," he said in the Xianbei language. "Make sure you wipe everything well. Finish cleaning up the royal tent before the Great Chanyu returns."

Chen Xing looked at the cloth in his hand, then back at the gathered group. He smiled. In his politest voice, he said in the Han language, "Fuck you."

# 28

I N THE CHI LE CHUAN region, nomadic settlements spanned vast areas, comparable in size to large cities within the pass like Ye City or Jinyang. These areas were organized according to tribal affiliations, with the Tiele tribe residing in the east. The Great Chanyu's residence was nestled between mountains, facing the settlement, which had no city walls. Many nomads traveled here with their families to spend a brief summer before joining the Ancient Covenant to prepare for the long winter ahead.

Chen Xing found the place beautiful. Even amid the bustle, there was a sense of peace, and the scenery was stunning. From halfway up the mountain at the back, there was a panoramic view of the plain. Xiang Shu's clansmen were relaxed and lively—they rode horses, played ball games, and idled away their time jovially as they waited for winter.

*But why should I, your honored guest who came from afar, clean your room for you?! I'm not a servant!* Chen Xing really wanted to throw the cloth onto the floor in frustration, but his curiosity got the better of him as he took in his surroundings.

Xiang Shu's living quarters didn't seem like those of a man with a wife and children, but it was clear that someone else had once lived there with him. Chen Xing, who'd grown up with his master, found the environment quite familiar. Xiang Shu might have lived with his father during his youth, and his mother had likely lived here even before that.

Chen Xing gave the bookshelf a cursory wipe down and flipped through the books on it. He barely recognized any of the words, but the illustrations, for the most part, he understood well enough. Most were related to martial arts, horsemanship, and archery, and a few others contained records of weapons or explanations of veins and acupoints written by outsiders. There were also numerous name registers and a map of the land beyond the Great Wall.

As the sun set in the west, he heard sounds of singing and dancing outside. Then Xiang Shu returned.

"What are you doing?" Xiang Shu yelled. "Don't touch my things!"

Chen Xing barely restrained himself from throwing the rag at Xiang Shu. "What do you think I'm doing? Is it a rule here that guests have to clean your rooms?!"

Xiang Shu was taken aback, but he smiled. His mood truly had improved upon his return to the Chi Le Covenant. Chen Xing had never seen Xiang Shu smile before; it made him even more handsome. His cold, aloof aura vanished when he smiled, replaced by a warmth even more mellow and pleasant than Tuoba Yan's.

But the smile vanished as quickly as it had appeared. "It's time for dinner," Xiang Shu said. "Follow me."

That night, the Tiele tribe was holding a grand celebration. Bonfires were lit across Chi Le Chuan to mark the return of the Great Chanyu. They drank wine, roasted fish, and feasted on meat under the mountain range, and their singing echoed through the night sky. Chen Xing sat next to Xiang Shu, and a subordinate presented him with a roasted leg of lamb and a silver knife. Chen Xing's appetite was stirred; he sliced off a piece of meat and was about to eat it when he was suddenly chided by those around him.

Chen Xing looked around, confused. The crowd berated Chen Xing and gestured for him to serve the Great Chanyu instead. Chen Xing's grip tightened around the knife. He really wanted to stab Xiang Shu to death.

"They said you're not being respectful," Xiang Shu said indifferently. He explained the situation to the onlookers, who gradually returned to their seats. Chen Xing had no choice but to slice the meat and serve it to Xiang Shu; after a few bites, Xiang Shu raised his hand and said, "Help yourselves."

With that, everyone began to enjoy their dinner. Not long thereafter, a woman helped an elderly man into the gathering; he was likely an elder of one of the tribes. He took his seat and exchanged greetings with several of the older individuals Xiang Shu had brought back from Chang'an, engaging in some casual conversation. Xiang Shu did not interrupt, choosing instead to sip his wine and occasionally glance at Chen Xing. Chen Xing ate his roasted lamb and observed the expressions of those around him—they were probably speaking ill of Fu Jian, as his name came up quite often.

Xiang Shu placed an empty cup next to him for Chen Xing to pour more wine.

"Are you planning to storm the pass, overthrow Fu Jian, and seize his place as emperor?" Chen Xing asked him.

"It depends on my mood," Xiang Shu replied, sounding not in the least bit concerned.

Chen Xing didn't know quite what to say to that. He filled Xiang Shu's cup with wine. "What about your promise to take me to that one mountain to look for the Dinghai Pearl? You said you would."

"Be patient."

"You're not lying to me, are you?" Chen Xing knew it was impertinent of him to urge Xiang Shu to act on his first day back home, but he couldn't help himself.

Xiang Shu looked at Chen Xing incredulously, as if to say, *Do you really think I'm that kind of person?* "If you don't believe me, then get lost!" he snapped.

His raised voice drew everyone's attention, and the tent fell silent. Hastily, Chen Xing tried to defuse the situation. "Calm down, calm down—it was just a slip of the tongue. Here, Great Chanyu, let me give you a toast!"

Fearing trouble from the gathered tribespeople, he hurriedly filled his own cup with wine and smiled as he attempted to toast to everyone. He wanted to show that they were not at odds. But before he could react, Xiang Shu grabbed his head with one hand, held the wine bowl with the other, and forced the wine down his throat.

Chen Xing spluttered. The attendees had only heard them speaking to one another in the Han language; they couldn't make sense of the situation, and they soon returned to their conversations. Choking and furious, Chen Xing managed, "You...!"

Xiang Shu ignored Chen Xing and turned to the others, speaking in the Xianbei language. "When will the Akele tribe arrive?"

"Great Chanyu," someone replied respectfully in the same language, "based on past evidence, they will reach Chi Le Chuan before the third of the tenth lunar month."

Somehow, suddenly, Chen Xing was finding the wine quite pleasant! It was sweet and didn't burn his throat. He poured some more and drank it with increasing enthusiasm.

"The Akele tribe is a branch of the Xiongnu, operating far to the north," Xiang Shu told Chen Xing. "They know the exact location of Mount Erchilun better than I do."

It was the fifteenth day of the ninth month, so it would be manageable to wait until the third of the tenth lunar month. Still sipping his wine, Chen Xing said, "If you're too busy, just draw me a map, and I'll go on my own."

Xiang Shu gave him a mocking look. "Do you know what it's like up north during winter?"

"If it comes to it, I'll just wear a few more layers—"

A guard nearby spoke up, also in Xianbei. "Wait for Che Luofeng to return; he might bring news about the Akele tribe."

"Che Luofeng is my anda,"[2] Xiang Shu said, not looking at Chen Xing but staring vacantly at the bonfire. "We grew up together. He left Chi Le Chuan to hunt in the north; he's traveled quite far this time, but I can ask him when he returns."

Chen Xing was eating a lot of salty roast lamb, which made him very thirsty. He lost track of how many bowls of wine he had consumed. The wine was sweet, brewed from honey and goat's milk, and it made him want more and more. His head started to spin, and eventually, it dropped right onto the table. He passed out, utterly intoxicated.

Xiang Shu glanced at him, speechless. A guard across from him exclaimed in surprise, "He drank an entire vat! Impressive!"

Chen Xing was still drunk when he woke up in the middle of the night, feeling thirsty. A blanket was draped over him, and he had the impression that Xiang Shu had carried him back to the tent. Singing and drunken laughter still echoed from outside.

"Water," he mumbled.

Xiang Shu gave him water from a flask. Chen Xing drank, then turned over and fell back to sleep.

---

2   "Anda" means "sworn brother."

Early the next morning, he woke to the pale light of dawn. The revelry in Chi Le Chuan had quieted down, and everyone was sound asleep. Chen Xing scratched himself, sat up, and said, "Xiang Shu, I want to take a bath..."

"What?" Xiang Shu had been disturbed by Chen Xing all night. He sat up in his unlined garment and looked at Chen Xing irritably.

"I want to take a bath. Where can I find some hot water?"

"Wash yourself in the river."

"I'll catch a cold. I want a hot bath."

"You don't want a hot bath," Xiang Shu said firmly. "If you keep insisting, I'll throw you into the river."

There was nothing Chen Xing could say to that.

Xiang Shu didn't fully wake up again until the sun was well into the sky. When he did, though, he took Chen Xing to a nearby stream for a bath.

"It's so cold!" Chen Xing cried out as soon as he stepped into the water, but Xiang Shu, uncaring and grumpy, just stripped off his clothes and entered the stream. Chen Xing had seen his unclothed body many times before, and they had even bathed together when they first arrived in Chang'an, but today, for some reason, his face flushed with embarrassment.

Xiang Shu's physique was striking—slim yet ruggedly masculine. His skin was fair and smooth, with no sign of the Tiele people's roughness, and the contours of his back and long legs were particularly captivating.

"Wash my back!" he demanded. "What are you staring at?"

"Why should I?" said Chen Xing. "I'm not your servant! I've had enough of this! Xiang Shu, if you keep treating me like a servant, I'll—"

"You'll what? What are you going to do?"

"Do you all look down on the Han people? I finally understand now. When they asked who I was, you called me your servant, didn't you? You never had good intentions; you just brought me to your tribe to serve you!"

"And what of it?" Xiang Shu retorted. "Do you expect the Great Chanyu to serve you?"

"You're a protector!" Chen Xing shot back.

"Fuck off! Just wipe my back!"

Chen Xing held up the cloth. Xiang Shu reached out to grab him, but Chen Xing quickly dodged—and, in his haste, slipped and nearly fell into the water. Xiang Shu caught his arm and hauled him upright, leaving Chen Xing no choice but to angrily wash Xiang Shu's back.

"If you had the strength to show them," said Xiang Shu coolly, "no one would dare treat you like a servant."

"Fine. But even if you aren't a protector, is this how you treat all your guests?"

"You're not a guest," Xiang Shu replied, studying Chen Xing's bare form. He was about to add *You followed me of your own volition*, but his breath caught for a moment, and he turned away.

"Don't underestimate me," Chen Xing warned him. Avoiding Chen Xing's gaze, Xiang Shu turned his head and raised an eyebrow: *Do as you please.*

Chen Xing hurriedly finished his bath, got dressed, and returned to the tent. Xiang Shu followed him in just his underclothes and made no attempt to avoid anyone. He entertained guests over breakfast in his tent. Many people came and went, some paying their respects to their sovereign, others offering greetings, and still others discussing important matters. Though Xiang Shu was dressed entirely in white, with his wet hair draped loosely over his shoulders, it did nothing to diminish his regal presence.

"How do you write 'sick' and 'see a doctor' in the Tiele language?" Chen Xing asked after breakfast, sneezing as he did. Tired of serving Xiang Shu, he turned to the young man who had spoken Xianbei earlier. The man looked puzzled but wrote the words on the ground for him. "And how do you say 'doctor'?"

Once he'd learned the words, Chen Xing went outside, found a plank, wrote them down, and hung the plank outside Xiang Shu's tent. Xiang Shu seemed unimpressed.

That afternoon, someone came seeking medical help. Half of Xiang Shu's tent was used for hosting guests, while Chen Xing had turned the other half into a makeshift clinic. A Tiele man entered and glanced around, and Chen Xing pulled over a small table, sat down, and gestured for the man to come in. He took the man's pulse and began to assess his condition.

"Do you speak Xianbei?" Chen Xing asked, pressing a wooden stick against the patient's tongue. "What's wrong with you?"

The man responded with a stream of incomprehensible words, leaving Chen Xing utterly confused. Eventually, Xiang Shu had to thank his remaining guests for coming and dismiss them. When they were gone, he turned and said, "His stomach hurts."

"Help me translate," said Chen Xing. "What are you just sitting there for?"

Xiang Shu stared at Chen Xing in disbelief. "Where do you get the nerve?"

"He's one of your clansmen! Ask him what he's eaten recently and how long his stomach has been hurting."

Suppressing his irritation, Xiang Shu translated. Chen Xing quickly diagnosed the patient's condition and prescribed some medicine. He had Xiang Shu write down the necessary ingredients in the Tiele language with a charcoal brush to help the man find them.

Xiang Shu hadn't expected to spend his entire afternoon being bossed around by Chen Xing, but as the only person in Chi Le Chuan who really understood the Han language, he couldn't just abandon his ailing clansmen. Translating was one thing, but no one else would have known what the Han medicinal herbs were, so the Great Chanyu was stuck sitting around and playing assistant to Chen Xing.

"Can't you set up shop somewhere else?" he asked Chen Xing once there was a lull in patients.

"No. If more patients showed up, I'd never be able to close shop. You're the Great Chanyu—they wouldn't dare bother you at night."

"You..." Xiang Shu was tempted to hit Chen Xing, but just then, another patient arrived. In Chi Le Chuan, whether they were Tiele, Xiongnu, or from any of the Sixteen Hu, everyone considered Xiang Shu their kin and regarded him as their guardian. Xiang Shu couldn't bear to see his people suffering. The doctor of the plains only visited every few months, and he lacked a permanent residence and traveled extensively to treat people. When people fell ill, they often had to endure or resign themselves to fate until the doctor arrived, and then the doctor typically only performed bloodletting anyway. Chen Xing's presence was undeniably a significant benefit to the Ancient Chi Le Covenant.

In a matter of days, the valley was packed with people waiting to see Chen Xing. Xiang Shu's royal tent became so crowded that not even a drop of water could have passed through. Each day, he did nothing but sit next to Chen Xing and help him with communicating with patients in the various Hu languages.

As another day passed, the patients who had seen Chen Xing showed noticeable improvement in their colds or fevers.

His reputation as a "divine doctor" spread like wildfire, drawing most of the sick people in Chi Le Chuan to the Tiele settlement. Eventually, Xiang Shu had to move his royal tent to the open space outside the valley to accommodate the influx.

"How long has this been growing?" Chen Xing asked, examining an elderly Xiongnu man with concern. The patient had a tumor on his back. Chen Xing thought to himself that if Feng Qianyi knew he was treating Hu people, he would be berated thoroughly from the underworld.

"Three years," Xiang Shu translated emotionlessly.

"Why did you only come to get it treated now?" Chen Xing asked. Xiang Shu couldn't be bothered to translate such a pointless question.

Chen Xing prescribed some medicine to apply to the tumor and then called the next patient over. During the examination, he noticed Xiang Shu staring at him with a slightly dazed expression. Chen Xing felt a shiver down his spine from the intensity of Xiang Shu's gaze.

"Hey!" Chen Xing said. "Say something!"

The sudden outburst startled everyone in the tent. Xiang Shu snapped out of his daze and said impatiently, "Rheumatism! Knee pain! Foot ache!"

"What about this one?" Chen Xing asked, tending to another elderly man. He didn't flinch at the man's festering wound; he cleaned it thoroughly and prescribed some medicine. When the man was gone, a woman approached. "What about you? What's your ailment?"

"I've been having nightmares and can't sleep well at night," Xiang Shu translated.

"I can't help with that. Prescribe her an anshen decoction to soothe her nerves.[3] There are still some ingredients in the back; help me bring them over."

---

3 Anshen (安神) literally translates as "to soothe the nerves."

Xiang Shu helped him, frustrated all the while that he, the Great Chanyu, was being ordered around. After treatment, each patient thanked Chen Xing profusely and then bowed deeply to Xiang Shu in gratitude. Xiang Shu merely waved them away.

"Why are you always staring at me?" said Chen Xing. "Focus on the patients."

"You..." Xiang Shu took a deep breath and bit back whatever he was about to say. Chen Xing shot him a questioning look. "Nothing. His ribs hurt, and it's been going on for half a year."

Chen Xing pressed down on the man's chest. "Do you always sleep on your stomach? Go home and soften your bed a bit, and try not to sleep on your stomach. Next!"

A sudden commotion erupted outside the tent, accompanied by a girl's wailing. A critically ill patient must have arrived. Chen Xing asked the patients waiting in line to hold on and called out, "Come in!"

Xiang Shu frowned slightly as a young man was carried in on a stretcher. Then he saw who it was, and he jumped up. "Che Luofeng?!" he cried, falling to his knees next to the stretcher.

Chen Xing signaled for everyone else in the tent to leave. The man on the stretcher was deathly pale and covered in wounds, and he had an earthenware bowl on his stomach. A foul odor had followed him into the tent.

"Che Luofeng!" Xiang Shu said again.

"Shulü...Kong," the young man murmured weakly.

"You know each other?" Chen Xing asked, looking at Xiang Shu. He had never seen Xiang Shu become such a flustered mess—it was like looking at a whole different person.

"Quick, save him," Xiang Shu begged in a trembling voice, grabbing Chen Xing's wrist. "He's my anda. You have to save him! I'll do anything you ask!"

Chen Xing winced from the pain—Xiang Shu's grip was nearly breaking his wrist. "I will! Let go! I'd save him even if you didn't make any promises!" Nearby, a young woman and an older Rouran woman were crying, distracting Chen Xing. "I'll do my best to save him! Where is the injury? What caused it?"

He untied the bandage on Che Luofeng's belly and carefully removed the bowl. As he suspected, there was a gaping hole in Che Luofeng's stomach from which his intestines were protruding. Two deep knife wounds were visible on his abdomen—his stomach had been sliced open. Aside from that, the young man also had numerous scratches on his body, evidently from a wild beast's claws.

"Wolf claws and knife wounds," Chen Xing muttered. Grief-stricken and cradling Che Luofeng's upper body, Xiang Shu let out a long, sorrowful breath. Chen Xing went to prepare medicine for Che Luofeng. "I'll stitch up his stomach first. Simmer a bowl of mafei soup for him to drink.⁴ I'll get the needles ready."

---

4   Mafei soup is an herbal medicine made from boiled hemp, used as an anesthetic by ancient Chinese physicians.

# 29

ONCE THEY'D SIMMERED a concentrated bowl of mafei soup, Chen Xing wanted to pry Che Luofeng's teeth open and pour it down the unconscious man's throat, but Che Luofeng's ghastly pale complexion gave him pause. Che Luofeng had suffered grievous injuries in the northern mountains and forests and had exhausted his stores of strength just to make it back.

Without saying a word, Xiang Shu took the bowl from Chen Xing, lifted his head, and poured the soup into his own mouth. Holding it there, he lowered his head again and fed it to Che Luofeng.

Chen Xing came out holding a bent sewing needle and asked Xiang Shu to wash his own hands with shaojiu so that he could provide assistance.[5] "It's fortunate that his companion covered his belly with a bowl to contain his intestines," he murmured. "If something had severed them, not even an immortal could have saved him. Move all of the lights and mirrors over here."

Xiang Shu's subordinates had already driven everyone else out of the tent. First, Chen Xing cleaned the unconscious Che Luofeng's wounds with shaojiu, removing the pus, blood, and filth. More and more blood streamed from Che Luofeng's wounds, and his body was becoming ice cold. Chen Xing asked two young Rouran

---

5   A strong, colorless liquor, also known as baijiu.

subordinates to press down on acupoints to staunch the blood flow as he inserted needles to stop Che Luofeng's bleeding.

"You have saved people from this sort of injury before," Xiang Shu observed, noting how familiar and nimble Chen Xing's movements were.

"Nope, I've only stitched up bears before," said Chen Xing. Xiang Shu stared at him. "That was a joke. Don't be so nervous."

Xiang Shu's hands weren't the only ones that were trembling, however. Chen Xing was nervous too. Che Luofeng was bleeding too much; the cotton and gauze wrapped around him had soaked through almost instantly. In a wavering voice, Xiang Shu asked, "What about the medicine you gave me in the Exorcism Department?"

"I don't have any left. That was the last of it," Chen Xing told him calmly. Xiang Shu took a deep breath. "Don't be nervous."

It was clear that this Che Luofeng was of utmost importance to Xiang Shu. While Chen Xing was confident about treating the injuries, he couldn't do anything about the bleeding, and he feared that Che Luofeng might die from blood loss before Chen Xing could sew up his abdomen. He dared not tell Xiang Shu as much, but Chen Xing really wasn't certain he could save Che Luofeng. Two-thirds of that depended on his medical skills—the rest would depend on Che Luofeng's desire to live.

Che Luofeng's face was ashen, and his eyes were squeezed tightly shut, as if he had sunk into an endless dream. He looked to be around the same age as Xiang Shu, and he bore the distinctive features of the Rouran people: thin lips, long eyelashes, high cheekbones, and a well-defined face that gave him an air of stubbornness. He looked just like the helmeted Rouran cavalrymen Chen Xing had seen in portraits. His arms, shoulders, and back were all very sturdy, and with his long legs and robust waist, it was clear that he was a martial arts practitioner. Chen Xing could only hope that his constitution would carry him through this.

When Chen Xing had sewed up half of his abdomen, he leaned over to listen to his heartbeat. It was very slow, and Chen Xing took a deep breath. He lit up the Heart Lamp in his palm and pressed it against Che Luofeng's chest, whispering, "Che Luofeng, your anda is waiting for you to wake up. You must make it through this no matter what."

Xiang Shu's breathing grew rapid. "Che Luofeng!" he shouted in a still-trembling voice. "Live! You promised me—you promised Shulü Kong!"

After the light from Chen Xing's Heart Lamp was pushed into Che Luofeng's heart, his heartbeat stabilized a little. The bleeding, however, was worsening, so Chen Xing had to sew him up as quickly as possible.

"How much longer?" Xiang Shu asked. He could feel that Che Luofeng wouldn't be able to hold on through much more of this. His blood was still gushing, and it had already drenched his and Xiang Shu's clothes.

"Soon." Chen Xing's hands kept trembling as he stitched up the wound. "Once we get his intestines back inside him, his viscera will return to their original places and heal themselves. Be careful not to make any knots."

They worked together to restore Che Luofeng's abdomen to its original state. Chen Xing inserted silver needles into Che Luofeng's acupoints using acupuncture techniques that would stop the bleeding and strengthen his heart. This process demanded every skill Chen Xing had learned in his life, ever since he started studying under his shifu; it was the true pinnacle of Chen Xing's medical career.

The last stitch was made. Bandages were wrapped and medicine applied. By this point, Chen Xing's and Xiang Shu's hands and bodies were covered in blood.

"Ginseng soup, hurry!" Chen Xing ordered, and Xiang Shu obediently poured the ginseng soup, which had been prepared to keep the patient alive, into Che Luofeng's mouth. Chen Xing applied anti-inflammatory herbs and ointments to stop the bleeding and promote muscle growth.

Finally, Che Luofeng made a sound: "Urk..."

Chen Xing was utterly exhausted. "We're done."

Though his complexion was still pale, in Xiang Shu's arms, Che Luofeng breathed a slight sigh of relief.

"I hope he'll wake up without any further complications." Chen Xing listened to Che Luofeng's heartbeat, then tested his breath: weak, but very stable. He went outside to wash off his head-to-toe coating of blood. He only realized when he saw the flood of stars in the sky that it was midnight.

Xiang Shu dismissed his subordinates to rest—they'd been busy for the past twelve hours—and went back to worrying whether Che Luofeng would wake up. That night, Chen Xing washed himself, changed into a new set of clothes, ate a bit, and took over for Xiang Shu. Xiang Shu quickly cleaned himself up and then returned to keep vigil.

"Go and rest," said Xiang Shu, half-embracing Che Luofeng.

"Just raise his upper body a little higher," Chen Xing told him, but Xiang Shu insisted on sitting on the blanket with Che Luofeng himself. He held Che Luofeng's upper body and covered him with a blanket.

Chen Xing didn't say much; he was thoroughly spent. He soon fell sound asleep. When he woke in the morning, he found that

Che Luofeng was still unconscious, and that Xiang Shu had held him like that for the entire night.

The next day, the Great Chanyu kept his doors closed and declined to meet any guests. The sun rose and set, but Che Luofeng didn't wake up. One day and one night passed just like that.

At midnight the next day, Chen Xing sensed something was off with Xiang Shu. He approached them and knelt at one side to listen to Che Luofeng's heartbeat and test his breathing. Xiang Shu glanced at him, seeming a little unsteady. Looking at the situation, Chen Xing feared that the worst-case scenario would come to pass—that Che Luofeng really wouldn't wake up.

"It's okay," Xiang Shu said in a small voice. "There's no need to comfort me."

"When I was a child," said Chen Xing, "my father told me that every part of a person's life—when they're born; when they start talking; the first time they take a fancy to someone; when they marry, have children, and bid farewell to their parents; even when they leave this world—is predestined. We just can't see it in advance, so we don't believe people who talk about fate."

"Do you believe that?" Xiang Shu's voice seemed a lot warmer now. He extended a hand and laid it gently on Che Luofeng's forehead.

Chen Xing remained silent for a while, then sighed. He had never met Che Luofeng before, but he couldn't help but envy the man a little. If it really was time for his life to end, he had his sworn brother, Xiang Shu, by his side. Chen Xing, on the other hand, had no idea who would be with him three years from now, on the day of his death.

In truth, Chen Xing didn't know if he believed it or not. Ever since his shifu had told him that he wouldn't live past the age of twenty, he had often banked his hopes on what-ifs. For example, what if his shifu was wrong? But his shifu had never deceived him, and his predictions were rarely mistaken.

*I'm living so well right now*, Chen Xing always thought. *I won't just keel over and die when I turn twenty, will I? Don't tell me that I'll just be walking along the road and a rock will fall from the sky and smash me to death...*

This was why Chen Xing was conflicted and couldn't decide between believing and not believing. On the one hand, he had so little time left; on the other, he secretly intended to challenge the heavens. If worse came to worst, he planned to find a place with nobody else around—some kind of vast plain that stretched for ten thousand miles—and hide there on the day he turned twenty. He'd make full preparations, put a pot on his head, and wait there from sunrise to sunset. Once he got through that first day, everything would be fine, wouldn't it?

Preoccupied by these thoughts, Chen Xing got up to leave, but Xiang Shu said, "Don't go. Keep me company for a while." Chen Xing sat back down; however heavy his heart was, he understood that Xiang Shu needed company. "Thank you."

Chen Xing dismissed this with a laugh. *You didn't say thank you when I saved you from death row in Xiangyang City*, he thought, *yet you thank me for Che Luofeng's life. What a rare honor.* "Doctors should have benevolent hearts," was all he said out loud. "I just did what I was supposed to do."

"I grew up with Che Luofeng," Xiang Shu told him. "I'm an only child. My mother died of illness after she gave birth to me. In all the years after that, my father never had another heir, and as a child, I often envied the brothers in other Tiele families.

"Che Luofeng was sent to Chi Le Chuan at age four as a hostage from the Rouran side, in exchange for us sending troops to save their people from being wiped out in the Dai State. Che Luofeng said, 'I have no brothers, so he'll be my brother.' When I was seven, I left Chi Le Chuan and went north to chase a wounded stag, only to find myself besieged by a pack of wolves. I was trapped in the wasteland for three days and three nights, and my tribe thought I was dead. Che Luofeng was the only one who still had faith that I was alive. He took his guards with him and searched the entire wasteland just to find me.

"If we're alive, we must see each other; if we're dead, we must see the other's corpse." Xiang Shu was immersed in his memories. "That has been our arrangement since childhood. As each other's anda, if one is killed, then the other will avenge him. You Han people have that thing you call an 'oath of brotherhood.' I think it's just like that."

Xiang Shu glanced at Chen Xing. Chen Xing was a little sad, but he tried to smile. "I envy you a lot."

Xiang Shu, who didn't know that Yuwen Xin had personally hanged Chen Xing's father, just nodded. "When I was ten, the Rouran people finally returned to the lands beyond the pass, but Che Luofeng still came back every year to see me. Things stayed like that until my father fell gravely ill. After I took over as the Great Chanyu, all the tribes were at odds with one another. It was Che Luofeng who led the Rouran people to stand with me and offer support. When I first took office as the Great Chanyu, I really didn't have the energy to continue taking care of my father, so Che Luofeng treated my father as if he were his own. He stayed by my father's bedside to wait on him so that I could focus on bringing the tribes together. This kid used to bug me about bringing him south to see the place where the Han live. He'd heard that the Central Plains was a very prosperous place. But I really didn't have the time to spare, so I kept putting it off and putting it off. If I had known this would happen..."

"He'll get better," Chen Xing said comfortingly, and Xiang Shu nodded. "You're much better than me. My sworn brother... Forget it, it doesn't bear mentioning."

Xiang Shu kept his silence for a moment. Chen Xing didn't really know how to comfort people. Like a child, all he could think of to say was, *I'm worse off than you, see? Your situation isn't so bad in comparison.*

"You're a very good Han," Xiang Shu said, sounding sincere. "Your temperament is good, and so is your heart. At first, I regarded your tolerance as cowardice, but looking at you now, I don't see a coward."

"It's only that I've put other things aside for the time being because there's a lot on my plate," Chen Xing said, somewhat wearily. "I have more important things to do."

Xiang Shu sighed. "But I still don't understand why you were willing to be an exorcist."

"The Heart Lamp is in me." Chen Xing forced out a bitter, helpless laugh. "What choice do I have?"

"What if you did have a choice?"

Chen Xing fell silent. "I'd still be an exorcist," he said eventually. "Perhaps that's why the heavens chose me instead of someone else. Sleep for a while, Xiang Shu. You haven't slept in two whole days."

Chen Xing exhaled a long breath and then got up and left the tent. Xiang Shu nodded but didn't move. He kept holding his anda and never let go.

On the horizon, the dawn sky glowed a marbled pink. Chen Xing breathed in the cold air of the north and stopped walking.

Xiang Shu had said a lot today, and Chen Xing felt like he'd seen a new side of him. Xiang Shu, too, had people he cared about and affection for his family in his heart. Just as Xiang Shu had said, "Looking at you now, I don't see a coward," so too had Chen Xing's impression of Xiang Shu changed. *We should've talked like that a long time ago,* Chen Xing thought.

Once, he had held the naive belief that when he met his destined protector, they would entrust themselves to each other without hesitation. He'd thought they would face life and death together in mutual faith. His greatest disappointment in his journey had been discovering that it wasn't, in fact, so easy for people to trust one another. And Xiang Shu being a Hu while Chen Xing was a Han made understanding each other even more difficult.

Whatever the case, the conversation they'd just had felt like a good start. Chen Xing squatted by the stream and washed his face with the icy water. Now he just hoped that Che Luofeng would wake up soon, or at least not deteriorate. Otherwise—

Just then, he heard Xiang Shu shout like a madman from inside the tent! Chen Xing almost fell into the stream. He whirled around and rushed back into the royal tent, shouting, "What's wrong?!"

Xiang Shu was shaking uncontrollably. He still held Che Luofeng, and his head was buried against his friend's body. When he heard Chen Xing's voice, he raised his head; tears were pooling in his eyes. He looked at Chen Xing meaningfully.

In his arms, Che Luofeng opened his eyes, his gaze confused. His lips moved slightly and he said something too faint for Chen Xing to hear.

"This is great!" Chen Xing felt tears at the back of his nose. "This is great! You finally woke up!"

Xiang Shu had wanted to cry, but instead he started laughing. Chen Xing had never seen him lose himself like this before. Together, the three of them laughed like a pack of fools.

The news that Che Luofeng had woken spread like wildfire that morning. Rouran people arrived in droves and kowtowed to thank Xiang Shu and Chen Xing. They also delivered enough gifts to fill the entire tent. Chen Xing ate the newly delivered fried sabzi and jerky and drank milk tea, wearing gold and silver jewelry all over his body. He treated patients looking like a wealthy local landlord.

Xiang Shu, for his part, was so tired that he passed out in the tent and slept for the whole day and night.

Che Luofeng temporarily stayed in Xiang Shu's tent so that it was convenient for Chen Xing to take care of him at any time. This Rouran heir, who could only speak the Han language minimally and did so in a strange accent, was a very cheerful, active man. From time to time, he would say a few words and then start laughing by himself.

Xiang Shu had regained his usual reserved air now that Che Luofeng was conscious again. Even in front of his sworn brother, he was as mild as ever, and he acted like he couldn't stand him. *Looks like he's like that to everyone*, Chen Xing thought cheerfully, *so I'm not the only one he can't stand!*

Che Luofeng tried to describe to Chen Xing how he'd run into trouble. "The wolf rushed over, and it started kneading me over and over, like it was kneading dough. Then it wrapped me up like a dumpling—"

Chen Xing laughed so hard at this strange analogy that he almost choked on his milk tea. "You can't say it like that!"

"If I hadn't been scratched by that wolf before the Akele ambushed me, this injury wouldn't have been much."

"Why did the Akele ambush you?"

"The Rouran fought with them over the river water," Che Luofeng explained breezily. "They killed the strongest warrior under my command, then we killed their tribe leader's son, that bastard..."

"Are you sure it was them?" Xiang Shu asked coldly.

"Who else could it have been?" said Che Luofeng.

Xiang Shu reprimanded him in the Rouran language, so Che Luofeng didn't speak any further. Chen Xing didn't understand the words Xiang Shu had used, but he figured it must have been along the lines of *If you didn't see it for yourself, don't jump to conclusions.*

On the prairie, it was common to see murders and robberies and even fights breaking out over a minor disagreement or because one party couldn't stand the sight of the other. Massacres were even more common north of the Yin Mountains; there were plenty of hunters out there who preferred to strike first and ask questions later rather than land themselves in trouble due to carelessness.

Che Luofeng didn't know the origins of the people who'd ambushed him. He'd been wounded by a wolf and had staggered into a bush, on the verge of losing consciousness. Right after the attackers assaulted him, his Rouran subordinates rushed over to rescue him and chased his enemies away. His subordinates hadn't seen who his attackers were, and they couldn't even describe their weapons.

After puzzling it over extensively, not even Xiang Shu could say for certain who had hurt Che Luofeng. He pushed it to the back of his mind for future investigation and went back to chiding this fearless anda of his, insisting that he not act so recklessly in the future.

Even after he'd recovered enough to move out of the royal tent, Che Luofeng kept coming over before dawn to get Xiang Shu out of bed and so that Chen Xing could change his dressings, at which point he'd remain in the tent without any care for courtesy. On the few occasions he arrived before Xiang Shu had woken up, he burrowed under Xiang Shu's blanket to sleep with him. Every time he did this, Xiang Shu irritably shoved him back out and kicked him aside.

During the day, Che Luofeng was just as energetic. He was off disturbing Xiang Shu every other minute, if not playing tricks on him then nagging him to talk.

*You're even worse than me*, Chen Xing thought. *Luckily, as his anda, you don't need to be afraid of dying. If I were the one doing all that, Xiang Shu would beat me to death without hesitation.*

One day, while Xiang Shu was taking an afternoon nap, Che Luofeng said, "Look at Shulü Kong, isn't he beautiful?" He tutted as if he showing off a prized possession. "I think he's just like Wang Zhaojun."

Chen Xing's mouth twitched. "He *is* really beautiful...but what do you mean, just like Wang Zhaojun? How?"

"Legend has it that Wang Zhaojun is the most beautiful woman in the world, right?"

The Hu people who lived beyond the pass didn't have much of an idea of the appearance of those in the Central Plains, but they knew of the legend of Zhaojun's Departure from the Pass. It was rumored that Zhaojun, who married the Great Chanyu Huhanye, was the world's most beautiful woman. The legend went that even wild geese passing overhead would land on the prairie to see her beautiful face.

"The Great Chanyu Huhanye married the most beautiful woman in the world," Che Luofeng went on. "As for the Great Chanyu Shulü Kong...what should he do about marriage? Don't you think that, at this rate, the only option is giving him away in marriage to himself?"

"He's not asleep," said Chen Xing. "He heard you."

Xiang Shu stayed silent, and Chen Xing scrutinized him, thinking, *With Fu Jian's male marriage decree, maybe I'd be willing to marry a guy with such a pretty face...if he wasn't actually a rabid dog. If I did marry him and take him back home, I'd get beaten every day and live in fear for my life.*

Something was telling Chen Xing that Che Luofeng's feelings toward Xiang Shu were a bit out of the ordinary, regardless...

After Xiang Shu woke up, Chen Xing asked Che Luofeng, "Since you fought the Akele, will they still come to Chi Le Chuan?"

Che Luofeng became vigilant at once. "Why are you looking for them?"

Chen Xing looked at Xiang Shu, feeling apprehensive. He knew that the Akele people were one of the northern nomadic tribes in the Ancient Covenant. In just a few days, they would return from the north and spend the winter at Chi Le Chuan. But he didn't know whether their current enmity with the Rouran would make things difficult between them and Xiang Shu again.

Xiang Shu guessed what Chen Xing was thinking. "Don't worry. Standing against the Great Chanyu means standing against the Ancient Chi Le Covenant."

Chen Xing was relieved. The weather was getting colder by the day, but the first snow of autumn had yet to arrive. Every morning, the prairie was covered in a layer of frost. On the promised date of the third of the tenth lunar month, there was still no news from the legendary Akele tribe.

The prairie's Autumn Close Festival was set for the fifteenth of the tenth lunar month. Chen Xing went around inquiring about this tribe that was active in the north and learned that the Akele were a large branch of the Shiwei, comprising nearly three thousand people. Their area of activity was farther north, including around Lake Baikal.

"They'll come," Xiang Shu said impassively, "or else they'll freeze to death in the north once the snow comes."

"Shulü Kong," Che Luofeng said with a smile, "when will you take me to the place where the Han live?"

He was sticking together a Great Chanyu feather crown for Xiang Shu while Chen Xing changed his dressings. Xiang Shu didn't reply to him.

Che Luofeng hooked Chen Xing's chin with his finger. "I heard that there are a lot of places to enjoy yourself in your Central Plains."

Chen Xing batted his hand away. "Another one who wants to take over the Central Plains? Unfortunately, the north side doesn't belong to us now. Feel free to compete with Fu Jian for it."

Che Luofeng smiled at him. "If I were to bring troops into the pass and go to war with Fu Jian to become a Rouran emperor, would you help me, Chen Xing?"

Xiang Shu harshly reprimanded Che Luofeng in the Rouran language, but Chen Xing still gave him a serious reply. "You all act like the Central Plains is just a large tract of land where no one lives, like it should belong to whoever wins it in a fight. Have you guys ever thought about how it would feel if the Han came trampling all over your homeland and robbed you of your property?"

"It was just a joke," Che Luofeng said pleasantly. "If the Great Chanyu doesn't agree, the Chi Le Covenant won't head south."

Patients continued to pour in until almost all of the sick people in the area had been seen. Chen Xing saw nearly two hundred people each day, and within a month, he'd treated thousands of patients. By this point, his reputation as the divine doctor had spread throughout all of Chi Le Chuan. No one treated him as a servant anymore; as he came and went, every Hu treated him with respect. Even Xiang Shu's attitude toward him had improved since their conversation that night.

Che Luofeng had almost completely recovered and could now ride a horse. Sometimes, Xiang Shu took him out for a stroll. Chen Xing had followed along on a few occasions, but he didn't like walking around in the cold, and since he still had patients coming to see him every now and then, he stopped joining them after a while.

Che Luofeng was, it transpired, very interested in the world of the Han people. Not only did he know a bit of the Han language, he also pestered Chen Xing with all sorts of questions. He seemed a bit covetous as well, which made Chen Xing uncomfortable.

"Teach me how to write Shulü Kong's name using Han characters, okay?" asked Che Luofeng. Chen Xing wondered, *Why don't you want to learn how to write your own?*

The Autumn Close Festival grew nearer. It was a grand annual festival for the Hu living outside the pass. The fifteenth day of the tenth month marked the beginning of winter on the prairie, and the Hu gathered on that day to sing, dance, slaughter lambs, drink wine, and also to begin to prepare for many Tibetan winter activities. Chen Xing had, by this point, learned a fair bit of the Rouran,

Xiongnu, and Tiele languages, and he had gleaned that the first snow was supposed to come late in the ninth month or early in the tenth. This year's snow, however, had yet to be seen, as had the Akele.

If the Akele didn't come here, Chen Xing would have no way of confirming the location on the map...and once the snowfall became heavy, it would become even more difficult to traverse the path leading north. He would be forced to wait until spring. The more time went by without the Akele's arrival, the more anxious Chen Xing felt.

"After today," Xiang Shu decided as he drank tea in his tent, "if they still haven't come, I'll send some people out north to find them."

Since returning to Chi Le Chuan, Xiang Shu had changed into the royal robe of the Great Chanyu. His attire was gorgeous, with a feather crown on his head that had three additional feathers inserted into it. His martial robe was embroidered with the magnificent deity insignia of the Ancient Covenant's Sixteen Hu.

After a great deal of observation, Chen Xing had discovered that Xiang Shu did, in fact, have work to do. The position of Great Chanyu was unlike that of an emperor. While he rarely concerned himself with the internal affairs of the Hu tribes, he was active in mediating disputes, dividing up responsibilities, and acting as a symbol of the Ancient Covenant. When he was busy, he was very busy; he often had to listen to the elders of each tribe air all of their grievances while denouncing and criticizing one another. But once these affairs were dealt with, he was free again, and that meant becoming very idle. He often had nothing to do for an entire day, and he and Chen Xing just sat around in the tent staring at each other.

"If there's no snow this year, we won't be able to ski down the mountains in late autumn," Xiang Shu added. "Can you stop frowning all the time?"

*After the end of this year, I'll only have three years left to live!* Chen Xing griped in his heart. *Who are you to tell me not to frown?!*

# 30

ORRYING TOO MUCH didn't do anyone any good. As a child, Chen Xing's favorite thing to do had been to go to festivals, but sadly, he had spent most of his youth on remote mountains. After so many years of isolation, he wanted to seize the opportunity to have some fun.

"All right," he said at last. "Do you remember saying that if I cured Che Luofeng, you'd do anything I asked you to?"

"Ah, finally," said Xiang Shu. "I've been waiting for you to say that. You want me to be your protector, right? Well, I am a man of my word."

Chen Xing was taken aback. He hadn't expected Xiang Shu to accept so straightforwardly.

"Over these past few days, I've done a lot of thinking about what you said," Xiang Shu went on.

"Hey, slow down," Chen Xing protested. "That's not what I want. What kind of person do you think I am? What's the point of forcing you to be my protector when your heart isn't in it?"

It was Xiang Shu's turn to be surprised. He frowned, regarding Chen Xing with suspicion.

Chen Xing smiled. "Take me with you to tomorrow's Autumn Close Festival for some fun. How's that sound?"

Xiang Shu studied Chen Xing in silence for a while. Then, at last, he said, "All right."

The day of the Autumn Close Festival arrived, and Chi Le Chuan welcomed a festival grander than had ever been seen before. All of the tribes piled up their good wine, beef, and mutton in an area they'd cleared out for that purpose, then set up a mile-long table for people to freely eat and drink at. The Sixteen Hu also set up ten competition grounds, hosting contests ranging from horse racing to equestrian archery, wrestling to bull taming—in short, this was to be a wild, rowdy party!

When he saw the lively scene, Chen Xing let out a joyful cheer. He stopped at one of the competition grounds, but it was packed with people waiting to watch Xiang Shu carry out the arrow-shooting ceremony, a way for them to honor the gods. Chen Xing spent some time just wandering around; he cheered loudly at the boisterous wrestling matches and, using the money he'd made from his medical work, gambled and won quite a bit from the Hu festivalgoers. With his winnings, he bought a wine-colored pony from some Xiongnu and rode it all through the festival.

"Divine Doctor!" shouted a Tiele youth, who had apparently been searching for him for some time. "The Great Chanyu is looking for you! Go to the platform, quick!"

"Xiang Shu!" Chen Xing called out. "What do you think of the horse I bought?"

A crowd had already gathered in front of the platform by the time Chen Xing led his horse to it. Xiang Shu was standing high up on the platform with a jade bow in his hand. He was clad in a set of golden Tiele armor; it clung to his muscles, emphasizing his eye-catching chest and his neat, attractive rows of abdominal muscles.

"You said you wanted me to bring you so that you could have some fun," Xiang Shu spat, "but you vanished first thing in the morning!"

Chen Xing chuckled as he looked up at Xiang Shu, standing tall on the platform, turned slightly away. Viewed from this angle, he was the textbook image of a handsome, upstanding young man. Chen Xing racked his brain, but none of the poems, books, or other writings he'd studied in his life had adequate words to describe him.

"Here comes a gentleman, as beautiful as flowers," he tried. As he approached Xiang Shu, he felt his heart pound, so much so that he became a bit breathless. But even though his heart felt like a raging sea, he kept up a calm, smiling facade.

"What?" said Xiang Shu, raising a confused eyebrow.

Chen Xing jumped onto the platform and straightened Xiang Shu's armor for him. "I'm praising your beauty! You Hu people are so unromantic!"

When Chen Xing reached one edge of the platform, the people below began to whistle. Xiang Shu then pointed behind him, motioning for Chen Xing to move back and watch from the rear. Che Luofeng climbed up onto the platform too. "We're starting?" he shouted.

Xiang Shu agreed, so Che Luofeng started ordering people around. Soon, the Rouran trumpeters around the platform blew their horns in unison. All across the Chi Le Covenant, people stopped what they were doing and rushed toward the central platform.

Someone handed Che Luofeng a pair of wild geese. They were tied together with a red string around their necks, and from the string hung a palm-sized golden gong.

"What's this for?" asked Chen Xing.

"Keep your eyes open," Xiang Shu said with the jade bow in his hand.

"Two birds with one arrow?" Chen Xing said cheekily. "There's no need for this, right? Can you even hit them? What if you miss?"

"I'd lose face if I missed."

"No, but...even if you did hit them, what did the geese ever do to you? They're innocent!"

Xiang Shu raised his voice and, in the Tiele language, announced the beginning of the Autumn Close Festival. Yet none of the hundreds of thousands of people packed densely below them cheered.

"Go!" shouted Che Luofeng as he set the geese free. The geese honked in unison as they spread their wings and flew toward the horizon. They started out pulling each other in opposite directions and began to fly in circles, but before long, they synchronized their movements and flew away, becoming nothing more than a black speck in the distance.

The three hundred people down below held their collective breath and watched as Xiang Shu slowly drew his longbow. Chen Xing was stunned. Did he really have the skills to hit them?! Xiang Shu turned full circle, drawing the bow in a full-moon arc. He borrowed the force of the rotation to tilt the longbow upward and fired three arrows in quick succession—*whoosh, whoosh, whoosh!*

Back in Chang'an City, Xiang Shu had shot the yin yang mirror out of Feng Qianyi's hands from a hundred steps away. That itself had been miraculous—but now he was going to try to hit that airborne gong?!

As the geese flew further away, Xiang Shu released one last arrow. The first arrow hit, slicing through the red rope and sending the golden gong falling out of the sky, and the second arrow hit it with a resounding *bong*.

*Bong!* The third arrow hit its mark too!

Then the last arrow caught up to the rest. It pierced the gong clear through, making it vibrate from within.

The people on the field erupted in an earth-shattering cheer that seemed to make the very ground beneath their feet tremble. Xiang Shu put down his bow, and things below him quickly got rowdy as the festive energy built to a climax. The crowd surged away in all directions, men and women, young or old, all singing and dancing buoyantly.

Che Luofeng let out a raucous laugh and grabbed Xiang Shu's free hand. Xiang Shu tossed the jade bow aside and beckoned for Chen Xing to join them, so Chen Xing grabbed his wrist, and the three men ran off the platform.

There were plenty of delicacies and good wine to be had, and within the throng of people, a drinking contest had begun. The crowd buffeted Chen Xing around, and he decided to join in. Of course, he'd already imbibed a fair bit earlier in the day, and the wine was so strong it made him a little dizzy. Che Luofeng shouted something, and Xiang Shu said in Chen Xing's ear, "Don't drink too much! I don't want to carry you back!"

"It'll be fine!" Chen Xing yelled back.

Xiang Shu cleared the crowd, then drank a bowl of wine while Che Luofeng handed another one to Chen Xing.

"Che Luofeng," Chen Xing said, "you're still recovering, so don't drink too much."

Someone handed Che Luofeng more wine, but Xiang Shu snatched the bowl out of his hand, leaned up against the table, and downed every last drop on Che Luofeng's behalf, which made the onlookers kick up a ruckus. Che Luofeng barked a loud laugh before he pressed Xiang Shu down on the table, ducked his head down, and—to Chen Xing's great astonishment—moved to kiss him.

This got the crowd even more excited, and they erupted in laughter. Xiang Shu raised a hand to shove Che Luofeng's face away, though, and before Che Luofeng could land a kiss on his lips, he kicked Che Luofeng aside. "Get lost!"

Chen Xing laughed with everyone else, but in his chest he felt a perplexing twinge of pain, like something had grabbed his heart and squeezed it the tiniest bit. He felt short of breath suddenly. It was probably the alcohol.

Che Luofeng had landed on the ground and he lay there, groaning. Afraid that he'd accidentally kicked Che Luofeng in one of his wounds, Xiang Shu rushed over to check on him. Chen Xing hurriedly stepped in. "Let me take a look?" he said, but Che Luofeng just smiled and pushed Chen Xing away.

In the Rouran language, Che Luofeng announced for all to hear that he wanted to wrestle with Xiang Shu. Then he bounced to his feet and leaped onto Xiang Shu's back, but Xiang Shu yanked him back down again and told him that he wasn't about to fight an injured man. Xiang Shu waved his hand and made to leave, but Che Luofeng stopped him, smiling.

"Shulü Kong! I challenge you! If I win, then I'll be the Great Chanyu! You have to fight with only one hand, though, because of my injuries!"

This delighted the Rouran youngsters, who began to chant, "Fight! Fight! Fight!"

Xiang Shu smirked and put one hand behind his back. Immediately, people surged forward to watch, blocking Chen Xing's view.

Chen Xing put down his bowl. Cheers erupted from inside the circle of onlookers, and suddenly, a sense of loneliness washed over him. He turned and walked away from the crowd with his little horse, only stopping when he reached the southern end of Chi Le Chuan.

*What's wrong with me?* Chen Xing thought. He was baffled by the sudden heaviness that had seized him. The once-clear blue sky had darkened considerably, as if in promise of a coming snowstorm. He climbed up onto a haystack and sat down quietly, feeling more melancholy than he ever had before. *Is this homesickness? But where even is my home?*

He put a piece of straw in his mouth and lay down, letting his drunkenness weigh down on him as he sank into the haystack. He looked up at the darkening gray sky and listened to the Hu's loud cheers. Where he'd earlier been cheery, Chen Xing now felt irritable, and the celebrations, which had seemed so lively until then, suddenly struck him as dull. When he recalled how valiant and formidable Xiang Shu had looked wielding his bow on the platform, he felt bitter, as if he'd been robbed of something. His emotions were a tangled, chaotic mess.

The shouts of the Hu drew closer and closer, aggravating Chen Xing even more. "So noisy!" he shouted, sitting up. "What are you doing?!"

But what he saw when his eyes focused was a group of on-duty guards running toward the grasslands, shouting and spreading outward in a fan-shaped formation. The surprise interrupted Chen Xing's self-pitying thoughts. For one confused moment, he just watched them. Then he leaped off the haystack, mounted his little horse, and rode toward the commotion.

Dozens of Rouran cavalrymen had surrounded a lone person on horseback. The rider was dressed in a black cloak, and his face was obscured by rough-woven cloth. He was holding a staff in hand, and he watched the cavalry warily.

Faltering a little in the Rouran language, Chen Xing asked, "Who's this?"

The cavalry relaxed a little at his arrival; almost everyone in Chi Le Chuan knew him by now. To his surprise, though, the masked rider brightened when he saw him too.

"Tianchi!" the rider called out. He took off his mask and hood, revealing familiar bright eyes and red lips, and bared his white teeth in a smile. "I've found you at last!"

"Tuoba Yan?" Chen Xing immediately dismounted and ran over to him. What was Tuoba Yan doing there?

Tuoba Yan got off his own horse and embraced Chen Xing with a hearty laugh. "I heard that the Great Chanyu brought you back to Chi Le Chuan. I asked for His Majesty's permission to come here and find you."

Chen Xing swiftly informed the Rouran cavalry that Tuoba Yan was his friend. The cavalrymen's expressions changed, and they saluted and left.

"Celebrating the Autumn Close Festival?" Tuoba Yan asked, looking around.

Tuoba Yan's arrival had swept away the discontent in Chen Xing's heart; now he felt only the joy of meeting a friend. "That's right," he laughed. "Why didn't you write first before traveling so far? Did you come alone?"

Tuoba Yan nodded. He slung one arm over Chen Xing's shoulders, and they led their horses unhurriedly toward Chi Le Chuan. "How are you doing?" he asked as they walked. "They're pretty respectful of you. Is that because of the Great Chanyu?"

"Him?" Chen Xing wrinkled his nose and gave Tuoba Yan a quick rundown of recent events. "Do you want to see Xiang Shu? Should I get someone to call him?"

Tuoba Yan seemed a little uneasy. He looked out into the distance, then back at Chen Xing, not responding.

"How is the court?" asked Chen Xing. "Did you need something from me?"

The news Tuoba Yan had brought of the Central Plains was nothing out of the ordinary. After Xiang Shu and Chen Xing left, Fu Jian had returned to Weiyang Palace, since the drought fiends had retreated for the moment. Seeing the ruins of Weiyang Palace had nearly made him cough up blood, and he issued orders to have it rebuilt as soon as possible. Murong Chong remained in the palace that first night, and Fu Jian had managed to dissuade him from setting off after Xiang Shu. Murong Chong agreed, on one condition: He wanted Feng Qianjun arrested and handed over to the Murong family.

Everyone, from Fu Jian to the rest of the civil and martial officials, knew that the Murong family held grudges. The only reason no one was pushing the issue with Xiang Shu right now was fear of the formidable Ancient Covenant that backed him. The Hu tribes had been locked in a cycle of "you kill me, I kill you" for so many years, fighting one another relentlessly. Even after their migration into the Central Plains, that animosity and hatred remained deep-seated. Knowing that Xiang Shu was able to corral such a major power, Fu Jian's only choice was to let things cool off until a later date and hope they'd be in a better position to settle things with the Great Chanyu.

Still, he wanted to appease Murong Chong and help him save face. Princess Qinghe's death couldn't be explained away, so Fu Jian did as Murong Chong asked and issued an arrest warrant for Feng Qianjun.

"Feng Qianjun already left," said Chen Xing.

"I know," Tuoba Yan replied. "I asked His Majesty for a writ of amnesty for you. The Great Chanyu was the one who killed Princess Qinghe, and the Feng family was behind the plot—you were barely involved. I've smoothed things over with Murong Chong on your behalf, too, so you can rest easy."

Chen Xing was slightly confused, but he nodded in thanks.

"I told them that I wished to bring you back," Tuoba Yan continued, "and His Majesty told me to come and talk to you myself."

"Back where?"

"Back to Chang'an. Don't you want to go back? With me there, nobody would dare cause trouble for you."

Understanding dawned on Chen Xing at last, and he began to laugh. Tuoba Yan ducked his head a little and shot Chen Xing an earnest look. His eyes shone with youthful energy—he was very cute.

"Want to go have a drink?" Chen Xing asked. "The festival's still going, and the wine is delicious."

"Sure!" Tuoba Yan said immediately. "I haven't been to the Autumn Close Festival in so long!"

Chen Xing took Tuoba Yan back to the festival. Now that they were drunk, the Hu were all busy either wrestling each other or whispering sweet nothings in each other's ears; the Autumn Close Festival's other purpose, aside from celebrating the fall harvest, was to provide a means for those daring young men and women to show each other a good time. Emboldened by the alcohol running through their veins, men began to chase after the women, doing things they normally dared not do and saying things they normally dared not say. The atmosphere was really quite charming. The tables were crowded with wine, the colorful spectacles of Chi Le Chuan on display for all to see.

Chen Xing took a bowl of wine and handed it to Tuoba Yan. It turned out that Tuoba Yan had unexpectedly good tolerance. Carrying the wine jar, he led Chen Xing to the riverside and sat down under a tree. He drank half the bowl in silence, then looked at Chen Xing with a hint of red painting his cheeks.

"Tianchi," he said, "I have something to tell you. Since that day in the royal study, when His Majesty mentioned to you...mentioned that... Well, since then, I've spent a long time thinking about this."

Chen Xing understood, of course, what Tuoba Yan was skirting around. Why else would he chase Chen Xing all the way to Chi Le Chuan after he left Chang'an? If he'd come to pass along Fu Jian's message, that would have been one thing, but the first thing he'd said to Chen Xing was "I came to find you." Chen Xing found the gesture quite touching.

"I know what you're trying to say," he said, smiling. "Come, cheers." He clinked his wine bowl with Tuoba Yan's, then downed it. Tuoba Yan watched him, stunned.

"You're beautiful," Tuoba Yan said, smiling back. "Tianchi, why don't you come home with me? I've always wanted to marry to someone like you. I will promise you anything—just say the word. I'll do whatever you ask of me."

"Tuoba-xiong..." Chen Xing sighed and looked straight into Tuoba Yan's eyes. "Thank you for coming a thousand miles to find me. When I was leaving Chang'an, there's one thing I forgot to do. I forgot to return this to you."

He poured a bit of wine into his hand to loosen the ring that Tuoba Yan had given him, took it off, and held it out to him. Tuoba Yan was silent, so Chen Xing took his hand and put the ring in his palm.

"All right," Tuoba Yan said.

"You should give it to someone else. Give it to someone who, at first sight, makes you feel like you cannot live without them."

"You are that person," Tuoba Yan insisted.

"No," Chen Xing said with a smile, "I'm not. I just happen to be someone who fits the characteristics of the person you've imagined for yourself—the person you've been looking for, the person you feel is appropriate to marry. Nothing more."

Tuoba Yan looked at Chen Xing with his brow slightly furrowed, not understanding.

"You don't understand," Chen Xing went on, feeling a touch melancholy. "You ought to give this ring to that one person who makes your heart pound uncontrollably whenever you see him. You will always try to find more reasons to talk to him. When you see him with someone else, you will feel troubled. When you see him sad, you won't be able to bear it. When he smiles at you, you will feel like spring has finally come after a long winter. You shouldn't give it to someone who everyone else thinks you should marry. That's just a person who fits your idea of someone you *should* want to spend your entire life with. You'll think you two *should* be together, so you'll end up believing that person is destined to be with you, but they're not someone you really want."

Chen Xing raised an eyebrow and smiled again. As he spoke, he'd come to understand the odd weight that had been squeezing his heart.

"I don't understand," Tuoba Yan said with a sad little frown.

"That's all right. Just promise to remember what I said. One day, you may understand."

Tuoba Yan looked away. The silence stretched between them, and for a while, all that could be heard was the sound of the two of them breathing. At last, Tuoba Yan said, "All right."

"Shall I walk you back? I don't want to return just yet. Xiang Shu promised me—"

Suddenly, Xiang Shu's voice rang out from behind a tree. "You'd best keep him away from the Rouran, or I'll have a murder case on my hands."

"You eavesdropped on our conversation!" sputtered Chen Xing, startled and furious.

As a martial arts practitioner, however, Tuoba Yan seemed to have known that Xiang Shu was hiding behind the tree. He simply looked at Xiang Shu and said, "Great Chanyu, I'm sorry to have disturbed you."

"What now?" Chen Xing asked. "You welcome your guests either by making them clean the room or by murdering them. Has the Chi Le Covenant ever even heard of etiquette?"

Xiang Shu came out from behind the tree. He had already changed back into his royal robe. "The Tuoba clan, on behalf of their country, once captured several thousand of the Rouran and enslaved them. The Rouran are currently rousingly drunk. If they figure out who he is, I can't say for certain what will happen, but they could very well end up drawing their knives and stabbing your sweetheart to death. Forgive me if I am unable to stop them."

"It doesn't matter," Tuoba Yan said, putting on the ring. He turned to Chen Xing. "Now that I know you're safe and sound, I will take my leave."

"Wait," Chen Xing protested. "Why don't you stay for a few days longer? You've come such a long way..."

"Go back and tell Jiantou," said Xiang Shu, "that I don't have any time to deal with his missteps, but he should still behave himself. If I ever hear of trouble brewing in the Central Plains again, who knows? If he can't even guard his own capital, I wouldn't mind putting those Xianbei in their place for him."

"I'll certainly let him know," Tuoba Yan said. With that, he got on his horse and galloped away. Chen Xing took a few steps, intending to stop him, but Xiang Shu caught his arm.

"Xiang Shu, let me go. Tuoba Yan!"

Tuoba Yan looked back at Chen Xing, and he suddenly smiled. There was a hint of bitterness in that smile, but it was hidden well, and he followed it up with a whistle. "Tianchi!" he called out. "Until we meet again!"

Chen Xing sighed. He shook off Xiang Shu's arm and glared at him.

Xiang Shu frowned back. "All I did was go back to change my outfit," he said. "Where did you run off to?"

"How could you eavesdrop on us?!" Chen Xing demanded.

"I happened to pass by and noticed you two drinking under a tree. Chi Le Chuan is my territory; I can go anywhere I want. What gives you the right to question me?"

"You...!" Chen Xing was walking ahead angrily with Xiang Shu following him, keeping just the right distance. They circled around the area where the Hu were holding the Autumn Close Festival.

"You dare vent your anger at the Great Chanyu?!" Xiang Shu snarled.

"What? Want to hit me again? Bring it, then!"

To Chen Xing's surprise, Xiang Shu stopped. He scrutinized Chen Xing, frowning. "What did I do to you now? Why are you so angry? If you don't want to stay, just get lost! Go back to Chang'an with Tuoba Yan!"

Chen Xing took a deep breath; he was at his wit's end. He stepped forward and shoved Xiang Shu, but Xiang Shu didn't even budge. "Bastard!" Chen Xing shouted furiously. "You damn bastard!"

With those words, he turned to the side and rammed his shoulder into Xiang Shu, who remained still as a stone rooted deep in the ground. He raised his eyebrows at Chen Xing mockingly, then pushed him aside with no effort at all. Chen Xing stumbled and nearly fell.

Xiang Shu grabbed his wrist again, and Chen Xing shouted in pain. Just as Xiang Shu was about to hit him, a shout came from nearby.

It was Che Luofeng. His eyes were red from the wine, but they gleamed with fury as he approached them. Behind him were hundreds of Rouran cavalry, each dressed neatly in armor.

"Where is that Xianbei Tuoba?!" Che Luofeng demanded. "Divine Doctor! Hand over your friend!"

# 31

THE AUTUMN CLOSE FESTIVAL had barely begun, and already trouble was brewing. Tension hung thick in the air between Xiang Shu and Che Luofeng. How had news of Tuoba Yan's arrival in Chi Le Chuan spread so fast? Chen Xing wondered if the group of Rouran cavalrymen who had left him with Tuoba Yan earlier had rushed back to inform Che Luofeng.

"That man has already left," Xiang Shu said in a low voice, "and fighting is forbidden in Chi Le Chuan. This rule has stood for over four hundred years in the Ancient Covenant."

But Che Luofeng refused to back down. "The Tuoba clan of Xianbei," he declared, "has defiled our women and abducted our elderly and children! Even if he is your friend, Divine Doctor, this is a blood feud that cannot be reconciled! Please step away!"

He raised his hand to lead his troops in pursuit, but Xiang Shu stopped him. "Who dares to kill in Chi Le Chuan?!" he roared. His voice was like thunder. It made Chen Xing's ears throb with pain; his vision darkened until he nearly fainted. Intimidated by Xiang Shu's fury, the Rouran cavalry instinctively took half a step back.

"Che Luofeng," Xiang Shu intoned, "go ahead and seek your revenge. But if you kill Tuoba Yan, you and your entire clan will be exiled from the Yin Mountains, never to set foot in Chi Le Chuan again. The Great Chanyu always keeps his word."

Che Luofeng gasped for breath, stunned. That shout had sobered him up considerably. Chen Xing opened his mouth to speak, hoping to ease the tension, but Xiang Shu raised his hand, cutting him off, and swept his gaze over the Rouran cavalry with an air of unmistakable authority.

The state of Dai had been a separatist regime founded by Tuoba Yan's grandfather, Tuoba Shiyijian, with the northeastern branch of the Tuoba clan, but it had been destroyed by Fu Jian. Pursuing vengeance against a descendant was clearly not worth the cost of offending the Great Chanyu. The cavalrymen, now more sober, exchanged glances with Che Luofeng, begging him with their eyes to let it go.

"Shulü Kong, you...you..." Che Luofeng laughed, bitter and furious. "Do you really think the Rouran are afraid of you?"

"Go," said Xiang Shu, "and you won't survive to see the sun rise tomorrow morning."

The Rouran comprised nearly sixty thousand people within the Ancient Chi Le Covenant. Their expulsion from the alliance would be no small matter. Many on the plains had heard the argument and gathered to watch, but Xiang Shu remained unmoved.

"This is your choice," he told them, and he pointed to the gathering site. "I'll count to three: Either mobilize your troops for revenge, or return to the festival. One."

Che Luofeng angrily threw his weapon to the ground, spurred his horse, and charged back through the crowd. The onlookers scrambled to get out of the way, clearing a path for him. Within moments, all of the Rouran cavalrymen had withdrawn.

Even seeing Che Luofeng heading north, Chen Xing still felt uneasy, but after the crowd dispersed, Xiang Shu summoned a Tiele tribesman and gave him orders in a low voice. Chen Xing understood most of it: Xiang Shu had dispatched a cavalry unit to follow Tuoba Yan and protect him until he reached the Great Wall, to prevent Che Luofeng from pursuing him for revenge.

Chen Xing breathed a sigh of relief. "Thank you."

Xiang Shu didn't respond. He turned and left with a dark look on his face. Chen Xing stood there for a moment longer, feeling melancholy under the bustling, festive mood of the Autumn Close Festival. Then, with heavy steps, he returned to the tent.

Xiang Shu entered the royal tent first, and Chen Xing followed him, lifting the curtain to find the inside of the tent in disarray. It was clear that Che Luofeng had been here already and taken away everything he'd used over the past few days. Xiang Shu looked around with evident anger.

Chen Xing bent to tidy up. "Tuoba Yan is my friend. I'm sorry for troubling you."

"Che Luofeng is always like this," said Xiang Shu. "After a few days, when he's had time to think it over, he'll apologize to you."

"I've bought a horse," added Chen Xing, recalling the day's events. "Tomorrow, I'll trade with your people for some food and warm clothing, then set off north."

Xiang Shu sat silently in the tent. Chen Xing had come to understand that despite the beauty of Chi Le Chuan, it was not his homeland, and however warm and welcoming Xiang Shu's people had been, they were not his kin. After a month in Chi Le Chuan, he had started to feel that perhaps the world south of the Yangtze River, with its lush, terraced fields and the song of orioles, was where he truly belonged.

Xiang Shu glanced at Chen Xing, as if seeing through his thoughts. Chen Xing kept tidying up the tent.

"If I stay any longer, I might cause you more trouble, so I'll just get out of here," he added. Xiang Shu did not respond. When he was finished with tidying, Chen Xing poured himself a cup of milk tea, sat down, and thought for a moment. He scratched his head. "Just forget about the whole protector thing. You're the Great Chanyu; you have your own responsibilities. You can't just wander around with me when there are so many people who need you. Luck has always been on my side anyway, so you don't need to worry about me."

Xiang Shu remained silent as Chen Xing checked his traveling medicine pouch, sheathed his dagger, and unfolded the map. He studied it briefly, comparing the sketch Xiang Shu had made on a piece of sheepskin with the terrain of mountains and rivers beyond the Great Wall in an effort to pinpoint the locations of Duan Gorge and the Great Lake. Based on the map and the guidance of the Big Dipper, if he continued north, he might even encounter the Akele, in which case he could ask them for directions with the little bit of Xiongnu he had learned.

The journey would be difficult, but there was still hope. He couldn't afford any more delays; he had to find the legendary Dinghai Pearl before spring. Once that burden was lifted, he could at least return to the south and wait for death with some peace of mind.

Later in the evening, Chen Xing heard cheers from outside. He stepped out and glanced around—snow was falling! Returning to the tent, he pointed outside. "Xiang Shu! It's snowing."

Xiang Shu furrowed his brow, scrutinizing Chen Xing with an annoyed expression.

The snowfall quickly intensified, marking the arrival of winter; the northern wind howled and sent thick, downy snowflakes swirling across Chi Le Chuan. Bonfires were moved inside of tents. Chen Xing stood alone for a while in front of the royal tent until someone brought a simple dinner for himself and Xiang Shu.

After they ate, Xiang Shu gazed blankly outside, apparently lost in thought. Well accustomed to Xiang Shu's aloofness, Chen Xing drank a bit of wine before settling on his small couch. He covered himself with a thin wool blanket and soon fell asleep.

At long last, Xiang Shu finally spoke. "You can't leave now," he said. "The heavy snow will block the roads in the north. You'll have to wait until spring." But Chen Xing didn't hear him.

The cold draft leaking from the gap below the tent was relentless, and Chen Xing's thin blanket wasn't enough. During the night, he woke just long enough to feel Xiang Shu covering him with two more blankets.

By early morning, the world outside was draped in silver, and the fleeting discomfort of the previous day was forgotten.

"Wow!" Chen Xing exclaimed in astonishment.

Snow blanketed both the mountains and the land like a thick, shimmering coating of sugar, and it sparkled brilliantly under the bright sun. A thin layer of ice had formed over the streams overnight, and early risers among the Hu people were breaking the ice to water their horses.

Xiang Shu was nowhere to be seen. Chen Xing sneezed, his nose a bit stuffy. "It's so beautiful!" he said to himself.

He quickly washed up, found breakfast on the table, and, once he'd eaten, bundled up in a thick fur coat. He stepped outside, navigating the deep snow that had transformed all of Chi Le Chuan into an enchanting fairy tale world overnight.

"Xiang Shu!" Chen Xing called out from the top of a hill. Down below, Xiang Shu, dressed in a knee-length tiger fur coat with a belt cinching his waist and a fox fur hat, was giving instructions to a group of Tiele people. The Tiele warriors were loading tents and supplies onto horses, apparently preparing for a trade expedition.

When he heard Chen Xing call to him, Xiang Shu looked up. The sight of his red lips and white teeth under the sunlight stirred something in Chen Xing's heart.

Xiang Shu raised a hand, gesturing for Chen Xing to wait at the top, and turned to climb the hill. "Want to go skiing?" he asked when he reached him. "We didn't get to try it yesterday during the festival."

"Sure," said Chen Xing. He had woken up in a much better mood. He planned to leave the next day, and he wanted to make some memories on his last day in Chi Le Chuan.

Carrying a cavalry shield, Xiang Shu led Chen Xing to a slope and stood on the shield. Chen Xing stared at him. "Get on," Xiang Shu said, "and hold tight from behind."

"How is this supposed to work?" Chen Xing protested. "We'll fall! There isn't even a rope?! If one foot slips, we'll roll all the way down!"

"Useless!" Xiang Shu snapped, impatient. "Hurry up!"

The cavalry shield was small, and Chen Xing hesitantly stepped onto it behind Xiang Shu. But before he could react, Xiang Shu reached behind himself, grabbed Chen Xing's arms, and wrapped them around him. With a powerful tug, he had Chen Xing hold on tightly. Then he tilted the shield sideways and they swooshed down the slope.

"Ahhhh!" Chen Xing screamed as Xiang Shu led them in a sharp dive off the edge. His heart nearly leaped out of his throat. Xiang Shu pressed down on the tail of the shield, launching them into the air and into a smooth landing.

Chen Xing stood there, speechless.

"Again?" said Xiang Shu.

Chen Xing's heart was still racing, and he felt overwhelmed.

Sliding down that steep slope had felt almost as terrifying as jumping off a cliff! "I didn't open my eyes," he admitted.

"Coward."

Xiang Shu whistled for his horse. The two of them mounted, and he brought Chen Xing to an even steeper slope. When Chen Xing looked down and saw that it stretched for nearly three miles, his legs went weak. "This time, you're in front," Xiang Shu told him. "And keep your eyes open!"

"Waaahhhhhh!" Without further warning, Xiang Shu had whisked him away, and they were speeding down the slope. During the final stretch, Chen Xing turned to Xiang Shu and said, "Xiang Shu, tomorrow, I'll—"

They were closer than he'd realized, and as he turned, their lips nearly brushed. Xiang Shu suddenly lost his footing, and Chen Xing, unable to maintain his balance, was sent flying and landed in the snow.

"Ha ha ha!" Chen Xing laughed as he got up, his face covered in snow. "Did that make you blush?"

Xiang Shu quickly stood up, flushed with anger. "What were you doing?!"

Chen Xing quickly waved his hands in apology. Despite his usual menacing demeanor, it seemed that Xiang Shu was embarrassed by close contact—so much so that he actually blushed! It was even more pronounced than his reaction had been when Che Luofeng almost kissed him at the festival. Chen Xing picked up the shield. "Want to go again?"

As Xiang Shu took the shield and headed toward the horses, Che Luofeng approached from off to the side. He stood alone in the open space and watched them from a distance.

Xiang Shu gestured to Chen Xing: *See? I told you so.*

"Snowball fight?" Che Luofeng asked.

Xiang Shu looked Che Luofeng up and down. "Sober now?"

"It's fine!" Che Luofeng waved his hand dismissively, then suddenly broke into a smile.

Xiang Shu motioned for Chen Xing to mount the horse, then sat behind him, carrying the shield. Winding his arms around Chen Xing's waist, he shook the reins and headed up the mountain. After they had gone a few steps, he looked back, and Che Luofeng finally followed, looking somewhat disgruntled.

By this point, the other Tiele, Rouran, and Xiongnu people who had been drinking heavily the night before had also awakened. Carrying shields of their own, they each followed the Great Chanyu, making up for the missed snowball fight from the festival. Soon, more than a thousand people were sliding from the mountaintop to the cliff, creating a spectacular scene. Xiang Shu guided Chen Xing as they slid ahead of the pack, while Che Luofeng chased after them.

"Che Luofeng!" Chen Xing called back, but Xiang Shu forcefully turned his head forward again and told him to look where he was going.

Che Luofeng didn't respond, just continued to join in the fun. More and more people, both women and men, joined them, and before long, a massive snowball fight broke out among the tens of thousands of people at the base of the mountain. Shouts and laughter filled the air.

After he was hit by several of Che Luofeng's snowballs, Chen Xing sensed his hostility. When he glanced over, Che Luofeng gave him a provocative smile. His meaning was clear: *You stole my anda.*

"I'll head back!" Chen Xing said, not knowing what else to say. He turned to Xiang Shu and added, "You guys have fun!"

Xiang Shu had sensed the tension too. He gauged the situation, holding a snowball in his hand. As Chen Xing walked away, Xiang Shu glanced at him, then looked at Che Luofeng with a slight smile. Che Luofeng threw him a carefree grin and struck a playful pose under the sunlight, looking the very picture of an easygoing young man. But Xiang Shu just tossed his snowball to the ground and turned to leave.

Chen Xing returned to the royal tent. He felt groggy; he must have caught a chill the previous night. He prepared a dose of medicine and boiled some hot water. Once he'd taken the medicine, he lay down on the couch to rest.

Before long, Xiang Shu arrived with a bowl of sweet food cooked by the Tiele people. It was a local tradition to eat black ginger and brown sugar stewed rice cakes during the first snow. "Caught a cold?" he asked, frowning.

Chen Xing made an equivocal sound. He smelled the ginger and, recognizing it as a remedy for cold, sat up with much difficulty to drink it. "I just need to sweat it out."

"Even the doctor's sick."

"Of course doctors can get sick. Not everyone is like you, immune to everything."

"And you call yourself an exorcist?" Xiang Shu said mockingly, sitting with him in the tent. "Where's your Heart Lamp?"

Chen Xing sighed. "The Heart Lamp is just a form of magic, not a shield that grants immortality. In fact, using its power is what weakened me. I'd love to be as strong as you guys, you know? Han people can be pretty strong too."

It was true that Han people could be strong. Even after hundreds of years, the various tribes outside the Great Wall held great respect and fear for the strength of the Han army during Emperor Wu's reign. Chen Xing was implying that while his own physical condition was poor, it didn't mean that all Han people were weak. His frailty was due to the Heart Lamp's magic; it had drained his spirit and strength since he was young, leaving him in his current worthless state.

Chen Xing mumbled a few more explanations and then lay back down to sleep, hoping that he could sweat it out and feel better in the morning. Xiang Shu decided to stay in as well. He had risen early, and he soon lay down to sleep.

By evening, the sky grew dim, and a fierce wind picked up, bringing a heavy snowfall. All the same, Che Luofeng braved the snow to call out to Xiang Shu from outside the tent. "Anda, come out. Let's talk."

Xiang Shu glanced at Chen Xing, who was still asleep, and quietly stood up and went outside. Despite the care Xiang Shu took, however, Chen Xing woke suddenly—perhaps the heavens wanted him to overhear the conversation. His mind was clear, and he'd picked up enough of the Rouran language in his time in Chi Le Chuan to understand some of what Che Luofeng said. From the tone, Chen Xing inferred that Che Luofeng was displeased with him.

"Let's discuss this outside the settlement," Xiang Shu said, preparing to leave. "Or do you want to settle things with a fight?"

"Why should I have to avoid speaking in my own home just because of that Han?!" Che Luofeng demanded. Xiang Shu didn't respond, and his eyes began to show clear anger. Che Luofeng raised his voice. "Anda, just how much of that Han boy's provocation have you listened to?!"

"Be quiet, Che Luofeng! He saved your life!"

"So he's using my life to coerce me? Can I return it to him, then?!" Che Luofeng pulled out a dagger and made a slashing motion in front of his abdomen. "Get him out of Chi Le Chuan!"

Chen Xing sat up in the tent. He needed to intervene. There was no need for an outsider like him to strain Xiang Shu and Che Luofeng's relationship.

Outside, Xiang Shu was about to step forward to take the dagger from Che Luofeng when he suddenly stopped. In the midst of the raging wind and snow, several Tiele riders were leading a Hu envoy into the valley.

"Akele's envoy requests an audience with the Great Chanyu!" the leader called.

Chen Xing quickly opened the curtain and stepped out of the royal tent, glancing at Xiang Shu.

"Go back inside," Xiang Shu told him. "You're still not fully recovered."

Che Luofeng's expression was stormy. Now that he knew Chen Xing was awake, Xiang Shu gestured for everyone to come in and speak.

# 32

THE MESSENGER was shivering from the cold. Once he was inside the golden tent, he sunk to one knee and delivered his message in clear Xiongnu.

"The Four Seas and the prairies are the Great Chanyu's land, and all people under the sky are the Great Chanyu's people. We, the Akele, praise the Great Chanyu's martial prowess. I come seeking the leader of the Chi Le Covenant, the greatest warrior and the master of the lands beyond the Great Wall, so that I might request assistance for my people—to save my entire tribe as it hangs in the balance between life and death."

As he spoke, the messenger respectfully presented a black wooden box. Inside the box were four neatly arranged gemstone rings in four different colors: azure, red, ocher, and jade. They all glittered brilliantly.

The moment he saw the rings, Xiang Shu knew the messenger needed something from him. He was only wearing a fur robe, but it didn't detract from his royal demeanor. "Take them back," he said in a deep voice. "I will help you if it's within my power."

The messenger took a deep breath. "We need medical support. Something's happened. It was very sudden..."

When he saw the four rings, Chen Xing remembered one of the scrolls he had read when he stayed with his shifu. It had spoken of a magical artifact—a set of imperial seal rings in four colors. These rings seemed to match the description. According to the scroll, rumor had it that the rings contained the four powers of earth, fire, ice, and wind. They had been created by a Sogdian named Sassan, and they'd been passed along the Silk Road during the Han Dynasty until Zhang Qian brought them back. Afterward, the rings were passed around among many people and eventually disappeared. But without the Spiritual Qi of the Heavens and Earth, Chen Xing had no way to verify whether these were the same fabled rings.

"Did you hear him?" Xiang Shu asked Chen Xing, jolting him back out of his thoughts.

"What?"

Xiang Shu translated the messenger's words. The wife of the Akele tribe's chief was with child, and she had just gone into a difficult labor. The Xarusgol River was frozen, but only with a thin layer of ice, so it was difficult to cross. The snowstorm had hindered them further, trapping them inside a world of ice and snow. The consort's pregnancy had slowed the whole tribe's journey south to Chi Le Chuan for the winter, and now she was in labor.

The arrogant and unassailable Akele had never blended in with the rest of the Ancient Chi Le Covenant. They were always the last ones to arrive for the winter, and they stuck close to their chosen spot and seldom had dealings with the Tiele, Xiongnu, Rouran, or other Hu. They came in late autumn and left in spring. The other people of the Covenant had a poor impression of them that had only worsened when, three years ago, they and the Rouran had a disagreement over living habitats that eventually led to a large-scale battle and resulted in a deep, irreconcilable blood feud.

"Are you going or not?" Xiang Shu asked Che Luofeng. "This is the best opportunity to dispel your blood feud."

This infuriated Che Luofeng, who let out a crazy laugh. "Did I hear that right? Shulü Kong! What have the Akele ever done for the Ancient Covenant? Not a single one of them showed up during the war! They stalled when it was time to support the Great Chanyu's ascension! And now that the heavens' eyes have finally been opened and the world itself plans to exterminate the tribe, here they come with a single box filled with broken jewelry, expecting you to forget the past!"

Xiang Shu's face turned stony, and Chen Xing jumped in to mediate. "I will go with the messenger to have a look."

It was taboo for Che Luofeng to oppose the Great Chanyu in public, but they were anda, so Xiang Shu dispelled his anger and turned to Chen Xing. "Do you know how to deliver the baby?"

Of course Chen Xing knew, but he feared that admitting it might provoke Che Luofeng and Xiang Shu into another quarrel. "I will try my best," he said. "Either way, I need to find the Akele to ask for directions, right?"

"Then pass on my order," Xiang Shu commanded. "Assemble all divisions and prepare carriages and horses. Set out and help the Akele cross the river."

Chen Xing packed up his medicine box, but as he set out to leave, he found Che Luofeng blocking the path in front of the tent.

"I will regard whoever thinks of helping the Akele as my enemy," he announced. "Until Hulunbuir dries up and the Helan Mountains collapse, the grudge between the Rouran and the Akele will never be resolved!"

Xiang Shu got up and slowly stepped forward. Chen Xing said, "I am a doctor; my only concern is to save people. You can settle your grudges at a later date. It has nothing to do with me. Che Luofeng, if you really want to take revenge, why not challenge the Akele? This is just a pregnant woman—"

"Make way," Xiang Shu commanded Che Luofeng in a deep, steady voice, interrupting Chen Xing.

"Shulü Kong," said Che Luofeng, "are you serious? You really want to protect this Han—"

A muffled clap rang out. Xiang Shu had slapped Che Luofeng in the face, so fast that Chen Xing hadn't even seen him move. Xiang Shu had used less than a tenth of his power, but even that was enough to knock Che Luofeng's head against the tent pole.

Chen Xing was shocked, and everyone else around them exclaimed as one. Xiang Shu must have been furious! Chen Xing hurried to try to appease him. "Don't be angry. Calm down, let's talk things out."

"Drag him out!" shouted Xiang Shu. "Pour cold water on him! Tie him to a pillar for four hours!"

A handful of his subordinates arrived at once and escorted Che Luofeng away. Chen Xing hurriedly motioned to the Akele messenger. "Let's go, otherwise the Rouran will come back and trouble you again."

The messenger leaped onto his horse and helped Chen Xing up behind him. Just as they were about to leave the valley, Chen Xing noticed Xiang Shu following them on horseback. "Xiang Shu!" he called back to him.

Xiang Shu spurred his horse until he was riding side by side with them. "Go and lead the carriage team," he told the messenger, who nodded.

Despite Chen Xing's doubts, which he was certain were written right across his face, Xiang Shu reached out and pulled Chen Xing over. Using the borrowed momentum, Chen Xing jumped onto the back of Xiang Shu's horse, and the two riders separated. With Chen Xing safely at his back, Xiang Shu spurred his horse on into the snowstorm.

Hugging Xiang Shu's waist, Chen Xing couldn't stop himself from looking back at the settlement. "Is he okay?!"

"He needs to calm down," said Xiang Shu, looking at the snowstorm.

As they galloped through the blanket of snow, Chen Xing sneezed, and Xiang Shu slowed down the horse. "I've recovered!" Chen Xing insisted. "I'm just a little weak!"

"Are there many Han like you?" Xiang Shu asked out of nowhere.

"What? I told you yesterday! Most Han aren't as weak as me. Haven't you met other Han before?"

"I'm not familiar with many Han," Xiang Shu said. Chen Xing didn't understand. "What I'm asking is, do all Han have the same temperament as you? Is it always this difficult to provoke them, even when they're being bullied on a regular basis?"

"This is called being educated and reasonable! Gentle and cultured! Fuck you! What do you mean, 'bullied on a regular basis'?!"

"Are you cold?" Xiang Shu asked. "Don't you want to sit in the front?"

"Isn't it colder in the front?! You just want to use me to block the wind!"

Heedless of his complaints, Xiang Shu had Chen Xing sit in front of him, then untied the front of his fur overcoat and wrapped it around him. Leaning against Xiang Shu's chest, Chen Xing was surprised to find that he didn't feel cold at all; Xiang Shu's body was very warm, like the fire in a furnace on cold winter night, and it actually made him a little sleepy. There was a very faint scent of the snowdrop bush from the western regions lingering on Xiang Shu's skin.

"Go!" Xiang Shu said to the horse, picking up the space until they were galloping across the snowfield. Chen Xing yawned, hugged Xiang Shu's waist, and let himself doze off, forgetting for the moment that Xiang Shu was the Great Chanyu of the Chi Le Covenant. In his half-sleeping, half-waking state, he remembered only that Xiang Shu was the Protector Martial God for whom he had been waiting a very long time.

It felt as if Xiang Shu, too, had been waiting all his life for Chen Xing. They ignited the Heart Lamp to illuminate the dusky northern night and rode the wind toward the ends of the Divine Land.

Inside the boundless snowstorm, they reached the Xarusgol River. Xiang Shu left the horse on the bank. He woke Chen Xing, laid down his shield, and told Chen Xing to stand on it and wait.

Chen Xing was still muddled from sleep. "What?" he asked, turning around.

"The horse can't get through, the ice is too thin!" said Xiang Shu, clarifying nothing. Chen Xing gave him a bewildered look.

Instead of explaining further, Xiang Shu walked a distance away and then sprinted back toward Chen Xing. He leaped into the air and grabbed Chen Xing, wrapping his arms around him from behind, and his momentum launched them into a slide.

*Crash!* They shot forward into the river, and Chen Xing screamed in horror. Xiang Shu was as fast as lightning, but the strength he used was very precise; the ice split in their wake and shattered into smaller pieces, but for the moment, the two of them were safe and sound. The icy water of the Xarusgol blasted into the sky, and a violent wind blew over them. For a moment, Chen Xing felt like he could hear his own heart pound.

Between one breath and the next, they reached the other side of the river. Chen Xing turned his head to see another torrent rise into the sky to swallow the scattered shards of ice.

"I can't believe you!" Chen Xing said. "What if we fell?!"

Xiang Shu strapped the shield onto his back and walked through the snow, pulling Chen Xing along. The more Chen Xing thought about the fact that Xiang Shu had been relying only on his exceptional physical prowess, the more lingering fear he felt.

"Why are you so troublesome?" said Xiang Shu impatiently.

Not too far away, Chen Xing saw a group of cobbled-together tents—they had finally reached the Akele camp. Someone at the camp saw Xiang Shu and blew the horn, and the tribe's king, who had been anxiously waiting, quickly dispatched a group of warriors to check. They shouted confirmation back when they found it was Xiang Shu. A quarter of an hour later, Xiang Shu was drinking milk tea and chatting with King Akele in the royal tent.

Chen Xing washed his hands with shaojiu so that he could go into another small tent to deliver the consort's baby. King Akele was a rough, robust man of about fifty, and despite his fierce appearance, he was very courteous to Xiang Shu.

When he entered the other tent, Chen Xing found that the situation was already dire. Looking at the consort, he feared that if the baby wasn't delivered quickly, neither she nor her child would survive the night. He hurried back to the royal tent to look for some red sage medications and heart-strengthening pills.

"If she isn't able to push the baby out," Chen Xing told King Akele, "I will save the consort."

Xiang Shu said a few words to King Akele, and they both nodded. King Akele said something, and Xiang Shu translated: "Save the consort."

He put down his teacup then, wanting to help, but Chen Xing made him stay behind to look after King Akele. On the surface, the king looked unconcerned, but his trembling hands betrayed his true feelings.

The consort's complexion was deathly pale, and several tribeswomen were already at her side, helping her. Giving birth on the prairie was like living on the edge; it was very dangerous compared to the Han who lived in the south.

Chen Xing gave medicine to the Akele consort and performed some acupuncture on her. Before long, her complexion recovered a little, and she looked carefully at Chen Xing. "You...you are..."

"I'm a friend of the Great Chanyu." Chen Xing held her hand. "You can speak the Han language? Madam, you must be strong."

"Where is...Xiang...Xiang Yuyan's child?" the consort asked wearily. "Is he here too?"

"Xiang...what Yan?" Chen Xing asked, but a hypothesis was already forming in his head. *Xiang Shu's mother? A Han?!* It was true that Xiang Shu looked like a Han, but Chen Xing was flabbergasted. "You two know each other?"

"You...are also a Han," said the consort as she held Chen Xing's hand. "What's your name?"

Chen Xing opened his mouth to reply, but the gravity of the situation returned to him. "Now's not the time for idle chat! You focus on giving birth, we can talk later... Madam, come on, push hard!"

Her hair all disheveled, the consort pushed with all her strength. "Aaahhhh!"

"Please excuse me, madam. I'm going to overstep a boundary for a moment." Chen Xing condensed the Heart Lamp and pressed it to the consort's heart acupoint. Then, with the bright light protecting her acupoint, he began to perform acupuncture on her. Chen Xing intended to use every means at his disposal to save this woman and her baby.

One hour later, all the tribeswomen cried out in joy.

"Did it work?" Chen Xing asked. "What did they say?"

The voice that answered him was not the consort's but Xiang Shu's, from outside the tent. "The head...the head came out," he translated.

"It's cold outside," Chen Xing admonished him. "Go back inside and drink tea. Madam, keep going! You're going to make it!"

The weather was freezing, but a large crowd had surrounded the outside of the tent. Meanwhile, inside, Chen Xing was sweating all over. He changed needles, applied acupuncture, and fed medicine to the consort, all while encouraging her last bit of willpower. When at last the cry of an infant rang out, Chen Xing felt as if a great weight had been lifted from him, and he nearly collapsed.

Another quarter of an hour later:

*Glug, glug, glug!* Chen Xing poured more than half a pot of milk tea down his throat in King Akele's tent. He was so tired he had difficulty breathing.

After the birth, the household of the consort's maternal uncle had personally come over to express their thanks. Chen Xing had wanted to return their thank-you gifts to them, but Xiang Shu waved his hand to stop him. "If you return a gift from a Xiongnu, they will consider it humiliation," Xiang Shu explained, so Chen Xing had no choice but to accept the gifts.

The snow outside was getting heavier and heavier; they would have to wait until at least the morning to cross the river and go back to Chi Le Chuan. King Akele ordered his subordinates to clear out, arrange a warm tent, and set up a charcoal fire in it so that the two men could sleep. When morning came, a snowstorm was on the horizon—the sky was so dark it was impossible to distinguish night from day. With nothing else to do, Xiang Shu took Chen Xing to King Akele's tent to drink tea, eat roasted meat, and chat.

The Xiongnu dialect spoken by the Akele was much older than anything spoken by the rest of the Hu in Chi Le Chuan. Many of the phonemes were ancient, and even Xiang Shu sometimes didn't understand them. To Chen Xing's ears, they sounded like the rattling of a crow, and it made his head spin.

The consort came out hugging the baby, whose eyes still hadn't opened, and showed it to the crowd. Chen Xing touched the baby's clenched fist. "It's a little prince," he said, smiling.

King Akele had been without an heir for many years following the death of his firstborn. Now, as he approached his fiftieth year, his consort had given birth to another son. Deeply moved, he asked Xiang Shu to name his child. Xiang Shu didn't refuse; he gave the child the name "Nadoro," which meant "the ocean under the mountain" in the ancient Xiongnu language.

Chen Xing caught Xiang Shu's eye, telling him with a look that he wanted to ask King Akele about the matter of the map. Xiang Shu nodded and took out the parchment.

"You actually brought it with you?" asked Chen Xing. It was his turn to feel a little moved. He recalled that Xiang Shu had lagged behind him and the messenger a bit when they first departed—it must have been because he had gone to get the map.

Xiang Shu said many words to King Akele and showed him the map. King Akele was skeptical. He looked it over carefully for a moment before ordering his men to look for someone.

"He said he doesn't know, but some old hunters in the tribe might know something," explained Xiang Shu.

Chen Xing's heart pounded. He hoped with everything he had that someone would be able to give him a clue.

For a time, the only sound inside the tent was the crackling of the furnace fire. The consort handed her baby over to the wet nurse and turned to Xiang Shu, smiling. "Is Chen Xing a relative from your maternal uncle's side?" she asked.

"What?" Xiang Shu looked stunned. "No, he's just...a friend I met in the Central Plains."

Chen Xing nodded and concentrated on drinking his tea.

"Have you found anyone from your mother's family since then?" the consort asked.

"No," replied Xiang Shu. "The land is in chaos due to war, and I didn't go there intending to look for them. My father spent many years trying to find them to no avail." Chen Xing didn't want to interrupt, but Xiang Shu seemed to know what he was thinking. "My mother was a Han," he explained, and Chen Xing nodded.

"Twenty years have passed in the blink of an eye," said the consort.

Xiang Shu huffed. For a moment, he seemed to be lost in his own thoughts, and when he returned to the present, he was met with Chen Xing's uneasy gaze. "It's fine," he assured Chen Xing. "The fact that my mother is a Han is nothing shameful."

"He didn't know?" The consort laughed. "You can clearly tell from his looks," she added to Chen Xing.

Chen Xing had asked Xiang Shu once and nearly gotten himself beaten up, so he'd never dared to ask again. Now, however,

Xiang Shu explained lightly, "My father was so full of sorrow after my mother died that the clansmen refrained from mentioning her. As time passed, the Ancient Covenant started to think that I also didn't like anyone mentioning my mother, so no one ever speaks of her now."

"Shulü Kong's mother was stunning back in the day," the consort said.

"You need only look at her son to see that," agreed Chen Xing.

"My Han name follows my mother's family name," said Xiang Shu. "So now you know."

Chen Xing thought for a moment. "In the future, if you have a chance, you could go south to try to find your maternal uncle's family. I remember there being a large and influential Han family with the family name Xiang..."

"Xiang Yu," Xiang Shu supplied.

Chen Xing nodded. "Yes, he was a famous person in Pengcheng. After the large-scale migration to the South, most of the Central Plains' scholars moved to Kuaiji. I can't say for sure, but you can try asking around Kuaiji."

"Let's talk about it later," said Xiang Shu indifferently.

"When Yuyan was still alive, she once said she had a Han friend, her sworn brother, whose name I have sadly forgotten," the consort put in. "You could also try tracking this man down to find out more. Maybe he's still alive?" Xiang Shu looked a little confused. "I remember that year," the consort added. "It was on the edge of Lake Barkol."

"When did she go to Lake Barkol?" Xiang Shu asked.

"Twenty-two years ago, before you were born. She was walking all the way north the first time I saw her, and she told me she was looking for someone—a man."

"She first came to Chi Le Chuan twenty years ago; that's what my father said when he was still alive."

The consort smiled, not wanting to argue. "I must've remembered it wrong."

"Where is Lake Barkol?" Chen Xing asked, perplexed.

"Further north from here," the consort explained. "It's where we spend the summer."

"She had already come beyond the pass two years before she gave birth to me?" Xiang Shu cut in.

The consort tried hard to recall, but she couldn't remember it clearly after all.

"What's wrong?" Chen Xing asked Xiang Shu. "Is that inconsistent with what you remember?"

Xiang Shu frowned. "My father told me that when he met her, she was being pursued by her enemies and had fainted in the prairie. He came across her while he was hunting and saved her. She settled in Chi Le Chuan after that, and two years later she gave birth to me."

Chen Xing was a little curious about these "enemies," but this was Xiang Shu's past they were talking about; if Xiang Shu didn't explain further, it was better not to pry.

Things became quiet again in the tent until King Akele's men came in with two old hunters. The hunters bowed to Xiang Shu and greeted him as their Great Chanyu, then stepped closer to read the parchment.

They said something to Xiang Shu, and the consort translated for them. "There is indeed such a place," she said. "They ask the Great Chanyu how he learned of it." This was for Chen Xing's benefit, but also for Xiang Shu's; the ancient dialect had a strong accent, and the consort was saving Xiang Shu the effort of deciphering their words.

Chen Xing was overjoyed. "Where is it?"

The two old hunters began to draw the route to the place on another piece of parchment. "They say that this is a cursed place where mountain ghouls often appear," the consort explained. "They went there to hunt once, ten years ago..."

"Mountain ghouls?" Chen Xing asked, bemused. "What's a mountain ghoul?" He had heard of mountain demons, but the ancient texts had never recorded those as "mountain ghouls." A mountain demon was a one-legged supernatural being with a child's face. They had once lived deep in the mountains, but they'd vanished long ago.

"The dead," the consort explained, "are buried in the mountains. If their bodies don't rot after a few years have passed, they become mountain ghouls."

Chen Xing whipped his head around to look at Xiang Shu, who gazed back at him levelly. *Drought fiends?!*

"Go on," Xiang Shu ordered.

Once the two men had completed their map, they shared their stories, each supporting and building on the other's. Carosha, the place mentioned in the Xiongnu legend, was real. Nobody knew exactly from which period it originated, but rumor said it was from an ancient time before the invention of written records.

According to the legend, a dragon god once fell in the north. Its corpse turned into three steep mountains, and its flowing blood formed a large lake. This place became a sacred mountain where the Xiongnu buried their dead warriors, but over time, as the dragon god's body decomposed, it expelled a gas that gradually revived their corpses. Any person who accidentally trespassed on the mountain would find themselves trapped there forever.

Of course, Chen Xing knew that there were many such mystifying legends among the tribes. In his view, the main purpose behind the spread of these legends was to dissuade people from disturbing burial grounds. If these mountain ghouls and drought fiends were indeed one and the same, he couldn't understand why they'd be there, of all places. To trek so far north just to refine a pile of drought fiends, all while the bitter cold had frozen everything and made it almost impossible to walk properly... Who had the time for that? Not to mention the high risk of getting oneself buried in an avalanche.

"What did the mountain ghoul you saw look like?" asked Xiang Shu.

The two old hunters described it vividly, but neither of them had actually seen the mountain ghoul's true face. Chen Xing breathed a sigh of relief. He did, however, notice King Akele and his consort exchanging looks—something felt a little off.

Xiang Shu nodded and thanked the hunters before handing the map to Chen Xing. "Tomorrow," he said to King Akele, "when the Xarusgol River has completely frozen, the Tiele and Xiongnu will be able to cross the river and escort you to Chi Le Chuan. The location for the camp has already been chosen; it's the same as last year."

King Akele thanked him again.

"Is there anything else you know about the mountain ghouls?" Chen Xing cut in. It was sheer intuition, but Chen Xing had a hunch that King Akele and his consort were afraid of something.

The consort shook her head with a blank expression. King Akele changed the subject and said something to Xiang Shu. Xiang Shu noticed this, but he didn't push King Akele to say more; he just nodded.

That night, the entire tribe began to gather up their things in preparation for the next day's river crossing. Chen Xing returned to his tent. It was freezing outside, and this was only the beginning of winter—

it was ruthlessly cold along the Xarusgol river. Without the Yin Mountains to shield them from the wind, the Akele probably wouldn't survive longer than a month or two up here.

Even inside the tent, Chen Xing was shivering a little.

"You still want to go north even with this constitution of yours," Xiang Shu remarked. "It's even colder up there."

"I've just been feeling weak lately," said Chen Xing. "Everything will be fine once I've recovered a little."

Xiang Shu opened his quilt and moved over a bit. "Come and sleep here."

That was exactly what Chen Xing had been hoping for. Still shivering, he walked over and folded his quilt over Xiang Shu's, then wormed his way in. *Che Luofeng once tried to get into your quilt,* he thought, *and you kicked him out—but you're actually treating me nicely?*

"Is the consort hiding something?" Chen Xing asked. "And why do I get the sense that King Akele knows something too?"

"You should be careful about prying into matters other people don't want to divulge."

"You've been a lot more calm and good-tempered lately, you know. You haven't been mean to me in a while either."

"I'm not crazy," Xiang Shu retorted. "If you're polite, why should I be mean to you?"

Lying down with Xiang Shu warmed Chen Xing up a lot. He felt like his whole person was coming back to life. They were sharing a quilt, though, which put them in awfully close quarters; their faces were mere inches from each other, and the proximity made Chen Xing's face turn red. Before Chen Xing could turn over, though, Xiang Shu turned to lie flat on his back, putting a bit of distance between them. He bent one knee under the quilt, tenting it.

Chen Xing's heart was in his throat, and for a moment, he felt consumed by confusion and ambiguity. He recalled what he'd said to Tuoba Yan that day under the tree. *I couldn't have feelings for Xiang Shu...right?* No, no—Chen Xing forced the idea out of his mind. *Maybe it's just a sense of dependency on my protector.*

From the moment Chen Xing had first learned that he would have to find a protector, he had built up expectations for that person, whose name and origin he hadn't even yet known. When he got closer to Xiang Shu, his expectations seemed to have manifested into reality.

As the night wore on, Chen Xing kept tossing and turning. He couldn't sleep well; his heart was a mess. At one point, he saw from the corner of his eye that Xiang Shu was looking at him, so he rolled over onto his side to talk to him.

## 33

"THE CONSORT IS GETTING ON in years," said Chen Xing. "The successful delivery of her baby was truly a blessing from the heavens."

"King Akele once had another son," Xiang Shu told him. "He died in battle against the Rouran tribe. That's why I felt I ought to come and check on them this time. Che Luofeng bears some responsibility for their circumstances, after all."

No wonder Che Luofeng's expression had been so strange whenever he mentioned the Akele. Chen Xing turned his head a little to get a better look at Xiang Shu. "Does this kind of situation happen often outside the Great Wall?"

"Yes, it happens a lot," Xiang Shu said with a shrug. "It's even fiercer than the aggression between the Hu and the Han in the south. There has always been infighting among the Hu outside the Great Wall. For the past few decades, everyone has lived in a state of 'I'll kill you before you can kill me.' The tribes may seem to be living in harmony inside the Ancient Chi Le Covenant, but in reality, there are blood feuds between all of them."

"So...no matter the place or tribe, there is always a need for education and order."

"That's easier said than done." Xiang Shu seemed to be deep in thought. "Reconciling the Rouran and Akele took a lot of effort in the first place, and Che Luofeng, well..." He sighed again.

There was a moment of silence. "Che Luofeng wouldn't deliberately cause trouble with the Akele, would he?" asked Chen Xing.

"That depends on him." Xiang Shu frowned deeply. "Three years ago, Zhou Zhen, the finest Rouran warrior, died at the hands of the Akele. He was Che Luofeng's..."

"Brother-in-arms," Chen Xing offered, recalling some conversations about the Rouran's past he had overheard back in Chi Le Chuan.

"Not just that. Zhou Zhen was Che Luofeng's sweetheart. They were a couple."

Chen Xing blinked. "A girl? Family name Zhou? Or was she a Han?"

"A man," Xiang Shu said, "with mixed Han and Rouran blood. Zhou Zhen-xiong was two years older than me. When the Rouran king was still on his throne, he and Che Luofeng were always inseparable..."

"Maybe he was simply guarding Che Luofeng?"

Chen Xing was lying on his side, facing Xiang Shu. At this point, Xiang Shu turned over so that he was also lying on his side, his ear pressed against the wooden pillow. Now he and Chen Xing were facing each other.

"The way those two looked at each other was unmistakable," said Xiang Shu. "I don't want to talk about it anymore."

Some strange, unidentifiable emotion gripped Chen Xing then, but beneath it, he also felt a twinge of sympathy for Che Luofeng. Three years ago, in the same scuffle in which the Akele lost their eldest prince, Che Luofeng had lost his lover. Chen Xing wondered now if Che Luofeng had simply transferred his affections onto Xiang Shu, his anda.

Apparently, Xiang Shu was well aware of all this. He simply hadn't mentioned it.

"I think Che Luofeng—"

Xiang Shu's tone became harsher. "I said I don't want to talk about it anymore."

"You treat him very well," Chen Xing said a little sourly.

"Are you angling for another beating?"

Chen Xing was forced to drop it. Under the cover of the dark night, though, he summoned up his courage to ask, "Can you stop being so mean, Xiang Shu? I know this isn't what you're really like."

Xiang Shu remained silent.

When he'd first learned about Xiang Shu's deeds from Zhu Xu, Chen Xing had slotted him into a category in his mind: a Hu man who was fierce, violent, and addicted to killing. But since then he'd gotten to know Xiang Shu and discovered that Xiang Shu didn't love fighting at all. When he was ambushed in the middle of the night on the streets of Chang'an, he chose to withdraw and retreat, preventing the patrolling city soldiers from wasting their lives trying to fight enemies too powerful for them to contend with. Almost every time he had to fight hand-to-hand, he relied on his martial prowess to hit the other person's pressure points and teach them a lesson by knocking them down. The only person Chen Xing had ever seen him kill was Princess Qinghe...and when Chen Xing thought back on that situation, he couldn't see any other choice for Xiang Shu.

In front of him, a strange expression crossed Xiang Shu's face, but Chen Xing was still lost in thought.

When he'd returned to Chi Le Chuan, Xiang Shu had done his best to maintain the Ancient Covenant and ensure that each tribe peacefully coexisted with the others. He took this duty very seriously. The Akele and the Rouran were at odds, but Xiang Shu never discriminated against either tribe, and he was even assisting the Akele right now. That was why...

"I really think that your viciousness is just a facade," Chen Xing said, getting right to the heart of the matter. "You keep it up because you need to maintain your reputation as the Great Chanyu; you need to make all the tribes in the Ancient Covenant respect and fear you. That's why using brute force all the time to suppress them became a habit for you. Am I right?"

Xiang Shu sat up suddenly. Chen Xing backed away at once, afraid that Xiang Shu would hit him again, but Xiang Shu wordlessly put on his robe, tied his belt, and went outside.

Chen Xing sat up too. "Xiang Shu!" he called after him. "Can't we just have a proper chat?" He must have been right; Xiang Shu did, in fact, have a gentle and tender heart. He wasn't a typical Hu person at all.

The entrance of the tent opened and Xiang Shu poked his head inside, frowning deeply. "Get out here, quick! Put on your clothes!"

Chen Xing was confused. In fact, what had happened was that Xiang Shu had detected a weak tremor in the distance, deep in the night while the entire Akele camp was fast asleep. He strapped his sword to his back and rushed into King Akele's royal tent, shouting in the Xiongnu language so loudly he woke almost the entire camp.

It was the fifth watch of the night, and the wild winds outside were whipping up a snowstorm. Feeling dazed, Chen Xing ran outside and saw Xiang Shu wading through the snow, leading the Akele warriors and directing them to take up guard positions around the camp.

"There's nothing out there!" Chen Xing shouted.

"Go to the rear! Stay with the king's consort!" Xiang Shu readied his bow and nocked an arrow.

Everyone was on edge; they could all smell an odd scent on the wind. The wind was numbingly cold, but this time, Chen Xing caught yet another strange scent—the foul stench of corpses.

The Akele shouted loudly in the Xiongnu language. Xiang Shu said something angry-sounding to King Akele, and King Akele panicked. Trudging through the snow, the warriors took up their battle formation. As soon as they were in place, Xiang Shu turned his head to the side, drew his longbow, and loosed his first arrow into the snowstorm.

They heard an anguished scream. It was followed by the miserable shriek of an Akele warrior as he was thrown to the ground by a living corpse that had rushed out of the darkness.

"What are they doing here?!" yelled Chen Xing.

"Withdraw to the riverbank!" Xiang Shu called out. "Chen Xing, you go first!"

"I won't! Why should I?!"

In the brief lull, Xiang Shu looked around them and turned to Chen Xing with a cold look on his face. "The Akele have known for a long time that there are drought fiends in the north."

"What?" Chen Xing looked over, blank-faced, at the Akele, but Xiang Shu was right: The situation seemed a little fishy. When the Akele saw the drought fiends, they didn't show the slightest hint of panic. In fact, they kept on shooting arrows as they retreated, as if they had fought drought fiends before.

It wasn't easy to light torches in a snowstorm, so they were surrounded by darkness. The camp had fallen into enemy hands. Behind them, screams and cries of pain rang out. They had no idea how many living corpses were lurking in the dark night. Chen Xing quickly lit up the Heart Lamp to illuminate a small area in front of him.

Living corpses! Thousands of them! And that was just what was in front of him; he didn't know how many more might be behind him, trampling over the snow to reach the camp. They were unbelievably lucky that Xiang Shu's ear had been pressed against the wooden pillow. That was the only reason he'd been able to detect the tremors in the ground. If he had understood what was happening even a moment later, the Akele camp would have had no hope of escaping the ambush.

Someone sounded a horn inside the camp, and the Akele fled. King Akele set fire to the tents, and the flames burst into the sky, hindering the living corpses' movements. Chen Xing spread his arms to send out a bright burst of light from the Heart Lamp. The living corpses around them backed away, then let out wild cries and turned to hunt down the scattering Akele.

Xiang Shu loosed several arrows in quick succession while Chen Xing cast his magic. The shining arrows pierced the group of living corpses in front of the two men, clearing a path. When his quiver was finally empty, Xiang Shu grabbed his sword off his back and swept it in an arc.

Chen Xing, meanwhile, snagged a horse's reins. "Get on the horse!" he yelled as he mounted it, and Xiang Shu got up behind him. "Still want to tell me to hide? Can you kill the enemy if I'm hiding? Hmm?"

"Shut up!" shouted Xiang Shu. "We have to help them! Come on!"

Chen Xing tried to control the horse, but the Xiongnu horses' temperaments were fiery, and in the low visibility of the snowstorm, it went running every which way and crashed into a lot of things. "This horse doesn't listen to orders!"

Xiang Shu wrapped his left arm around Chen Xing's waist to take the reins, steering the horse right into the group of living corpses. The living corpses were chasing the retreating Akele, and the women and children who were fleeing on foot at the rear of the group were about to be overrun.

"Light!" Xiang Shu called out. Chen Xing put one hand on Xiang Shu's sword arm and did his best to push the Heart Lamp's light into it.

Suddenly, a bright light burst out of the sword, transforming it into a shining beacon in the dark night. This beam was even more dazzling than the ones they'd managed in the past, and when Xiang Shu waved his sword, he sent out an invisible shockwave that overturned the living corpses in front of him.

Xiang Shu yanked the horse to a stop at the riverbank and dismounted. The Akele had escaped to the banks of the Xarusgol. Xiang Shu grabbed King Akele by the collar and asked him a furious question that drained King Akele's face of all color.

"What's going on?" Chen Xing asked. "Let him go! The drought fiend horde is coming again!"

Xiang Shu was forced to let go of King Akele. He took the bundle of rope off the king and slung it over his own shoulder instead, then pointed behind him and gestured for the king to quickly cross the river. Chen Xing stopped beside Xiang Shu, formed a circle with his hands, and began to cast a spell to call forth the light of the Heart Lamp.

Suddenly, a shout in the Tiele language came from the south bank of Xarusgol River.

"The reinforcements are here!" Chen Xing cried out in relief. "Do we still fight?"

"Withdraw!" Xiang Shu tied one end of the rope around his waist and tossed the other end to Chen Xing. "The time for your revenge has come! If you want to get back at me, all you have to do is let go!"

Chen Xing held the rope, baffled.

The Akele withdrew across the frozen river, with the living corpses slipping and sliding across the ice in pursuit. Chen Xing retreated to the south bank—only to see Xiang Shu take a few running steps and jump off a rock on the bank. As he leaped, he pulled out his sword, did a full turn in the air, and arched backward, hefting that heavy sword over his head. Then he brought it down on the ice with all the strength he had.

The sound of the ice cracking was so loud it made Chen Xing's ears ring. The ice splintered along the surface in a pattern like a cobweb, then burst into pieces, and a torrent of water gushed forth to block the living corpses' path.

Chen Xing immediately gripped the rope and pulled on it madly until he managed to fish Xiang Shu out of the icy water. "You're insane!" he yelled.

Xiang Shu splashed out of the water with a bloodthirsty grin on his face. They turned in tandem to see that the unstoppable living corpses had fallen into the water. They still weren't sure how many were left on the north bank, but they did see a living corpse almost ten feet tall, dressed in the leather armor of the Xiongnu and armed with a scimitar, standing there. It seemed to be the pack's leader.

Chen Xing stared. The Tiele and Xiongnu had arrived to welcome the caravan, and they headed back south with the Akele. In no time at all, the snowstorm covered everything, obstructing their line of sight.

Why were the drought fiends here? When Chen Xing had first seen them in the camp, his heart had stopped beating.

Xiang Shu had only spent a few seconds in the water, but ice was forming in his hair and eyebrows. Chen Xing had no time to spare for the Akele. As fast as he could, he secured Xiang Shu in the carriage at the end of the line. "Let's go! Back to Chi Le Chuan!"

Xiang Shu took a deep breath, but he couldn't stop shivering. Chen Xing worked quickly: He removed Xiang Shu's wet fur coat for him and pulled his robes open, then wiped his body dry and covered him with a rug. Next, he took off his own outer robe and, after a moment of thought, decided he might as well take off his inner robes as well. Thus, wearing nothing but his underwear, he lifted a corner of the rug, snuggled into Xiang Shu's lap, and wrapped the rug tight around them both.

Xiang Shu immediately wrapped his arms around Chen Xing and buried his head in Chen Xing's shoulder.

"Motherfucker!" Chen Xing wailed. "You're so cold! Ugh!"

Xiang Shu's skin was cold beyond compare; he was almost frozen solid. Chen Xing, on the other hand, was still warm, so he had no choice but to endure Xiang Shu's embrace.

"Ha..." Xiang Shu breathed deeply and evenly. Chen Xing rubbed Xiang Shu's chest, protecting his heart meridian, while Xiang Shu kept up his breathing pattern. Before long, his body slowly began to warm up.

Chen Xing touched his shoulders and back, then pressed his cheek to Xiang Shu's chest. The cold wind blew violently outside the open carriage. As Chen Xing helped Xiang Shu clear away the ice shards clinging to his eyelashes, he thought, *This guy's eyelashes are so long, just like a girl's.*

"All right, I've come back to life now," Xiang Shu said at last, letting go of Chen Xing.

"I really should've taken the opportunity to hit you in revenge when you were still frozen stiff," Chen Xing said expressionlessly.

"Then hit me now. I won't fight back."

"You won't?"

"Not right now. Wait until we reach Chi Le Chuan; I'll fight back then."

Chen Xing didn't dignify that with a response. Instead, he poked his head out from under the rug and peered toward the head of the caravan. "Why on earth were there drought fiends here? Who's going to explain that to me?"

Xiang Shu stuffed Chen Xing's head back under the rug, encouraging him to sleep. "When we get back to Chi Le Chuan, you'll know."

It took the caravan almost eight hours to reach Chi Le Chuan. After Xiang Shu got out of the carriage, the first thing he did was grab King Akele by the front of his robes and drag him inside the royal tent. He then ordered a meeting with all the tribal chiefs of the Ancient Covenant.

On the northern side of Chi Le Chuan, every tribe's riders assembled on the plains, preparing to face down a great enemy. They'd increased the number of patrols and pushed some anti-cavalry barriers into place. Despite the violent snowstorm, the archers had their quivers slung over their backs, and now they lit torches and lay in wait in front of the camp. All scouts were dispatched to watch for any movement along the Xarusgol River.

Inside the tent, a thunderous quarrel was ongoing. Each of the tribal chiefs spoke a different language, which made communication nearly impossible as they asked questions and cursed in equal measure. King Akele's face was ashen, and Xiang Shu, who had changed into his royal robe, sat silently on the Great Chanyu's seat and listened.

From all the shouting, Chen Xing gleaned roughly what was being said, but the more he listened, the more shocked he was.

As early as half a month ago, King Akele had been attacked by living corpses in the eastern part of the Barkol region. As a result, the Akele had hurriedly withdrawn to Chi Le Chuan. Any time he was asked a question, King Akele answered with just a single sentence, clearly unwilling to elaborate.

"Why aren't you addressing this?" the Loufan king demanded.

"When the Great Chanyu heard your tribe was stranded, he immediately led his men to assist you," the Tiele king added. "This is how you repay Chi Le Chuan?!"

"I never thought they'd come back!" King Akele replied. "How was I to know that these mountain ghouls would pursue us so relentlessly?"

Che Luofeng, whose face was still red and swollen where Xiang Shu had hit him, was rejoicing in King Akele's misfortune. He let out a cold chuckle at King Akele's words—not his first in this meeting. Xiang Shu shot him a threatening look, reminding him not to be arrogant.

"King Akele," Chen Xing said in the Han language, "you've been aware of the living corpses this entire time, and the appearance of this horde must have something to do with you. If you don't tell us what you know, they will come back again. Tell me: How are we going to deal with them then?"

Everyone stared blankly at him—they didn't understand the Han language. Xiang Shu had to translate for them.

"Aren't you a sorcerer from the Central Plains?" said King Akele. "Surely you have a way to handle them!"

"Impudence!" Xiang Shu snarled, making King Akele quiver. He was already anxious, and that shout stunned him into speechlessness.

Chen Xing felt as if his head was going to explode. He wasn't familiar with these barbarians' languages or speaking habits. He felt like a chicken trying to hold a conversation with a group of ducks; he couldn't communicate with them at all.

"Let me tell them," the consort said in a quiet voice. She was sitting off to one side of the tent. "You see, the one who is leading the mountain ghouls...he's my son."

Chen Xing was stunned.

"Three years ago, Che Luofeng of the Rouran tribe killed my son." The consort looked toward Che Luofeng with tears in her eyes. "He carved my son's heart out of his chest."

Xiang Shu leaned to the side and quietly translated this for Chen Xing. Chen Xing grew even more suspicious.

Che Luofeng sneered at her. "Your child murdered many of my warriors, and my Zhou Zhen! He deserved to die! I'd like nothing more than to rip your hearts out as well!"

"Shut up!" Xiang Shu shouted. "Che Luofeng, are you asking for another beating?!"

Che Luofeng shut his mouth, but his resentment was still clear on his face.

The consort composed herself and continued. "During the wake, a doctor came to Lake Barkol. Just like your Han friend, he possessed divine medical skills..."

Suddenly, Xiang Shu stopped translating. Chen Xing tugged the corner of his robe, urging him to hurry up and translate, but he didn't. "Kjera," he said. A name.

The consort looked startled, but she nodded. For a moment, Chen Xing was lost, but then he remembered: Wasn't that the name of the doctor who took care of Xiang Shu's father, the former Great Chanyu?!

"What did he do to your son?" Xiang Shu asked in the Han language.

"He told us that he happened to have a 'heart' with him," the consort replied in the same language, "which he was going to give to us as a present. He procured a black heart from within a wooden box he was carrying and put it inside Youduo's chest cavity, and he gave him a dose of some kind of medicine. Three days later, Youduo came back to life. But after he came back to life, he didn't eat or drink, nor did he sleep. He couldn't even recognize me, his father, or any of his tribesmen. Finally, one day, he left us and went north. It wasn't until this autumn that he came back, and when he did, he brought with him the mountain ghouls under his command..." The consort buried her head in her hands and wept, her voice choked with emotion. "I dreamed of him. He pointed at his own heart, asking me why I didn't help him take his revenge, why..."

Xiang Shu got up and walked toward the entrance of the royal tent, issuing commands as he went. "From now on, all tribes will be on a rotating patrol schedule. We must prepare to fight the drought fiends. Any tribe that complains about personal grievances will, without exception, be expelled from the Ancient Chi Le Covenant."

Che Luofeng looked at Xiang Shu, a complicated mix of emotions on his face. Xiang Shu just gestured at Chen Xing, turned, and walked out of the tent.

The snow had lessened that afternoon, and the Tiele took the opportunity to construct wooden defensive lines along the northern side of Chi Le Chuan.

Chen Xing came to a stop by the defensive lines. Xiang Shu, clad head to toe in metal armor, was in the middle of issuing instructions to the commanders of all the tribes, preparing them for what was to come.

"Don't allow yourselves to be scratched or bitten," Xiang Shu warned them repeatedly. "When you see a corpse, behead it. Do not draw out the fight."

Now he'd sorted out the consort's narration of how she was acquainted with Kjera, Chen Xing was almost certain that this doctor was a member of the mysterious group that was using resentment to create the drought fiends. It was even possible that he was the reason for everything—the puppeteer behind the scenes, the mastermind hiding in the dark. Three years ago, he'd headed beyond the pass, where he'd turned the Akele prince into a living corpse; then, on his way south, he'd fed the former Great Chanyu a mysterious drug.

"Youduo was the same as your father," Chen Xing muttered. "They were both turned into living corpses. If we can locate Kjera, maybe we can shed some light on the origin of this drought fiend chaos."

"That bastard left for the south three years ago," Xiang Shu replied. "He must be hiding in the Central Plains by now. He may have even reached the southern bank of the Yangtze River. Once things are settled here, even if I have to chase him to the ends of the earth, I *will* find him."

Chen Xing took a deep breath. "The living corpses have probably crossed the river by now."

Xiang Shu nodded. "The scouts have already sent back reports that they're wading through the snow."

Frowning, Chen Xing looked up at the sky. "It would be better if the snow were heavier." The living corpses had a hard time moving to begin with, so if the snowstorm had come a few days earlier, they might have been buried in the snow before they ever reached Chi Le Chuan.

*Why are they so persistent in going south? What purpose drives them?* No matter how many times he asked himself these questions, Chen Xing couldn't find an answer. *Where do they come from? And where are they going?*

Countless questions whirled through Chen Xing's mind. He frowned again. "Xiang Shu, I'm not sure why, but I suspect the origin of this group of drought fiends is related in some way to Mount Erchilun, the area where the dragon fell in the Xiongnu legend. We have to leave as soon as possible and head north."

From the foot of the Yin Mountains, a signal horn sounded. "We must repel them first!" said Xiang Shu. "Everything else can wait. Get ready! Prepare to fight!"

The snow had stopped. In the fields that stretched as far as the eye could see, innumerable living corpses in worn-out, rusted armor waded through the snow, charging toward Chi Le Chuan.

A FIERCE BATTLE erupted. Chen Xing mounted his horse, and from behind him, cavalry from every tribe charged out in full force. In the blink of an eye, more than ten thousand riders stormed out of the camp brandishing long blades. They plunged into the horde of undead and slashed through them.

"Cut off their heads!" Xiang Shu commanded.

Chen Xing rode forward too. His initial thought was to assist Xiang Shu with his Heart Lamp, but he quickly realized it wasn't necessary. This was the first time he'd witnessed Chi Le Chuan's cavalry in action, and the warriors from each tribe advanced and retreated in perfect coordination, clearly well trained. They'd heeded Xiang Shu's warning regarding their hands and legs; they were all equipped with arm and leg guards, and even the warhorses were clad in iron-plated armor. Light reflected off of sabers everywhere Chen Xing looked, and none of the warriors seemed to require more than a single stroke to behead their enemies. The undead horde was swiftly overcome.

The drought fiends, Chen Xing noticed, moved sluggishly in this icy, snow-covered terrain, likely frozen by the cold. They were far less nimble than the ones he and Xiang Shu had faced in Chang'an City. Between their diminished pace and the ferocity of Chi Le Chuan's cavalry, which was unmatched even by the heavily armored

Qin cavalry of Guanzhong, it was less than a quarter of an hour before the frozen battlefield was strewn with headless corpses.

Meanwhile, Xiang Shu led the Tiele warriors through two fierce charges. When he observed that the situation was no longer critical, he pulled back and oversaw the battle from the outskirts.

"They're retreating!" someone shouted.

It was true: The undead horde was scattering, fleeing northward, though its leader had yet to appear. Chen Xing finally reached the front lines then, and he surveyed the dead bodies on the battlefield with confusion.

Xiang Shu ordered the troops to stand down and not pursue the enemy. The outcome was already decided; the Chi Le Chuan cavalry, with their overwhelming numbers and strength, had claimed a decisive victory.

It was then that Che Luofeng finally arrived at the battlefield with the Rouran troops.

"You're too late; it's over," Xiang Shu said, removing his helmet and tossing it to the ground. From horseback, Che Luofeng looked down at the field littered with corpses. "Have your men gather the bodies and burn them. Don't touch them!"

Chen Xing waved his hand as if to say that it wasn't a big deal and began inspecting one of the corpses. Xiang Shu took off his steel gloves and tossed them to Chen Xing. The gloves weighed several pounds, but Chen Xing slipped one on, flipped over a headless body, and removed the breastplate, examining it closely in the sunlight.

Unlike the Chang'an drought fiends, which had been mostly a mix of Han and Hu commoners, these corpses from beyond the Great Wall were all Hu people, and nearly all of them were warriors. These were home-grown, locally farmed undead.

"Have you seen this kind of armor before?" Chen Xing asked.

Xiang Shu frowned in silence. King Akele came over with his warriors and said something to Xiang Shu, and they looked at the armor and began deliberating.

"Xiongnu armor," Xiang Shu said finally. "These awakened corpses are all Xiongnu warriors who died anywhere from a hundred years to just a couple of decades ago."

Chen Xing put down the breastplate, his confusion deepening. "Where were these people buried after they died?"

"In Carosha. It used to be the Xiongnu burial ground."

Chen Xing recalled what the king's consort had told him: Years ago, her firstborn son, Youduo, had "returned from the dead" and left the tribe soon after, heading even further north. When he returned years later, he brought with him tens of thousands of Xiongnu warriors who were supposed to be dead...

The answer was becoming clear. Something had happened in the mountains of Carosha.

The group dismounted and passed by the camp. On one side of Chi Le Chuan, the decapitated heads of the living corpses had been separated from their bodies and piled up in small mounds. Each mound was stacked on a pile of wood, topped with chunks of butter. Xiang Shu took a torch and ignited the wood pile, and flames erupted skyward, engulfing the heap of corpses.

Of the Hu tribes in Chi Le Chuan, the Xiongnu were the most numerous, followed by the Tiele and then the Rouran and Shiwei. The Xiongnu gathered in droves, kneeling outside the burning pyre and singing a mournful ballad.

"There's still no sign of Youdou," Xiang Shu said. "He must be nearby."

"What did they come here for?" asked Chen Xing.

A Xiongnu warrior spoke a long string of words to Xiang Shu, leaving Chen Xing puzzled. "The Xiongnu believe that the dead became mountain ghouls and returned to life because they have unfulfilled wishes from their past lives," Xiang Shu explained.

Chen Xing pondered for a moment, then shook his head. "I doubt that."

"It's just a legend," said Xiang Shu. He was clearly skeptical, though he didn't elaborate further and averted his gaze slightly.

A terrifying thought struck Chen Xing: What if these living corpses were after him? They had quelled the drought fiend disturbance in Chang'an, but the mastermind behind it had yet to reveal himself. What if their goal was to eliminate Chen Xing and prevent him from thwarting their plans, even if they had to travel a thousand miles to do it?

As this thought crossed his mind, a disquieting sensation washed over him—he felt as though someone was watching him from the shadows. "I have to leave," he said. "They might be after me."

Xiang Shu understood what Chen Xing was thinking and dismissed it at once. "That's impossible! Kjera came to the prairie three years ago. How would you explain that, if this is all because of you?"

"Do you know where the mountain ghouls come from?" asked Che Luofeng, who was listening off to one side.

Xiang Shu turned to him. "I'll be heading north tomorrow. Anda, I'm leaving Chi Le Chuan in your care."

A wave of relief washed over Chen Xing.

"I had luggage packed on the day of the Autumn Close Festival," Xiang Shu said to Chen Xing. "We can leave any time."

Since their last argument, Che Luofeng had avoided speaking to Chen Xing. He addressed Xiang Shu in the Rouran language. "Where are you going?"

"Carosha, where the ancient dragon fell."

"You can't!" Che Luofeng exclaimed. "The Akele told me that the mountain ghouls will be back again!"

"I need to find out what's really going on. Chen Xing followed me to Chi Le Chuan for this very reason. You wouldn't know this, but there was a similar drought fiend disturbance in Chang'an. We didn't understand the situation in time then, and it led to a tragedy."

"No wonder," Che Luofeng said. He glanced at Chen Xing. "So it was you who brought them here!"

"It has nothing to do with him!" Xiang Shu snapped, before Chen Xing could respond. "Che Luofeng! Forget it..." He sounded quite frustrated. He reached out to Che Luofeng, but his hand was brushed aside. It was clear that Che Luofeng still held a grudge over Xiang Shu beating him up.

Chen Xing, standing in front of the royal tent, could feel the rising tension. "I'll go pack my things," he said quickly.

"What on earth is wrong with you?!" Xiang Shu demanded, knitting his brows.

"That's what I want to ask!" Che Luofeng shot back. "You're Chi Le Chuan's Great Chanyu! The enemy hasn't been dealt with—who knows where that monster Youduo is hiding—and you're leaving now? To go north with this Han?"

"You're here!" Xiang Shu said, his tone serious. "I'm entrusting Chi Le Chuan to you. You're the only one I can trust!"

Chen Xing heard these words as he entered the tent and felt another strange emotion wash over him. It was tinged with a bit of sadness. This, perhaps, was the kind of trusting, life-and-death friendship he had yearned for.

"I'm not the Grand Chanyu!" Che Luofeng insisted. "I won't take responsibility for what happens here!"

Xiang Shu looked closely at Che Luofeng, still frowning, and let out a weary sigh. "Are you a child?"

"You've changed. Anda, you've changed. You left for the Central Plains, disappeared for a year, and came back with this shady Han dog by your side. Now you're so smitten with him that you don't even want to be the Grand Chanyu anymore?!"

"You..." Xiang Shu began, clearly taken aback, but before he could say anything more, Chen Xing finally snapped.

"Who the hell are you calling a Han dog?!" he shouted, throwing down the medicine box. He grabbed the longbow from the tent, strung the bow, and stepped outside. Drawing the bowstring back, he aimed at Che Luofeng. "A Han dog? A Han dog saved your life! Is this how you treat your savior?! You worthless piece of Rouran trash! If I'm a dog, you're something even worse!"

Chen Xing had reached his breaking point; this was more than he could bear. Throughout his stay in Chi Le Chuan, he had tried to be patient and accommodating, not wanting to create conflict with Che Luofeng as a guest. He had pretended not to notice the jealous glares Che Luofeng shot at him, but enough was enough. He didn't want to tolerate this man any longer.

With Chen Xing's arrow pointed at Che Luofeng, silence fell outside the tent. Snow began to fall again, dancing and swirling in the air; a few snowflakes landed on the arrow. Xiang Shu extended his hand and pressed down Chen Xing's bow. Trembling in anger, Chen Xing lowered it.

But Che Luofeng started to laugh. "Oh? How about this: Let's step outside and settle this with archery. Three arrows each, a fight to the death. Are you brave enough, little Han?"

Chen Xing was no match for Che Luofeng at equestrian archery. He would be shot dead.

"Che Luofeng!" Xiang Shu shouted. "If you keep this up, whatever I do to you will be your own fault!"

"Wait!" a woman's voice cut in. "I'll take his place in this duel."

It was none other than the King Akele's consort. Chen Xing gaped at her. King Akele and the consort had approached Xiang Shu's tent, where they'd seen Che Luofeng and Chen Xing in a standoff.

"The Divine Doctor saved both me and my son," the consort continued, "so that Youduo, who died at your hands, could have a younger brother, and the Akele bloodline would be preserved. I will gladly accept your challenge on behalf of the Divine Doctor. Che Luofeng, do you dare accept?"

"Hold on!" Chen Xing interjected. "*I* haven't accepted his challenge yet."

Never mind that the consort should have been resting at home for at least a month following childbirth. Looking at Xiang Shu, Chen Xing found it impossible to agree to duel Che Luofeng. It wasn't that he was worried about losing his life, since he had always been able to hit whatever he aimed at with his arrows...but if he accidentally shot Che Luofeng off his horse, he would end up having to treat Che Luofeng's injuries again. Wouldn't that just be creating more trouble for himself?

Sure enough, Xiang Shu spoke up in a taunting voice. "Anda, don't underestimate this Han. I have seen him use a crossbow with great precision—he shot down a fully armored Han general from a hundred paces."

"So?!" Che Luofeng shouted angrily. "Do you accept or not?"

Xiang Shu waved his hand dismissively. "He won't. If you really want to compete, why not challenge him in saving lives?"

"Compete with a doctor in saving lives? How could I possibly win?" Che Luofeng sneered.

"So you're trying to get a doctor to compete with a warrior in equestrian archery instead? Do you have no shame?"

With a mocking smile on his lips, Xiang Shu defused the tense situation. Chen Xing, still brimming with frustration, reluctantly lowered his bow and stormed back into the royal tent. Xiang Shu motioned for King Akele, the consort, and Che Luofeng to follow him somewhere else.

"What are you up to now?" Che Luofeng asked, frowning.

The leaders of the various tribal cavalry had gathered around too, so Xiang Shu decided to take Che Luofeng, King Akele, and the consort somewhere more private. Before he left, he glanced back into the tent at Chen Xing. "I'll be back by evening," he said.

*Can all of you just get lost?* thought Chen Xing. He sprawled out on the ground inside the tent, feeling frustrated and sorry for himself.

By the time night fell, Xiang Shu still hadn't returned. Someone came by with food, saying, "The Great Chanyu is still busy with discussions and asks that you wait a little longer."

"Got it," Chen Xing replied, a little annoyed. He knew that by now the steppes of Chi Le Chuan must have been swarming with cavalry scouts, sent out to search for any traces of Youduo, and the discussion Xiang Shu was having was to figure out the next steps. They were probably arguing again in the process, of course. Xiang Shu probably wouldn't be able to leave for the north with him until they had found Youduo and burned him to ashes. But the longer the delay dragged on, the colder the weather would grow, and who knew what else could happen?

Hearing that argument earlier in the afternoon had left Chen Xing feeling uneasy. Over the past few days, he'd realized with certainty that Xiang Shu wasn't going to serve as his protector—he simply couldn't afford to. He was the Great Chanyu, revered by three hundred thousand warriors and the people of Chi Le Chuan. How could Chen Xing live with himself if he asked Xiang Shu to abandon that responsibility?

After thinking it over, Chen Xing decided it would be best to leave on his own. He'd survived breaking through the two-hundred-thousand-strong Qin army outside Xiangyang with nothing but Sui Xing's protection. Armed with a map and enough supplies, he would could handle the north. At worst, he'd get a little cold.

So he packed some medicines and slung a longbow across his back. He didn't bother with money; there'd be no use for it where he was going. Outside the royal tent, the horse he had purchased was ready, laden with dried rations, butter, flint, and wool. But as he turned to leave, he suddenly noticed King Akele standing quietly in the darkness, holding a horse.

"Ahhh!" Chen Xing yelped. "It's pitch black out here! Why are you just standing around scaring people?!"

King Akele said a few words in Xiongnu, then gestured toward a bewildered Chen Xing. Without further explanation, King Akele mounted his horse and motioned for Chen Xing to follow him.

Outside the Akele camp, to the north of Chi Le Chuan.

The consort had prepared three horses, and she handed the reins of one to Chen Xing. "That little pony of yours won't be able to withstand the bitter cold; it would collapse in the snow within three days. Ride this one instead, and put your belongings on the one without a rider."

"What's going on?" Chen Xing asked. "I'm not trying to find Youduo."

"I know. You're heading north, right? Let this old man lead the way," she said with a nod to King Akele. "It'll be good to have someone looking out for you. Wear this, too. This horse was left with me by Xiang Yuyan a long time ago. It's twenty-two years old, but it still runs very well. An old horse knows the way; you don't have to worry about getting lost on the way back. Oh, and take this too..."

She handed Chen Xing a dagger, and he looked at it blankly. He glanced back up at the consort, then at King Akele. The descendants of the ancient Xiongnu had prepared all the supplies for them. In somber succession, the people of the tribe—men and women, old and young—emerged and knelt before Chen Xing and the Akele king.

"Go," the consort said, "and may you return safely."

"Yah!" said King Akele. Dressed in a long cloak, he led the way out of Chi Le Chuan.

Chen Xing's eyes dampened. He shook the horse's reins to make it follow King Akele, then turned back to shout to the consort. "Thank you!"

She was standing in the snow, bidding them farewell at the head of the crowd. Snowflakes swirled around them, covering the vast, cold prairie of Chi Le Chuan with a gentle blanket.

The journey to Lake Barkol was a considerable two-hundred-mile trek. They would first have to cross the Xarusgol River to the north, then head east, passing through the ancient ruins marked on the map before turning north again to cross the lake. Then, if they didn't stray from their path for another three hundred miles, they would finally reach Carosha.

The roads were covered in deep snow from the storm, making travel difficult and slowing the horses down. Fortunately, the weather was merciful, and as they set out, they encountered no more thick, opaque snowstorms that obscured the sky and sun. After they crossed the Xarusgol River, the skies cleared up and the winter sun shone brightly. They could see wild foxes hunting birds in the sweeping white snowscape.

It was obvious to Chen Xing that King Akele knew the wilderness like the back of his hand. His clan was well-known for taming and raising horses, and he had a good memory of the terrain, including where it was easy to travel and where it was not. Chen Xing, who had difficulty communicating with him, had worried at first that this fifty-year-old man might struggle on the journey—but to his surprise, King Akele's stamina was greater than his own, and he often shared wild game with Chen Xing along the way.

Days into their journey, they reached their first stop: a desolate city half-buried in snow, yet with a few flickering lights still visible.

"People actually live here!" Chen Xing was astonished. Outside of Chi Le Chuan, this was the second trading hub he had encountered north of the Great Wall. He turned to King Akele. "What is this place?"

King Akele understood his question. "Karakorum," he replied.

As Chen Xing followed King Akele into the city, he looked around. The city was quite large, but it seemed to only be home to a few hundred households. Then he caught sight of a monument in the middle of the city which bore the city's name in both Han and Xiongnu scripts: Longcheng.

This was the place where Wei Qing had decisively defeated the Xiongnu over four hundred years ago;[6] it had once been a site where the Xiongnu worshipped the dragon and held gatherings of their

---

6    Wei Qing (衛青) was a Western Han general who, in the second century B.C., became famous for initiating a successful long-distance raid of Longcheng, killing over seven hundred Xiongnu soldiers.

various tribes. After Wei Qing conquered Longcheng, the area declined from great prosperity to severe desolation as the Xiongnu people moved en masse to Chi Le Chuan, leaving behind only itinerant merchants and the elderly to endure the winter in the city.

KING AKELE helped Chen Xing settle down in a stone house, fed his horse, and then breezed right back out again. By this point, Chen Xing was used to communicating with him through gestures, and besides, it was all still just a chicken talking to a duck. He didn't bother to ask King Akele what he was heading out to do; he just told him he'd take a stroll around the city himself.

He had always enjoyed strolling around when he visited a new place. With the New Year fast approaching, he only had three years left to live, and he had no desire for material possessions, so what else could he do? All that was left was to explore and broaden his horizons. King Akele had given him a necklace made of wolf teeth that was adorned with colorful gems—its main purpose was to differentiate his identity from everyone else, lest he get snatched away by Xiongnu.

Four hundred years... It had been a whole four hundred years. Time had gently smoothed out the traces of the Han Dynasty war; the only remaining monument was the old Xiongnu imperial court, which was made of black stone and stood in the middle of the city. The Xiongnu, the Rouran, and even the Tiele had all once occupied this place. Under the blowing snow, Chen Xing walked toward the stone palace, hoping to see the glory it once possessed.

A group of Xiongnu were warming themselves by a fire in the imperial court. When they saw a Han coming, they scrutinized him for a while; eventually, someone invited him for a drink. Chen Xing stayed long enough to greet them, then headed back to get some of his rations and returned to share them with the Xiongnu.

As he turned around, he noticed a square tower in the depths of the imperial palace garden. "What kind of place is this?" he asked, gesturing to the Xiongnu, since they couldn't understand each other's languages. Standing in front of the tower, he saw patterns laid on the stone tiles on the ground...

It was a magical array! A defensive formation!

Chen Xing strode over in a hurry. He never would have expected to see ruins left behind by exorcists before the Silence of All Magic in a place so far away from the Central Plains! What was this defensive formation used for? It was the first time he'd encountered such an array in real life, not counting the one inside the mirror world.

There was a stone gate in front of the square tower that looked like it must have weighed more than five tons. Chen Xing tried a few times to push it open, but it didn't budge an inch. The tower was situated in the center of the array, and aside from the gate, it was all sealed-off stone; it didn't have even a single window.

*There must be a magical artifact inside,* Chen Xing thought. *Forget it, I'd better not touch it.*

On the stone gate was a small, spirit-based lock painted with molten gold, which Chen Xing recognized as the mechanism to open it. The tower's design was ingenious; before the Silence of All Magic, exorcists with powerful magic would have only needed to summon the Spiritual Qi of the Heavens and Earth and inject it into the gate through the spiritual lock.

Once he had restored the spiritual qi, Chen Xing could come back to take a look. He was confident that he'd be able to open this lock.

King Akele arrived with a deer over his shoulder, having apparently gone hunting, and several of the Xiongnu who had been warming themselves by the fire in the imperial court helped him barbecue the meat. King Akele was short of breath; he was clearly getting on in years, and he needed some time to recuperate in front of the campfire after spending a good while chasing that deer. He noticed Chen Xing's worried gaze and smiled at him.

*If my father were still alive*, Chen Xing thought, *I bet he'd be like this.*

In his day, back in Jinyang, Chen Xing's father hadn't been blessed with a son until he was forty. As a result, he'd pampered Chen Xing a lot, but not to the point of spoiling him rotten. He'd often warned Chen Xing about the chaos in the world that had yet to settle down; about the difficult ways of the world, the rise and fall of dynasties, and the devastating wars that lasted for many years. He'd also told him that whenever the Hu and the Han killed each other, it was the common people who suffered.

"In life," he'd told Chen Xing, "a man must have an indomitable spirit and focus on four things: cultivating his moral character, governing his household, ruling the country, and creating peace in the land. Remember, a man must never, at any cost, succumb to the mire of hatred and allow his personal grudges to create disputes between the Hu and the Han. He should be upright and dignified, with unflinching integrity, so that he can bring honor to the Chen family."

His guidance was what had led Chen Xing to cultivate an excellent temper after reading the books of sages. Chen Xing tried his best not to be at odds with other people unless it was absolutely necessary. In theory, a man was to cultivate his own self first before setting up a family, ruling the country, and then, finally, creating peace in the land. When he was faced with the responsibility of "creating peace," Chen Xing barely hesitated to accept it.

King Akele kept gasping for breath for a while, but before too long he felt better.

"You shouldn't torment yourself like that at your age," Chen Xing told him. "It doesn't matter whether we eat fresh meat or rations."

King Akele couldn't understand him, but he smiled to show Chen Xing that he was fine. It made Chen Xing's heart ache a bit. He unfolded the map to figure out how much further they had to go.

"Youduo, my son," King Akele said suddenly, in broken Han language, "I will come—protect you. You—be okay."

Chen Xing looked at him in silence.

"I...can't not care. Thank, thank you."

Chen Xing teared up a little. He must have learned those few sentences in the Han language from his consort.

"Thank you, Chen Xing." King Akele took the roasted deer leg and offered some to Chen Xing, who nodded and reluctantly smiled.

Wolves howled outside of Longcheng that night, and Chen Xing worried that they might bump into a pack of them when they left the next day to continue their journey. They had already encountered several lone wolves on their way, and one or two had followed them. Fortunately, King Akele was a master of archery and had always managed to take the wolves out before their horses received a fright. But hearing that noise in the dark, Chen Xing had the uncanny feeling that wolves had surrounded them on all sides. It was winter, the twelfth lunar month, and wolves struggling to find prey in the snow were forming packs to fight the Hu people inside the city for food.

The wolves stopped howling the next morning. Though King Akele didn't say anything as they set off to continue their journey, he was on high alert along the way. Leaving Longcheng, they entered the Lake Barkol area and, once they'd crossed the frozen lake, continued traveling north. They began to encounter more and more trees, and occasionally they passed meadows and mountains that were covered with frost. They moved through the forest in a zigzag fashion, spent the night in a cave, and gradually reached the end of their journey that had stretched for almost four hundred and fifty miles.

Enveloped by a thick fog, they couldn't yet see Carosha, this place that was meant to exist only in legends. King Akele had brought Chen Xing to a place with barely any sign of human habitation—only snow, snow, and more snow as far as the eye could see. This part of the world saw only three short months of spring and summer each year.

The two of them often didn't say a single word to each other for an entire day.

One night, when the snow had stopped, they spent the night under a tree. The world around them was incomparably tranquil, and the starry river in the night sky flickered overhead. Chen Xing scrutinized the map. It didn't seem like they'd gone the wrong way; they had stuck to the direction of the North Star.

King Akele combed his white, grizzled beard, making it seem even longer, and he kept his deep blue eyes affixed to the bonfire. Chen Xing put away the map, but just as he was thinking about going to sleep, he heard a wolf's deep howl from the end of the mountain ridges in the distance. A moment later, other wolves joined in, their voices ringing out one after another in all directions.

"There are a lot of wolves," Chen Xing said. King Akele fanned the bonfire to make it even brighter, a signal that Chen Xing should stop worrying and go to sleep. "Akele, have you been here before?"

King Akele couldn't understand him. He shook his head and made a bed for Chen Xing.

"Thank you," said Chen Xing.

"Thank you," King Akele echoed. It was one of the only phrases he knew in the Han language.

Chen Xing lay on his side. The howling continued, which annoyed him a great deal, and he couldn't sleep for a long time. Eventually, he sat up in frustration and shouted, "Stop howling!"

King Akele shushed him and gestured to a mountain slope in the distance: Chen Xing could have accidentally caused an avalanche.

Chagrined, he lay back down—but then he heard a strange sound coming from the ground. This, he remembered, was how Xiang Shu had detected the invasion of the living corpse army. It was an extremely weak sound, but it put Chen Xing on alert. King Akele was sitting vigil, and Chen Xing gestured for him to listen to the ground.

As King Akele bent down, Chen Xing saw glittering green lights appear in their surroundings, winking to life like fireflies. "What are those?" Chen Xing asked. "It's winter, how could there be fireflies..."

Then he realized: Those were the wolves' eyes! The wolf pack had come!

Cautiously, King Akele got up and surveyed their surroundings. He threw all of their firewood into the bonfire at once and added some butter, making the flames surge up into the sky. The thousands of wild wolves circling them backed away slightly. Chen Xing grew nervous, and King Akele said something.

"What?" Chen Xing said. "I don't understand!"

King Akele nocked an arrow on his bow. The wolf pack was wandering around the periphery of the bonfire, but they feared the flames and didn't dare come too close. King Akele shook his head to tell Chen Xing that he need not worry, and Chen Xing knew that as long as they had fire, the wolves wouldn't get too close to them. This was how they had traveled all the way here.

Then, suddenly, a figure swept by above them, and a huge pile of snow fell from the trees and extinguished the bonfire. Another "awoo!" rang out, as if one wolf was urging the rest on. In a flash, King Akele aimed at the place the sound had come from and released his arrow into the darkness.

The wolf pack didn't wait for him to nock another arrow. They took advantage of the extinguished bonfire and lunged at them.

King Akele immediately retreated and shouted to Chen Xing, who didn't even have to guess at his meaning—King Akele was telling him to run. Instead, Chen Xing grabbed up a bow and shot into the forest.

The wolf pack swarmed them, and it soon became clear: Their target was King Akele. Without their fire, Chen Xing and King Akele couldn't see anything around them, and King Akele shouted as he struggled against the wolves.

"Akele!" Chen Xing yelled. He wasted no time raising his hand and releasing the light of the Heart Lamp.

The wolf pack seemed startled by the burst of light and began to retreat. Chen Xing turned back to look for their horses, but the horses were gone. There were wolves everywhere. He evaded them, desperate to find King Akele.

A black figure descended from the sky. Chen Xing heard the movement and looked up—but a metal claw that flickered with a cold light was already at his throat.

Just then, a familiar voice shouted, "Get down!"

Without even thinking about it, Chen Xing arched his neck, and the metal claw brushed obliquely across his face. The claw's strange light flickered again, but then a sword flew out from behind Chen Xing and blocked it. With one swing, the sword hurled the assassin brutally into a tree. The assassin roared in fury, and the tree split at its middle and collapsed, snow and all!

"Xiang Shu?!" Chen Xing was stunned. "Xiang Shu! Why are you here?"

"Idiot!" Xiang Shu spat, plainly furious. "I've been chasing the two of you for seven days! Get up into the tree!"

Chen Xing climbed up, slid down, climbed up, slid down, climbed up slid down climbed up slid down climbed up slid down... Finally, Xiang Shu lost patience. He lifted his leg and kicked Chen Xing at his waist, sending him flying up the tree. Chen Xing hugged the tree's trunk tightly and continued climbing upward. "Find Akele!" he shouted down to Xiang Shu.

Xiang Shu swung his huge sword, and the surrounding trees fell, one after another, each hitting the ground with an earthshaking rumble. The wolf pack fled in all directions, leaving Chen Xing clinging to a pine tree over thirty feet tall. He swayed from side to side at the top of the tree.

"Behind you!" Chen Xing hollered as he spotted something. *Is that a human or a yao?!*

The assassin was tiny, not even half as tall as Xiang Shu. On all fours, the assassin had darted over from the snowfield and was behind Xiang Shu in the blink of an eye. Xiang Shu whirled around and brandished his sword horizontally to block.

*Clang!* The weapons collided, metal on metal. Without hesitation, the assassin swept around behind Xiang Shu again and reached out to claw at his neck.

It was too fast! Chen Xing had been certain until now that no one could rival Xiang Shu in speed, but this black shadow seemed to be flying around the snowfield. Xiang Shu turned around, then turned again, but the shadow kept one step ahead of him. It threw itself onto his back and firmly attached itself there.

With both legs wrapped around the tree, Chen Xing gathered a snowball in his hands and threw it down. It hit the black shadow right in the face. Xiang Shu let out an angry yell, grabbed the black shadow, and flung it away.

"It's a yao!" Chen Xing called. "Wait for me, I'll come down and help you!"

At last, Xiang Shu saw the black shadow clearly—it was some kind of half-wolf, half-human creature. The wolf's mouth opened, revealing a human face inside, and it howled hoarsely at Xiang Shu a few times. Then it looked up, saw Chen Xing in the tree, and leaped over. By hooking two claws into the tree, it managed to leap several feet high in the blink of an eye.

Xiang Shu immediately gave chase, but Chen Xing didn't dare to jump down. Suddenly, the enemy was right in front of him.

Panicked, Chen Xing illuminated his surroundings with the Heart Lamp. Finally, he saw the assassin in full view. "You're..."

It wasn't a wolf yao. It wasn't a monster at all. It was a person! A child!

The child was dazzled by the white light. He used his arm to cover his eyes and swung his metal claw. In the illumination of the Heart Lamp, Chen Xing saw a peculiar inscription on the edge of each claw. The claws were shaped like a dragon's, and they flickered with a radiant light.

There were very few claw weapons in the world in the shape of dragon claws, and the gold inscription... Unexpectedly, Chen Xing

recalled a record he had seen in an ancient text. In ancient times, the Dragon God descended upon a place far north of the Divine Land. Gongshu Ban obtained its claws and refined them into a divine weapon. That weapon was called...

The Sky-Rending Claws!

"Wait!" Chen Xing said. "Why do you have—"

"Wait!"

"Awoo!"

"Listen to me!" Chen Xing was becoming frantic. "Listen to what I'm saying, you brat!"

The child had the skin of a gray wolf draped over him and wore a hat made from a wolf's head. Clamping down on the tree trunk with both legs, he swiftly clawed toward Chen Xing's throat to slit it.

Xiang Shu released several arrows in succession from under the tree, and the child stopped what he was doing. Without even looking back, he turned and swung his metal claws, somehow managing to block the arrows—*clink! clank! clank!*—and send them flying.

"I said! Listen to me!" Chen Xing exploded. He grabbed a handful of snow and smacked it into the child's face.

Perhaps Chen Xing had appeared useless, because the child hadn't guarded against him at all. The snow to the face made him lose his balance, and he tumbled down the tree, shaking the leaves along the way. Xiang Shu ran over until he was underneath the tree, but the child abruptly lunged and rolled over in midair, somehow leaping several feet and then landing steadily on the snowfield.

The child raised his head slightly, then looked up at the sky and unleashed a wolf's howl. "Awoo!"

The wolf pack retreated. Before Xiang Shu could even ready his bow and arrow, the child and the wolves had vanished into the forest.

There was nothing Chen Xing could say about that.

Xiang Shu gasped for breath. His horse had already fled in terror outside the forest, and he had rushed the whole way over on foot when he heard the wolves howling. He'd run almost a mile just to reach them.

"It was human!" Chen Xing called down to him. "A little kid!"

"I saw! I'm not blind!" said Xiang Shu impatiently.

Chen Xing ran to Xiang Shu's side and looked in the direction the wolf pack had gone. "He wasn't wearing clothes! He didn't seem to understand what we were saying either."

Xiang Shu lost his temper. He put his weapon on his back, grabbed Chen Xing's collar, and pushed him to one side. "Why did you run out of Chi Le Chuan without saying a word?! Do you have no regard for me at all?!"

"Uh..." It was only now that this serious problem finally occurred to Chen Xing. "Don't...don't get angry. I just didn't want you to..."

Xiang Shu had departed from Chi Le Chuan seven days ago, but no matter what he did, he couldn't catch up to King Akele and Chen Xing. The heavy snowfall had covered their horses' hoofprints, and King Akele, as an experienced old hunter, knew how to minimize their tracks. Xiang Shu had chased them all the way to Lake Barkol, but he was always just a little bit behind.

The longer the chase continued, the angrier Xiang Shu became. At first he'd only intended to give Chen Xing a good scolding once he caught up with him, but along the way that had morphed into wanting to slap him. Then his patience had worn away further, and he'd fantasized vividly about hanging Chen Xing up and giving him a few hard slaps.

Suddenly, Chen Xing laughed. "This is great! I'm so happy!" He took a step forward, hugged Xiang Shu around the waist, and buried his head in Xiang Shu's chest. "This is *great*!"

"Get lost!" Xiang Shu growled. He was so angry he was about to lose his mind. He grabbed Chen Xing and shoved him away.

"King Akele said that he could show me the way," Chen Xing explained with a smile. "I didn't want to trouble you... Wait! Where's King Akele?"

Finally remembering him, they both immediately went to search for King Akele in the direction in which the wolf pack had left. Xiang Shu looked down to try to distinguish the footprints in the snow, but the ground was a mess. Chen Xing ran over to the extinguished bonfire. "Here! This was where I last heard his voice."

Chen Xing was afraid of finding King Akele's corpse there, but fortunately he didn't. From the dark cover of night, he heard Xiang Shu's voice: "If he's dead, it's on you!"

Chen Xing couldn't refute this. He was at a loss for a moment, just standing in the snow.

Xiang Shu had been so furious with Chen Xing for leaving Chi Le Chuan in secret that he spoke without thinking, but as his anger cooled a bit, he realized that he had overstepped. King Akele had escorted Chen Xing all the way north because he himself wanted to uncover the truth; how could Chen Xing be to blame for his death?

Xiang Shu looked over at Chen Xing and saw that he was about to cry. Guilt washed over him.

"He isn't dead," Chen Xing said, quickly regaining his calm and pulling himself together. "The wolves didn't attack us because they wanted to eat us. They followed us the whole way here. It must have something to do with that child. I don't think they'd kill people indiscriminately. Akele! Are you there?!"

Xiang Shu breathed a sigh of relief and followed Chen Xing as he stumbled through the forest, shouting in all directions. They couldn't find King Akele, but they found the lost horses. Xiang Shu whistled, and his horse returned as well.

Eventually they reached the boundary of the woods. The wolves' footprints seemed to lead off into the distance. The sky was slowly brightening, illuminating the vast expanse of snow.

Chen Xing looked at Xiang Shu, but Xiang Shu couldn't decide what to do either. Eventually, he decided, "Let's follow them and see."

They mounted their horses and rode for half a mile in the wilderness. The sun was high in the sky when Xiang Shu suddenly stopped them. "Wait!"

Following his gaze, Chen Xing saw King Akele's wolf fang necklace lying in the snow. Chen Xing was relieved; King Akele had, in fact, been captured by the wolf pack.

Chen Xing picked up the necklace. He'd established a strange kind of friendship with King Akele on their journey; he had to save him. This middle-aged man had just welcomed a new son at his advanced age after surviving the pain of losing his firstborn. He had treated Chen Xing gently, as a child. No matter what it took, Chen Xing needed to bring him back alive.

Looking around, Chen Xing shouted for him. "Akele!"

"His name is not Akele! Akele is a tribe name!"

"Oh...then what's his name?"

But Xiang Shu didn't know the king's name himself. There was a long pause. "Let's go," he said at last.

"You obviously don't know either," said Chen Xing. He mounted his horse to follow the wolves' trail.

"Oi!"

Chen Xing twisted around to look at Xiang Shu. "Hm?"

"Do you not trust me?"

"I just didn't want to put you on the spot! You're the Chi Le Covenant's Great Chanyu, and now the drought fiends are causing havoc. So many people rely on you. How could you just throw them aside and leave with me?"

"Who was the one who said he wanted a protector to watch over him?"

"Do you even have any intention of being my protector? I can't afford you, Great Chanyu!"

"I chased you for two hundred and fifty miles!" Xiang Shu said in disbelief. "Don't you have anything nice to say? Fine, I'll turn round and go back right now!"

Chen Xing was still preoccupied with all the questions he was turning over and over in his head: *Who on earth was that child? How did he get his hands on such a powerful divine weapon?* He had no answer to the first question and even less of a clue as to the second. Hearing Xiang Shu's words, however, he looked at Xiang Shu more closely, and suddenly, it hit him:

Xiang Shu was apologizing to him.

"Ah. Thank you, then," he said, with a smile that didn't reach his eyes.

Xiang Shu urged his horse forward, wanting to drag Chen Xing from his own horse to teach him a lesson, but Chen Xing galloped away. Xiang Shu was astonished. "You're so stable on a horse now?"

"Akele taught me! Just try and shoot me to death with your arrows now! Ha!"

Urging his horse forward again, Xiang Shu caught up with Chen Xing in no time, and they rode their horses side by side in the snow. For some reason, their horses weren't being very obedient, especially the old brown horse that Xiang Shu was riding. Every so often, it tried to break free from the reins that bound all of the horses together, and the further they went, the more frequently it tried it. It kept straying and turning northeast, taking Xiang Shu with it.

"This horse has gone crazy!" Xiang Shu exploded. "Go back!"

"Why are you taking out your frustration on a horse?" Chen Xing turned around to look at Xiang Shu and saw the old horse running east. Xiang Shu was yanking on the reins, trying to turn it back around.

"I'll just let it go!" Xiang Shu said. He was scolding the horse, but Chen Xing knew that Xiang Shu was just as frustrated with him. "This stubborn thing!"

As he drew his dagger to cut the reins, though, Chen Xing interrupted. "That's your mother's horse," he said. "You can just release it if you want. What does it have to do with me?"

Xiang Shu stared at him. "What? Impossible! Where did you find it?" Chen Xing relayed the consort's words, but Xiang Shu's doubts only increased. "This was the horse she rode when she first came to the north?"

"Maybe." Chen Xing watched as the old horse gradually calmed down and returned to run along with the rest.

"Where does it want to go?"

But of course Chen Xing had no idea.

The sun rose, and the world lit up around them. Light reflected off the white snow and blinded their eyes. It hadn't snowed again during the night, and the wolves' paw prints were still distinct and easy to recognize. After crossing the vast plains, they continued toward the horizon, where their destination finally appeared.

There, within the misty fog, stood the Xiongnu people's legendary mountain.

A long, narrow, towering mountain range stretched for dozens of miles, with white clouds curling around its snow-capped peaks.

The entire mountain range seemed to have been split into three by lightning, divided by a narrow cliff. In front of the cliff was a lake that covered thousands of acres and reflected the blazing sun like a mirror.

The white snow plains on both sides of the cliff were covered in countless black dots. Crouching high above them...

...were more than ten thousand black wolves.

The horses panicked and tried to retreat.

## 36

XIANG SHU CLIMBED up over the precipice, then took a sudden half step back. His heel scraped up a bit of snow, which fell and landed on Chen Xing's head. Chen Xing looked up and opened his mouth to shout something up to Xiang Shu, but then he saw Xiang Shu stick one hand out from the edge of the cliff and wag his index finger. He was telling Chen Xing not to speak.

Was there an enemy up there? The path that looped around the mountain was narrow, so Chen Xing's guess was that Xiang Shu was worried about accidentally knocking Chen Xing over the edge if they did encounter the wolves and had to fight.

Xiang Shu slowly descended the narrow path. When he turned a corner around a piece of rock that jutted outwards, he came face-to-face with a living corpse holding a scimitar and wearing heavy, pitch-black armor, covered with frost. It stood face-to-face with Xiang Shu. A black, shadowy general, in armor just like they'd seen Sima Lun wearing in Chang'an!

The general and Xiang Shu moved at the same time. Xiang Shu stepped back, dodging and leaping into a backflip, while the general unsheathed his blade and swung it down at Xiang Shu's head. Countless crows erupted from the mountains, cawing hoarsely as they dived at Xiang Shu, who was stuck on the narrow passage halfway up the mountain.

Xiang Shu paused, then—"Fuck off!" he bellowed, as if he had lost all reason.

Chen Xing didn't make a sound. He looked up. Halfway up the mountain was a black cloud that seemed to blot out the sky—it was made up entirely of crows. They attacked Xiang Shu like crazy. Chen Xing took a deep breath and lit up the Heart Lamp in his hand, and above, Xiang Shu let out a loud shout. The heavy sword in his hand glowed with a bright light, and he swung it to force the birds back.

"Don't use the Heart Lamp!" he yelled, afraid that the light would attract the crows. He swung his heavy sword again, then went to shout down from the edge of the cliff, "Wait for me right where you are!"

With that, he leaped away from the mountainside, heading to even higher ground.

The shadowy general bent down a little, and black energy burst from his body, coalescing to form a grappling hook. He threw the grappling hook up the cliff, and Chen Xing got his first clear view of the enemy's appearance. In those few moments, Xiang Shu had already made his way to the other side of the cliff, out of Chen Xing's sight. The general chased after him, followed by the ominous cloud of crows.

Chen Xing tried to climb up too, but he was nowhere near as good a climber as Xiang Shu. He almost fell off. It was a good thing that Xiang Shu hadn't carried him up to the narrow path; they would have run right into the enemy's ambush, and Xiang Shu wouldn't have been able to fight as effectively with Chen Xing in his arms. All Chen Xing could do now was hope that he—

Right then, Chen Xing detected a sudden sense of danger. The next moment there was the howl of a wolf, and a claw swiped at him from behind. Chen Xing turned around to discover that at some point, a huge pack of wolves had gathered on the rock by the cliff.

*Crap.*

"I'm warning you guys," Chen Xing said, "I know martial arts too."

Three wolves pounced at him at once and sent him flying backwards off the rock with a piteous scream.

Xiang Shu, who was crossing the mountain range, whipped around, shock evident in his eyes. But as soon as he slowed, the general dashed forward to meet him.

The world spun around Chen Xing as he plummeted down the mountain. He was in freefall, but as he went, a wolf grabbed him by the collar of his robes and tossed him into the air. He was thrown around, passed from wolf to wolf, until they got him to the canyon, at which point the biggest wolf closed its jaws around his waist, holding him in its mouth. Its bite didn't hurt Chen Xing, and it rushed deep into the canyon with Chen Xing in its mouth.

"This is so gross!" Chen Xing groaned. "Why do you have so much saliva?!"

He was dangling from the wolf's mouth, and it was slobbering all over him. It was even getting on his face. Struggling against its jaws, he managed to free one hand from the wolf's mouth, so he used it to slap the wolf harshly in the snout. Unfortunately, the wolf was just too big, and it seemed indifferent to his efforts to escape. The pack, which had swelled to nearly ten thousand, rushed into the canyon together.

They kept running for what must have been nearly a quarter of an hour. Finally, they arrived outside a cave, and the big wolf tossed Chen Xing onto the ground. Chen Xing wiped his face and crawled out of the snow, gasping for breath. *Where am I now?*

The wolves had brought him to a dim valley. No, not a valley—

a cave. The mouth of the cave yawned open at the bottom of a clearing surrounded by steep cliffs. Piles of rocks were scattered around it, and black wolves crouched throughout the area.

A piece of tiger skin hung over the mouth of the cave, and under the light of day, a small, foxlike figure emerged slowly from within. For all that this beast was small, however, it must have been dangerous, because the wolves all lowered their heads.

Chen Xing backed away. *You guys specialize in bullying scholars, right? Wait 'til Xiang Shu frees himself, then you'll see. He'll beat you beasts to death!*

But when the small animal came further into the daylight, Chen Xing saw it clearly. It wasn't an animal at all.

"You?!" Chen Xing shouted. With an angry roar, the child lunged forward and wrapped both legs around Chen Xing's waist, pushing him down into the snow outside the cave. "You stupid brat! What are you trying to do?!"

The child was no longer wearing the dragon claws, and both of his hands were downright filthy. He grabbed two handfuls of snow and slapped Chen Xing back and forth, smearing the snow all over his face and stuffing his mouth full of it.

"Let me go," Chen Xing protested, hacking up snow. "Ugh... I said...enough!"

Being held down and bullied by a child to the point where he couldn't even fight back pushed Chen Xing past his limit. The child was obviously taking revenge for the time when Chen Xing had hit him in the tree. His revenge complete, the kid jumped back up and squatted on a rock with his legs spread. He looked down at Chen Xing, his wolf hood draped over his head.

Chen Xing struggled to get up. He felt battered and exhausted as he dusted the snow off his body. "Get your parents to come out and talk!" he demanded angrily. "Where's Akele? Where did you take him?"

The child stared at Chen Xing, his face filled with suspicion, and Chen Xing studied him back. Finally, he had a chance to see this kid clearly. He was skinny and sunburnt, and he seemed to be about eight or nine years old. Even though it was winter, his chest was exposed; he didn't seem to fear the cold in the slightest. His legs were wrapped in beast pelts, and the steely gray wolf-head hood was in fact an intact wolf pelt that draped over his back like a cloak. The only thing preserving his modesty was a decoratively patterned beast skin wrapped around his waist, though now that he was squatting there with his legs spread wide...

"Aren't you ashamed?!" Chen Xing asked. "Don't you have pants at home? Put some pants on!"

The child clearly didn't understand him. He shifted just slightly, and the pack of wolves moved to crouch behind him, all of them staring threateningly at Chen Xing.

Chen Xing surveyed his surroundings. *I've truly had enough. Who on earth is this child? Was he raised by wolves?* He'd heard that sometimes, in the mountains, wild wolves snatched away human babies, and the babies grew up to look just like this kid.

"Can you speak the Xianbei language?" Chen Xing asked, thinking it would make sense for this brat to not understand the Han language. When the kid didn't respond, he switched to Xiongnu. The child continued to study him appraisingly, as if wondering whether Chen Xing would taste better roasted or raw. Next, Chen Xing tried the stiff, ancient Xiongnu language that he had picked up on the way there. "Where are your parents? Who are you?"

There was some hesitation in the child's gaze, and Chen Xing knew that he had been understood. He took a step forward, but the child let out a threatening shout, and the pack of wolves were instantly on edge again.

Chen Xing only understood a little ancient Xiongnu. In broken language, he managed to ask a few questions with words that didn't quite convey his meaning. The child took on a pensive look, but didn't answer him. Chen Xing knew that expression well; he often saw it on Xiang Shu's face. It signaled wariness and hesitant trust at the same time—an expression of consideration.

"How about I sing you a song?" Copying the people of Chi Le Chuan, Chen Xing sang, "Chi Le Chuan, under the Yin Mountains..."

The child's expression relaxed a little, and the pack of wolves began to retreat. They clearly sensed that Chen Xing wasn't hostile.

Once he was done singing, a thought came to Chen Xing. There was something odd here. The asshole who'd chased Xiang Shu on the mountain was a drought fiend, but this child was clearly not on their side.

Chen Xing copied a crow's caw and flapped his arms a few times. "Did you see the crows? Caw! Caw!" The child laughed at that, but Chen Xing couldn't bring himself to laugh too. He pointed in another direction. "My protector ran after the crows."

The child adopted a stern expression as well, and Chen Xing smacked his forehead with his hand. What was he supposed to do now?! God damn it! Then the child went inside and brought out a dragon claw, which he slid onto his left hand.

The Sky-Rending Claws came in a set of two. Why had he only brought one this time? "May I take a look?" asked Chen Xing.

As he reached out, the child watched him warily, then lifted his hand to swipe at him. Chen Xing quickly pulled his own hand back.

The child motioned for him to get out of the way, then used the claw to scratch out something in the snow.

Chen Xing watched him curiously. With his hands on his knees, he looked down at those zig-zag lines drawn by a childish hand.

"No, no," Chen Xing said. "I was talking about crows. What kind of nonsense are you drawing? A map?"

Chen Xing turned around and picked up a branch. He drew a few birds, then a small person holding a sword in front and another person chasing from behind. He finished off by drawing in a few mountains below them.

The child let out an angry growl and wiped away Chen Xing's drawings. He reached out again to swipe at Chen Xing, who knew that if the claw so much as grazed him, he'd be slit from throat to belly. "Okay, okay," he said, admitting defeat, "you go ahead and draw. I won't try to take your canvas."

The child drew for a long while. He spent a long time in the middle just scratching his head, as if he'd forgotten something, but finally, he produced some semblance of a finished drawing and showed it to Chen Xing.

"Ah! What a good drawing!" Chen Xing said, though his thoughts weren't focused on the child or his drawing at all. All of his energy was currently being spent worrying about Xiang Shu.

The child beckoned again for him to take a look, so Chen Xing stepped closer. Immediately, the tips of the dragon claw were resting against his neck, glinting with a cold light.

"Please excuse this humble one for not understanding the drawing!" Chen Xing wailed in anguish. "Why are you like this?! Isn't it enough for me to say that you drew really well?" Then, suddenly, he put it together. "Wait...are those words?"

The "drawing" he was looking at was actually a series of characters written in the great seal script![7] Chen Xing was flabbergasted. This damn brat knew how to write in the great seal script?!

"Xiao...Shan?" he read. "Where's that?"

When the child heard those two words, his eyes lit up, and he nodded at Chen Xing.

"That's your name? Your name is Xiao Shan?" Chen Xing asked. The child pointed at himself and nodded. "That truly is a nice name, xiandi. Now, can you let me go?"

Xiao Shan lifted the claw away from Chen Xing's throat and turned to direct the wolf pack. As he did so, he adopted the intimidating aura of an alpha wolf, and his expression turned stern. The wolf pack gathered around him, leaving Chen Xing off to one side, and Xiao Shan let out a few nonsensical sounds. After that, he turned his face up at the sky and let out an "Awoo!"

"Where is he?!" Chen Xing asked. "Where did you take the Akele king? Return him to me!"

The wolf pack bounded gracefully across the rocks, taking several different paths to the top of the cliff. Xiao Shan lunged up the cliff as well, landing on all fours before turning and running away along the passageway.

"Where are you going?" Mystified, Chen Xing had no choice but to run after them. Xiao Shan looked back and realized that Chen Xing wasn't right behind him, so he went back to drag him over impatiently. "My arm's gonna dislocate, argh!"

Xiao Shan ran very quickly, and he was small too, forcing Chen Xing to hunch over as Xiao Shan dragged him along. Chen Xing's arm felt like it was about to break, and after a while of running,

---

7   The great seal script, or large seal script, is a specific writing style that was used prior to the Qin dynasty (pre-221 BCE).

he found himself out of breath. "I'm not running anymore," he gasped out. "You guys go ahead and entertain yourselves..."

Xiao Shan whistled, and the giant wolf from before turned around, picked Chen Xing up in its mouth again, and, with just a few leaps, jumped to the top of the cliff. Unfortunately, this time, it had grabbed Chen Xing with the back of his head facing forward, and no matter how many times he asked the wolf to shift him around, the wolf couldn't answer. He had to just let it do what it wanted.

At last, when it was dusk and the sky was dark, all the wolves stopped. They'd reached a ridge looking over yet another gap between the mountains. They had come from one crack in Carosha to the other.

"Let me down," Chen Xing complained, shoving against his restraints a few times. The giant wolf opened its mouth a little, and Chen Xing caught sight of the bottomless abyss that was basically right below him. As it turned out, the group of over ten thousand wolves had stopped on a natural stone bridge less than six feet wide. Chen Xing's soul departed his body. "Forget it, let's keep going."

The wolves moved very quietly; all Chen Xing could hear was the sound of Xiao Shan's Sky-Rending Claws scratching against the ground. "Little brother," Chen Xing whispered, "could you please not make that sort of noise?" Xiao Shan glanced at Chen Xing, who, still dangling from the wolf's mouth with his face pointed backward, couldn't see what was happening in front of him. "What happened? Are you guys lining up to cross the bridge?"

Xiao Shan twisted his head, indicating that Chen Xing should turn and look. Chen Xing struggled to turn his body, clamped as he was between the wolf's jaws, but he managed to turn a little bit. A bizarre scene greeted him.

Under the stone bridge lay a narrow valley full of withered trees. The cliffs that lined it on both sides were covered in crows' nests. A dense fog pervaded the valley, with tendrils of it reaching up into the sky. Strangest of all, the valley seemed to be an immense forest, and a strong burst of resentment was seeping out from deep within it.

Two figures appeared in the valley below. Xiang Shu was there, staggering along, and against his shoulder, he half-carried the unconscious form of King Akele.

"Xiang Shu!" Chen Xing called out. "Hurry, we have to get down there to help them!"

Xiao Shan nodded. He swung his claws, and the wolf pack leaped down from the stone bridge.

As he and the giant wolf plummeted through the air, Chen Xing bit back his scream with all his might, convinced that if he let it out, he was going to lose it. When they landed, the wolf pack gathered outside the entrance to the narrow valley. The crows were instantly on edge, beating their wings and cawing madly as they began to converge on the entrance.

"Xiang Shu!" Chen Xing shouted as soon as the giant wolf lowered him to the ground.

Xiang Shu seemed to have been injured. He wobbled out from within the valley, then suddenly stopped, hesitating as if he couldn't recognize Chen Xing. A tinge of resentment coiled around him.

"Xiang Shu?" Chen Xing came to a gradual halt. The fog was getting thicker and thicker, and it had already submerged the entire valley.

A voice echoed from within the fog. "Wielder of the Heart Lamp, you have finally...come. Unfortunately, you are too late..."

Chen Xing was instantly on guard. "Who are you? Who's there?!"

Xiang Shu set the Akele king down, his voice trembling a little. "Go...go! Go, now! Leave this place..."

The crows danced around the two of them, unleashing a cacophony of hoarse caws. Xiang Shu seemed very wary of them, and his eyes bore a blood-red tinge. The wolf pack, meanwhile, had scattered through the fog and begun to fight the crows.

"Xiang Shu!" Not only did Chen Xing not back away, he rushed forward instead. He was less than twenty steps away from Xiang Shu when a saber came swinging down at him from the side. Xiang Shu raised his sword to parry, but the black-armored general appeared from inside the fog, heralded by the wild caws of the crows.

"Crows...crows..." Xiang Shu's voice was still trembling. In fact, his whole body was shaking.

Chen Xing stepped in front of Xiang Shu, raised his hand, and shone the Heart Lamp into the fog. The black-armored general vanished back into the fog, his first strike having missed. Chen Xing turned around and shouted, "Xiang Shu! You—"

But before he could finish his sentence, Xiang Shu wrapped his hands around Chen Xing's throat.

"I told you...not to follow me..." There was a dangerous aura about Xiang Shu, and his eyes had turned blood red, just like Feng Qianjun's had when he was possessed. "Why are you always making these thoughtless decisions?!" he bellowed.

"You've...been possessed..." Chen Xing gasped in the ice-cold fog, his head spinning.

The resentment here seemed different from the resentment in the mirror world's Chang'an—here, he realized, when people breathed in the dense white fog, it seeped directly into their souls. He had to snap Xiang Shu out of it immediately.

In the frigid fog, Chen Xing conjured up in his mind's eye the scene of his family being destroyed. With that, he resolutely lit up his Heart Lamp to guard his heart against the cold fog's invasion, then lifted his hand and shot forth a burst of white light. "Expel!"

Xiang Shu was blinded by the dazzling light. A shock went through Chen Xing that was far greater than the one he'd felt when he did this to Feng Qianjun. Perhaps it was because of their predestined connection as exorcist and protector. In that moment, Xiang Shu's grip around his neck loosened slightly, and Chen Xing seized the chance to press one hand against Xiang Shu's forehead.

Xiang Shu's hands unclenched, and his eyes shot open, reflecting Chen Xing's shining figure. He fell to his knees. Chen Xing increased the strength of his Heart Lamp, pressing its light against Xiang Shu's forehead as he pushed him to the ground. Suddenly, there was a flash of light in Chen Xing's mind's eye, and through the white light that connected them, he found himself stepping into Xiang Shu's boundless sea of thoughts!

"Heart Lamp..." a voice murmured from deep within the fog.

The fog washed over them again. The black-armored general seemed to have been waiting for this moment, and he swung his blade down...but as he did, Xiao Shan dashed out and raised his claws to block the general's strike.

# 37

THE SOUND of clashing weapons echoed through the air as the black-armored general revealed his left hand—he was holding another dragon claw. As they fought, Xiao Shan covered his nose and held his breath, his movements noticeably slowing. He was forced to retreat from the fog now and then, but each time, he managed to rush back just in time to intercept the black-armored general's blade before he could strike Xiang Shu and Chen Xing.

Chen Xing's eyes glazed over. The Heart Lamp's strength surged into Xiang Shu's body, and his meridians, like glowing streams of white light, converged toward a single point at his chest. With another explosive flash, Chen Xing suddenly found himself standing in a desolate wilderness. Right—this was Xiang Shu's consciousness.

The world stretched around them, endless. In the heart of the wilderness, Xiang Shu knelt before a corpse that was struggling beneath a white shroud. He gasped and shivered, slowly untying the shroud's head covering, and was greeted by the gray, ferocious face of the living corpse that his father, Shulü Wen, had become.

Crows circled in the sky, eyeing the corpse covetously.

"Xiang Shu!" Chen Xing sprinted toward him. "Wake up! You're losing yourself!"

Xiang Shu was deaf to his pleas. He held a dagger, his hand shivering madly, unable to strike his still-moving father with the blade no matter how hard he tried.

The crows' cawing grew louder until it reached a deafening crescendo. Just as Xiang Shu was about to stab his deceased father so that he could give him a sky burial, Chen Xing lunged at him, wrapping his arms around Xiang Shu, and firmly gripped the blade's edge with his right hand.

"Wake up!" Chen Xing yelled.

Xiang Shu raised his head and stared at Chen Xing in disbelief. Fresh blood spurted from Chen Xing's palm, and a wave of pain shot through him even though he knew it was merely an illusion. He ignored it and pulled Xiang Shu's head to his shoulder. The dagger fell from Xiang Shu's hand with a clatter, and a powerful light burst forth from the Heart Lamp, flooding their surroundings with a sea of light.

In the valley, the fog gradually receded from the two of them. Crows swooped toward the center of the valley, and resentment converged on the black-armored general. With a swipe of the claw in his left hand, the general flung Xiao Shan away, sending him crashing into the cliffside—he fell to the ground, blood streaming from his head. Down came the general's blade in another strike, this one aiming to pierce through Xiang Shu and Chen Xing where they were huddled together.

At that moment, the Akele king woke up and let out a mad roar. He grabbed a nearby weapon and charged at the black-armored general.

The white light contracted once again before bursting forth in a thunderous wave, pulling them back to the prison beneath Xiangyang City. Xiang Shu woke up, but his eyes were barely open and his lips moved slightly, as if he wanted to say something. In the darkness, Chen Xing was bathed in a soft, warm glow as he looked down at Xiang Shu.

"I know what you're afraid of now," Chen Xing said, breathing heavily.

"I wanted to save my father," said Xiang Shu slowly. "I didn't expect to kill him. There was no other way. I was also afraid...so I could only...give him...a sky burial...while he was alive..."

For a moment Chen Xing was speechless. He stared at him. "He was already dead," he said finally. "He had turned into a living corpse. He could no longer recognize you."

"I...I don't know. Ever since then, I really couldn't...couldn't forget that day. I didn't let any of my clansmen see. I just sat alone in the wilderness, slice after slice... My father..."

Chen Xing lowered his head to press his forehead against Xiang Shu's. "We are but lodgers in life," he murmured to him. "We only return to our true home in death. What you performed a sky burial for was just a husk that was being used by others. His three immortal souls and seven mortal forms had returned to the heavens the moment he died. Look, the stars are eternal." Chen Xing looked up, and the dark prison around them transformed into an endless night sky. "Every single one of us is a living thing swimming in that river."

Xiang Shu gradually became calm. He lifted his hand as if to touch the elusive, indistinct starry river in the sky. Even in the long night, when silence had fallen on all magic, innumerable stars shone brilliantly above.

Chen Xing held Xiang Shu's hand and whispered, "Just look at the Akele king, who traveled miles to get here just to learn the truth behind his son Youduo's death... If your father knew what happened, he definitely wouldn't blame you."

Xiang Shu nodded.

"Wake up, Protector." Kneeling on the ground, Chen Xing hugged Xiang Shu. He closed both eyes and said in a deep voice, "Expel."

Without warning, the white light blazed forth like an avalanche, sweeping across the narrow gorge in all directions.

Chen Xing lay feebly on his side on the ground. Xiang Shu drew his heavy sword, brandished it, and swung out a fan of dazzling light that pierced the darkness. The black-armored general somersaulted in midair, the crows lunged forward—and, in that burst of light, the sword transformed into a gigantic bow.

Chen Xing was astonished. Xiang Shu didn't understand what had just happened either, but, thinking quickly, he pulled back the glowing bowstring, and a cluster of arrows of white light spilled into the sky. Every last crow exploded into black mist.

The giant bow transformed back into the heavy sword, and Xiang Shu pointed it at the black-armored general, ready to charge. But before he could move, the general morphed into a meteor of black fire and hurtled south, disappearing from view.

Xiang Shu didn't chase him. He turned to look at Chen Xing, who was still lying on the ground. He'd exhausted all his energy to activate the Heart Lamp. His heart throbbed sharply and painfully, and he couldn't even take deep breaths.

"Chen Xing?!" Xiang Shu sank to one knee, moving to lift Chen Xing off the ground, but Chen Xing managed a weak nod to indicate he was okay.

"My soul is a bit damaged," he panted. "I just need to rest for a while."

Now that the general was gone, the bitingly cold fog gradually dispersed, and Xiao Shan came running toward them, blood streaming from his head. Xiang Shu raised his sword in alarm, but

Xiao Shan ignored him and rushed past them, heading into the depths of the gorge.

Xiang Shu's brows were locked in a deep frown. "I just wanted to lure that monster away," he said before Chen Xing could ask what had happened, "but somehow, I stumbled into the valley and found the Akele king..."

"Get up, let's go in and see." There was something amiss in this deep gorge. "Where is Akele? Akele!"

Chen Xing spotted something by the stone wall—and when he realized what it was, he cried out in surprise and dashed to it. It was King Akele, lying under a piece of rock with blood pouring from the side of his neck. While Chen Xing and Xiang Shu were unconscious, he had protected them, and he'd been struck by the black-armored general's blade in the process. It had severed the blood vessels at the side of his neck.

Chen Xing frantically tried to stop the bleeding, and Xiang Shu pressed down on the wound, but it was too late. Half of the king's body was already soaked in blood. His mouth opened a little, but no sound came out.

Xiang Shu looked up at Chen Xing, who was beside himself with sorrow. Tears streamed down his face, and he gritted his teeth and shook his head at Xiang Shu—there was no saving him. All Xiang Shu could do was tighten his grip on the king's blood-soaked hand.

Despite his condition, King Akele forced a weak smile. His lips moved faintly, and they made out the word "Nadoro"—the infant Chen Xing had delivered, the child whom the Great Chanyu, Shulü Kong, had named. King Akele nodded.

Chen Xing wiped away his tears, and Xiang Shu set his heavy sword aside. In the Xiongnu tongue, he told King Akele, "Rest assured, your people will be safe. I will deal with Youduo. You have already made amends for your past mistakes. Now please, return to the heavens and earth with the Dragon God." Then he gestured for Chen Xing to stop crying.

At peace, King Akele closed his eyes. Xiang Shu and Chen Xing remained silent for a long time. Chen Xing let out a prolonged, grief-stricken sigh.

From deep within the narrow valley, a voice drifted over to them. "Please come in," it said slowly. "Thank you, wielder of the Heart Lamp. In these last moments, I am...finally free."

Chen Xing jerked his head up. Xiang Shu got up, holding the Akele king's corpse in his arms, and the two of them faced the depths of the valley together.

As the fog dispersed, a shaded path appeared in the valley, lined with blackened, withered trees and dried-up rivers. It looked as if it had been haunted by lingering resentment for a long, long time, turning it into a desolate, lonely gorge. From what was left, Chen Xing thought that this place must have been a serene paradise back when the world was rich in spiritual qi.

Chen Xing picked the Sky-Rending Claw up from the ground and followed Xiang Shu into the valley. They came to a huge cemetery, but all of the graves were already empty. At the cemetery's far edge, adorned with tangled, withered vines, was a dried-up lake.

From the other side of the lake, the voice continued speaking. "This is the ancient Xiongnu burial ground. You may place the Akele king here." Xiang Shu laid the body of King Akele in one of the tombs. "Come up here. I don't have much time left."

The dry lake was encircled by layers of withered trees. During bountiful times, this place would have boasted mountains, lakes, waterfalls, and immense trees with twisting, intertwining roots. Now, it was an eerie, ghostly wasteland.

There was an islet in the middle of the dry lake. On the islet, under the trees, sat a young man in white who looked to be about the same age as Chen Xing. Xiao Shan was squatting beside him, murmuring and gesturing animatedly to the white-clad youth and, like a wolf, scratching behind his ear with one foot all the while.

"My name is Lu Ying," that young man said softly. "I'm sorry, I can only talk to you sitting like this. Because of the blood of Shi Hai's Demon God, all of my strength has been sapped away."

Chen Xing's instincts told him that they had come to the right place.

Once Xiao Shan had scratched his itch, he moved a little to stand in front of Lu Ying, studying Xiang Shu with distrust in his eyes. Chen Xing handed him the other claw, and Xiao Shan took it and put it on.

"I've seen you before," Xiang Shu said suddenly.

"I've seen you before, too," said Lu Ying. "You're the son of the human Great Chanyu, Shulü Wen. Chi Le Chuan's little master. I saw you from a distance many years ago, by Lake Barkol."

"Human," Chen Xing echoed. "You're... Wait! You! You're..."

"Yes," Lu Ying said wearily, "I'm a yao."

He turned to the side. Under the light of the stars, Chen Xing finally saw his full appearance. He gasped.

The half of Lu Ying that had been facing them was the body of an elegant, handsome young man of only sixteen or seventeen. But the half that was concealed in the shadows was so decayed that Chen Xing could see eerie white bones, and he even caught a few faint glimpses of blackened viscera. Chen Xing quickly stepped forward and knelt in front of Lu Ying to examine his condition.

Xiao Shan tensed up, but Lu Ying gestured for him to relax. "Xiao Shan is just worried about my body. I hope you two can understand."

Xiang Shu slowly walked over and studied Xiao Shan and Lu Ying. As Chen Xing examined Lu Ying, he glanced at Xiao Shan. "Is he a yao too?" he asked.

"He's human, like you," said Lu Ying, as Xiao Shan crawled behind him, looking for something. "But before the Wolf God died, he passed his yao powers to him in order to save his life."

"Who's the Wolf God?" Xiang Shu asked, frowning.

"The other god who guarded the sacred mountain of Carosha with me after the Dragon God, Zhuyin, descended upon the human world. I suppose you exorcists would call him a great yao."

"Mm." Chen Xing found that most of Lu Ying's body had already rotted away. It had clearly been corroded by some kind of strong toxin, and there was nothing Chen Xing could do to help.

"I can't be saved," Lu Ying said calmly. "Before the Silence of All Magic, there might have been a chance, but over the centuries, I've tried everything. The only thing in this world that could rid me of this demonic qi is the Heart Lamp, but as you are now, it's impossible."

Chen Xing frowned. "Demonic qi."

"After I was infected with the Demon God's blood, it started rotting my internal organs. The only way to save my life would be to harness the Spiritual Qi of the Heavens and Earth and use the Heart Lamp to purify my body."

From the tree behind Lu Ying, Xiao Shan fished out a very small amber waist pendant. He offered it to Chen Xing, motioning for him to take it. Chen Xing looked at him, perplexed.

"The ashes of a phoenix are sealed within this pendant," whispered Lu Ying. "I once thought that the power of a phoenix's rebirth— which occurs only once every hundred years—could perhaps help me reconstruct my body. Unfortunately, after the Silence of All

Magic, the phoenix can no longer reincarnate. Keep it safe so that, when all magic is reawakened, it will still have a chance to be reborn in flames."

Chen Xing looked down at the waist pendant, and through the amber, he saw a handful of flickering ashes. He recalled reading in books that the phoenix reincarnated once every hundred years, just as Lu Ying said. It burned in the True Fire of Samadhi until nothing was left, and then a new fledgling phoenix was born amidst the ashes. If one were to properly harness the powerful energy released during its rebirth, that energy could rebuild a human body—even perhaps resurrect the dead.

But now, all that remained of the phoenix was this small handful of ashes from its last burning.

"That day will come," Chen Xing said simply. He took off his cloak and used it to cover Lu Ying's decaying half. After a moment's thought, he glanced at Xiang Shu.

"I know it will come," said Lu Ying, smiling, "but I won't live to see it. Still, I'm grateful that you and the Protector Martial God have arrived so that I can face this final moment with dignity."

"What exactly happened?" asked Xiang Shu.

Lu Ying beckoned to Xiao Shan, who came over and lay comfortably in Lu Ying's arms. "It's a very long story," he said distantly. "Please take a seat. I'm guessing you must already know quite a lot, if you've come from thousands of miles away. Hopefully, after listening to my account, you will find the answers you seek."

They both sat down in front of Lu Ying. "The Silence of All Magic," Chen Xing said.

"Kjera," added Xiang Shu.

Xiao Shan, who understood nothing of their conversation, yawned and settled into Lu Ying's embrace.

Chen Xing cut straight to the point. "What's so special about this mountain? Why did everything start here?"

"It started in Carosha. That's the clue you found?"

Chen Xing unfolded the map and showed it to Lu Ying. Xiao Shan yawned again and, now more alert, took the map and looked at it from various angles, flipping it upside down and back again.

"As I said, this is the place where the Dragon God, Zhuyin, descended." Lu Ying pondered for a moment. "Let's start with Zhuyin. According to ancient records—"

"Day comes as Zhuyin opens its eyes; night arrives as its eyes close," Chen Xing interrupted. "It is the progenitor of all dragons, the first dragon in the world."

Lu Ying nodded politely. "That's right. Lord Zhuyin allowed time to move forward, nudging the heaven and earth veins into motion and forming the wheel of time. Just as the great god Pangu put his feet on the ground and held up the sky for eighteen thousand years, Zhuyin used sacred power to move time and to endlessly rotate the chakra of the heavens and earth. After many years, Zhuyin fell here and became the Carosha mountain range before you now.

"The Wolf God and I became its guardians after its fall. We obtained Lord Zhuyin's dragon powers and turned into yao. The Wolf God ruled over daylight, while I ruled over dreams of the long night. Lord Zhuyin also had a dragon son named Yeming, but no one knows where he is now."

"How long have you lived?" Xiang Shu asked doubtfully.

"About four hundred years," said Lu Ying. "The Wolf God and I aren't like the phoenix. Our souls aren't reborn in samsara; instead, our yao powers are passed down from generation to generation. Twelve years ago, the Wolf God sensed an unusual disturbance in the southeast, so he set out alone to investigate."

"The southeast is..." Chen Xing frowned.

"Karakorum," said Xiang Shu.

Lu Ying nodded. "I still remember that day twelve years ago. It was a winter night much like this one. The Wolf God brought this child back from Karakorum, but he was severely wounded. He passed the last of his yao powers to Xiao Shan before he lost consciousness. I tried everything I could to cleanse the toxin from the Wolf God, but in the process, I became infected myself."

The only thing Xiang Shu wanted to know was how this decaying youth was connected to the drought fiends, but Lu Ying kept circling around the issue. Lu Ying noticed his brow furrowing in impatience and gestured for him to remain calm.

"What kind of toxin is it?" Chen Xing asked. He knew that both exorcists and yao had seen their powers dwindle after the Silence of All Magic. If spiritual qi were still present in the world, a powerful yao like Lu Ying could, at the very least, have used his regenerative abilities to extend his life, even if he couldn't cleanse himself of the poison.

"Demon God's blood. That's what causes mortals to transform into 'drought fiends' after they die. It originates from an ancient, powerful yao, one far older than any history recorded by mankind."

Chen Xing was stunned into silence. Xiang Shu was silent too; Xiao Shan, meanwhile, had fallen asleep peacefully in Lu Ying's embrace.

"Which yao?" Chen Xing asked at last. "I remember only one being referred to as the Demon God in the historical records."

The Demon God in the records was Chiyou, who had fought the Yellow Emperor in Banquan.[8] After he defeated Chiyou, the

---

8    In Chinese mythology and history, the Yellow Emperor is considered one of the ancient Five Emperors and is often regarded as the ancestor of the Han Chinese people. He is a central figure in Chinese history, credited with founding Chinese civilization, introducing essential technologies, and unifying the tribes of ancient China.

Yellow Emperor, Xuanyuan, divided his corpse and buried Chiyou's head, limbs, torso, and heart in seven different places across the Divine Land.

"That's the one," Lu Ying confirmed. "You guessed right. The blood left behind by the Demon God has the power to awaken the dead and rally them to fight for him. That's the origin of the drought fiends."

Chen Xing was struck by a sudden realization. That meant the medicine that Kjera had given Xiang Shu's father, Shulü Wen, had been mixed with the blood of the Demon God!

"Kjera is his incarnation?" Xiang Shu asked in a low voice.

"Impossible!" said Chen Xing. "If Chiyou had truly succeeded in taking human form, the Divine Land would not be in the state it's in now."

Even as he said that, however, Chen Xing felt a surge of fear in his heart. Previously, all of his theories about the drought fiends had been based on the assumption that they were related in some way to yao. He'd thought they might have been brought about by evil arts or some abnormal transformation triggered by a yao. He'd never imagined that their true enemy might turn out to be Chiyou, the Demon God!

What kind of being was Chiyou? He was the ancient God of War, the Warlord of the world! The descendants of the Yellow Emperor had had to rely on the help of the Celestial Emperor, the Mysterious Lady of the Nine Heavens,[9] the Lords of Wind and Rain, and the Divine Dragon to finally defeat him after years of warfare, and even then, they could never completely eradicate the threat he posed.

---

9  The Mysterious Lady of the Nine Heavens, or Xuannu (玄女), is a goddess in Chinese mythology and Taoism. She is often associated with wisdom, warfare, and strategy. In legend, she played a crucial role in helping the Yellow Emperor defeat Chiyou by teaching him the art of war and giving him mystical weapons and tactics.

After thousands of years, the disparity in strength would have become immense! If Chiyou revived, he would be a godlike demon, a force of unimaginable destruction. No one in the world would be able to stand against him. A single confrontation would result in complete annihilation!

Xiang Shu was unfamiliar with these Han legends. He frowned. "Then who's Kjera?"

"Kjera?" Lu Ying thought for a moment. "Though I'm not certain who you're referring to, I suspect it may be Shi Hai."

Xiang Shu was about to describe further, but Chen Xing stopped him with a glance. He sensed that Lu Ying's life was rapidly fading; he had little time left, and this moment was merely a fleeting revival of strength before the end.

"Shi Hai is the Demon God's subordinate," Lu Ying continued slowly, closing his eyes. "I don't even remember when he first appeared in this world. All I know for certain is that he's lived far longer than the Wolf God or I have. He might be a remnant of the ancient era. With his last words, the Wolf God told me that Shi Hai may have escaped his tomb long ago. With the ongoing wars between the Xiongnu and the southern Han, there have been too many disturbances in the Divine Land—the exact cause of it all can no longer be traced."

Chen Xing noticed Lu Ying's voice growing weaker. "You're exhausted, Lu Ying. I think you need to rest for a while."

"It's okay." Lu Ying opened his eyes and forced a smile. "Twelve years ago, Shi Hai returned to the north for the first time, causing me to fall gravely ill. As the corrosion worsened, any yao powers I had left were affected by the resentment. The burial grounds you saw along the way are where the Xiongnu laid their dead to rest."

Chen Xing recalled Lu Ying mentioning that he "ruled over dreams of the long night." Once the poison took him, his dreams must have turned into nightmares; that explained the way Xiang Shu had remembered his past within the fog. "Is that also why these corpses have mutated?"

Lu Ying shook his head. "Several years later, while I was fighting against the corrosion, Shi Hai came to the north for the second time. He was very patient. He waited until I had been weakened by the Demon God's blood for a very long time before seeking me out. He brought with him the corpse of a mortal, a man who, in life, was named Sima Yue. That man had a deep-seated enmity with the Xiongnu."

"Sima Yue, Great Jin's Prince of the Donghai!" Chen Xing exclaimed.

Lu Ying nodded. "I have lived in seclusion in the mountains for a long time and was unaware of the grudges between mortals. Shi Hai urged me to submit to the Demon God, to build a human world without death..."

He took a moment to catch his breath, and Chen Xing paced back and forth on the desolate island. "Insane," he said in utter disbelief, "this is absolutely insane!"

"Birth, old age, illness, and death are all part of samsara," Lu Ying said. "Without death, how can there be life? Without pain, how can there be joy? Time is like an inn, and I am the traveler. Without farewells and departures, how can there be the splendor or continuity of life? Naturally, I rejected Shi Hai's proposal. Later, Sima Yue and I did battle, and he severed my horns and took them away. My horns allowed me to command a hundred beasts. Now, all I can do is stay on Mount Carosha, struggling at death's door."

Lu Ying started to cough, and Xiao Shan awoke and reached out to pat his chest. "A year later, when Xiao Shan was nine," he said, rubbing Xiao Shan's head, "someone came from the south—the crown prince of the Akele tribe, who in life was named Youduo."

"THE MOMENT I saw Youduo, I knew that he had drunk the Demon God's Blood," Lu Ying said. "Shi Hai's purpose in sending him here was to use his identity to awaken the sleeping Xiongnu ancestors, those who had rested for many years within Carosha, and then lead them south as a living dead army. I subdued Youduo with the last bit of strength I had and made him sleep for a while... After that, I searched for the humans down in Chi Le Chuan..."

"That was when we first met," said Xiang Shu.

"Yes." With what seemed to be a great deal of effort, Lu Ying took a deep breath. He was almost at his limit. "Shulü Kong, you're a kind child who cares for this world's living creatures. You didn't return to Carosha with me, but I never suspected that you would become an exorcist's protector one day. As we can see, no one can escape what is written in the stars."

"What happened next?" asked Chen Xing.

"My strength continued to weaken," said Lu Ying. "In late autumn this year, Sima Yue came again. He controlled the crows who ate the dead for sustenance, and he started to attack the White Deer Forest— this place. I had no choice but to give up on Youduo and the Xiongnu and seal the valley. As a result, Youduo rallied all of the living dead Xiongnu to break free of my restraints. They left Carosha that night.

"It seemed as if Sima Yue had been ordered to come here and pollute this land. It was I who drove Xiao Shan down the mountain. I wanted him to go forth to seek survival elsewhere, but he kept circling the periphery of the mountain, searching for a way to save me. In the end, he turned south and crossed paths with the two of you."

Xiao Shan glanced at Lu Ying, clearly not having understood what they were saying.

"Xiao Shan," Lu Ying went on, "judged from the Akele king's attire that he was Youduo's senior, so he brought him back here. But while he was wandering outside the valley, Sima Yue appeared and defeated him, seizing both his weapon and the Akele king. Xiao Shan became extremely anxious when he met both of you."

Chen Xing let out a sigh and looked at Xiao Shan. "It wasn't easy for you either."

Xiao Shan let out a few little yelps like a wolf pup. He pulled Chen Xing closer to Lu Ying, then pointed at the rotten half of Lu Ying's body, clearly urging Chen Xing to treat him.

"Sima Yue has escaped as well," Xiang Shu pointed out. "From the direction he left in, he might be heading to Chi Le Chuan. Carosha's crisis must be resolved, but we have to go back to Chi Le Chuan as soon as possible."

One of Chen Xing's questions had finally been answered, but the answer had raised even more mysteries. For a moment, numerous complicated events entangled with one another, confusing things in Chen Xing's mind, and it only got worse when he thought about his enemy being Chiyou...

"Let's go, then," Chen Xing said apprehensively. It would take about ten days to reach Chi Le Chuan.

CHAPTER 38 ➤ 181

Just as Chen Xing was about to bid Lu Ying and Xiao Shan farewell, Xiang Shu clutched Chen Xing's collar and made him stand properly. "Where's the Dinghai Pearl?" asked Xiang Shu.

That was right! Chen Xing had almost forgotten the most important thing!

"Dinghai Pearl?" Lu Ying frowned a little.

"Did a Han exorcist come here, close to three hundred years ago?" Xiang Shu pressed.

Thank goodness Xiang Shu hadn't forgotten the matter of the Dinghai Pearl. Chen Xing's mind was still spinning with everything they'd learned about Chiyou's resurrection, but he quickly put those thoughts aside. "How much do you know about the Silence of All Magic?" he asked.

Lu Ying appeared puzzled. "An...exorcist? I didn't really pay attention, but I think I remember the person you're asking about." Chen Xing waited with bated breath. He had a nagging feeling that there was still something odd there that hadn't been resolved. "How did you two know about Zhang Liu?"

"Zhang Liu?" Chen Xing repeated, deeply confused himself. "Is that his name?"

Xiang Shu could tell that Lu Ying was dubious. "Explain everything properly," he told Chen Xing, so Chen Xing backed up and told Lu Ying in detail about how he'd found the diary in the Exorcism Department.

"Well, there was a person who came here," Lu Ying said, "but I don't remember it very clearly..."

"Let's talk about the Silence of All Magic first, then." That was the most important thing for Chen Xing right now. If he could restore the Spiritual Qi of the Heavens and Earth, then maybe he could also cure Lu Ying. "You've been alive for more than four hundred years, so you must have lived through that period. Can you tell me what caused the Spiritual Qi of the Heavens and Earth to disappear overnight?"

Lu Ying was silent. It was a long, long while before he answered. "Yes, the Spiritual Qi of the Heavens and Earth did disappear just like that," he said at last. "What deductions have you exorcists made about that?"

"Some people say that the Xuan Gate was closed."

"Aside from that?" Lu Ying was still thinking. He seemed a little more spirited. Chen Xing shrugged, palms up, and Lu Ying looked up at him. He asked softly, "Do you know how humans control magical artifacts? The world's magical artifacts don't work properly now, of course, but I may be able to explain their workings to you two..."

But Chen Xing already knew; he didn't need Lu Ying to explain. "They don't work because they can only be used by harnessing the Spiritual Qi of the Heavens and Earth. For example, to use the Yin Yang Mirror, a human must draw in spiritual qi before it can be activated. Magical artifacts operate on a similar principle to yao tribes, who absorb spiritual qi to cultivate. That's also why some magical artifacts that are brimming with an exceptional amount of power can, over time, transform into humans."

"That's correct," Lu Ying said with evident relief. "The Silence of All Magic didn't only leave you humans at a loss; it has puzzled us for a long time as well. For three hundred years, we have been unable to absorb any kind of spiritual qi. Hearing what you've said today, however, has resolved a question I had for many years. Maybe... Hm..."

"Come on, tell us!" Chen Xing said impatiently, but Lu Ying spoke as slowly as ever.

"We yao don't understand the world as well as you exorcists," he said, "and I don't know if there really is a 'Xuan Gate' or, if there is, where it may be...but have you ever considered the possibility that the disappearance of spiritual qi isn't a result of the Xuan Gate closing, but rather thanks to a magical artifact absorbing all of the Spiritual Qi of the Heavens and Earth into itself?"

Chen Xing was dumbfounded. "Is that...possible? What kind of artifact could hold all of the Spiritual Qi of the Heavens and Earth? That's...that's just unreasonable!"

He looked at Xiang Shu. Xiang Shu didn't understand a thing about any of this and just motioned for Chen Xing to continue asking questions, but Chen Xing was too stunned to think of anything. When he looked at Lu Ying again, the yao had a grave expression plastered on his face.

"Close to three hundred years ago..." Lu Ying began.

"Wait!" Chen Xing said. "Wait! Hold on!"

Lu Ying's conjecture was absurd, but...it was also the only thing that made sense! Chen Xing recalled what the diary had said:

*The Silence of All Magic was fated to be the final destination of all exorcists. The Dinghai Pearl alone can still release a surging flood of spiritual qi.*

Chen Xing's blood ran cold. "The spiritual qi...is all in the Dinghai Pearl!" he murmured.

"Dinghai Pearl," echoed Lu Ying. "Indeed... Seven months after Zhang Liu's arrival in Carosha, the Silence of All Magic fell. If you hadn't asked about it, I would never have thought..."

"What was Zhang Liu's purpose in coming here?" Xiang Shu cut in.

"He wanted to find a treasure buried in this mountain. A dragon pearl."

Chen Xing snapped out of his daze. "There's a dragon here?"

Lu Ying looked up. The long night had passed, and the enigmatic mist of the early morning, which had made everything dim, was slowly receding under a ray of sunlight. Carosha's lofty, majestic figure was visible outside the valley. Lu Ying's meaning was self-evident.

"The dragon pearl of the Dragon God, Zhuyin," said Chen Xing. "That must be it."

"He told me that he wanted to use that dragon pearl to accomplish something very difficult."

"What was it?" asked Xiang Shu.

Lu Ying shook his head. "We met only for a brief moment, three hundred years ago, so we didn't discuss much."

*"No plan survives first contact with the enemy... One can only do one's best. The vicissitudes of life pass with a flick of the finger, so what benefit is found in posthumous plans?"* Chen Xing recited in a murmur. "He found the Dinghai Pearl in Carosha, then used it to absorb and store all of the mana in the world... What did he want to achieve?"

"Will you let us take a look at where the Dinghai Pearl was?" asked Xiang Shu.

"It was in this tree hollow," Lu Ying said. "At the time, this islet was the Wolf God's dwelling."

Xiang Shu and Chen Xing each looked inside the hollow in turn. There was nothing unusual about it.

"Wouldn't Zhuyin's dragon pearl be very big?" said Chen Xing. "At least as big as a house? Zhuyin was so big it could turn into mountains... Then again, as a magical artifact, it's possible the dragon pearl could shrink or grow in size. But wait, I still have some questions to ask. How did the Wolf God obtain it?"

"He stumbled across it deep in the forest and carried it back in his mouth as a present for me. It struck me as exquisite and beautiful, so I kept it."

Xiang Shu asked another key question: "What's it used for?"

Lu Ying thought about it for a moment, then shook his head. "I'm not sure. Perhaps it has something to do with Zhuyin's dragon power."

"If you don't know what its purpose is, how do you know it could store all of the Spiritual Qi of the Heavens and Earth?"

"It's an ancient relic of the Dragon God; humans couldn't touch it. To activate it requires the power of the Dragon God. It's more powerful than any ordinary magical artifact, so the power required to use it must also be stronger than the Spiritual Qi of the Heavens and Earth."

"Day comes as Zhuyin opens its eyes," Chen Xing muttered to himself, "and night arrives as its eyes close. The Dinghai Pearl's effect must be related to time. Once he'd obtained the Dinghai Pearl, Zhang Liu would've also needed a lot of power to activate it."

"Perhaps," Lu Ying said. This thought seemed to put them more at ease. "This responsibility is still yours to bear, Great Exorcist and Protector Martial God."

Chen Xing and Xiang Shu fell silent for a long while. They had, in the end, reaped some benefits by coming to Carosha; at the very least, they had learned what the Dinghai Pearl was. Now they had a new question to answer: Once he'd gotten his hands on the pearl, where did Zhang Liu take it?

"If I may be so bold," Lu Ying said, "I have a favor to ask of the two of you. I hope you can fulfill this wish of mine."

He tried to stand up, but Chen Xing stopped him. "You must rest here! After we release the Spiritual Qi of the Heavens and Earth, I'll come back and find a way to treat your injuries with the Heart Lamp."

"I can't wait that long." Lu Ying stood up and held onto the withered tree behind him, and Xiao Shan stood with him, looking confused. He tugged on Chen Xing's sleeve to ask him to help.

"I..." Chen Xing didn't know what Lu Ying wanted to do. "I'll try my best."

He lit up the Heart Lamp and pressed it against Lu Ying's chest. Its white light enveloped Lu Ying, but the rotten half of his body didn't recover.

Lu Ying smiled. "Thank you. I feel much better now."

"No," Chen Xing said. "Lu Ying, there must be a way. You..."

Lu Ying knelt to kowtow to them. "I'd like to entrust Xiao Shan to you both for the time being."

Chen Xing was surprised, but Xiang Shu seemed to have expected it. He stayed standing where he was, motionless.

"His parents both passed away when he was young," said Lu Ying solemnly. "His father's family name was Xiao. He was a Han bodyguard who came to Longcheng from the north to do business. Xiao Shan's mother was the daughter of the Great Chanyu Huhanye and the Han lady Wang Zhaojun. Unfortunately, that tribe was wiped out during the calamity in Longcheng twelve years ago, and Xiao Shan was the only survivor. The Wolf God once vowed to protect the Xiongnu, and before he died, he bestowed his yao powers upon this child. Xiao Shan is twelve years old this year."

"Xiao Shan's twelve years old?!" Chen Xing yelped. "He looks nothing like a twelve-year-old?! What have you been feeding him? He's so small!"

Xiang Shu looked on in astonishment as Chen Xing scolded someone for not raising an orphan properly while that same orphan was being entrusted to him. He shot a look at Chen Xing, signaling with his eyes that Chen Xing needed to shut his mouth, but Chen Xing ignored him.

"Look at my family's protector. That's what a twelve-year-old should look like."

Xiang Shu was utterly speechless. So was Lu Ying. Eventually, Lu Ying managed, "I don't like eating meat by nature. He didn't want to eat meat in front of me, so he hasn't grown much."

"No wonder." Chen Xing's heart ached. "How can a boy grow if he eats only fruit and no meat?"

Xiang Shu couldn't stand it any longer; he motioned for Chen Xing to stop. But Lu Ying laughed.

"It's okay," Lu Ying said. "You're the wielder of the Heart Lamp. If he is fortunate enough to grow up by your side, then when he reaches adulthood at fourteen, you can just let him do what he wants. But it's okay if you don't want to take him along; if he can be sent back to the humans of Chi Le Chuan, that would be enough for me to be at peace."

"It's not that I'm not willing. The question is whether Xiao Shan would follow us. Would you like to come with us, Xiao Shan?"

Smiling a little, Lu Ying patted Xiao Shan's head and uttered a strange sentence. Xiao Shan stared doubtfully at Xiang Shu, then shifted his gaze to study Chen Xing. Lu Ying urged him a little more, and eventually Xiao Shan gave a reluctant nod.

"I asked him to help you two find a way to save me," Lu Ying said to Chen Xing and Xiang Shu. "Great Exorcist, Protector Martial God, I'm entrusting my only worry to you two. Leave now; don't let him see."

Chen Xing had a bad feeling about that. "You're leaving," he murmured.

"It's time," Lu Ying agreed gently. "Go."

Perhaps Xiao Shan sensed something, because he started crying. Lu Ying wanted to hug him, but he no longer had the energy, so Xiang Shu picked him up so Lu Ying could plant a soft kiss on his forehead. Chen Xing took half a step back.

"Don't cry," Lu Ying told him. "He has very acute senses; he'll know. Once you've left Carosha, White Mane, the wolf who once served the Wolf God, will send you back to Chi Le Chuan."

Recalling the giant wolf, Chen Xing nodded. He extended a hand toward Xiao Shan, and Xiao Shan grabbed it, but he pulled Chen Xing with one hand and tugged on Lu Ying with the other, refusing to let go. Lu Ying pretended to be angry and turned his head away slightly, so Xiao Shan would let go of him.

Lu Ying handed the amber pendant containing the phoenix's ashes to Chen Xing. "This is for you two." Chen Xing accepted it and took a few more steps away from him. "Don't look back."

Chen Xing felt tears at the back of his eyes, but Xiang Shu said, "Let's go."

Holding Xiao Shan by the hand, Chen Xing tried to leave, but Xiao Shan kept looking back, reluctant to part with Lu Ying. Lu Ying turned around to look at the withered forest, his back to them.

"Exorcist." Still facing away, Lu Ying loosened his robes and looked down at the rotten half of his body. "What's your name?"

Chen Xing turned away so that his own back was to Lu Ying. "Chen Xing."

"You came from the human world, so you must have walked through many places. There is one final question I would like to ask you."

Chen Xing remained silent. He didn't turn around.

"I heard that there is a sage in the distant western regions. It was said that under His divine power, everyone in the world would obtain redemption, and all obsessions would dissolve into enlightenment. Is there really such a sage?"

"He's called the Buddha," Chen Xing murmured.

"Where can I find Him?"

"Perhaps in the west, or perhaps in the Central Plains. I've only heard about Him in passing. It has been nearly eight hundred years since He was around."

Lu Ying tidied up his robes. His long white robe and black hair fluttered in the early morning breeze, and he looked up at the clear, sapphire-blue sky. He smiled and closed his eyes. "When my soul goes to the west, I hope to find my final destination. Exorcist, Protector Martial God, may we meet again someday."

Chen Xing picked up his pace as they left Mount Carosha. Xiao Shan kept turning back. Every time Chen Xing tried to pick him up, Xiao Shan struggled against him.

A short while later, under the early morning light, a resounding deer cry rang out from Mount Carosha. A gentle breeze blew, and the snow that had blanketed the mountains melted in an instant.

Standing in the middle of the withered, barren islet, Lu Ying released his grip on his collar, and his white robes fell to the ground. The half of his naked body that was still that of a fair young man began to glow; particles of light dotted the rotten half, beginning a gradual restoration.

Lu Ying turned around gracefully. His long hair became a splendid coat of fur, and his pure white body elongated, transforming into a giant, glowing stag. All that was missing were his shining horns. He lifted his front hooves and stepped into air. Ripples spread in the air where his hooves trod, and they were accompanied by the sounds of water.

Withered trees, barren land, stone mountains—the Deer God commanded vitality. The last of its yao powers gushed out of it like a torrent, covering the entire mountain range in a gentle blanket of light and wind. One by one, the wolves, white deer, foxes, and birds outside the mountains turned to face the depths of the sacred mountain, Carosha. Standing in the snowfield, Xiang Shu, Chen Xing, and Xiao Shan looked on, dazed.

The luminous stag stepped out of the valley. Wherever it passed, the snow melted, and all life returned. The cypress trees in the forest flourished, and everywhere, flowers bloomed. The newly melted snow flowed into the forest lake, creating a waterfall that cascaded down like pure silk. Deep in the valley, vegetation spread gently over King Akele's imposing body.

"From this earth you were born," came Lu Ying's gentle voice, "and to this earth you will eventually return."

In the lush, verdant canyon, the fog had dispersed, revealing thousands of blooming flowers in a scene that could have been plucked from a fairy tale. The shadow of the Gray Wolf flickered under the trees, and the White Deer flew back into the valley. Together, they vanished, dissolving into white particles that rose from the valley and converged in the sky to join the vast, majestic river of the divine veins.

Xiao Shan finally understood what was happening, and he let out a thunderous, sorrow-filled wail. Xiang Shu, prepared for this moment, locked onto Xiao Shan's wrist with one hand so that he couldn't rush back to Carosha.

The wolves dashed over to them from within the valley to surround Xiao Shan, Xiang Shu, and Chen Xing, bowing to them like a well-trained army. The giant wolf, White Mane, approached them and bowed as well.

"Lu Ying wants you to live well," Chen Xing said to Xiao Shan.

Xiao Shan wiped away his tears, but for a moment, he seemed lost. Xiang Shu gestured that the three of them should leave, so Chen Xing hugged Xiao Shan and mounted the wolf. Xiao Shan came back to himself, but before he could start struggling again, the wolf pack clustered around them and led them away from Carosha.

# 39

THE SNOWSTORM gently receded, and the northern lands quietened in the wintry night. The starry river stretched, north to south, over the length of the horizon, guiding them forward. Behind them, the North Star hung in the midnight-blue sky, gradually receding into the distance.

The wolf pack was traveling south. White Mane bore Chen Xing and a sleeping Xiao Shan, and Xiang Shu rode on the back of another sturdily built gray wolf. The wolves loped over peaks and through ravines; they sped through snow-capped mountains as swiftly as the wind. Far more familiar with the terrain than horses were, they didn't have to stop to look for the correct path. Where the journey from Longcheng had taken the original group four days, the wolves took only a day to cross that same distance.

The residents of Karakorum panicked when they saw tens of thousands of wolves rushing into the city—but when they realized Xiang Shu was leading the way, they called out his name and knelt, pressing their foreheads to the ground in worship, as if they had seen a god. Xiang Shu instructed them not to worry and to lead the wolf pack into the stone palace. The wolves and humans spent the long night together there, neither group harming the other.

"You should eat a little," Chen Xing said as he roasted the meat the Xiongnu had given them. When he thought of how the late Akele king had taken care of him the last time he was in the city, he choked up. Xiao Shan's eyes had reddened, but he kept his face set in a stubborn expression, and he refused to eat.

Xiang Shu looked at Xiao Shan. "A child who doesn't eat meat or drink milk won't grow tall," he said, but Xiao Shan ignored him. Chen Xing was thoroughly spent, but before he could say anything else to try to persuade Xiao Shan, Xiang Shu waved him off and told him to go to sleep.

In the middle of the night, Chen Xing heard Xiao Shan quietly get up and squat beside the embers of their bonfire. Then there came the soft sounds of him chewing something. Relief washed over Chen Xing.

Perhaps Xiao Shan had prepared himself long ago to one day bid Lu Ying farewell. In that respect, he had a great deal in common with Chen Xing's younger self. Chen Xing's shifu hadn't told him that his family had been killed, but he had guessed that was the case. There was nothing to be said in times like this. He could only keep Xiao Shan company; in time, the boy would learn how to move on.

Xiang Shu, it seemed, had gone off somewhere again. Chen Xing waited for a long while and then got up as quietly as he could. He scrounged up a blanket to cover Xiao Shan, who had lain back down. The kid really was too skinny. He looked like a starved puppy that had been left out in the rain; Chen Xing's heart ached just looking at him.

Xiao Shan's small head peeked out from under the blanket that Chen Xing had covered him with, and his bright eyes were wide open. He didn't say a word as Chen Xing leaned over to ruffle his hair and then got up to leave.

In front of the pagoda, at the highest point of Karakorum, Xiang Shu leaned against his heavy sword as he looked up at the low-hanging stars. He stared indifferently toward the south, a blanket draped over his knees.

"What are you doing now?" Chen Xing asked.

"Night watch."

"There are so many wolves. Why're you still on night watch?"

Instead of replying, Xiang Shu glanced at Chen Xing and raised an eyebrow.

"He ate a little," said Chen Xing. "He's asleep now."

"You knew what I wanted to ask again?" Xiang Shu's voice was cold.

A fascinating realization came to Chen Xing. He was the only one who seemed to possess this tacit understanding of Xiang Shu; they each understood what the other was getting at, even without words. Was that the Heart Lamp's doing? Or was it the relationship between an exorcist and his protector?

Chen Xing climbed the steps to join him. Xiang Shu shifted a little to make space, then covered them both with the same blanket. Chen Xing picked up the sword at his side and studied it. "It's really rare for a divine weapon like this to be able to transform into a bow."

Xiang Shu glanced over and frowned slightly. When Che Luofeng had picked up the same sword, he'd had to exert a lot of energy to lift it—but now, in Chen Xing's hands, it seemed as light as a wooden sword. He'd picked it up without any difficulty.

"The ensnaring nets of life and death bind firm and strong. Only by the Sword of Wisdom may they be cut," Chen Xing murmured. "I wonder, though, who passed this artifact down."

A gust of wind blew, and Chen Xing shifted closer to Xiang Shu under the blanket.

"What are you thinking about?" Chen Xing asked. Xiang Shu remained silent. Chen Xing frowned and muttered to himself, "The Dinghai Pearl... Could it be in one of the other two spots?"

"I'll draw the map out for you when we get back," Xiang Shu said evenly. "I memorized it all."

"And where on earth could Kjera and Shi Hai be hiding?"

Shi Hai had traveled all over the Divine Land, even to the far north, in his quest to revive the ancient Demon God Chiyou. The Silence of All Magic seemed to have had no effect on those two at all, thanks to their ability to control magical artifacts through resentment. That meant that while Chen Xing and Xiang Shu had no mana to draw on, the same wasn't true for their enemies. Without mana, they could only rely on the Heart Lamp and the divine weapon in Xiang Shu's hands. It was vexing.

Even if they found the Dinghai Pearl, how were they to release the Spiritual Qi of the Heavens and Earth stored within it? Were they supposed to destroy the artifact? And there was, Chen Xing was starting to realize, an even more serious problem. If, as Lu Ying had mentioned, the Dinghai Pearl possessed the ability to travel through time and change the past, then after the exorcist Zhang Liu obtained it three hundred years ago, he might have taken it with him and left for another time. What if he'd taken it thousands of years into the past or future? Their chances of finding it in their present were even slimmer than he'd thought.

If they did manage to find the Dinghai Pearl and use it to restore mana to the world, how were they supposed to seal Chiyou away? They were only humans, and they could only use human strength!

"*Aaargh!*" The more Chen Xing thought about it, the more frustrated and anxious he felt, so he grabbed Xiang Shu around the neck and shook him back and forth.

Xiang Shu just stared at him. Chen Xing frowned hard, despairing at how complicated his mission had become, but when he saw Xiang Shu's expression—which seemed to ask *Are you trying to assault me?*—he restrained himself. He scrubbed at his head in frustration and then shrank back under the blanket.

"Where to next?" Xiang Shu asked.

"Back to Chi Le Chuan, duh. We have to make sure your people are safe first."

But Xiang Shu was asking something else. "What I meant was that there are two different places where the Dinghai Pearl could be."

"Ugh, why is this so difficult?! And I didn't have a lot of time to begin with, damn it."

Apparently it had been foolish of Chen Xing to hope that he could resolve the problem early and then use what little time he had left to roam the Divine Land and admire its various famous landmarks. From the looks of things now, with only three years left for him, it was well within the realm of possibility that the Demon God Chiyou would simply reach out a palm and smack him like a fly. His future was a dark and thorny path.

"You should go back to take care of your people," Chen Xing said gloomily. "Give me the map, and I'll find a way. If I really can't figure something out, I'll write a letter to ask for your help. Let's sleep."

"Chi Le Chuan will be fine," said Xiang Shu. "Che Luofeng is looking after it."

The next morning, when Chen Xing woke up, he realized that he was back in the stone palace, sleeping alongside Xiao Shan. Xiao Shan was curled up comfortably in his embrace like a small animal— it was probably the same way he would have treated Lu Ying.

Outside, Xiang Shu whistled. "Time to go!"

The Xiongnu people had prepared a sled for the Great Chanyu. It was meant specifically for speeding through snow fields, and it was now harnessed to a wolf. The three of them got on the sled, and Xiang Shu instructed the city's residents to spend the winter at Chi Le Chuan. Then he took the reins of the sled and steered them away from Longcheng.

Xiao Shan's mood was much improved. He sat on the sled with a blanket around him, wiping off his two steel claws.

The pack of wolves flew through the snow; in less than two days, they were almost at the end of their hundred-and-fifty-mile journey. Chen Xing, of course, had spent the entire time bogged down by the weighty issues he was pondering. It wasn't until he saw Chi Le Chuan appearing through the mist that his mood finally improved.

Chen Xing figured that he should teach Xiao Shan how to speak, so he had been talking to him in the Han language all the way there, regardless of whether Xiao Shan understood. "When we're home, we'll have to give you a bath first thing," he told Xiao Shan now. Xiao Shan watched him warily. "The place we're about to arrive at is Chi Le Chuan."

The wolves gradually slowed.

Turning to Xiang Shu, Chen Xing said, "There are so many wolves, we can't bring them all in. We'll have to bid farewell to them outsi—"

Suddenly, without saying a word, Xiang Shu jumped off the sled. They were only a few hundred steps away from Chi Le Chuan.

Xiao Shan looked confused. He let out a strange noise, and the sled slowed further. Chen Xing stood up slowly on the sled and looked at the scene before him.

The entire region of Chi Le Chuan had been burned to the ground. Pitch-black tents dotted the landscape at the foot of the Yin Mountains.

Charred bodies littered the ground. An avalanche had buried the slopes to the northeast. Xiongnu, Tiele, and other Hu corpses floated in the river. At some point, the river had thawed and frozen over again, sealing the corpses in a layer of ice.

Chen Xing stared in horror.

Xiang Shu walked into Chi Le Chuan in utter silence. Things were so quiet it seemed eerie. A few crows were perched on the royal tent in the distance, and when they turned and spotted Xiang Shu, they spread their wings and flew away.

"Xiang Shu," Chen Xing whispered. He ran to catch up to him.

Xiao Shan clambered off the sled. He looked around him and sniffed the air before turning around, setting his steel claws against the earth, and dashing through the snow in another direction.

Intense resentment pervaded their surroundings, and Xiang Shu passed through Chi Le Chuan's ghastly ruins without a word. When they reached the royal tent, Chen Xing let out a loud shout. His vision went black, and he almost fainted.

Outside the royal tent lay the corpse of the Akele king's consort, curled up tightly with the little prince in her arms. She and her son had been dead for a long time.

Chen Xing felt such a swell of rage that he spat out a mouthful of blood. His eyesight blurred until all he could see was shadows. His vision faded in and out. Xiang Shu, next to him, grabbed Chen Xing's arm with one hand, but Chen Xing couldn't hold on any longer; he fell to the ground, unconscious.

Some time later—he couldn't tell how long it had been—he felt snowflakes landing on his face, and an icy cold hand patted his cheek. Chen Xing opened his eyes to find Xiao Shan squatting next to him with his dragon claws tucked against his back. He tugged on Chen Xing's sleeve a few times, asking him to get up.

Chen Xing sat up in a daze. When the reality of what had happened returned to him, he wanted to cry, but he had no tears to shed. His grief was so immense he wanted to die. King Akele had protected him all the way to Carosha, and then he'd sacrificed his own life to save Chen Xing and Xiang Shu. His wife, far away in Chi Le Chuan, had been his only hope; for that hope, he would have sacrificed anything. And he died not knowing that his wife and their newborn prince had been murdered in Chi Le Chuan.

Chen Xing's grief and indignation burst out of him. *"Who did this?!"*

Xiao Shan jumped back in fright. Not even the Heart Lamp could calm Chen Xing's rage. As he sat in front of the royal tent, his whole body trembling, all he could think about was killing someone for this. He wanted to hack whoever did this into a thousand pieces!

Xiao Shan pointed off into the distance and motioned for Chen Xing to look. Chen Xing followed his gaze and saw Xiang Shu's figure walking past in the distance, under a dark and gloomy sky. He was passing through the open space where Chi Le Chuan had held the Autumn Close Festival, carrying a corpse on his back and another under his arm. As Chen Xing watched, he brought the dead to the riverside, where cremations had traditionally been held, tossed them to the ground, and silently turned to head for another tent to find his dead tribesmen.

"Xiang Shu..." Chen Xing's voice trembled. They were balanced on a knife's edge. Knowing Xiang Shu's temperament, Chen Xing wasn't sure what he would do next. If Che Luofeng... Che Luofeng? Chen Xing didn't even want to imagine what it would be like when Xiang Shu saw Che Luofeng's corpse.

He got up and chased after Xiang Shu. Ever since Xiang Shu had entered Chi Le Chuan, he had not spoken a single word. Chen Xing watched him from behind, then asked, "Xiang Shu?"

Xiang Shu glanced at Chen Xing. He carried two more corpses to the riverside on his back.

Chen Xing took a deep breath, then went and pushed a worn-out cart over for Xiang Shu to load corpses onto. But Xiang Shu raised his hand to stop Chen Xing from touching the dead. Chen Xing was forced to stand to one side and watch Xiang Shu carry half a dozen corpses to the cart.

Chen Xing noticed that Xiang Shu used one hand to cover the eyes of each of the dead and whispered in the Tiele language before putting them on the cart. His movements were very gentle, as if he was afraid of startling them awake. Only when he'd done this for each of them and arranged them properly on the cart did Xiang Shu gesture for Chen Xing to push the cart into motion.

"Xiang Shu," Chen Xing said worriedly.

Xiang Shu just motioned for Chen Xing to go ahead. Chen Xing wiped his tears. He and Xiao Shan, who had come to join them, each took one of the leather belts tied to the axel and moved the corpses to the riverbank.

There were more than three thousand deceased. The sun set, then rose again—an entire night had passed. When Chen Xing finished counting the dead, he stared blankly at Xiang Shu.

Xiang Shu finally spoke. "Che Luofeng wasn't among them," he said.

Chen Xing breathed a slight sigh of relief. More than three hundred thousand people had been living in Chi Le Chuan when they left; it was fortunate that there weren't more than three thousand corpses. That meant that Che Luofeng could still be alive. When whatever had caused this had happened, Che Luofeng must have rallied the other tribesmen to fight and then retreated from this place.

Xiao Shan had picked up a rusty sword from somewhere. Now, he handed it to Xiang Shu. Xiang Shu glanced at it, then nodded his understanding. It was one of the weapons the ancient Xiongnu corpses had carried after they were awakened on Mount Carosha.

"Where did all the people go?" Chen Xing asked. "Were they captured?"

A heavy snow had fallen after the fighting in Chi Le Chuan, covering any tracks on the plains. But Xiao Shan went to the outskirts of the ruins and let out a howl to summon the wolves, who were watching from afar. The wolf pack gathered around him, and Xiao Shan held out the weapon for the wolves to look at it and sniff it. The wolves split up and scattered all through the mountains to search for tracks.

After Xiang Shu had cremated the corpses, he sat down on high ground in utter silence.

"Xiang Shu," Chen Xing called out to him.

"I'll be your protector," Xiang Shu vowed. "I want to hunt them to the ends of the earth. I will save my tribesmen."

"Xiang Shu," Chen Xing breathed. "You must calm yourself."

When Xiang Shu looked at Chen Xing, Chen Xing felt a sudden sense of dread, and a cold chill ran down his spine. Xiang Shu's eyes were filled with hatred. Those eyes looked much like Murong Chong's had when he'd glared at them outside Chang'an City.

"I'm no longer qualified to be the Great Chanyu," he said. "I can't even protect my own people."

"Shulü Kong," said Chen Xing, "your heart is overcome by a thirst for vengeance. You must calm yourself."

Outside, two of the wolves returned. Xiao Shan jumped to his feet and climbed onto White Mane's back, where he let out a string of howls. Immediately, Xiang Shu slung his sword over his back and sprinted out of Chi Le Chuan, darting across the snow as he followed the second wild wolf.

Chen Xing chased after him, but Xiang Shu didn't slow down and Chen Xing couldn't catch up. Xiao Shan, riding White Mane, turned around and signaled to Chen Xing to climb on as well, and the wolf carried Chen Xing along as they followed Xiang Shu.

"Xiao Shan," Chen Xing said. Xiao Shan turned around and cast a doubtful glance at Chen Xing. Lu Ying had entrusted this child to them hoping they would take care of him, but Xiao Shan had actually turned out to be a great help to them. "Thank you."

"Chen Xing," Xiao Shan tried. "Chen Xing?"

Chen Xing laughed bitterly and nodded. "Chen Xing."

"Chen Xing. Chen Xing?"

"We've arrived!"

Chen Xing was surprised at the enemy's audacity. They'd really remained so close to Chi Le Chuan?! The wolf had led them deep into the southeast Yin Mountains, outside a long and narrow canyon. From within, they could hear the sounds of a pitched battle. Someone blew on a bugle horn; there was the sound of people shouting, and then a group of Hu cavalrymen galloped out from the canyon.

Without a word, Xiang Shu unsheathed his sword and dashed forward. When Chen Xing caught up to him, he saw them, just outside the canyon—legions of living corpses!

"Hold on! Xiang Shu!" Chen Xing shouted.

But Xiang Shu had already turned sideways, and as Chen Xing watched, he slammed into the outer ring of living corpses and pierced them with his sword. Xiao Shan let out a howl, slotted the steel claws onto his hands, and pounced off White Mane's back and into the air!

Chen Xing latched tightly onto White Mane as it jumped off a cliff and took a shortcut past the battle formation. The pack of wolves surged into the canyon like a roaring wave. The Hu, who had been struggling to maintain their position, found their situation suddenly reversed.

"The Great Chanyu is back!"

"Great Chanyu!"

War drums began to beat within the canyon, reverberating like thunder. Their energy renewed, the Hu cavalry surged forth with a loud rumble. Meanwhile, Chen Xing was trying to spot the leader of the living corpse army. When he looked up, he saw a black-armored general standing on a cliff high above. The design of that black armor was familiar. This was the same general they had encountered at Carosha—the Prince of Donghai, Sima Yue!

"Xiang Shu!" Chen Xing shouted. "Above you!"

Xiang Shu shouted back, "Give me mana!"

Chen Xing wasted no time activating the Heart Lamp. Xiang Shu was deep in the enemy's ranks, with the living corpses surrounding him on all sides. He gripped his sword, preparing to turn it into a giant bow...but this time, the sword didn't glow at all!

With Chen Xing still astride its back, White Mane turned around and rushed toward the edge of the drought fiends' encirclement. A bright light burst from Chen Xing's hand as he bore down on Xiang Shu. Xiang Shu swept his heavy sword horizontally, hacking away at his enemies, but he didn't have the formidable power of the Heart Lamp.

"Give me mana!" Xiang Shu called again. "And don't come over here!"

Chen Xing tried again and again to call on the Heart Lamp's power, but he couldn't make the sword glow. *What's going on?!* he thought frantically.

"Give me mana!" Xiang Shu forced away the group of corpses crowding him from the front. He was already very close to the black-armored general—he'd need only a single arrow to bring the general down into the canyon—but Chen Xing's support didn't come. "What's happening?! What are you doing?! Do something!"

"I..." Chen Xing looked up. "I can't! Retreat!"

The black-armored general drew the string of a black longbow, and an arrow seething with black energy shot toward Xiang Shu. Seeing that Xiang Shu couldn't get out of the way in time and that Chen Xing was too far away to assist him, Xiao Shan dashed forward. *Clang!* With one claw, he smacked the arrow away.

The formation of cavalry behind them sounded their horns again. In response, the Hu army loosed a swath of fire arrows that blotted out the sky. The fiery rain descended like a meteor shower, and the wolves began to scatter.

"Run!" Chen Xing shouted. "Protect your people!"

Alarmed by the flames, the living corpse army receded like a tide. Xiang Shu let out an angry bellow. He grabbed Xiao Shan and tossed him to a wolf, then retreated into the canyon, which was filled with panicked Hu families. Riddled with wounds from head to toe but using his heavy sword as support, Xiang Shu dragged himself toward the entrance of the canyon.

There were more than two hundred thousand people packed inside. None of them had had time to bring their livestock or valuables with them. From the expressions on their faces, it was clear they'd been terrified when they escaped.

Xiang Shu looked around. "Where's Che Luofeng?"

No one answered. Chen Xing's heart thudded in fear.

# 40

THE TRAGEDY had been abrupt and fierce. According to the people of Chi Le Chuan, on the third day after Xiang Shu's departure, the legion of living corpses had appeared from nowhere and breached Chi Le Chuan.

Following the Great Chanyu's orders, they'd strengthened Chi Le Chuan's defenses in his absence, and everyone was on high alert. They patrolled the area, kept the perimeter well lit, and even released scout hawks to monitor their surroundings. But it hadn't been enough to prevent the unexpected upheaval—which had, in fact, originated from within Chi Le Chuan.

Reports of chaos first emerged from the northeastern corner of the Yin Mountains. At first, the leaders of the various tribes thought it was a mere fight between the tribes of the Ancient Covenant, but the unrest quickly escalated and spiraled out of control. All of Chi Le Chuan was thrown into disarray. Then, in the night, the frenzied, biting undead appeared all around them.

In the pitch-black night, the tribes' leaders were afraid of injuring their own people. They had no choice but to retreat, and retreat again. All attempts to form defensive lines were quickly overrun. Ironically, when another group of undead that had previously attacked Chi Le Chuan stormed into the camp, led by Youduo, they disregarded the living and instead fought the first group of living corpses. The undead slaughtered one another.

"Youduo," Chen Xing murmured, realization dawning on him. "Of course, Youduo was there for revenge."

A chill ran down his spine. The accounts relayed to him made it clear how chaotic and desperate the situation had been.

In the canyon, the leaders of various tribes, including the Tiele, Gaoche, Xiongnu, Lushui, Northern Jie, and Wuheng peoples, among others, gathered solemnly around a campfire. The fierce warriors of each tribe stood in silence along the perimeter, waiting for Xiang Shu's decision.

Chen Xing had a hunch that since the turmoil had started within Chi Le Chuan, it must be connected to the people residing there. "What's in the northeast corner of the Yin Mountains?"

"Rouran camp," Xiang Shu whispered.

Before he left, Xiang Shu had instructed Che Luofeng to act on his behalf as the Great Chanyu. But the living corpses had first appeared in the Rouran camp, and no one had seen Che Luofeng during the downfall of Chi Le Chuan.

After that harrowing night passed, the various Hu leaders regrouped with their defeated troops and retreated from the lower plain of the Yin Mountains, setting fire to their settlements and abandoning their supplies and livelihoods. Chi Le Chuan had thus been burned to ashes, and nearly 240,000 Hu of various tribes fled into the Yin Mountains. A few days later, the living corpses returned, this time blocking the entrance to the canyon in an attempt to trap them inside.

"Their leader is Youduo?" Chen Xing asked. Based on the fragmented information he'd been given, he surmised that Youduo held a deep-seated grudge against Che Luofeng's Rouran tribe.

The turmoil had begun in the Rouran territory, so presumably, Youduo had attacked there first.

"No," the Wuheng chieftain replied in the Xianbei language. "The Akele consort said that she caught sight of Che Luofeng and Zhou Zhen, and Youduo too. She wanted to stay and avenge her eldest son."

Chen Xing didn't know what to say to that, and Xiang Shu looked up from the bonfire, staring in disbelief at the Wuheng chieftain. Immediately, someone scolded the man and told him not to speak so carelessly.

Looking around the campfire, Chen Xing saw mistrust on the other chieftains' faces. Their trust in the Great Chanyu, Xiang Shu, was weakening, and their attitude made it clear that they blamed Chen Xing for it. After Xiang Shu took on the role of Great Chanyu, he had gone missing and abandoned his duties several times. Then he'd come back with a Han person and handed over his responsibilities to Che Luofeng, who was incapable of commanding respect, before rushing off north without any explanation.

Even if Chen Xing had nothing to do with it, Che Luofeng was Xiang Shu's anda. The fact that he hadn't appeared during such a grave crisis had stirred great dissatisfaction in Chi Le Chuan.

"Great Chanyu!" the Wuheng chieftain said. "What do we do now? We have no food. The people are eating snow to suppress their hunger."

"Our homes have been destroyed," added the Gaoche chieftain. "And we don't even know where the culprit is, so how can we get our revenge?!"

"This is an insult!" someone else shouted.

Tension mounted fast. Xiang Shu took a deep breath, his brow furrowed deeply, and suddenly stood up. Chen Xing immediately sensed what was going through his mind: Xiang Shu was resolved to lead a team out of the canyon to search for Che Luofeng.

"Everyone, please go back and get some rest." Chen Xing glanced around, knowing that he had to say something to calm Xiang Shu down. "The Great Chanyu will give you all an answer in the morning."

"And who are you?" the Lushui chieftain asked rudely. "Who are you to speak on behalf of the Great Chanyu?"

The others shot him warning looks. "This is the Divine Doctor!" said the Tiele chieftan. "Don't you recognize him?"

It was dark at night, and Chen Xing's whole body was covered in dust from travel, so the Lushui chieftain hadn't recognized him. Now that he saw Chen Xing more clearly, he fell silent. Over the last few months, Chen Xing had gained considerable respect for his work treating the sick in Chi Le Chuan. Xiang Shu's authority still held strong, too. The Lushui chieftain knew that, after they'd waited so many days, one more night wouldn't make a difference.

Everyone dispersed; Xiang Shu and Chen Xing returned to the Tiele camp. Along the way, they passed countless Hu people huddled in sheltered places, all of whom cast them doubtful glances. Xiang Shu avoided their gazes. This was the first time since he'd become Great Chanyu that he had faced such a serious crisis.

"Why isn't the Heart Lamp working?" Xiang Shu asked Chen Xing.

"Ask yourself that!" Chen Xing struggled to pry his wrist out of Xiang Shu's hold. "Let go! Shulü Kong!"

"Explain yourself!" Xiang Shu demanded, threatening.

Chen Xing didn't yield. Instead, he stared at Xiang Shu with a gaze filled with authority and righteousness, which startled Xiang Shu into releasing his hold.

"There was only vengeance in your heart," Chen Xing said. "With hatred clouding your mind, it's no wonder you can't sense my Heart Lamp."

Those words hit Xiang Shu like a slap to the face. From the moment he'd returned to Chi Le Chuan and found it devasted, with his people missing or dead, Xiang Shu had been overwhelmed by guilt and hatred. His actions had become reckless, driven by a single desire—to tear apart those who had ravaged Chi Le Chuan. Fueled by grief and rage, his vision was clouded by a thirst for vengeance, making it impossible for his heart to resonate with Chen Xing's light.

"You saw your people's suffering, and you let hatred drive you," Chen Xing continued, his brow furrowed in reproach. "When I saw my people lying dead across the land, did I seek revenge? The dead are gone. Right now, your priority is protecting those who are still alive! The present matters most!"

Xiang Shu took a deep breath and closed his eyes. "I understand," he said.

"Chi Le Chuan is facing its most dangerous hour. If you act recklessly again, you can forget about giving an explanation—by morning, everyone here might end up dead."

Xiang Shu raised his hand, which was trembling slightly, to stop Chen Xing. He took a brief moment to finally regain his composure.

Chen Xing tried again. "Our best course of action is to—"

"We'll send out scouts to search for another way out of the mountains," Xiang Shu interrupted. "If that fails, at dawn, you'll join me as we find a way to break through with the troops."

Chen Xing nodded in agreement. With over two hundred thousand people hiding here, they had to move quickly. The survival of their people was the top priority.

At that moment, the Tiele chieftain arrived. His name was Shi Mokun, meaning "Voice of the Arrow." He had once been a warrior who fought alongside Xiang Shu's father, the former Great Chanyu—

the Shulü clan was from the Tiele tribe, and after Xiang Shu became the Great Chanyu, he'd left the management of his tribe to Shi Mokun. Shi Mokun was in his early forties now, and he was widely respected by the entire tribe for his reliability.

Even in front of Chen Xing, Shi Mokun did not hesitate to address Xiang Shu frankly. "Shulü Kong, your anda, Che Luofeng, slaughtered the Akele people—every man, woman, and child. He didn't even spare the babies. His warrior subordinate, Zhou Zhen, has risen from the dead and become some kind of living corpse monster. All of this happened because of Che Luofeng. I didn't wish to say it in front of the chieftains earlier, but you owe everyone an explanation."

Chen Xing couldn't believe what he was hearing. Xiang Shu motioned for him not to intervene, but Chen Xing saw his hand trembling a little. Too much had happened in one day; one piece of bad news after another.

"Did you see it with your own eyes?" Xiang Shu asked, frowning deeply. This blow hit him even harder than the horrifying scenes he'd witnessed upon his return to Chi Le Chuan. He'd nearly lost his footing.

"It's what I was told," Shi Mokun replied. "While we were evacuating Chi Le Chuan, our clansmen and the Akele were covering the rear. Many saw Che Luofeng and Zhou Zhen chasing down the Akele side by side. They took the Akele's little prince, which was why the consort turned back with her forces."

A hand reached out from the side and tugged at Chen Xing. Turning, he saw that it was Xiao Shan, who was squatting on the ground, holding a piece of some kind of flatbread he'd gotten from somewhere. He offered it to Chen Xing.

Breathing heavily, Xiang Shu glanced at Chen Xing. Chen Xing nodded in understanding; Xiang Shu wanted him to take Xiao Shan away.

Together, he and Xiao Shan went to the edge of the Tiele camp. Xiao Shan jumped around all over the place before leaping onto Chen Xing's back as if he wanted to be carried, so Chen Xing lifted him up.

*Che Luofeng, Zhou Zhen... What should we do now?* Looking toward the Tiele camp in the distance, Chen Xing saw Xiang Shu following Shi Mokun to the center of the camp to begin discussions with the Tiele people in search of a solution.

"Who gave you that to eat?" Chen Xing asked Xiao Shan. "What about the wolves?"

Xiao Shan pointed to the place where the Xiongnu gathered, and Chen Xing understood that he meant that was where the flatbread had come from.

The wolf pack had scattered; each wolf was now perched on the rocks of Yin Mountain and gazing into the distance from their high vantage point. Chen Xing climbed halfway up the mountain, and from there he saw that the living corpses had not yet dispersed. Instead, they were moving slowly in groups of three to five from the snow-swept plains, approaching the canyon entrance but not yet charging in.

Chen Xing frowned. "What are they waiting for?"

Sitting next to Chen Xing, Xiao Shan had just finished his piece of bread when a skinny, one-eyed wolf approached, carrying a strange beast on its back. The creature had long hind legs and short forelegs. Its entire body was covered in brownish hair, and it had a rather foolish appearance.

"What's this?" Chen Xing asked, curiously examining the odd animal. The creature made a series of huffing sounds, and Xiao Shan patted its head. "Is this a bei? There are bei in the Yin Mountains?"

As the old saying went, "the wolves and bei collude."[10] Bei were very intelligent animals that were said to often suggest wicked schemes to wolves. Chen Xing had never seen a living bei before.

The bei growled a little, like it wanted to say something, but Xiao Shan nudged Chen Xing and signaled him to follow.

"Did you find something?" asked Chen Xing.

"Something?" Xiao Shan mimicked. He occasionally imitated Chen Xing's speech without understanding the words he was saying. Once they had some free time, Chen Xing intended to teach Xiao Shan properly; the boy would have to return to the human world eventually.

"Walk on two legs," Chen Xing told him. "Stand up straight."

Xiao Shan preferred to move on all fours, and with his two extra claws, he could run like the wind. He was reluctant to comply with Chen Xing's request, but from his observations, he seemed to understand that the Hu people around him walked upright, so he made a half-hearted attempt to do the same. Chen Xing had originally planned to prepare clothes for Xiao Shan and help him bathe once they returned to Chi Le Chuan, but, circumstances being what they were, he hadn't had the opportunity.

Xiao Shan led him to a cave. A slight breeze blew from its mouth.

"What is this place?" Chen Xing asked.

Xiao Shan drew a few mountains in the dirt and pointed around,

---

10  狼狈为奸 (lang bei wei jian): This idiomatic expression literally translates to "wolves and bei conspire together." It refers to the collusion of two or more parties in wrongdoing, emphasizing deceit and treachery. The bei is a mythological creature said to be similar in appearance to a wolf, but with short front legs that mean it has to lean on a wolf's back to get around; in return, it assists the wolf with its superior cunning and intelligence.

and then at the cave. He sketched a stick figure outside the mountains, then drew a line passing through the mountains and looping around to the figure's back, ending with an arrow.

"Great! A cave! We can get out through this cave!" Chen Xing exclaimed. "That's wonderful! You're so clever!"

The wolf carrying the bei left the cave. Xiao Shan waved his claws again, and Chen Xing immediately understood—he wanted to ambush Sima Yue, one of the black shadow generals. This horde of living corpses had invaded Mount Carosha in the past, which had ultimately led to Lu Ying's deteriorating condition. Xiao Shan didn't understand exactly how, but he sensed that the living corpses and the general were connected to Lu Ying's death, and he wanted revenge.

"Wait," said Chen Xing. "First, let's get everyone out of here. Let's go." Xiao Shan tried to dart into the cave, but Chen Xing stopped him. "Stop messing around! Follow me!"

He pulled Xiao Shan along, determined to bring him back to the Tiele tribe's camp. This method proved effective indeed. No wonder Xiang Shu often preferred to just drag people around without explanation.

The atmosphere in the Tiele camp was tense. When Chen Xing rushed in, everyone seemed to be engaged in a difficult discussion, and Xiang Shu's expression looked even worse than before.

"What are you planning to do?" Chen Xing asked. He saw there was food in the camp, so he grabbed some and shared it with Xiao Shan—who momentarily forgot about revenge and sat down to eat.

Xiang Shu said, "At dawn, the Tiele will take the lead and break through with the sixteen tribes of Chi Le Chuan. We'll get as many people out as we can, then settle the elderly and children and look for Che Luofeng."

"Xiao Shan found a place," Chen Xing started to say, but he stopped when he saw Xiao Shan holding an earthen jar. "Hey! Don't drink that! It's alcohol!"

But Xiao Shan had already drunk nearly half of it.

That night, more than two hundred thousand people of Chi Le Chuan retreated through the cave without making a sound. Xiang Shu and Chen Xing stood at the cave entrance to hold the rear, and the chieftains counted their people before following them inside.

This continued through the night until dawn, when the cawing of crows echoed from outside the canyon. The Tiele were the last to leave.

"Where do we go after we leave the Yin Mountains?" asked Chen Xing. "The passes?"

"Northwest," Xiang Shu replied. "To Karakorum. Let's go."

Xiang Shu handed the inebriated Xiao Shan over to Chen Xing. Chen Xing was a little surprised—he'd assumed Xiang Shu would insist on staying behind and charging into the living corpses' ranks alone, but he didn't seem to have any such plans.

Xiang Shu took a deep breath and furrowed his brow. "You're right. I need to be with my people now. I can't leave them again." He lead the horse forward, but then, out of nowhere, asked, "Who taught you all of this?"

"What?" Chen Xing was preoccupied, thinking about the enemy.

"You see things more clearly than I do. You understand the necessity of cherishing the people around you instead of acting on impulse."

Chen Xing smiled wryly. Perhaps it was because he himself didn't have much time left. A person who knew their time was limited naturally paid attention to what mattered most.

But he didn't say that aloud. "I'm not sure if I'm right either," he said, "but look, they all have their hopes pinned on you. They just suffered an attack from the drought fiends, and they haven't settled down yet. If we just run off and launch a counterattack now, it will only make things more dangerous. Everyone needs time to recover."

All of the horses they could spare had been distributed, leaving only one horse for Chen Xing, Xiang Shu, and Xiao Shan.

"That's strange," said Chen Xing. "What happened to the horse your mother left behind?"

The horse had run off when they left Carosha, but it'd never returned. Chen Xing had felt certain that the horse had wanted to take them somewhere. That bei gave him a strange feeling too. The Silence of All Magic had robbed many yao races of their ability to speak, let alone cultivate human forms. There weren't many yao in the Yin Mountains, but there were certainly a few; Chen Xing wondered if the horse and the bei were among them. Perhaps they knew some hidden truths.

The situation was urgent, however, and they had no time to investigate. With all three of them seated on the same horse—Xiang Shu holding the reins and Chen Xing holding Xiao Shan—they joined the troops.

The sixteen tribes knew this was their last chance to survive. They marched swiftly, leaving the horses and carts for the elderly, the weak, and the women and children. It took only a day for them to reach the Xarusgol River. By the time they reached Longcheng, three days and nights had passed, and Chen Xing was exhausted.

Over two hundred thousand people poured into Karakorum, instantly reviving the long-abandoned ancient city. The first thing Xiang Shu did was send out various tribes to reinforce the city walls, increase the patrols, and keep torches burning through the night, transforming Longcheng into a massive military stronghold. Hunters scattered across the plains to scout and gather supplies for the winter, bringing back game to feed their respective tribes.

For several days, Xiang Shu spoke very little, which worried Chen Xing.

On the first day after their arrival in Longcheng, a slight commotion broke out outside the city. The wolf pack had surrounded the city walls. At first, the tribes had been wary of them, but Chen Xing had explained on their journey to Longcheng that the wolves were their protectors and the guardians of the Xiongnu, which eased some of their fears. But on the twenty-second day of the twelfth lunar month, the wolves began to howl intermittently.

Chen Xing and Xiang Shu followed Xiao Shan up onto the city wall, where Xiao Shan squatted and called down a few times. White Mane stepped forward and looked up at him. They exchanged several wolf howls. Suddenly, Chen Xing noticed tears in Xiao Shan's eyes.

"They're leaving, aren't they?" Chen Xing asked Xiao Shan. Though Xiao Shan didn't fully understand, he had heard the word "leave" often enough in the past few days, and he nodded in recognition.

With that, White Mane led the wolf pack northward, disappearing into the vast snowy expanse.

"The wolves know that staying here will only lead to competition for food with humans," Xiang Shu said. "Nobody would survive the winter."

The Xiongnu came out, one after another, to bid farewell to White Mane, the "Wolf God" they revered.

*From now on, Xiao Shan will be alone*, Chen Xing thought. Aloud, he said, "All right, since this is happening and your friends have all left... Xiao Shan, how about we..."

Xiao Shan just looked at him questioningly.

Chen Xing was fed up with this kid. "Take a bath?"

"No!" Xiao Shan shouted. "No! No! No! Go! Go!" The first thing he'd learned to say was Chen Xing's name, but the second was "No!" and the third was "Go!"

Chen Xing was forced to take a long detour through the city, but with the help of the Xiongnu, Tiele, and Gaoche peoples, he finally managed to capture Xiao Shan and deposit him in a steaming hot bath. "No! No! No!" Xiao Shan yelled, but Chen Xing scrubbed him down by force, which only made him scream louder.

"Look, I need to take a bath too!" Chen Xing said. "You're a human, not an animal! And even animals have to take baths!"

Xiao Shan's flailing left Chen Xing completely soaked, so he decided he might as well jump into the bath himself to better control Xiao Shan. There was a royal palace for the Xiongnu king in Karakorum, and the bath was about forty feet square. A wood fire had been lit in the water room, melting snow in a storage tank into hot water for bathing.

With concerted effort, Chen Xing eventually managed to get Xiao Shan thoroughly wet, and with nothing left to lose, Xiao Shan settled down at last.

"Look at you!" Chen Xing exclaimed, holding Xiao Shan's wrist as he scrubbed him hard. "You're filthy!"

Xiao Shan leaned in closer, bumping his head against Chen Xing's face. Chen Xing sputtered and fended off Xiao Shan's messy hair, which was all over the place.

"He wants you to lick him," Xiang Shu said as he walked into the bathhouse.

No matter how hard Chen Xing tried, he couldn't bring himself to do it. He recalled that wolves washed their pups by licking their fur and that it was a gesture of intimacy for creatures like them, but...

He leaned in to sniff Xiao Shan instead, hoping he'd think that was just as good as licking.

Xiang Shu loosened his Great Chanyu robe and stepped into the bath to soak, letting out a tired sigh.

"How's it going?" Chen Xing asked.

"Scouts have reported that the living corpses are already on the way," Xiang Shu replied. "They've just crossed the Xarusgol River."

In the freezing cold, the living corpses couldn't move quite as quickly. A few days earlier, Chen Xing had heard the Tiele people discussing Xiang Shu's plans to postpone their revenge and focus on ensuring the safety of their clan. But if Che Luofeng had turned into one of the living corpses, he would undoubtedly return. Chen Xing could tell that Xiang Shu was feeling extremely stifled. If he was by himself, he would have set out to find Che Luofeng by now, but as the Great Chanyu, Xiang Shu's foremost duty was to protect all of Chi Le Chuan.

Chen Xing didn't think it wise to ask about Che Luofeng. He focused instead on grooming Xiao Shan's hair. "We have to burn them all up outside Longcheng," he said.

"Yes. This is the biggest danger we've faced since the establishment of the Chi Le Covenant, but I believe we can get through it. Fortunately, we have you."

This surprised Chen Xing, and he glanced at Xiang Shu. Xiang Shu leaned in a bit in a request for Chen Xing to massage his shoulders.

"Why?!" Chen Xing demanded. "Why should I do that?!"

"You'll wash Xiao Shan, but not me?" Xiang Shu said in a casual tone, his eyes closed.

Reluctantly, Chen Xing let go of Xiao Shan and helped Xiang Shu wash his hair. As he did so, Xiao Shan clung to Chen Xing from behind, hanging off him. Suddenly, Xiang Shu turned around and pushed Xiao Shan underwater, making Chen Xing and Xiao Shan scream in unison.

# 41

XIAO SHAN immediately hid behind Chen Xing. Xiang Shu looked at him and asked, "What are you going to do with this kid?"

Chen Xing was a bit concerned about that too. Should they take him with them to look for the Dinghai Pearl? Shi Hai was targeting Chen Xing; he feared that bringing Xiao Shan with them would only put him in danger. But Lu Ying had entrusted Xiao Shan to him, so how could Chen Xing leave him behind?

"What do you think?" he asked Xiang Shu.

"He should go back to wherever he came from. He is a descendant of the Great Chanyu Huhanye; the most suitable place for him is with his clan."

Lu Ying had said that the entire Huhanye clan had perished in Longcheng, but the rest of the Xiongnu were still around. Could they take proper care of Xiao Shan, though? Chen Xing was skeptical. Besides, he didn't even know whether Xiao Shan wanted to stay in Longcheng.

Xiao Shan seemed to sense that they were talking about finding him a place to settle in. He looked a little worried. Noticing his unease, Chen Xing stopped talking altogether.

Chen Xing washed the dirt off of Xiao Shan and managed to get him to some semblance of cleanliness. He was surprised to discover that Xiao Shan wasn't actually as dark-skinned as he'd always appeared; free of dirt and grime, he was pale and delicate-looking.

After their bath, Chen Xing borrowed some children's clothes from the Xiongnu and had Xiao Shan put them on. Xiao Shan and Xiang Shu really didn't look alike, but their bearings made them look like father and son. One grown man and one child, each with habitually grumpy and hostile facial expressions paired with auras of majesty. All it took was one look to see that these weren't people to be messed with.

"Where's the music coming from?" Chen Xing asked, holding Xiao Shan's hand as they stood in the streets of Karakorum. Enjoying the blood-red sunset, he followed the distant sound of a flute to its source.

It was Xiang Shu. Fresh from his bath, he stood atop the city gate tower, facing Chi Le Chuan with a Qiang flute in his hands. With his gaze lowered, he played an ancient song of the lands beyond the pass. Many people, including both the Hu from Chi Le Chuan and the locals of Longcheng, emerged from their houses, went to the city walls, and knelt in the streets.

Chen Xing slowly approached the city gate tower, momentarily fascinated by the fact that Xiang Shu could play the Qiang flute. Xiang Shu's Hu robe swayed and fluttered like a dragon's whiskers against the snow-covered backdrop, and the Qiang flute in his hands produced a deep and sonorous tone. Under the moody sky, the wind surged and clouds billowed, creating an atmosphere that stirred the soul.

The sound of the Qiang flute was resolute and crystal clear. At first, it sang of an intense battle between armies of golden spears and iron cavalry; then, it played the music of a raging sea with surging,

raucous waves. The tone shifted and became a flock of wild geese flying far away. It suddenly built up again into ten thousand horses galloping on the plains beyond the pass, then gradually calmed until it was as gentle and tender as falling snowflakes. Finally, it hit its deepest note, a ballad to calm the resentful souls of those who had sacrificed themselves in Chi Le Chuan and direct them to at last return to the earth.

"What song is this?" Chen Xing murmured.

Now that the song was over, Xiang Shu opened his eyes and glanced at Chen Xing. "Fusheng Melody."

Chen Xing thought about the song. Its melody had risen abruptly and then calmed down, evoking the instability of life in the vast ocean, one moment floating, another moment sinking. He opened his mouth to ask who had taught Xiang Shu to play like that, but he was interrupted when Xiao Shan, full of curiosity, reached out and snatched the Qiang flute out of Xiang Shu's hands.

"Give it back!" Xiang Shu immediately chased after him.

As he ran away, Xiao Shan leaned in and tried to play the flute, but he only made a strained blowing sound. Chen Xing couldn't believe how energetic this kid was.

It had taken Chen Xing a full two days to correct Xiao Shan's habit of walking on all fours. Xiao Shan had reluctantly complied in the end, but sometimes, when Chen Xing wasn't around, he returned to his old habits. Chen Xing had been forced to temporarily confiscate his claws so that his hands were shorter than his feet, which made it less comfortable for him to crawl around like that. Fortunately, though, Xiao Shan was devoted to carrying out Lu Ying's dying command, and he mainly behaved very well.

Chen Xing got back to teaching Xiao Shan how to speak Han, starting with people's names: "Xiang Shu, Xiang Shu." Then they moved on to heaven and earth, rivers and plains, and the sun, moon, stars, and other celestial bodies. Xiao Shan learned surprisingly quickly. Chen Xing didn't know what language Lu Ying had used to speak to Xiao Shan, and he'd been surprised that Lu Ying spoke Han so clearly; he'd assumed that these great yao were mostly accustomed to the northern Xiongnu language.

Perhaps Lu Ying had occasionally spoken Han to Xiao Shan so that Xiao Shan wouldn't forget that he had a Han father. As Xiao Shan picked up the language, he began to string some short sentences together on his own, but he also said a lot of confusing words that only Chen Xing could understand.

As Chen Xing looked after Xiao Shan, it occurred to him that this kid was more fun to be with than Xiang Shu. Going to see Xiang Shu was like asking for a rebuff. Besides, Chen Xing wasn't going to live past twenty years old. He had no hope of settling down, starting a family, and having children. Taking care of Xiao Shan felt just like raising a son, so Chen Xing decided to treat it as a shortcut to the joy of having children.

When Xiang Shu had asked Chen Xing earlier about finding a place for Xiao Shan, Chen Xing had felt conflicted. He wanted to keep Xiao Shan with him, but he also worried about being unable to take care of Xiao Shan in the long term. What would he do with the child when he died? Give him to Xiang Shu? It wasn't like Xiang Shu seemed all that reliable. The solution was clear: Xiao Shan had to be returned to his clan as soon as possible.

At twelve years old, Xiao Shan was only about as tall as a typical eight- or nine-year-old. His education also lagged far behind his peers because he'd been living with the wolves for so long. But on top of changing his attire to a Xiongnu leather hunting suit, Chen Xing had taken special care to doll Xiao Shan up. He parted Xiao Shan's hair in the middle and combed it up to the crown, arranging it just like Xiang Shu's. His identity wasn't yet known to the people of Chi Le Chuan, but nobody asked about it; they just saw Xiao Shan as the little prince of the Tiele.

Chen Xing wanted to dress Xiao Shan in Han attire, but he couldn't find suitable clothing anywhere. Xiao Shan was still very young, and his facial features were very upright. His facial structure was deep, and he had a high nose bridge and bright amber eyes. There remained a trace of stubbornness in his face that betrayed his half-Xiongnu lineage.

"You are Zhaojun's descendant," Chen Xing admonished him. "Your ancestor was a famous beauty. You should always have some dignity as her descendant; don't rub against the wall like a dog."

Xiao Shan blinked at him, visibly bemused.

They were sitting beside the city walls, warming themselves up in front of a fire. Xiao Shan's back had itched, so he had leaned back to rub against the brick wall. Chen Xing gave him a back scratcher, and Xiao Shan made quiet use of it, looking very pleased.

Since he'd started following Chen Xing everywhere, Xiao Shan seemed to be in good spirits. Most of the time, he was all curiosity, going around and peering at everything. It was only in the dead of night that he seemed to occasionally think of Lu Ying and become depressed. When that happened, Chen Xing touched his small arm and comforted him by saying, "Everyone in the world, without exception, has to go through this. Things will slowly get better."

He'd also given Xiao Shan the amber pendant containing the ashes of the phoenix as a token by which to remember Lu Ying. Xiao Shan wore it around his neck, underneath his clothes.

"How do you get so dirty every day?" Chen Xing asked. He really didn't understand it! Xiao Shan was almost always just following him around, but he still managed to get filthy. It took less than half a day for his new clothes to get covered in dust. When Chen Xing was a child, he had been well accustomed to sitting politely at home to study all day, and Yuwen Xin had waited on him on the rare occasions he'd gone out. He certainly never went wild like Xiao Shan, who wanted to climb every tree and touch any cattle or sheep he spotted.

"How?" Xiao Shan repeated. He was just echoing Chen Xing's words automatically, but it sounded like a provocation. Sometimes Chen Xing looked at him and felt the fondness in his heart grow even greater. If he'd had a younger brother like Xiao Shan back at home, he would have adored him, and he also would have wanted to tie him up with a rope to stop him from running around everywhere.

"Take care of your amber," Chen Xing said. "Maybe, if all goes well, when the mana returns to the world, you can bring Lu Ying back to life."

Xiao Shan nodded, roughly gleaning what Chen Xing was telling him.

Chen Xing didn't actually know how the phoenix would revive the dead. The ancient records said that the power released during the phoenix's rebirth could reshape a person's body, but the effect was limited to the physical body. Lu Ying was already dead, and he should have returned to the divine veins and entered the reincarnation cycle by now. Chen Xing didn't know whether the phoenix's power would have any effect anymore.

As he finished scratching his back, Xiao Shan's ears perked up and he turned to look at the plains outside the city. "Coming!" he said. "Coming!"

Chen Xing was sitting in front of the fire, trying to keep his hands warm. Hearing Xiao Shan's words, he raised his head and then nervously stood up, looking out past the city walls. Xiao Shan stood in front of him holding the back scratcher, the might that could hold out against ten thousand warriors evident in his posture. Chen Xing scanned their surroundings for a long time, but he could see nothing amiss outside the city.

"Coming! Coming!" Xiao Shan pushed Chen Xing, trying to make him go to a safe place, and then opened up his own outer robe and tied it on his waist as if he intended to leave the city to fight. "Chen Xing, leave! Chen Xing, leave!"

And then Chen Xing saw it. Out on the plain, far off in the distance, an incoming black tide—thousands of living corpse soldiers were closing in.

The scouts saw it too. They blew their horns, and the sound echoed all through Longcheng.

The living corpses had come faster than expected, but in the two short days since they'd arrived in Longcheng, Xiang Shu had already readied all of the city's defenses. As long there was no snowstorm, Karakorum's solid defenses would have no problem withstanding this living corpse army for two or three days.

Xiao Shan wanted to jump straight down from the city tower and go to war, but Chen Xing grabbed him.

"Not now!" he told him. "Wait for Xiang Shu!"

He activated the Heart Lamp several times. Having already led the Tiele cavalry to high ground, Xiang Shu rode his horse up to the city gate tower and looked into the distance with them.

"We have to find a way to capture the general," Chen Xing told Xiang Shu. "Try to keep Sima Yue alive; I want to bring him back here and clarify something."

He looked at Xiang Shu as he made this request. All the fights they'd been in together had left Chen Xing with the impression that Xiang Shu was nigh unbeatable—he knew in his heart Xiang Shu would get it done. Bringing the black-armored general Sima Yue back to the city alive would certainly help them to find Shi Hai and Chiyou's hiding place.

"Defend the city first," Xiang Shu said. "Avoid joining the battle outside the city walls. I'll find a way to watch Xiao Shan out there and keep him out of trouble."

The first incoming wave from the living corpse army was infantry, and the next wave was the cavalry. A surging ice fog obscured their field of view, preventing them from seeing the commander-in-chief clearly. Their enemy's leader obviously had no intention of exposing himself.

"All these bodies," Chen Xing murmured. "Where did they come from?"

The Tiele chief answered him. "They must've turned over every single burial ground within a thousand-mile radius."

Sky burial remained customary among the Hu. It was only prohibited for prisoners of war, slaves, and those who had committed grave taboos. Over the past few decades, all sorts of burial pits had been erected all around the mountains, most using stones. The enemy had made use of local resources to find and awaken corpses.

Xiao Shan kept climbing on Chen Xing, trying to retrieve his confiscated weapon. "Claws! Claws!"

"Not now!" Chen Xing told him. "When we go into battle, let's go together." Xiao Shan gave up and stood at the top of the city walls, watching the battle with Xiang Shu and Chen Xing.

Archers lined the city walls, igniting fiery arrow after fiery arrow. The Hu outside the Great Wall were natural-born sharpshooters. Led by the various clan chiefs, they stood high on the city walls, forming an indestructible line of defense.

For the past few days, Xiang Shu had been meeting up with the clan chiefs and bringing them up to speed on the drought fiends' upheaval. Now that they knew where the monsters came from and what they actually were, the Hu were no longer afraid. All they had to do was take more precautions and fight harder.

Everyone looked serious as they waited. There was a strange silence inside and outside the city; only the rustling of the living corpses moving through the snow could be heard. Ice fog filled the air. When the corpses got close to their perimeter, Xiang Shu shouted, "Shoot!" and fiery arrows soared into the sky and down over the snowy plain.

Chen Xing watched the enemy try and fail to get close to the city walls. It didn't matter how hard the living corpses struggled; their movements were slow, and most of them had been rotting when they were dug up from the ground. The intense cold was the only thing keeping their flesh, blood, and limbs together. Once the snow melted, they would simply fall to pieces.

But Chen Xing sensed a danger lurking in the swirling fog, and sure enough, from within the fog, a drum began to beat. The drum beats weren't loud, but everyone heard them clearly.

Chen Xing made a quick deduction. "It's a magical artifact! Get ready!"

Xiang Shu stayed silent. It sounded like a rattle drum was shaking in their ears. Then, suddenly, a dozen huge monsters rushed out of the fog, each one at least ten feet tall and covered with tattered hair. They trampled directly through the group of living corpses and charged toward the outer wall of Longcheng.

The Hu archers shouted loudly, but Chen Xing couldn't understand what they were saying. He'd never seen monsters like these before. "What is that?" he yelled.

Xiao Shan yelled something too.

"Mammoths!" said Xiang Shu.

Chen Xing had only read about mammoths in books. The enemy must have found their carcasses in this cold northern region. The mammoths were covered with ice and snow; it seemed that after they'd been dead for thousands of years, their internal organs and limbs were frozen stiff, making them natural battering rams. When the first mammoth hit the city wall, tiles and bricks flew in all directions, and the earth shook beneath them.

Xiang Shu steadied himself, reached for Chen Xing, and then jumped down from the top of the city wall. Archers tumbled to the ground one after the other, and the brazier toppled inward. The other mammoths quickly flattened the anti-cavalry barriers and crashed through the wooden outer walls to slam into Karakorum's city walls.

Chaos reigned above and below the city tower. The mammoths soon retreated, but they weren't afraid of arrows at all. Under the sound of the rattle drum, they began to organize a second charge.

The Tiele chief rushed down from the top of the tower. "We can't stop this! Another hit and the walls will fall apart! Great Chanyu!"

"Four hundred of you," Xiang Shu shouted, "follow me out! Chen Xing!"

The mammoths had to be stopped. If these multi-ton monsters kept it up, it would take less than two hours for them to smash through the walls and flatten the whole of Karakorum!

"I'm going to cleanse that magical artifact!" Chen Xing shouted.

"No! It's too dangerous!" Xiang Shu said. "Prepare net traps and caltrops!"

"It's no use! These mammoths are already dead! They're not afraid of pain! Shi Mokun, you keep an eye on Xiao Shan!"

When the city gate opened, Xiang Shu rushed out of Karakorum with the Tiele and the Xiongnu cavalry. Under the dark sky, the cavalry threw out net traps. Every time a mammoth stepped on a net, a team of five immediately closed it and made the vast, rotting animal stumble. The ground shook every time a mammoth fell into the snow.

With the Heart Lamp shining brightly in his hands, Chen Xing urged his horse on into the battle. Xiang Shu chased after him, shouting, "Wait for me!"

Chen Xing turned his head. Listening to the drum beats, he deduced the enemy's secret weapon. This drum, an ancient magical artifact, was made from the skin of an immortal beast called a zheng. The zheng was said to have been able to suppress the souls of the deceased and emit a roar that made the dead cower in fear.

It must have been similar to the Yin Yang Mirror: The enemy had used resentment to activate the magical artifact and alter its original function. The magical artifact had once harnessed spiritual qi to exorcise evil spirits, but refined by resentment, it became a demonic weapon that could control living corpses.

*We must get it back as soon as possible!* Chen Xing thought. If they could seize the magical artifact, their foes would be forced to retreat.

"Time to fight," Che Luofeng said levelly. He and a tall man sat quietly atop corpse horses in the rear of the formation. Sima Yue was behind them, wearing his black armor and holding a strange antler staff that emitted jet-black resentment. "Zhou Zhen?"

Che Luofeng turned his head and looked at the man beside him. This man had been dead for years, but his condition hadn't deteriorated much; he looked just as he had when he was buried. He wore Xiang Shu's Great Chanyu crown, with its three feathers protruding from the side of his head, and his whole body was covered in a wolf fur robe. On his left hand he wore a knuckle ring, and he held a small rattle drum in his right. It was none other than the Rourans' greatest warrior, Zhou Zhen.

"I'll deal with Shulü Kong," Zhou Zhen said indifferently.

"Leave that Han to me," said Che Luofeng.

Zhou Zhen nodded. He glanced at Che Luofeng and said in the same casual tone, "If we keep them far away enough from each other, the Heart Lamp won't work."

Che Luofeng looked at his people again. The sixty thousand Rouran, now members of the stiff-faced living corpse army, were astride their horses and awaiting his orders. Che Luofeng's resolve wavered. "I..."

"Rest assured, my lord has ordered us not to kill Shulü Kong. He is still of great use to us."

Che Luofeng took a deep breath. In the distance, the mammoths had fallen, one after another, and they and the corpses from the first wave were piled under the city walls. Zhou Zhen shook his rattle drum again, sounding three drum beats. The disciplined Rouran took up their weapons and launched the second siege attack. With the first-wave mammoths and corpses as their siege ladders, the Rouran cavalry charged across the wasteland and at Karakorum's walls.

Xiang Shu looked back to see a flood of enemy troops rushing the walls.

"Xiang Shu!" shouted Chen Xing.

Xiang Shu urged his horse to catch up with Chen Xing, but the storming army drove the two of them apart in no time. With the Heart Lamp in his hands, Chen Xing made the attacking cavalry scatter to avoid him, but Xiang Shu was unprotected and had to swing his huge sword to clear a path to reunite with Chen Xing.

Wherever the army marched, snow was kicked up underfoot, making it hard to tell allies from foes. Chen Xing was galloping forward, searching for Xiang Shu with the aid of the Heart Lamp's light, when suddenly, a figure emerged from the ice fog—

Che Luofeng!

Fury overtook Chen Xing in an instant, and he urged his horse out of the ice fog.

Che Luofeng smiled strangely. The Demon God's blood had corrupted his whole body, turning his skin the ash-gray of a corpse. "Little Han dog. You finally came out."

"Che Luofeng!" Chen Xing shouted, bow in hand. "Why would you do this?! Xiang Shu has never treated you badly! Are you really so unable to let go of your hatred for the Akele?!"

Che Luofeng's laugh was sinister. He tilted his head and looked at Chen Xing carefully. "I could have let it go now that my good brother Zhou Zhen has come back to life. Blame it on that Akele consort for meddling in other people's business. She went looking for her eldest son, and instead she found Zhou Zhen hiding inside my tent..."

"Zhou Zhen?" Chen Xing's brow twisted.

"Remember our agreement?" Che Luofeng took out his longbow too. "One shot for you, and one for me. Come and play."

Chen Xing was flabbergasted. "Where is Zhou Zhen? What's your relationship with Shi Hai?"

"Shi Hai?" Che Luofeng thought for a moment, but he seemed to come up short. "Come! If you can get within twenty feet of me, I'll answer your question."

With that, he turned his horse and rushed into the blizzard.

Chen Xing was furious. "Don't underestimate me!" he yelled, and he urged his horse on with both legs to chase him.

Out of nowhere, the cavalry around Xiang Shu eased up. Heralded by several beats of the drum, a figure emerged from inside the ice fog.

Xiang Shu couldn't believe his eyes. "Zhou Zhen?!"

Dressed in wolf fur that exposed a big, round scar over his heart, Zhou Zhen approached him slowly. "Long time no see, Shulü Kong. The exorcist isn't by your side—you don't have the power of the Heart Lamp now. Come back with me. My lord is waiting for you."

Xiang Shu held up his heavy sword and kept his distance, looking straight at Zhou Zhen. "Were you resurrected too? You're already dead. Why haven't you made your peace and returned to the earth?"

Zhou Zhen smiled. It looked incomparably strange on a corpse's face. "It's more apt to say that I never really died. Originally, Shi Hai-daren wanted to give the former Great Chanyu, Shulü Wen, an immortal life. But you had to go and personally send him off, Shulü Kong."

"Shut up!" Xiang Shu cried, flying into a rage. "It's you! You make it so that not even the dead can rest in peace!"

Zhou Zhen raised his hand and spun his rattle drum. Rouran cavalry emerged from the ice fog once more.

Xiang Shu sneered as they encircled him. "The 'greatest warrior' of the Rouran. It was only the Rouran who granted you that title.

Do you really think that the Great Chanyu will fear you just because the exorcist isn't here?"

"The Great Chanyu's martial arts are unrivaled," Zhou Zhen said in a low voice. "Why should you be afraid? I just don't know your odds of success against my clan, who fear neither pain nor death and will fight until the last moment. Do you?"

Meanwhile, Chen Xing chased after Che Luofeng, but Che Luofeng kept leading him in circles in the fog. It was like he was mocking him. Chen Xing drew his bow and nocked an arrow more than once, but Che Luofeng was moving too fast for him to take aim.

"Idiot!" Che Luofeng laughed like a madman.

When they approached a forest, Chen Xing made up his mind. *At a critical moment like this, it's time to rely on Sui Xing!* He stopped looking for Che Luofeng. He drew his longbow, closed his eyes, and nocked an arrow—

—and Che Luofeng drove his horse directly into Chen Xing's. The impact sent Chen Xing flying. His fingers on the string loosened up, and the arrow shot into the sky.

Chen Xing landed hard on the ground. Horrified, he grabbed his bow and got up. In front of him, Che Luofeng drew his bow and aimed at Chen Xing's head.

"Enough fun." Che Luofeng smiled. "It's my turn now."

What could Chen Xing do now? He glanced up, hoping that a sudden gust of wind would blow the arrow back down to pierce Che Luofeng's skull, but there was nothing. The arrow was gone.

Inside the dense ice fog, Xiang Shu clutched his sword tightly and stared at Zhou Zhen, who smiled as he fiddled with the rattle drum. He gave it a gentle spin, and thousands of Rouran cavalrymen instantly tried to slam into Xiang Shu, pressing against him from all sides and dragging him off his horse.

But in the same moment, the arrow that had been knocked off its trajectory flew down from the sky toward Zhou Zhen. *Pow!* It struck him in the wrist. The rattle drum flew out of his hand and spun in the air, emitting a single beat.

Zhou Zhen was caught off guard. He didn't know what had just happened, only that his hand was suddenly empty. He whipped his head around, but Xiang Shu didn't waste a second: He raised his heavy sword and rushed forward, shouting, to try to snatch the magical artifact. Out of nowhere, a shadowy figure flew through the air to appear behind Zhou Zhen. The figure caught the rattle drum, and just as Zhou Zhen reached out, he was struck with a back scratcher in a blow so ruthless it fractured his finger.

It was Xiao Shan! Xiang Shu took a step forward, but the Rouran cavalry closed in on him. "Xiao Shan!" he shouted. "Take the magical artifact and run!"

Xiao Shan looked down at the rattle drum in his hand and ran. He was gone before Zhou Zhen could even turn around to catch him. Frantic, the Rouran cavalry besieged Xiang Shu, but Xiang Shu was done fighting. He used his sword to sweep away the warriors in front of him and then turned around to look for Chen Xing.

Chen Xing kept waiting, but the arrow didn't come back. Still on the ground, he shuffled backward, away from Che Luofeng, and Che Luofeng's arrow missed its mark by a tiny margin.

Thinking quickly, Chen Xing pointed behind Che Luofeng. "Eh?! Look who's here!"

It almost worked, but Che Luofeng caught himself just before he turned his head. He sneered. "Do you really think I'm so—"

Suddenly, behind him, a living corpse rushed out of the forest. With a mad roar, it slammed into Che Luofeng and clung to him!

"Youduo!" Chen Xing exclaimed.

That living corpse was none other than the late Akele prince. Youduo bit Che Luofeng on the shoulder. Che Luofeng shouted and struggled with all his might, throwing Youduo into the snow.

"I told you so! You were the one who refused to look!" Chen Xing leaped up and escaped, leaving the two men to fight in the snow. He ran a few steps, looked around, and shouted, "Xiang Shu! Xiang Shu, where are you?!"

There was no response from Xiang Shu, but Xiao Shan rushed out of the foggy battlefield with a rattle drum in his left hand and a back scratcher in his right. He looked at Chen Xing and demanded, "Claws! Claws!"

*Yes! We got it! Excellent!* Chen Xing didn't have time to ask Xiao Shan where he'd come from, never mind why the magical artifact was in his hands. "Quick!" he shouted. "Give it to me! Give it to me!"

"Claws!"

"The claws are at home!" Chen Xing pointed in the direction of the city. "I didn't bring them. I'll fetch them later when we return!"

Xiao Shan was displeased, but he understood the point.

"Just give me the magical artifact first!" Chen Xing said anxiously. Xiao Shan threw him the back scratcher. "Wrong! Give me that one! The one that went dum, dum, dum!"

Behind them, Che Luofeng broke free from Youduo's grip, pulled out his sword, and rushed toward Chen Xing. Xiao Shan threw the rattle drum at Chen Xing and moved to protect him, trying to stop Che Luofeng with his bare hands. The moment Chen Xing got has hands on the rattle drum, he sensed that he'd been right:

This magical artifact had been refined by resentment. He took a breath, focused himself, and shook it.

With a beat, a small change seemed to occur within the ice fog. The resentment spread along the wooden handle of the drum and then up to Chen Xing's arm. Heavy resentment rose all around him. Standing in the snow, Chen Xing protected his heart with the Heart Lamp, then activated the ancient magical artifact. He spun it again and again, and the resentment rippled out, creating concentric circles that covered the entire battlefield with Chen Xing at their center.

# 42

THE NOW-TANGIBLE resentment rose into the air and began to swirl like a tornado. Its bleak, intense gale engulfed Chen Xing as he did his best to control the rattle drum. A mighty struggle was taking place inside the tornado of resentment, and it resolved into the massive form of an ancient mythical beast: a zheng!

The zheng had the appearance of a scarlet panther with five tails and one horn. Its resentful spirit struggled ceaselessly within the tornado, and its roars, which echoed for hundreds of miles, were like the crash of stone on stone. The moment the zheng appeared, the living corpses stopped attacking the city. They turned away from the battlefield and focused on Chen Xing.

"Get it back!" shouted Zhou Zhen, desperate.

The Rouran cavalry remained unaffected by the rattle drum, but they turned away from the city and toward the battlefield. This significantly eased the pressure on Karakorum, which had almost been overrun. The tribes took the opportunity to hack their way out of the city and serve as reinforcements for their Great Chanyu, Xiang Shu.

*This resentment is too strong... This artifact's even harder to control than the Yin Yang Mirror.*

For all that Chen Xing had become familiar with all kinds of magic as a child, magical artifacts with this level of power were incredibly difficult to deal with. And the resentment wrapped around the rattle drum was relentlessly looking for a way to break into his heart; if it succeeded, it would swallow him whole and assimilate him.

*I can't hold on any longer!* The living corpses around him were gradually starting to lose their formations, so Chen Xing twisted the rattle drum once, with all his might. *Thock!* Suddenly, hundreds of thousands of living corpses changed direction, following the command of the rattle drum in Chen Xing's hand.

Xiang Shu urged his horse onward, swinging his sword as he rushed toward Che Luofeng.

"Shulü Kong?!" Che Luofeng asked breathlessly.

Brandishing his heavy sword in one hand, Xiang Shu put himself between Chen Xing and Che Luofeng. "Che Luofeng!" he bellowed. "What did you do?!"

"Xiang Shu... Xiang Shu..." Activating that magical artifact had dealt Chen Xing's heart meridian a great blow. He staggered, breathing heavily, one hand pressed to his chest. He was close to collapsing into the snow.

Che Luofeng let out a cold laugh. Standing hunched over slightly in front of him, he watched Xiang Shu's every move.

With Che Luofeng in front of him and Chen Xing behind him, Xiang Shu was torn for a moment—but this was not the time to fight with Che Luofeng. Chen Xing was teetering on the verge of collapse. Xiang Shu had to get him out of here, or else the two of them would be surrounded when the Rouran cavalry returned. Even if Xiang Shu had the skills of a god, he wouldn't be able to guarantee Chen Xing's safety in a situation like that.

"Can you hold on?" Xiang Shu asked, keeping his eyes fixed on Che Luofeng. He wasn't going to be able to carry Chen Xing and deal with Che Luofeng at the same time.

"I'm fine," Chen Xing said, though he was having trouble breathing and could barely keep hold of the rattle drum. "You should go... They'll come back soon. Leave me! Go, quick!"

The Rouran cavalry in the distance had turned and begun hacking their way back to the three of them. The encirclement was growing larger by the minute. Che Luofeng's face twisted with rage, but before he could attack, Xiang Shu made his decision. He left Che Luofeng to his own devices and said sharply, "Xiao Shan! We go!"

With that, he dragged Chen Xing up onto his horse, turned around, and broke through the encirclement. Xiao Shan grabbed a horse, clambered on, and chased after Xiang Shu.

Che Luofeng was left stunned. He stood there blankly, watching Xiang Shu leave.

Following the rattle drum's commands, the army of almost two hundred thousand living corpses changed their targets and advanced on the Rouran cavalry. Xiang Shu settled Chen Xing onto the horse before quickly changing direction. They followed the living corpses, and the Tiele, Xiongnu, and other Hu cavalry members tailed them in turn.

Zhou Zhen floundered as his own strategy came back to bite him in the ass. He'd been under the impression that since the Silence of All Magic, no humans could activate any magical artifacts. He hastily issued an order, but it was too late—his Rouran cavalry had already been crushed. The living corpses swarmed over them. The battlefield was in chaos.

"How can you activate the artifact my lord refined with His own blood?!" Zhou Zhen shouted.

"I am the Great Exorcist," Chen Xing replied coldly.

Xiang Shu's horse had galloped to the center of the Rouran army, and a single sweep of his heavy sword sent half a dozen cavalrymen flying. Chen Xing clung to Xiang Shu's waist, gasping desperately for breath. His heart was wracked with wave after wave of pain; the resentment he had used to force the rattle drum to activate was slowly eroding the power of the Heart Lamp.

"Give me the Heart Lamp's power!" Xiang Shu shouted.

Chen Xing tightened his arms around Xiang Shu's waist and pressed himself against his back. He closed his eyes and increased the Heart Lamp's strength.

Xiang Shu flourished his heavy sword, preparing for it to turn into a longbow again. The sword shone and changed shape...but this time, it became a six-foot-long pole. Xiang Shu was taken aback, but he wielded the pole as if it were a long halberd, swinging it left and right, back and forth. It moved so fast that all anyone else could see was a wheel of light spinning its way through the battlefield, felling all who got in its way.

Zhou Zhen looked horrified. His instincts screamed that this divine weapon was the very antithesis of his own existence. How could he fight something like that? He turned and beat a hasty retreat, but Xiang Shu, calling upon all his might, rapidly closed in on him.

With a single downward swing of the pole, the Heart Lamp's pure white light created a fiery blaze. The fire caught the back hem of Zhou Zhen's robe and set it alight—but, at the last second, just before the strike could solidly connect with Zhou Zhen and his horse, there came a sudden humming noise, and the light vanished.

Chen Xing fell heavily against Xiang Shu's back. His grip slackened, and a mouthful of blood soaked the back of Xiang Shu's leather armor. "Chen Xing?!" Xiang Shu called.

"Bastard!" Che Luofeng bellowed, coming back toward them. "Shulü Kong!"

In his heavy armor, he slammed viciously into their horse side-on. He'd thought that surely Xiang Shu would turn and fight him, but no—Xiang Shu, the person he cared about the most, didn't even look at him. The resentment in Che Luofeng's heart reached its peak. Heedless of life and death, he slammed into the horse and its two riders again, desperate to take Xiang Shu down with him.

Chen Xing had collapsed, and half of his body was hanging out of the saddle. The instant Che Luofeng collided with them, Xiang Shu reached out to grab Chen Xing, but he was a moment too late. The two of them were on the front lines of the chaos, and when reinforcements poured in, Xiang Shu and Chen Xing were both knocked off the horse.

The only thing on Zhou Zhen's mind was retaking the rattle drum. "Che Luofeng!" he shouted. "The artifact!"

The two armies collided like crashing waves. Chen Xing's consciousness faded, turning the world to darkness. *Am I dying? But it's too soon... It's not time yet.* But even as Chen Xing teetered on the brink of unconsciousness, his grip on the rattle drum did not loosen. He knew instinctively not to let go.

Just as his consciousness blurred, he saw something strange. It was as if he was seeing a world from another person's perspective. The room he was in was oddly distorted; a web of blood vessels seemed to crawl across its walls. In the short moment where his vision overlapped with this other person's, that other person found him. They peered straight into his heart, and somehow, their consciousnesses linked up.

"The host of the Heart Lamp?" a hoarse voice said. "What a surprise that you are able to arrive here through the medium of my blood. Ah well, I suppose it is to be expected. In all the Divine Land, you and I are the only ones who possess magical power."

"Wake up!" came a strange, teenage-sounding voice inside Chen Xing's consciousness. "It's not time to give up yet!"

Chen Xing's eyes shot open, and the image of the strange room shattered before him like glass. That second voice seemed to have pulled his consciousness back from where it had gone, thousands of miles away. His vision was fuzzy, and a cold wind was blowing snow onto his face. A hand, clad in an ice-cold iron glove, pinched his chin and tilted his head up slightly.

The moment Chen Xing's senses returned to him, he realized he was being held captive. Where was he?! His surroundings were shrouded in fog, but a gap in the clouds revealed part of a mountain ridge. He was on the ridge of the Yin Mountains, at the peak of Mount Huhebashe. Two black-armored generals stood in a small clearing, and Che Luofeng was there too, sitting disheveled on the ground and gasping for breath. Zhou Zhen stood to one side, his eyes fixed on the rattle drum where it lay on a boulder.

Wriggling his wrists, Chen Xing found that he was tied up by an icy iron chain. Their surroundings were cold enough to crystallize a drop of water into ice, and the iron chain was covered in a layer of frost. *Is this really necessary just to hold me?* he thought. *Did you need to tie me up with such a heavy chain? Even if I wasn't tied up, I wouldn't be able to get away, okay?*

When they saw that Chen Xing was awake, Che Luofeng and Zhou Zhen turned wary gazes on him. One of the black-armored generals moved to pick him up, but the other stopped him. Chen Xing recognized the armor. The person who had wanted to lift him up was probably Sima Yue, but he didn't know who the other general was. They wore almost identical armor, and they both had helmets that covered their whole faces, making them impossible to tell apart at a glance.

Sima Yue turned and walked toward Zhou Zhen. A hoarse voice came from inside the armor. "Now what?"

*This guy can talk?!* Chen Xing was shocked. He'd assumed that the generals were driven by pure instinct like the other living corpses; apparently he was wrong, and they were more advanced. The capacity for speech proved that they had their own wills. Perhaps Sima Lun, whom he had met back in Chang'an, had just been reluctant to speak.

In lieu of a response Zhou Zhen glanced at Che Luofeng, who shot Chen Xing a hate-filled look.

Sima Yue spoke in a voice like weapons scraping against each other. "I gave you command of the drought fiend army that Lord Shi Hai assembled here because you told me that you still had the sixty-thousand-strong Rouran cavalry. Now what do you have to show for yourself?"

The other black-armored general, who was standing next to Chen Xing, didn't say a word. Chen Xing shot him a quick glance. He looked a bit familiar, somehow, and Chen Xing had a niggling thought that he had seen that kind of armor somewhere before. *Nah, I've only seen three of these guys so far: Sima Lun, who's already been dealt with; Sima Yue; and the one on Longzhong Mountain...*

*Sima Wei!*

This was the Prince of Chu, Sima Wei! He was the first black-armored general that Chen Xing had seen. On the night of their first meeting, Chen Xing hadn't gotten a clear glimpse of his face. He was here, too?!

DINGHAI FUSHENG RECORDS

"We've stationed the invincible Rouran army in the Yin Mountains," said Zhou Zhen, having evidently lost a bit of his arrogance. "Shulü Kong is certain to come to save this boy. When he does, we will be lying in wait, and he shall leave himself exposed..."

"You're certainly fond of theorizing, for a man without the first idea of how to command a real army," Sima Yue sneered. "You imagined yourself one step ahead of your enemies, but in the end, you were caught off guard."

"How was I supposed to know this brat would be able to use the Zheng Drum?" Zhou Zhen moved toward Chen Xing, but the two black-armored generals stepped in front of Chen Xing to block his path.

Sima Yue replied, "Zhou Zhen, you already have an army of two hundred thousand drought fiends under your command. Can you and your companion capture Shulü Kong alive or not?"

"I have an idea," Che Luofeng said in a low voice. Peeking around the general's leg armor, Chen Xing could see his ferocious glare. "We can kill this boy and string his corpse up here. When Shulü Kong sees it he'll be frantic, and we can take advantage of th—"

"Fool!" Sima Yue interrupted harshly. "I see that none are more deserving of death here than you!"

Sima Yue drew his sword, but Zhou Zhen immediately stepped in front of Che Luofeng. "General!" he said darkly.

*Ooh, they're fighting amongst themselves...*

Chen Xing didn't know the exact details of the situation, but he could guess at a thing or two. These people had probably been sent by Shi Hai. He wasn't sure if the "lord" they referred to was Chiyou or Shi Hai, but it didn't matter either way. Perhaps over the years Shi Hai had resurrected two hundred thousand living corpses and then handed them over to Sima Yue.

Now, Zhou Zhen had taken over the command of the army. With the additional might of the sixty-thousand-strong Rouran cavalry, he'd intended to capture Longcheng in one fell swoop, but at the last second, Chen Xing got hold of the rattle drum and turned the tide of the battle. The drought fiend army had been exhausted, and the two black-armored generals were deeply dissatisfied with how things were progressing.

Chen Xing was filled with anticipation. *Keep fighting each other, go on! Keep it up! Don't stop!*

"Step aside," Sima Yue ordered menacingly.

"Drought fiend king," Zhou Zhen replied in a cold tone, "this is Lord Shi Hai's order."

"Shi Hai did not order you to involve yourself with the Rouran again. You had your life; in your afterlife, you belong to our lord. You must leave your past behind. If you cannot let go of your infatuation with that mortal behind you, then I would be pleased to deal with him for you."

Zhou Zhen exhaled heavily. Sima Yue put down his sword, summoned a flock of crows, and jumped off the cliff, disappearing from view.

Zhou Zhen glanced at Che Luofeng, whose face reflected a turbulent mix of emotions. "I'll set up an ambush for Shulü Kong," he said. "Do you want him captured alive?"

Che Luofeng was silent for a long time. "If you can't capture him alive," he said finally, "then kill him and bring his body back to me. It's all the same in the end."

"Then all will be as it should have been a long time ago. It wouldn't have come this far if I hadn't needed to ask for mercy on your behalf."

"I was wrong!" Che Luofeng said. "I was wrong, okay?!"

Zhou Zhen turned around and jumped off the cliff.

With only Sima Wei, Chen Xing, and Che Luofeng left at the summit, it grew quiet again. Che Luofeng sat alone, minding his own business, his head bowed over a block of pine resin that he was rubbing on the string of his bow.

Chen Xing knew that as he sat there, Xiang Shu must be trying his best to find a method to save him. It was possible that he already had an army surrounding the mountain. But while the cavalry of the Sixteen Hu were experts in fighting on the plains and would never hesitate to launch an assault there, they had far less experience in the mountains.

This mountain summit was no more than a hundred feet across. It was covered in a light dusting of snow, and there were several stone pillars jutting out of the ground. One tribe or another had once used this place as an altar. Chen Xing shifted the iron chain, making it clink a little as he thought about how he could escape.

Standing off to the side, Sima Wei turned his head slightly and looked at Chen Xing.

Why wasn't this guy talking, Chen Xing wondered? If he spoke, then maybe, by listening to him, Chen Xing could glean some information about Shi Hai's group. What about that room he saw when he was unconscious? And who was that teenager whose voice he had heard in the dream?

Whenever Chen Xing moved, he dragged the chain along with him, making small clanking sounds. Che Luofeng stopped what he was doing and looked at him, and Chen Xing stopped moving.

"Do you know how the Rouran torture our prisoners of war?" Che Luofeng asked icily.

"I don't. But in the past few days, I've seen how the Rouran torture their own people."

Che Luofeng's expression changed. "What do you know, Han dog?" he spat. Chen Xing had hit him where it hurt. "You're all bastards."

Suddenly the silent Sima Wei turned and drew his sword. Che Luofeng had actually forgotten that this corpse had once been a member of the Jin royal family, but now he got up and backed away. Sima Wei attacked, and Che Luofeng tried to parry, but the strike was lightning fast—Sima Wei's sword was already at his neck!

Chen Xing watched avidly, forgotten in all this bustle, and internally applauded that beautiful maneuver. He didn't know any martial arts himself, but he'd spent enough time hanging around Xiang Shu to see the general shape of what had happened. In a single move, Sima Wei had stopped his opponent from ducking away and simultaneously blocked his exit route. That was no easy feat!

Che Luofeng wisely kept his mouth shut, and Sima Wei withdrew his sword as if nothing had happened. Glancing at Sima Wei, Chen Xing found that he was no longer afraid of Che Luofeng.

Chen Xing observed Che Luofeng a little more. His complexion wasn't quite the right color anymore, he noticed. Most of the Rouran cavalry who had fought for him had the same green, pallid look to them. It was a little different from the ashen blue complexion of Zhou Zhen, who had been dead for a long time.

Che Luofeng's body was slowly changing. Chen Xing wasn't sure whether he still felt pain or not, though.

"Have all of you drunk the Demon God's blood?" Chen Xing asked. He thought for a moment, then added, "And how did Zhou Zhen trick you into doing it? Did he say that if you drank his potion, you would be able to lead your people to eternal life?"

"Eternal life?" Che Luofeng smiled in disdain. "I simply wanted to avenge Zhou Zhen. Now that he's alive again, what do you think the most important thing to me is? You, Han, are the one who's close to death."

Zhou Zhen was tall, and his mixed Han and Rouran parentage had given him striking facial features. From his postmortem appearance, Chen Xing surmised that he had probably been a beautiful and stately man when he was alive, but in a different way from Xiang Shu. He also knew that, in life, Zhou Zhen had been Che Luofeng's lover, even though it had always seemed clear to Chen Xing that Che Luofeng liked Xiang Shu.

Had Che Luofeng first fallen in love with Zhou Zhen and then shifted those affections to Xiang Shu after Zhou Zhen died? Or had he loved Xiang Shu first, been rejected, and then gotten together with Zhou Zhen? Or maybe Che Luofeng had always liked both of them...

"I'm curious about something," Chen Xing said. "Che Luofeng, do you still like Xiang Shu? Oh, and on that subject: Now that Zhou Zhen is dead, can he still get hard?"

Che Luofeng shouted and stood up like he was about to kick Chen Xing's ass. Sima Wei turned around again to stop him, but Che Luofeng was still glaring daggers at Chen Xing. He'd just been trying for some idle chatter—had the potion made Che Luofeng more irritable?

"Fine, fine," said Chen Xing, "let's not talk about it."

To Chen Xing, resurrecting the dead had always felt wrong, like it was going against the natural order of things. If the drought fiends could be called a "species," then they would be the most peculiar species to exist. Of course, they were probably unable to reproduce on their own, unlike other species of yao.

"How long has it been since Zhou Zhen came back to life? When did you meet him?" Chen Xing asked. When Che Luofeng didn't answer, he said earnestly, "Why don't we play a game? I'll answer one of your questions, and in exchange, how about you lick my chain?"

Chen Xing just wanted to play a trick on him. The chain was so cold that his tongue would get stuck to it, which would be a great way to deal with this opponent of his. But Che Luofeng, of course, wasn't about to be fooled. "Are you crazy? You think I'm three years old?"

"Then answer one of my questions, and I'll answer one of yours."

After a moment, Che Luofeng said, "You're an exorcist, right? You're here for the drought fiends. And here I thought you really were a doctor. You know you're going to die soon? When they bring you back to Huanmo Palace, you'll be used as a sacrifice. Why does someone who's about to die have so many questions?"

Finally, Che Luofeng had given Chen Xing his first piece of crucial information: *Huanmo Palace*.

"Even if I'd learned this morning that I was slated to die tonight," Chen Xing said, "I would die without regrets. No matter whether I'm about to die or not, I want to satisfy my curiosity, okay?"

Che Luofeng put down his bow and side-eyed Chen Xing, then looked at him properly, raising an eyebrow. When Chen Xing first saw Che Luofeng, he'd thought Che Luofeng was handsome with his thick eyebrows and big eyes; it was a pity about the evil in his features.

"Then ask, little bastard," said Che Luofeng.

"Where did you get your weapon?" Chen Xing was worried that Shi Hai might have given them another artifact like that rattle drum. He didn't know whether Xiang Shu would be able to fend them off when he came to save him, if they had another one.

"It was the token Shulü Kong gave me when he made me his anda," Che Luofeng replied coldly. "I will use this bow to kill you in front of him later. Now, it's your turn: Tell me, what on earth is your relationship with Shulü Kong?"

# 43

"WHAT'S OUR relationship?"

This question stumped Chen Xing. He couldn't quite explain it. Exorcist and protector? But Xiang Shu had never agreed to that. Friends? The way they interacted didn't quite feel like friendship either. Chen Xing had the sense that Xiang Shu cared about him, but the elusive, distant nature of their relationship made things complicated.

"We're not close," Chen Xing said at last. For one thing, he didn't want Che Luofeng to think that his relationship with Xiang Shu was deep enough for him to be useful as leverage, and for another, even now, he had no idea what was going on in Xiang Shu's head. "That's a question you should ask him."

They'd had this elusive relationship since the day they met. Sometimes it felt like they were strangers, and other times it felt like things between them were "maybe okay."

Che Luofeng scoffed—he obviously didn't believe him.

Chen Xing shrugged. "No, you really misunderstand. Xiang Shu and I just teamed up to investigate your people."

He recounted how he and Xiang Shu had come to know each other, though he carefully omitted certain key details. He obviously wasn't foolish enough to tell Che Luofeng about his plans to deal with Shi Hai and his pack of undead princes, generals, and soldiers.

Che Luofeng finally relaxed a bit as he listened to the story, though there was still a tinge of doubt on his face. But when he learned that Xiang Shu's father, Shulü Wen, had taken the same drug as Che Luofeng himself and become something neither human nor ghost in his final moments, Chen Xing saw a flash of fear in his eyes.

Chen Xing studied his expression. He was now able to infer that there were three methods for creating living corpses. The first was to target defenseless civilians who had died in the chaos of war; this required using resentment to power magical artifacts, like the rattle drum, to turn the dead into drought fiends. The second method was to force living people to consume a potion infused with the blood of the Demon God, which would gradually transform them into living corpses while they were still alive.

The third method was the one he had witnessed at Longzhong Mountain. The mysterious masked figure, a member of Shi Hai's group, had collected resentment and infused it into the corpses of the Jin Dynasty's Eight Princes, bringing them back to life. These black-armored princes seemed to be the strongest drought fiends Chen Xing had encountered so far.

"Really, you don't need to worry about me," Chen Xing said honestly. "I know you like Shulü Kong. He's not going to end up with me."

"Rubbish," Che Luofeng replied coldly. "He's the Great Chanyu. He'll marry and have children. You think he's going to marry a man?"

"That's not what I meant. We're not in the kind of relationship you think we are, but even if we were, I wouldn't be with him. In two or three years at most, I'll have to leave."

Che Luofeng looked at Chen Xing skeptically.

"Look, I'm dying. Why would I need to lie to you? And anyway, Shulü Kong doesn't have the slightest interest in me—"

"He has plenty of interest in you," Che Luofeng said, his voice like ice. "You're just oblivious. Why else would he ride north alone in that kind of weather just to bring you back?"

"He's the Great Chanyu," Chen Xing countered. "If any of your people went missing, he would—"

"Bullshit! I've been his anda for fourteen years. Heading north alone in the eleventh lunar month? You were just begging to die! The tribal leaders urged him over and over to stay, saying that old Akele bastard was with you, but the moment Shulü Kong found out you'd left alone, he still... Forget it!"

Chen Xing blinked. He'd never thought deeply about that particular sequence of events, and it was only now that he recalled the Hu north of the Great Wall had a unique set of survival rules. One of the strictest was the ban on hunting alone in the harsh winter. Traveling north alone in the dead of winter was even more frowned upon, since it was tantamount to suicide. To prevent disasters, the tribes of the north strictly forbade solo excursions. They also forbade rescue missions for those who broke this rule; attempting to save one life could risk many others. Anyone who violated the rule and journeyed north was left to die so that others wouldn't foolishly follow suit.

And on that day, Xiang Shu himself had broken this rule.

"It's my turn," Chen Xing said. "How did Zhou Zhen come back to life? What did he say to you? What are their plans outside the Great Wall?"

"Him? The moment he died, he was granted a new life by Shi Hai-daren."

After the bloody battle between the Rouran and the Akele three years ago, Shulü Kong mediated a peace treaty, and both tribes buried their dead and swore not to seek revenge. The price was that Youduo and Zhou Zhen were both deemed guilty, so they were denied a sky burial and had to be buried in the ground.

Months later, when Che Luofeng went to pay respects at Zhou Zhen's grave, he found signs that the tomb had been disturbed. He dug into the ground and discovered Zhou Zhen's corpse had disappeared. Then, just this winter, while he was hunting near Carosha, he thought he saw Zhou Zhen. He ran after him, only to be ambushed by a black shadow that leaped from the roadside and tore his belly open with its claws.

*Zhou Zhen appeared near Carosha? What was he doing there?* Chen Xing suddenly felt a deep sense of unease, as if something had moved in the fog beyond his sight. There was some critical piece of the puzzle here that had yet to be uncovered.

There had to have been something important he'd overlooked during his journey north with the Akele king.

Che Luofeng scrutinized Chen Xing. Noticing the deepening confusion in Chen Xing's eyes, he said casually, "I'm just following orders."

"Why are you doing this?" Chen Xing pressed. "Does your enmity with the Akele run that deep? Even if it does and you want to seek revenge, fine, but why target all of Chi Le Chuan? Including your own people?"

"Oh, please! You son of a bitch! What do you know about the feud between us?!" Che Luofeng roared, his voice thick with hatred. He glared at Chen Xing, breathing heavily, and only continued after taking a deep, steadying breath. "The Rouran are the true rulers of Chi Le Chuan! Shulü Kong is a coward! Fu Jian has already traversed the pass, and the Murong clan has also been subjugated! If we don't strike now and capture Guanzhong, when will we?!

"You Han people have a saying: 'to view the sky from the bottom of a well.'[11] Shulü Kong may be a great warrior, but he spends his days acting as a mediator for petty disputes. If some tribes are fighting over water sources, he'll go resolve it for them. If someone doesn't have enough to eat, he'll rush to their aid. He's become nothing more than a spineless, weak-willed fool!"

"Is that so?" Chen Xing murmured. "So you want to be the Great Chanyu? Lead the Ancient Chi Le Chuan Covenant south and share the spoils with Fu Jian? But have you ever sought your tribe's opinion?"

"When Fu Jian became emperor of the Central Plains," Che Luofeng shot back, "did he ask the Di people what they thought?"

Chen Xing laughed. He had always known when to concede a point. "That's true. Compared to talents of imperial caliber like you, who dream of eternal glory and an everlasting empire, my concerns really are short-sighted."

Che Luofeng heard the sarcasm in Chen Xing's voice, of course, but a Rouran was no match for someone like Chen Xing in eloquence. During the Jin dynasty, intellectual debates were highly esteemed, and Chen Xing had grown up learning classics like the White Horse Dialogue.[12] If he really put his mind to arguing with Che Luofeng, he could likely talk the man into spitting blood. But his goal wasn't to quarrel at the moment, so he chose not to get sidetracked.

"Now, here's the real issue," Chen Xing continued thoughtfully. "I have no objection to a Hu becoming emperor, but...an undead emperor? Now that's something new."

By now, Chen Xing had gradually pieced together Shi Hai's plan.

---

11  An idiom meaning "to be ignorant and narrow-minded." The sky is vast, and if you stare at it from the bottom of the well, you can only see a portion of it.

12  An ancient Chinese philosophical debate, often attributed to the philosopher Gongsun Long, that centers around the proposition "a white horse is not a horse."

It seemed to revolve around resurrecting Chiyou and creating a new world. But while these living dead might not fear death anymore, they would still eventually rot. What was the point of turning the Divine Land into a realm of corpses? In the end, wouldn't it just be an empire of the dead?

Che Luofeng opened his mouth to retort, but his breath caught in his throat and he couldn't get the words out. His complexion changed color.

"Hey!" Chen Xing called out. "Don't get angry. Let's talk this through. Che Luofeng?"

But Che Luofeng was collapsing in front of him. Xiang Shu hadn't even arrived yet! Sima Wei didn't even spare him a glance as he sunk to the ground slowly, as if this was an everyday occurrence.

"Che Luofeng!" Shocked, Chen Xing watched Che Luofeng transform from a living person into a living corpse before his very eyes. He immediately got up and moved to check Che Luofeng's condition, dragging his chains along with him until Sima Wei removed them from where they were fastened and held them in his hands. He allowed Chen Xing to approach, making no move to stop him.

Throughout their conversation, Chen Xing had noticed Che Luofeng gasping for breath. Now, when Chen Xing checked his breathing, it was weakening even further. Che Luofeng's eyes were also becoming cloudy, and Chen Xing leaned down to listen to his heartbeat and feel his pulse. Then he picked up an arrowhead, shallowly pierced Che Luofeng's skin with it, and sniffed.

Corpse venom. It was similar to the poison that came from being bitten by a living corpse, but more aggressive. Within a matter of days, it had ravaged his entire body. The scent was identical to the way Lu Ying had smelled. It was clear that the poison spread through bites and scratches from living corpses transformed by the Demon God's blood, though the speed at which it acted varied.

Sima Wei tugged on the chain, signaling Chen Xing to keep his distance.

In a trembling voice, Che Luofeng broke the silence. "I...I'm cold...so cold. Zhou Zhen...are you there? Zhou Zhen?"

From the base of the mountain came the sound of distant horns and battle cries. Chen Xing's senses sharpened—he could feel that Xiang Shu was leading a rescue mission up the mountain. Zhou Zhen must have been preoccupied fighting Xiang Shu while the Donghai Prince, Sima Yue, skirmished in the fray.

"Che Luofeng?" Looking at him, Chen Xing felt a flicker of sympathy for his enemy.

"So cold." Che Luofeng, now teetering on the edge of death, had lost his grip on reality. He was letting slip his innermost thoughts, struggling to form words. "Shulü Kong... Save me... I...I don't want to die... I...regret..."

Chen Xing remained silent. He held Che Luofeng's hand, feeling a storm of emotions.

"That cup of wine," Che Luofeng mumbled. "I didn't want to drink it at first. I was scared. Shulü Kong...Shulü Kong...I'm sorry..."

Che Luofeng's eyes grew duller, and tears rolled down his cheeks. Suddenly, Chen Xing understood. When Zhou Zhen had shown himself to Che Luofeng, he'd coerced him into drinking wine mixed with the Demon God's blood. Caught up in his pride and anger, Che Luofeng drank it, and he likely regretted it that very moment— but by then, it was too late. He sank deeper and deeper into his predicament, and now it had come to this.

For a moment, Chen Xing wasn't sure whether he should save him. Che Luofeng had committed a heinous crime in slaughtering the entire Akele clan, but without Zhou Zhen's temptation, he probably never would have taken things so far.

In the end, Chen Xing steeled his resolve. He had to give it a try. Letting Che Luofeng die like this would be too easy; he was Xiang Shu's anda, so ultimately it was up to Xiang Shu to decide his fate. If nothing else, he needed to be brought back to Chi Le Chuan to repent before his execution.

"Hold on to your true self, if you still have one," Chen Xing murmured. Then he ignited the Heart Lamp and held it against Che Luofeng's chest.

Sima Wei whipped his head around to look at Chen Xing and Che Luofeng. With his eyes shut tight and his body enveloped in light, Chen Xing pressed down on Che Luofeng's chest, just as he had done to awaken Xiang Shu that day at Carosha. Resentment already coiled around Che Luofeng's whole body, but the power of the Heart Lamp in Chen Xing's hand shot into Che Luofeng's heart.

Che Luofeng cried out in agony. Inside him, the Heart Lamp's power clashed fiercely with the Demon God's blood, fighting for control over his life and death. The Demon God's blood was dragging him toward the dark abyss of death, while the Heart Lamp acted like a sharp blade, protecting his three immortal souls and seven mortal forms. Che Luofeng's life was caught in a relentless tug-of-war between these two forces, and his soul was nearly torn to shreds.

"Let me die!" he screamed.

Chen Xing released his hand, withdrawing the power of the Heart Lamp. The moment he did, Sima Wei strode toward Chen Xing, grabbed him by the collar, and pulled him away from Che Luofeng, who writhed in place for a moment, then lay still on his side.

*Is he dead?* Chen Xing thought. *Will there be any changes later?* He was gazing intently at Che Luofeng when he suddenly heard Sima Wei speak.

"You have interfered with his transformation into a drought fiend." Sima Wei's voice was not as hoarse and unpleasant as Sima Yue's; it carried a hint of the warmth of the living. "You sealed the last remnants of his humanity within his heart."

Chen Xing looked up at Sima Wei in shock, but Sima Wei secured the iron chain to the stone pillar, preventing him from moving. "Sima Wei," Chen Xing asked, "do you remember what happened when you were still alive?"

Sima Wei made a simple gesture, as if he wanted to remove his helmet, but he abruptly halted when Che Luofeng began to convulse. Che Luofeng slowly rose from the ground, his cloudy, lifeless eyes fixating on Chen Xing.

"Shulü Kong...Shulü Kong..." Che Luofeng murmured.

The warriors' shouting and the whinnies of horses grew ever closer on the mountain below. Suddenly, Chen Xing felt a metal claw gently scratch at his back. He nearly turned around in shock, but he caught himself and just kept backing away. Xiao Shan, wearing his dragon claws, had silently scaled the peak of the mountain.

Chen Xing backed up against the pillar and watched Che Luofeng intently. Che Luofeng scrutinized Chen Xing, murmuring, "I will...kill you. Shulü Kong is mine... No one...can take him away from me..."

His mind seemed to have unraveled, and Chen Xing wasn't sure whether his use of the Heart Lamp was to blame. Regardless, Che Luofeng's demeanor and the dagger he clutched made it clear that he was obsessed, ready to pounce and kill Chen Xing at any moment.

Sima Wei drew his sword and placed it protectively in front of Chen Xing. Below, the sounds of battle intensified, as if another army had arrived at the gorge. Chen Xing couldn't tell if they were friend or foe. He retreated to the edge of the platform...then snapped his fingers.

In an instant, Xiao Shan transformed into a shadow and swept past from behind him. Sima Wei whirled around, realizing that an enemy had approached, and he abandoned Che Luofeng and drew his sword.

Xiao Shan's dragon claw struck the chain, but he couldn't sever it. *Damn it*, Chen Xing thought, *it's not an ordinary chain!* Xiao Shan swung his claws fiercely again, but the chain didn't budge at all!

Sima Wei was already in front of them with his sword at the ready. Chen Xing shoved Xiao Shan aside. "Run!" he shouted. "You can't cut it!"

"I go save him!" Xiao Shan shouted, leaping onto the stone pillar. "I go save him! Wait!"

Chen Xing quickly understood what Xiao Shan meant: *I'll save you, don't worry.* Sima Wei promptly pulled back the sword that had been right in Chen Xing's face and leaped onto the stone pillar. Like a wolf, Xiao Shan sprang away and crouched behind another pillar, baring his teeth and growling at Sima Wei.

"Don't worry about me for now!" Chen Xing shouted. "Get Xiang Shu up here! Hurry!"

Sima Wei swept toward Xiao Shan, transforming into a black whirlwind. Xiao Shan had to do a backflip off the stone pillar and leap off the platform to avoid him, and Sima Wei pursued him relentlessly.

With Sima Wei drawn away, no longer protecting Chen Xing, there was no one to restrain Che Luofeng. He slowly advanced on

Chen Xing, grasping his dagger, his eyes filled with confusion. "Kill you, kill you."

Where was Xiang Shu?!

"Xiang Shu! Xiang Shu! I'm here!" Chen Xing shouted in desperation, slamming the iron chain against the stone pillar. In his panic, he even activated the Heart Lamp.

Xiang Shu wasn't far away, but he was advancing very slowly. Chen Xing could sense him! He was in the canyon, less than a hundred steps away. But Che Luofeng was closing in.

"Shulü Kong!" Chen Xing yelled. "If you don't get over here now, your anda's gonna kill me!"

A furious roar echoed from within the canyon: "Shut up!"

Hearing Xiang Shu's voice reverberating through the mountains sent Che Luofeng into a frenzy. "I'll kill you now!" he roared, and lunged at Chen Xing.

Chen Xing raised the iron chain to block the attack, deflecting the dagger with a *clang*. He retreated again, only to find himself backed up to the edge of the cliff. Che Luofeng crashed into him, and he tumbled off the edge, screaming.

"AAAAAHHHHHHHHHHHH!!!!!!!!"

Xiang Shu, who had just fought his way into the heart of the canyon, looked up to see Chen Xing's body plummeting from a peak more than two hundred feet high. The sight left him reeling as if he had been struck a heavy blow, but Chen Xing's fall lasted only an instant before he halted in midair.

"My hands hurt!" Chen Xing shouted, suspended by the iron chain and swinging wildly against the cliff face. "Aaahhh!"

"Hold on!" Xiang Shu yelled with all he had. "I'm coming!"

Chen Xing turned his head to shout for help, but before he could open his mouth, he froze. Down below, Zhou Zhen was commanding the vast Rouran army, encircling and charging through the canyon. Sima Yue stood on a rocky outcrop, watching the battle with a dark, ominous artifact in his hand. The canyon was littered with corpses, and the snow was soaked with black blood.

And in the midst of all of this was Xiang Shu.

Xiang Shu alone.

Chen Xing boggled.

Clad in armor and wielding his heavy sword, Xiang Shu charged forward on foot, scattering enemies wherever he went. He was surrounded by tens of thousands of warriors, but not one of them could get close to him.

Chen Xing changed his tune at record speed. "Xiang Shu, have you gone mad?" he muttered. "Get out of here, Xiang Shu! Get out of here! Are you crazy?! Why are you the only one here?!"

Xiang Shu removed his helmet and threw it to the ground, looking up at Chen Xing where he was swinging on the cliff above. His head and face were covered in blood. "Watch out above!" he shouted.

Che Luofeng was leaning over the cliff's peak, aiming a bow down at Chen Xing. He began to shoot, and the projectiles grazed Chen Xing's face, forcing him to swing around to dodge. Xiao Shan, who had shaken off Sima Wei, leaped to the cliff and swiped at Che Luofeng with his claws. He raked Che Luofeng across the chest, and Che Luofeng stumbled backward.

With a loud cry, Xiao Shan dug his iron claws into the base of the stone pillar and started to pry it up. Chen Xing grasped the iron chain to climb up, and he put something together as he did so: Xiang Shu had made the reckless decision to come to rescue him with only Xiao Shan's assistance.

What about the people of Chi Le Chuan? Where had they all gone? Had something happened to them again?!

"Xiang Shu!" Chen Xing shouted as he climbed, looking down to the canyon below. "Don't worry! I can take care of myself! If you can't handle it, just run! Don't be stubborn!"

THIS BATTLE could easily be called the pinnacle of Xiang Shu's military career. One man versus sixty thousand people—he could be compared to the peerless Martial God Zhuge Liang who had, nearly two hundred years ago, charged alone seven times through the enemy's ranks in the ancient battlefield of Dangyang.

No matter how many he killed, though, the Rouran cavalry just kept coming, and Xiang Shu's strength was flagging.

But when he heard Chen Xing's voice saying, "You can't handle it, just run!" he felt as if a mouthful of blood was surging up inside him. Contrary to Chen Xing's intention, his words stirred the blood in Xiang Shu's body. Fearless of death, he fought with renewed vigor toward the bottom of the cliff!

Chen Xing tried to climb up using his hands and feet. Above him, he saw Xiao Shan still working to pry up the stone pillar, jamming the claws beneath it and jumping on them with all his strength. But then Che Luofeng picked up his blade and aimed it straight at Chen Xing, who was still climbing! Chen Xing dared not cry out for fear of distracting Xiang Shu, so he gritted his teeth hard and swung against the cliff.

Che Luofeng was fuming. "Han dog, your death—"

The stone pillar on the platform chose that moment to fall down and smash into Che Luofeng's waist. Before Chen Xing could process exactly what had happened, he saw Che Luofeng flying toward him with open arms, and the stone pillar close behind him. Che Luofeng's face looked ferocious as he fell past Chen Xing.

Chen Xing took a second to stare in astonishment before looking up and shouting, "Xiao—"

Before he could finish speaking, that multi-ton stone pillar dragged the iron chain down with it, with Chen Xing still attached. *Swoosh!* Chen Xing was flying straight to the bottom of the cliff! The pull was so sudden he felt it distort his face.

"AAAAAAAAAAHHHHHHHHHHHHHHHHHHH!!!!!!!!!!!!!"

Xiang Shu's right hand was trembling from exhaustion, so he switched the sword to his left. Just as he was about to urge his horse up the mountain, he saw a stone pillar rolling down the cliff behind the Rouran army. The ground itself trembled as the pillar fell, dragging Chen Xing down with it!

"BEWARE OF FALLING STONES!" Chen Xing shouted as he was pulled along by the chain like a kite drifting in the wind.

Zhou Zhen, still commanding the army, turned his head abruptly and saw a massive boulder rolling down the cliffside to crush the nearly ten thousand members of the Rouran cavalry. This was a dreadful turn of events! He quickly dodged to avoid the colossal pillar falling from the top of the mountain. Xiao Shan was hot on the pillar's heels, and Sima Wei, in his black armor, was chasing after him. In a desperate move, Sima Wei threw his black shield; it flew, spinning, and landed in perfect alignment beneath Chen Xing's feet.

"AAAAAAHHHHH!" Chen Xing's tongue almost flew out in the wind. With the pillar still dragging him along, he stepped onto the shield and began to ski down the cliff face. He slid to the left and dodged to the right, all with shackles around his hands and feet. The pillar crushed everything in its path. The Rouran cavalry had no time to dodge; like a rolling pin, the pillar flattened riders and horses alike into meat pancakes.

Xiang Shu was speechless. Chen Xing had fallen, but luck had given him a way to stabilize himself. Dizzy, he kept changing directions too fast for Xiao Shan to jump on him, no matter how he tried.

Zhou Zhen was so busy getting out of the way that he forgot for a moment that Xiang Shu was still there. He rushed into the canyon, and Xiang Shu leaped back onto his horse and chased after him. When Zhou Zhen changed his horse's direction, he came face-to-face with Xiang Shu.

"Heart Lamp!" roared Xiang Shu.

Getting dragged along like this had left Chen Xing dazed and his vision full of stars, but when he heard Xiang Shu's voice, he automatically activated the Heart Lamp. Its brilliant light flashed in the dark canyon. Xiang Shu lifted his heavy sword and pointed toward the horizon, and white light burst out of it to sweep across their surroundings. The sword's blade shone brightly, each character of the Nine-Syllable Incantation appearing on it in succession.

Zhou Zhen's eyes went wide. The glare of Xiang Shu's sword was blinding, and he had to raise his hand to block out the light.

"Go back to wherever you came from," Xiang Shu's voice said in his ear—and in the next instant, the sword split him in two. With an earsplitting scream, Zhou Zhen burst into glimmering dust that dispersed in all directions.

Meanwhile, the stone pillar rolled into the forest, Chen Xing in tow, and crashed into a giant boulder, where it shattered into a dozen pieces. Chen Xing was sliding on snow and dodging branches the whole way. He almost fell to the side, but he managed to step on the shield again and avoid danger—in the end, astonishingly, he came to a stop without having incurred the slightest injury. He stepped on one end of the shield and caught it in his hands, which were still bound to the iron chain. The pillar was broken, but he was still tied to a sixty- or seventy-pound fragment of it; his whole face turned pale, and he gasped for breath.

When Xiang Shu caught up with Chen Xing, he snatched up Chen Xing's hands. Drenched with black blood from head to toe, he stared at Chen Xing. "You...you..."

Chen Xing stared back at him, not knowing what to say. "Me... me what?"

Xiang Shu grabbed Chen Xing's wrist in a grip that was actually a little painful, refusing to let go. Looking around, he saw that most of the Rouran cavalry had been taken care of in the chaos thanks to Chen Xing's Sui Xing. The ones who'd survived were regrouping in a panicked rush. "Now's not the time to talk," Xiang Shu said quickly. "Let's go!"

"Xiao Shan..."

"He can protect himself!"

It was true, Chen Xing thought, that Xiao Shan was moving at breakneck speed. Sima Wei couldn't catch him, so Xiao Shan should have been able to keep himself alive without too much trouble. The most important thing now was to keep Chen Xing from falling back into the enemy's hands as a hostage, because that would put Xiao Shan and Xiang Shu at a far greater disadvantage.

Chen Xing ran with Xiang Shu until he was out of breath. As they pressed on into the depths of the woods, they came across a cave. Chen Xing was about to say, "Ah! Nice!" but Xiang Shu pushed his head down and motioned for him not to speak. Together, they went inside.

The cave was pitch-black and covered with frost. Chen Xing illuminated a small area with the Heart Lamp.

"Why was it just the two of you?" he asked.

"I didn't ask Xiao Shan to come!" Xiang Shu said. "He followed me! Am I alone not enough to save you?"

Xiang Shu was furious with Xiao Shan. He had been ready to rescue Chen Xing, but since Xiao Shan kept following him around, he'd had to change his plans. He'd challenged the enemy head-on to distract them while Xiao Shan silently climbed up the peak to rescue Chen Xing. The end result was Xiao Shan getting up to the summit, rampaging there, and making a huge mess.

"How about Karakorum?"

"It's guarded." Xiang Shu walked ahead, carrying the boulder fragment in one hand and pulling the chain along. He remained vigilant, looking around and watching for an ambush.

Chen Xing finally calmed down. "You're taking too much risk," he said, frowning. "You came here alone?"

"I don't want my people to risk their lives just because I wanted to save you. You have a problem with that?"

Hearing it put that way, Chen Xing felt a little guilty. For some reason, he felt oddly dejected when he looked at Xiang Shu. *If I hadn't helped defend the city for you people, would I have been caught in the first place?* But this was merely a passing thought.

Xiang Shu's messy hair and armor, which was covered in black blood, made him look like a ghost who had crawled straight out of the underworld. It made Chen Xing a little uncomfortable. He wanted to say, *Why did you come, then?* but he sensed something else in Xiang Shu's words—the impression of a plucked string that emitted a barely audible vibrato. He wanted to listen attentively, but the guqin sound was long gone. What remained was just the echo, the feeling of tasting an illusion of reciprocated love.

They were both silent for a moment.

"Are you feeling better?" Xiang Shu asked stiffly.

"What?" Chen Xing was confused. "I've felt fine this whole time."

"Bullshit!" Xiang Shu turned around, his voice rising. "You were vomiting blood!"

Chen Xing realized then that Xiang Shu was talking about what had happened before—when he'd fainted and suffered severe injuries because he had exhausted his heart's power for the Heart Lamp. "It's nothing," he amended hurriedly. "It was just that I overused the Heart Lamp's power, which made me unable to breathe for a while. Let's just go, okay?! Or are you going to hit me now?"

Xiang Shu carried the boulder, dragging the chain along. They followed the wind in the cave, and in less than a quarter of an hour, they saw light. To their surprise, they found themselves in a spacious ravine in the heart of the Yin Mountains. There were weapons and armor scattered everywhere.

"Where are we?" Chen Xing murmured.

"The sinners' pit." Xiang Shu looked around. The ravine, which was in the shape of a half-moon, was surrounded by several peaks, and there was a dense, snow-covered forest in the distance. "Convicted criminals from the Chi Le Covenant are denied sky burials and buried instead. This is their burial ground."

Chen Xing looked at the sky, but it was so overcast that he couldn't even tell east from south or west from north. How were they going to get out of the mountains?

Suddenly, to his side, he heard the sound of a stone falling to the ground. He looked over and saw Xiang Shu supporting himself with his sword and gasping a little for breath. It was clear that the battle had taken a toll on him, and he was struggling to stay on his feet.

Chen Xing hurriedly made Xiang Shu sit down and undid his armor. There were bloodstains inside and out; even the clothes beneath the armor were soaked purple and black with blood. "How many did you defeat?" Chen Xing asked, recalling that astonishing battle.

"I don't know," Xiang Shu replied coldly, leaning against a big tree. "No time to count. Help me take off my armor."

He was clad in heavy Tiele armor, the kind normally worn by horseback riders. Not long after he had entered the canyon, though, the warhorse had been struck by an arrow and it hadn't been able to hold on. Tiele and Rouran craftspeople had made this armor with hardened steel. It was misshapen from all the arrows and swords, but it had still protected his body well.

Chen Xing bared Xiang Shu's chest, and Xiang Shu took a deep breath and gasped for more air.

"I'll rest for a short while," he said. Sitting under the tree with his back against its trunk, he closed his eyes. "I'm too tired, too tired..."

Chen Xing tore off his own robe—with great difficulty, thanks to the chains that still shackled him—and used it to cover Xiang Shu's upper body. Xiang Shu's tired, bloodstained face was somehow still strikingly handsome; Chen Xing wanted to reach out and touch it. A thought occurred to him then: that he should do something to express his gratitude toward Xiang Shu.

"How far is it from Karakorum to here?" Chen Xing asked.

"One day and one night," replied Xiang Shu.

*So you came to save me as soon as I was caught?* Chen Xing tried again: "Do you want something to eat? Are you hungry?"

"Eat what?" Xiang Shu asked dismissively. "I'd like to see whether you can actually find me something to eat. Or do you mean eating you? How much meat do you have on your bones?"

Chen Xing dropped it.

Eventually Xiang Shu's breathing stabilized and he stopped talking, clearly asleep. Chen Xing sat down next to him and leaned against him slightly. Their surroundings were quiet, the only sound the rustling of wind through the mountains and trees. It felt, for the moment, as if all the world's dangers had withdrawn to a distance, leaving only this peaceful snow and these lofty mountains.

*I'm sorry*, Chen Xing said silently. *If I hadn't gone and made you my protector without your agreement, I wouldn't have caused you so much trouble.* He sighed, feeling bewildered about the world. Now and then, Chen Xing went so far as to treat Xiang Shu as his last hope, almost emotionally blackmailing him to fight hard and risk his life for him.

Chen Xing was only leaning on him a little, but, with his eyes still closed, Xiang Shu raised an arm and draped it around Chen Xing's shoulders, pulling him a little closer. This simple action filled Chen Xing with what felt like endless courage, and his momentary frustration vanished like smoke in thin air. He leaned down slowly, resting his head against Xiang Shu, and looked out at the desolate graves in front of him.

"What?" Xiang Shu said suddenly.

"What?" Chen Xing asked back.

"The Heart Lamp," Xiang Shu said concisely.

"The Heart Lamp...? But I'm not using it?"

Xiang Shu opened his eyes. "I feel it," he said doubtfully. "It's like you're glowing all over."

"Me?" Chen Xing raised his head, but Xiang Shu pressed him back down to lean on him. It made Chen Xing feel better, but he couldn't say why.

"Did you see Che Luofeng?" Xiang Shu asked, changing the subject.

"Yes." Chen Xing gave him a rough outline of the events, and Xiang Shu frowned.

"Zhou Zhen became a living corpse not long after he died, and so did Youduo. Where have they been hiding all these years?"

This was also the point that had Chen Xing the most puzzled. If the world's spiritual qi were still present, they might have been able to ask the yao who could be found everywhere in the mountains and other areas.

It was Chen Xing's turn to ask a question. "What are you going to do with Che Luofeng?"

"I'm going to take him back," Xiang Shu said in a low voice, "or finish him here. It's my fault."

Chen Xing wanted to tell him that he shouldn't have handed the responsibility of guarding Chi Le Chuan over to Che Luofeng, but what was the use of saying that now? And when Chen Xing thought about the circumstances, he realized it was irrelevant—even if Xiang Shu hadn't handed the responsibility to his anda, no one could have subdued Che Luofeng once he was set on taking over Chi Le Chuan and slaughtering people. Xiang Shu's decision to leave Chi Le Chuan was a mistake, yes, but it was Chen Xing who had caused this mistake.

"Before I left," Xiang Shu murmured, "he promised me that he wouldn't take revenge on the Akele and that he would protect Chi Le Chuan for me. That night, he and I came to an agreement, surrounded by the clan chiefs."

Chen Xing suddenly recalled the night when the Akele king had waited outside his tent and offered to take him north. King Akele must not have believed that the argument between Xiang Shu and Che Luofeng would end just like that. He didn't want to drag all of Chi Le Chuan into danger, nor did he want the Great Chanyu to abandon Chi Le Chuan for the sake of the Akele, so he left without permission in the middle of the argument to assist Chen Xing.

"Che Luofeng isn't that kind of person," said Xiang Shu. "Some words were said, but it was just because he let his emotions take over in the heat of the moment. Once he calms down, he'll see the big picture. It's Zhou Zhen and Shi Hai... It was the medicine Shi Hai gave him that changed his temperament."

"Forget it," Chen Xing said, feeling a little uncomfortable.

"Can you save him again?"

"It's hard to say. If the Spiritual Qi of the Heavens and Earth were still here, I could've attempted to dispel the influence of the Demon God's blood."

"I know he can't be forgiven. I just want him to regain his dignity before he dies."

"For what crime?" a hoarse voice said. "Shulü Kong, you are the one who should ask for forgiveness."

Startled, Chen Xing raised his head, but Xiang Shu seemed to have known Che Luofeng was coming. He gave Chen Xing a casual pat to indicate that he needed to get up, then stood up using his sword for support. "Well, explain yourself."

Che Luofeng had been battered beyond recognition. When he fell off the cliff, his head had been bashed in so badly it was visibly dented. All over his body, his armor and clothes were in tatters, and one of his hands was broken, dangling at his side.

His eyes were wide open as he looked at Xiang Shu. "My anda, never forget the consequence of going back on your word."

Wielding his sword, Xiang Shu slowly walked away from Chen Xing, telling him, "Don't move more than ten feet away from this tree." His lower body was still clad in iron armor, but his upper body was bare, showing the scar from that time in Chang'an, not so long ago, when he had blocked an arrow for Chen Xing. He held his sword horizontally, blocking Che Luofeng's way.

Quiet noises were coming from all directions; a powerful resentment was quietly spreading in this ancient burial ground. Sima Yue appeared from within the forest. Holding an antler staff, he stood on high ground overlooking the three men in the graveyard.

Chen Xing looked up at Sima Yue and saw that he was using the antler staff to channel the resentment around him. Like a gathering storm, all the resentment from beyond the Great Wall surged into the graveyard—it poured into the ravine like running water!

"Sima Yue!" Chen Xing shouted in a deep voice. "Ask your lord to come out and speak!"

"Exorcist," Sima Yue said from above, cold and aloof, "you will see him soon enough. I'll give you a chance to stop resisting and come with me. Then you will have an opportunity to ask him what you wish."

An idea occurred to Chen Xing: What would happen if he pretended to be defeated and let himself be caught? It was obvious that these two living corpses, the drought fiend kings, had orders from their superior to capture him alive... But he quickly discarded the idea. Sure, Shi Hai wanted him, so they'd keep him alive, but the same couldn't be said for Xiang Shu. It wasn't worth the risk.

Chen Xing lifted his chain and confronted his enemy. He had never shown mercy to these creatures, nor the slightest hint of fear.

"I have no interest in negotiating with him. Go back and tell him that my mission is to annihilate him and send him back to samsara, where the dead belong."

Sima Yue erupted in a hoarse, frantic laugh. "You alone? I'd like to see what a single weak, defenseless exorcist can do under the Silence of All Magic!"

He thrust the staff in his hand into the ground, and the overflowing resentment whipped into a frenzy. Cold winds howled in the ancient graveyard, as if their surroundings had transformed into the underworld.

"This is bad," Chen Xing muttered as he watched the transformation. Like the Yin Yang Mirror and the Zheng Drum, this magical artifact had been refined with resentment! The resentment in the antler staff had combined with the ambient resentment from the war and the massacre in Chi Le Chuan, and begun to stir the earth veins toward the yin side. This was even more dangerous than the situation back in Chang'an!

At first he hadn't thought much about it because the vast area of Chi Le Chuan wasn't as densely populated as a city, and there had been no large-scale wars in many years. Surely any resentment hovering around would dissipate quickly. But then he realized that the fact that Chi Le Chuan had fewer people compared to the city of Chang'an was precisely what made the present situation so dangerous. The fewer the number of living people in a given place, the weaker the yang qi became, slowing down the neutralization of resentment borne by death.

From nowhere, Sima Yue had produced a magical artifact containing powerful resentment, and now he was activating it and releasing its power. Dark clouds surged over the canyon in the blink of an eye, and blood-red lightning flickered faintly on the horizon.

Numerous shadows appeared from within the mountain range, surrounding that immense, ancient tree in the graveyard.

"Shulü Kong," Che Luofeng shouted from within the dark clouds. "I've given you everything I have, and all these years, I've owed you nothing."

He slowly emerged from the dense resentment. Chen Xing looked around the graveyard and saw that countless corrupted animals had emerged—deer, wolves, wild dogs, foxes, and vultures, all limping toward the graveyard, staring at them with muddy eyes and exposed, eerie white bones.

"My anda is already dead," Xiang Shu said, holding his heavy sword. "The monster standing in front of me is nothing."

Chen Xing forced himself to calm down. To his surprise, Che Luofeng's torn and broken body was slowly being mended inside the dense resentment. With a glance up at the darkened sky, Chen Xing activated the Heart Lamp, but the thick resentment interfered with the light of Xiang Shu's sword, dimming it down. The resentment was so heavy it was eating away at the power of the Heart Lamp by the minute.

"Shulü Kong," Che Luofeng said, trembling, "you selfish, ungrateful, vile man. I've seen through you. Just die! Return everything I've given you!"

"Xiang Shu!" Chen Xing shouted. "Stay close to me! The Heart Lamp's mana has been weakened!"

He rushed into the battlefield, and Xiang Shu moved back. Che Luofeng was being enveloped in resentment the likes of which Chen Xing had never seen before, and he was even less willing to let go than Feng Qianyi. Revealing a bone whip brandished in his left hand, he pounced on Xiang Shu.

# 45

THE ROTTING MONSTERS around them shrieked, their cries converging into an ear-piercing cacophony. In the blink of an eye, they pounced toward Xiang Shu and Chen Xing, who were engulfed by a tsunami of resentment and animal bones.

A voice cried, "Chen Xing! Chen Xing!" Xiao Shan was there!

"Xiao Shan! Get Chen Xing out of here!" Xiang Shu shouted at the top of his lungs as he fended off the enemy.

"I can't leave!" Chen Xing yelled. "You'll die without the Heart Lamp!"

Chen Xing forcibly called upon the Heart Lamp in spite of the darkness engulfing them. Mana surged wildly through his body, making his already damaged heart meridian clench with pain. He couldn't stop, though; Xiang Shu was relying on the light's protection. The Heart Lamp was what made the heavy sword he wielded shine so brightly, and it was the only reason he could fend off the living animal corpses' relentless attacks. If Chen Xing let go, Xiang Shu would be swallowed by resentment!

"You knew everything!" Che Luofeng roared madly. "All this time, you've known!"

As Che Luofeng cracked his whip with hatred in his heart, a blurry image appeared in the dark resentment that surrounded them.

It was that moment by the tent when Xiang Shu had stood in front of Chen Xing and slapped Che Luofeng.

A blinding light burst out of Xiang Shu's hands, blocking Che Luofeng's whip strike. A new scene appeared, set in the autumn light of Chi Le Chuan. He and Che Luofeng were sitting by a stream with Zhou Zhen, the three of them fishing side by side.

"Yes," Xiang Shu said. "I knew from the very start. You only chose Zhou Zhen because you couldn't get what you wanted from me."

Che Luofeng froze. Xiang Shu took this opening to parry his blow and push Che Luofeng backward with a mighty shove.

"But so what?" Xiang Shu asked. "Are you unsatisfied, being just my anda? Che Luofeng, I've told you this before: No matter who I am with in this life, I will always regard you as family."

"Shulü Kong! You're a liar!" Che Luofeng cried, as if he had gone mad. Countless farewells flashed by in an instant, and a scene rose up out of the darkness. It was what Che Luofeng had seen by the lake: Xiang Shu's back turned to him as he rode away on his horse.

"Wake up, Che Luofeng!" Xiang Shu bellowed. "You've become a monster!"

His heavy sword flashed with a searing light that dispelled the thick fog. Another memory flooded Che Luofeng's mind—Xiang Shu riding a horse across plains under brilliant sunlight, smiling back at Che Luofeng and whistling at him. For a moment, he couldn't swing his whip.

"Zhou Zhen should have been the one you entrusted yourself to," Xiang Shu said. "I told you that long ago."

"He's dead," Che Luofeng choked out between gritted teeth. "And you didn't even let me avenge him!"

"It was already over!" roared Xiang Shu. "All that hatred was finished! You admitted that then yourself, when you nodded!"

Resentment roiled around Che Luofeng. "You didn't let me avenge him, and you weren't even willing to...on his behalf... Shulü Kong, you liar! I'll kill you myself!"

Chen Xing tried again and again to activate the Heart Lamp, but the resentment was too strong. It chipped away at his strength, countering the power of the Heart Lamp. He tugged on the iron chain with all his might, trying to get a little closer to Xiang Shu. Xiao Shan dashed over to him and struck at the chain with his claws, but it didn't budge an inch.

Just then, something massive shot out of the cloud of resentment. Chen Xing tackled Xiao Shan, rolling across the ground with him in his arms. A tail swept through the air, right where they had been standing, and from of the black cloud of resentment emerged the moving corpse of a giant black snake. It had its sights set on them.

Xiao Shan let out a wild shout. He lunged forward to fight, but Chen Xing seized his collar with his chained hand and dragged Xiao Shan behind him. As he did so, a blinding light burst from his heart meridian; it circulated from his tianchi acupoint to the tianquan point, then down his arm past the quze and neigong points to gather in his palm. The energy built at his fingertip in his zhongchong point, and he extended that finger toward the darkness.

An intense light burst forth and pierced the darkness like a sharp sword. The corpse snake cried out in pain as it slithered around, trying to dodge. The light converged into a beam and, without losing momentum, passed through the layers of thick fog to illuminate Sima Yue high above. Sima Yue leaped back hastily to avoid it.

In the light, Xiao Shan saw the staff Sima Yue was holding in his hand, and he froze, stunned. Chen Xing was taken aback as well.

He thought of what Lu Ying had said to him in Carosha—that antler staff could very well have been cut from the Deer God's own head!

"Xiao Shan!" Chen Xing shouted, ignoring everything else, but he was too late. Xiao Shan struggled against his grip so hard he tore his martial robe to get free, and he sprinted up the cliff.

On the other side of the battlefield, Xiao Shan leaped up high, his horror plain on his face. In the hands of an enemy, Lu Ying's horns had been reduced to nothing but toys. Xiao Shan's eyes turned bloodshot, and he let out a terrible roar.

Sima Yue swung the staff in a clean sweep, striking Xiao Shan around the waist and brutally smacking him into the ground. Blood streamed from the corners of Xiao Shan's mouth, but in the next instant he crawled to his feet again for another lunge. Sima Yue brandished the staff horizontally in front of him to smack Xiao Shan square on the forehead, and Xiao Shan fell once more, this time from several feet up in the air.

It still didn't stop him. Xiao Shan lunged again. Sima Yue drew a dagger.

"Xiao Shan!" Chen Xing cried. The moment he saw the dagger in Sima Yue's hand, he felt all the blood in his body surge upwards. Xiang Shu, seeing that their lives were in imminent peril, had no choice but to give up on Che Luofeng to go save them instead.

Without the protection of the Heart Lamp, his every move was dragged down by resentment. He breathed it in and it seemed to course through him, chilling him to his very bones. A vicious surge of guilt overwhelmed him.

Che Luofeng lunged at Xiang Shu, unwilling to let him get away, but then he let out another mad shout—a living corpse had charged him from behind and grabbed him in a viselike grip. Two hands snaked around his head and wrenched, trying to twist Che Luofeng's head clean off!

"Youduo!" Xiang Shu shouted.

Che Luofeng cried out wildly. He lashed out with his bone whip, wrapping it around Youduo's body and then brutally yanking away. The whip tore Youdou's body to shreds, but his teeth remained latched onto Che Luofeng's shoulder, and he bit down so hard Che Luofeng's shoulder blade shattered. Xiang Shu saw his chance; he swung his blade in a horizontal arc and sent Che Luofeng flying.

Finally, Xiang Shu was free to rush over to Chen Xing and push him away. But just as he leaped into the air to take on Sima Yue, Che Luofeng re-emerged from the black fog; evidently, Youduo had been dealt with. He lifted a hand and made a flicking gesture at Xiang Shu, and in an instant, the animal carcasses surrounding them were all reduced to white bones. As their rotten flesh drifted through the resentment, their bones sunk into the ground, connecting to one another and turning into countless bony thorns that burst out of the earth.

"Watch out!" Chen Xing shouted.

With nowhere safe to land, Xiang Shu was forced to use his heavy sword as a shield. A forest of bony thorns shot out of the ground and caged him firmly.

Xiao Shan plummeted down from above, right into a thicket of bony thorns that pointed upward like a mountain and stabbed him through the shoulders, arms, and thighs. He struggled to raise his claws, and when that didn't work, he looked down at his body, confused.

"I'll be taking your exorcist away," drawled Sima Yue. "Che Luofeng, I'll leave the rest to you. You must repay in full the debt that Zhou Zhen owes our lord. Remember to send the rest of the Chi Le Chuan corpses to Huanmo Palace..."

A death-scream burst from Xiao Shan's throat. "AAAHHHH!"

Even skewered as he was on the bony thorns, his blood trickling down to the earth in an endless stream, he kept struggling. When he took his next breath, the resentment surrounding them grew even stronger. It congregated into a tornado that headed straight for Xiao Shan.

Chen Xing lost all rational thought. *"Che Luofeng!"* he roared.

Ignoring him, Che Luofeng walked toward Xiang Shu, who was bound in that cage of bones. He unslung the bow from his back, nocked a bone arrow, and aimed it at Xiang Shu. "Anda," he murmured, and Xiang Shu stared at Che Luofeng, dazed.

But right at the last moment, Che Luofeng's gaze seemed to clear a little. His hand on the taut bowstring trembled a little, and he could not bring himself to loose the arrow. A single teardrop rolled down his cheek.

Chen Xing finally lost it. Harnessing an immense strength that came from nowhere, he swung the seventy-pound stone fragment connected to his chains and sent it flying through the air.

*"Rouran dog!"* Chen Xing bellowed, lost in his rage. "You should die instead!"

Desperation had spurred Chen Xing into rage—an extremely rare occurrence. Che Luofeng had won a front-row seat to this special event, and in addition to the sound of that furious roar, he was treated to a giant chunk of stone smashing brutally into the back of his head.

Xiang Shu stared at them, utterly speechless.

Che Luofeng had never anticipated that Chen Xing might mount a sneak attack. Chen Xing had been so far away, and his fighting capabilities were so feeble that Che Luofeng didn't consider him a threat at all. And Chen Xing using that heavy stone as a weapon? Even more incomprehensible. Thus, his "Cyclone Counterattack," so powerful it could shatter the skies, smashed into Che Luofeng with a muffled thud from five steps away. The impact split Che Luofeng's head open and crushed his skull down into his shoulders.

The white bone cage instantly collapsed.

"Quickly now!" shouted Xiang Shu, brandishing his sword.

For a moment the resentment roiled even thicker—and then it disappeared altogether. Chen Xing still hadn't actually processed what had happened, but at the sound of Xiang Shu's voice, he leaped into action and activated the Heart Lamp. The heavy sword in Xiang Shu's hand shone with a blinding light as he set it against Che Luofeng's chest.

"Anda," he choked out. "Sleep. When you fall asleep...everything will be okay again..."

With a bitter shout, he pressed his sword against Che Luofeng's staggering form. He drove it in fast, impaling Che Luofeng through the wound in his abdomen that Chen Xing had once sutured. The blade pierced through his lower back, blazing with the Heart Lamp's white light.

Che Luofeng slackened like a kite with a cut string and went flying backward, leaving the stench of rotting blood in his wake.

Suddenly, Chen Xing felt as if his heart was being yanked out of his chest. In that moment, the Heart Lamp's power seemed to connect his soul with Xiang Shu's. He was assaulted by an immense, ancient sorrow, and he began to cry uncontrollably. "Xiang Shu..." he sobbed.

On the ground, Che Luofeng spasmed and reached one hand up toward the sky. His lips moved on his sunken face as if he wanted to say something, but he couldn't speak.

Xiang Shu slowly turned around. He and Chen Xing looked at Xiao Shan, who was on the ground, struggling to get to his feet.

"Xiao Shan?" Chen Xing arduously made his way over to him, dragging his chains and stone behind him. Slowly, Xiao Shan managed to get up. His two steel claws were still on his hands...and the endless stream of resentment that had been curling in the sky had been all sucked into them.

The Sky-Rending Claws had turned jet-black, and they glinted with a cold light just as the Saber of Life and Harmony had when it was refined by resentment. Xiao Shan looked the same as Feng Qianjun had then: His eyes were bloodshot, and resentment seeped out of him as he stared at Sima Yue, who still stood high above.

*Crap!* How on earth had this kid learned to use this artifact? Lu Ying couldn't have taught him, right?

Sima Yue flicked his left hand, and a black shield appeared. "Oh, how amusing. What you wield is also—"

Xiao Shan waved his first claw. A blackened, phantom image of the ancient Dragon God appeared behind him, accompanied by a faint dragon's call. Xiang Shu turned and pressed Chen Xing to the ground. Chen Xing's shackles shook, and when it made contact with the claws' energy, the chain was sliced apart.

Before Sima Yue could finish his sentence, he saw the mountains, the earth, even the sky, being sliced apart like pieces of paper. His own shield was cut into three neat sections, and his sturdy black breastplate misaligned, making him lose his balance. His upper body fell backward. Deep within the Yin Mountains, ridges and peaks slid precariously and then fell with a deafening bang.

"...A divine weapon," he finished.

Xiao Shan stepped forward and struck with his second claw. *Whoosh!* Sima Yue's helmet and head were both torn into shreds, scattering on the wind. The ground where he stood collapsed, and neat slabs of mirror-like stone came crashing down.

Even as the mountain ridges behind him were carved into sharply angled slopes, the second claw strike demolished them further. Like stormy waves, the debris crashed violently to either side, causing a thundering avalanche!

Xiao Shan raised his left claw slightly and drew a circle with his right in the Gray Wolf Chases the Moon move. Before he could charge forward, however, Chen Xing managed to sneak up behind him unnoticed.

"Expel!" Chen Xing roared in his ears, calling upon all the strength he had left. He covered Xiao Shan's eyes with his left hand and pressed his right against the small of Xiao Shan's back. A bright white light pierced through Xiao Shan's consciousness.

The Sky-Rending Claws clanged to the ground, and the resentment dissipated. Xiao Shan, who had lost consciousness, fell to the ground too. Chen Xing followed suit and collapsed limply into the snow, his energy thoroughly sapped.

The avalanche swept over the entire battlefield, leaving no trace of the battle behind.


A few flakes of snow drifted to earth. A massive pair of broken antlers jutted out from the ground, towering like a lonely tombstone in a silent world.

Chen Xing turned his head sideways to look at Xiang Shu, who was lying in the snow, staring up at the sky. "Xiang Shu... Are you okay?"

Xiang Shu turned his head to look back at Chen Xing, but he didn't speak. Chen Xing's hand moved, and he struggled to roll over. Xiang Shu's fingers twitched, and he grasped Chen Xing's hand.

Chen Xing turned over and got up, letting out an exhausted breath. His hair was a bird's nest. "Xiao Shan?"

He examined Xiao Shan's wounds. The bony thorns had pierced through his legs and arms, but fortunately, he was small enough that his chest had slipped safely between the thorns and not been injured. Chen Xing grabbed a handful of snow and scrubbed it across Xiao Shan's face to wake him up. Xiao Shan opened his eyes, bewildered, and gritted his teeth in pain the moment he tried to move. Chen Xing stopped him with a gesture and got to work applying simple dressings to his injuries.

Xiao Shan pointed at the antlers in the distance, so Chen Xing went to retrieve them. Xiao Shan sadly held them in his arms and refused to let go. Chen Xing gave him a pat on the head.

A sound rang out in the distance. Xiang Shu got up slowly. After all those fierce battles in such quick succession, he was thoroughly exhausted. With his body covered in wounds, he limped slowly toward the end of the snowfield, where Che Luofeng's broken body was still skewered on Xiang Shu's heavy sword. His rotten blood soaked the snow around the spot where he lay.

Xiang Shu knelt down in front of Che Luofeng and pried his fingers away from the bow they still gripped. With his left hand, he took Che Luofeng's hand, and he covered the back of it with his right.

Xiao Shan looked at Xiang Shu, then at Chen Xing.

Chen Xing shook his head and made a shushing gesture. "Leave him alone for a while," he whispered with a sigh.

Xiang Shu couldn't stop trembling. He pressed Che Luofeng's hand to his face, sobbing softly. A wind began to blow, creating a flurry of snowflakes that blanketed the landscape, and Xiang Shu's trembling voice came to Chen Xing and Xiao Shan on the wind.

"Go," he was saying. "Shulü Kong will abide by the oath we made as anda and avenge you. It's over. It's really over this time. You'll never wake up again, Che Luofeng, but you shall rest in peace...for all eternity..."

"Lu Ying," Xiao Shan said. He seemed to have sensed something. "Lu Ying."

"Do you want to avenge Lu Ying?" Chen Xing asked him.

Xiao Shan didn't reply; he just looked into the distance. The two of them stood in the snow together for a very, very long time. Finally, Xiang Shu dragged himself out of the valley with slow, lethargic steps. His tall, robust body was covered with frost, and he was carrying Che Luofeng's misshapen corpse, wrapped in a cloth. On his back was the keepsake he had given Che Luofeng when they became sworn brothers—the longbow.

"Let's go," he said.

High up on the mountain to the south, Sima Wei watched the three of them leave.


Nightfall, in a cave on the Yin Mountains.

They had been on the move for three whole days, and after all of those violent battles, they looked like savages. Xiang Shu had started a bonfire in the cave, and Xiao Shan was already sound asleep.

"Where are we going?" Chen Xing asked.

Xiang Shu looked up from the bonfire. "Back to Karakorum."

Chen Xing nodded. So many things had happened so fast. It would be wisest to go back and regroup. "I don't think Che Luofeng can be revived."

"I know. He's been dead ever since he drank the potion Zhou Zhen gave him and massacred the entire Akele tribe."

Chen Xing thought about what had happened before Che Luofeng transformed into a living corpse. "At the very beginning," he said, a little sadly, "he didn't want to drink that cup of wine."

Xiang Shu had already heard Chen Xing tell it once, yet this time he asked, "Did he mention me then?"

"He shouted for Zhou Zhen, and also for you. I think he must have been terrified."

Xiang Shu stared at Che Luofeng's cloth-wrapped corpse and didn't reply. Xiao Shan turned over in front of the fire, subconsciously moving to scratch his wounds, and Chen Xing grabbed his hand to stop him from scratching off his bandages.

"After Zhou Zhen died," Xiang Shu said, sounding far away, "everyone in Chi Le Chuan knew that I was the only one who could convince Che Luofeng to let go of his desire for revenge. I kept Che Luofeng company that day and for the entire following month... I knew he wanted me to take Zhou Zhen's place in his life, but he didn't ask. He knew that if he did, I would leave."

Chen Xing frowned. "You wouldn't have left."

"I would have." Xiang Shu added some wood to the fire. "I couldn't give him what Zhou Zhen gave him because I didn't feel that way for him. I could only be his anda."

For a moment, Chen Xing didn't know how to respond. He thought about it for a moment. "You've treated him very well," he said.

"No. I let him down."

Chen Xing didn't know how to console Xiang Shu, but he could tell that what Xiang Shu needed in that moment was for someone to listen and keep him company, just like he'd kept Che Luofeng company when Zhou Zhen died. "Perhaps you just don't know what it means to like someone that way..."

"I do," Xiang Shu said softly. "I understand it all too well. Don't compare me to Tuoba Yan. I know what it feels like to love someone, and I also know that I didn't love my anda that way. There was nothing to be done about that."

He glanced at Chen Xing. The blazing fire flickered inside the cave. Chen Xing leaned against the cave wall, looking down at the Zheng Drum that they had retrieved from Sima Yue. That made two artifacts, now.

"Xiang Shu," Chen Xing whispered, "I'm sorry."

Xiang Shu stared at Chen Xing, confused. "What are you apologizing for?"

Chen Xing smiled bitterly. "If it wasn't for me, you might not have had to go through all this."

To Chen Xing's bewilderment, Xiang Shu's expression became angry. He studied Chen Xing as if he didn't know who he was looking at anymore. "So that's what you think? What kind of person do you think I am? Am I really such an ignorant fool in your eyes?!"

Afraid of waking Xiao Shan, Chen Xing quickly motioned to Xiang Shu to keep it down.

Xiang Shu sighed, evidently not in the mood to argue. He glanced at Xiao Shan. "If it weren't for you," he said, "the situation would only have been worse."

Chen Xing made a noise of agreement. For the past few days, he'd been musing over what Xiang Shu had said. If not for him, the Akele king wouldn't have died; if Xiang Shu hadn't gone north to find him, calamity wouldn't have befallen Chi Le Chuan so suddenly. But what was coming would still eventually have come. If Chen Xing hadn't been there when it did, the Sixteen Hu wouldn't have been able to defend themselves, even if they hid away in Karakorum.

But Chen Xing still felt a little guilty. "I want to do something for you. Is there anything I can do?" He looked at Xiang Shu earnestly. His original plan had been to talk to Xiang Shu about the future and about Shi Hai, so that he would have revenge to focus on rather than his sorrows.

Xiang Shu remained silent for a while before asking, "Do you know how to perform a transcendence ceremony?"

"Transcendence," Chen Xing repeated. "Hm, I don't."

"Then give Che Luofeng a sky burial. You are an exorcist, and you're also Chi Le Chuan's benefactor. But if you think it's too much of an imposition, then..."

Chen Xing understood what Xiang Shu was trying to convey. Che Luofeng was dead, so all of this had come to an end as well. If they brought his corpse back to Karakorum, a sinner like him would be given an earth burial.

The Akele tribe had been wiped out, so Xiang Shu figured that he was the only one left who could pardon Che Luofeng of his sins—or admit that Che Luofeng's actions weren't done of his own volition, but rather because he had been possessed by a demon.

"Give him a sky burial," Chen Xing said at last. "Any method is acceptable for returning to the earth. Death is immutable."

"Thank you," Xiang Shu replied earnestly. "This is the last thing I can do for him."

He bowed down and picked up Che Luofeng's body, then left the cave. Chen Xing thought, *Now?* But bringing him back to Chi Le Chuan would have only stirred up more issues. He followed Xiang Shu to the cave's entrance and saw that the first glimmer of light was starting to appear in the night sky. As it happened, there was a sky burial platform right there on the summit.

"After this..." Xiang Shu said, turning to Chen Xing.

"Xiang Shu, I don't think I should go back to Karakorum with you after all." Another year had already slipped by. Chen Xing's time was running out—he had to leave. He couldn't waste any more time in Chi Le Chuan.

There was a long pause. Finally, Xiang Shu said, "Let's talk about it again after I come down."

Xiang Shu trekked up to the summit. Chen Xing didn't follow him. Instead, he covered Xiao Shan with a robe and stood there, halfway up the mountain, watching the vultures wheeling high overhead. As the first ray of dawn broke, he heard Xiang Shu sing the Tiele mourning song up at the peak. Vultures flocked to the sky burial platform. Then the mourning song ended, and more and more vultures arrived.

Chen Xing stood in silence. Suddenly, he heard footsteps behind him, and an iron-gloved hand covered his mouth. Chen Xing struggled, his eyes wide, but another hand covered his eyes and his vision went black as he was dragged into the darkness.

# 46

"YAH!"

The horse ride was a bumpy one. Chen Xing's hands were tied behind his back, and his waist was strapped to the saddle. Sima Wei's black armor clanked as they charged out of the Yin Mountains, heading east along the trade route outside the pass.

Sima Wei had abducted him. In what seemed like no time at all, they rode hundreds of miles—they even passed by Chi Le Chuan, but Sima Wei continued eastward rather than taking the route south toward the Great Wall.

At noon one day, Sima Wei threw Chen Xing to the ground, untied him, and tossed him some flatbread and dried meat before pointing to a stream nearby. Chen Xing was deeply unimpressed.

"Xiang Shu will come and save me," he muttered, scarfing down the food. A wise man submitted to his circumstances; resistance was futile, so Chen Xing decided to scour his mind for ways to slow Sima Wei down instead.

Throughout their journey, Sima Wei hadn't responded to anything Chen Xing said, but now he finally spoke. "No, he won't," he said in a low voice. "He'll think you just left on your own."

This struck a chord. Crap, what if Xiang Shu really did think that? Chen Xing had said he would leave him moments before Xiang Shu headed up the mountain. It was entirely possible! This wouldn't be the first time he'd left without a word, either. Last time, Xiang Shu had witnessed his abduction, but this time he hadn't seen a thing—and Xiao Shan had been asleep, too, so no one would have been able to tell Xiang Shu that Chen Xing had been captured. Chen Xing had dropped more than one hint lately about them going their separate ways, since he knew that Xiang Shu had his own responsibilities as the Great Chanyu.

If Xiang Shu had returned to Karakorum on his own, assuming Chen Xing had quietly left because he didn't want to say goodbye, then no one would come to save him. He had to find a way to escape on his own!

Under the watchful eyes of several crows perched in the tree overhead, Chen Xing tried a few times to activate his Heart Lamp. But it was no use. He couldn't sense Xiang Shu. Maybe Xiang Shu was too far away, or maybe... Well, either way, he had to accept this bleak reality: Xiang Shu wasn't coming to save him. Chen Xing had to plan his own escape.

As they traveled, he'd been scheming on ways to slip away while the asshole general wasn't paying attention. Unfortunately, Sima Wei neither ate nor slept; they paused occasionally for a breather, but only for Chen Xing's sake. Each time, they set off again as soon as Chen Xing was done resting. He had no opportunities to flee. Chen Xing also tried again and again to fish information out of his captor, but Sima Wei remained tight-lipped. In this way, they'd been travelling at full speed for six days straight.

"Get up, time to move," said Sima Wei.

"Where exactly are you taking me?!" Chen Xing demanded. No reply. "I need a nap. I've been riding for so long, I'm going bow-legged. My feet hurt."

This worked. Sima Wei let him remain where he was and got up to survey the surroundings. The moment he saw Sima Wei leave the woods, Chen Xing took stock of his own surroundings and then turned and bolted.

"Caw! Caw!" A flock of startled crows flapped their wings and took off into the air as Chen Xing dashed into the forest. This kicked off a brief chase with Sima Wei, and in less time than it would take for an incense stick to burn, Chen Xing got himself caught in a cave, bound tightly like a dumpling, and tossed back onto the horse. They continued eastward.

They hastened on their journey for close to ten days. Sima Wei kept moving forward along the Great Wall. Every time they stopped, crows surrounded their temporary campsite.

"Can't you at least take me somewhere with people?" Chen Xing groaned, wiggling around on the horse.

Sima Wei continued to steer clear of the Great Wall's gates, eventually turning north again and crossing into the Youzhou region. Chen Xing glimpsed Qin forces from afar a few times, but Sima Wei had remarkable evasion skills; he always managed to slip past them and continued southeast. When he saw a plaque reading *Zhuojun*, Chen Xing knew that if they didn't change direction again, their route would take them to Goguryeo territory.[13]

Once they were out of the Central Plains, Sima Wei finally relaxed his watch over Chen Xing.

"I really won't try to run away anymore!" Chen Xing insisted. "We're almost at Silla now. Even if I managed to escape, I'd never find my way back. Just untie me, Sima Wei!"

---

13  Goguryeo was a Korean kingdom that existed from 37 BC to 668 BC, one of the Three Kingdoms of Korea; the others were Silla and Baekje. At the time of Dinghai Fusheng Records, Goguryeo made up the northern part of the Korean Peninsula.

"After three attempts, a man should give up," said Sima Wei. But Chen Xing got what he wished for; Sima Wei finally untied him.

They reached Pyongyang, a large city in Goguryeo. It was mostly populated by the Buyeo people, so most of the residents understood the Xianbei language. Sima Wei, having found some regular clothes from who knows where, put his armor away and donned a bamboo hat that covered half his face.

Curious Buyeo people watched as the two travelers passed by. Someone approached and questioned them, and Chen Xing responded in Xianbei.

"What brings you two here?" a Buyeo man asked. "Are you from Jin?"

Sima Wei turned to Chen Xing. "What did they say?"

If Sima Wei didn't understand, Chen Xing realized, that meant he had the upper hand. "They asked where we're headed," he said.

"Ask them where we can find a boat."

"I've been kidnapped!" Chen Xing told the man in Xianbei. "This man dragged me here all the way from Chi Le Chuan!"

The people of the city began to talk among themselves, with many onlookers gathering around them. Most were dressed in the attire of Confucian scholars, in scholars' robes and bamboo hats.

When King Sosurim of Goguryeo ascended the throne, he had established a Taixue in Pyongyang, fostering scholars and promoting education.[14] From the Han dynasty to Cao Wei and later the Jin dynasty, Confucian teachings from the Central Plains were highly respected by various vassal states, and learning the Han language and reading Han texts was considered a mark of prestige among the different peoples. This particular group of scholars had just finished

---

14  The Taixue (太学), or Imperial Academy, was a high-ranking educational institution where students were taught Confucian classics and prepared for civil service.

the day's lessons at the Taixue. Motivated by a sense of chivalry, they blocked Chen Xing and Sima Wei's path, carefully scrutinizing the odd pair.

One scholar stepped forward. "How can we save you?" he asked. "Can we be of any help?"

"What did he say?" Sima Wei asked immediately.

Chen Xing waved at the crowd. Although Sima Wei had a gentler demeanor than the other drought fiend kings, Chen Xing couldn't be sure he wouldn't suddenly snap and go on a killing spree in the city. He didn't want to endanger innocent lives. Instead of asking for help, he explained to the crowd, "This man is deranged. He's killed a lot of people along the way. Please, don't act rashly."

Sima Wei looked at him, puzzled.

"Then what should we do?" asked the scholars.

Chen Xing turned to Sima Wei. "They're telling us that no boats are running at the moment, so we'll have to stay in the city for a few days and wait."

Sima Wei observed the faces of the people in the crowd. "Don't lie to me," he said.

"I'm not lying!"

"That man just now only said five words. How did you translate that into such a long explanation?"

"That's just how Xianbei works!" Chen Xing shrugged. "Have you never met a Xianbei person? If you think I'm too wordy, then go ahead and ask them yourself. I'm done."

"We'll go to the pier to look for a boat."

"Wait, wait, wait..." Thinking fast, Chen Xing turned to the scholars, clasped his hands, and said with a smile, "Gege, please notify the city's guard. I'll trick him into retiring to an inn for now. If someone comes looking for me, tell them where I am."

"What are you saying this time?" Sima Wei asked, still perplexed.

"I'm asking when the boats will be available."

"Your tone sounded like you were making a statement, not asking a question."

Chen Xing quickly switched to Xianbei again. "Where's the inn in this city?"

Someone pointed somewhere far away, and Chen Xing gestured to Sima Wei. *See? I'm asking.*

"I'll go to the King's guards now to report the situation in detail," said one of the scholars. "Be careful."

Chen Xing nodded hurriedly in agreement, and Sima Wei shot him another confused look. "They said it'll take at least three to five days," Chen Xing told him. "Let's go."

With that, Chen Xing took the lead and guided Sima Wei through the market under the watchful eyes of the crowd. Chen Xing was secretly delighted. He knew that Sima Wei was suspicious, though, so he had to think of something to divert his attention.

Thinking quickly, he pointed at some goods in the marketplace. "Do you want to buy some rouge?"

Sima Wei stared at him.

"They're starting to get suspicious of you because, well, your face is blue."

Sima Wei did not respond.

"Just a bit of rouge," Chen Xing insisted. "It'll cover it up. Got any money? Let's spend a little." Even as he spoke, he was planning his next move. If the city guards showed up to rescue him, he could easily feign innocence and claim that the onlookers had simply been concerned about Sima Wei's strange complexion.

But Sima Wei hadn't expected to spend money on their journey. He was penniless.

"You can pawn your armor," Chen Xing told him. "I bet just that helmet would be worth a fortune."

"You want to pawn my armor?"

"What else are we supposed to do? Taking a boat will cost money, and we need food and clothes too. Maybe you don't need to eat, but I still have to."

It worked! Sima Wei was duped into pawning his helmet for a sum of money, and they managed to check into an inn. As they left the pawnshop, Chen Xing noticed a few crows flying away from the shop entrance, a sight that felt oddly familiar. Could those have been the same crows they'd seen on the road?

He shrugged it off. All crows looked the same anyway. It was probably just a coincidence.

A bolt of lightning split the sky, followed by a deafening clap of thunder and a sudden downpour that sent the people in the streets scurrying for shelter.

Once they were inside the inn, Chen Xing didn't pay Sima Wei much mind. He quickly instructed the innkeeper to prepare hot water so he could bathe. After a refreshing bath and changing into clean clothes, he felt much better.

"I'll help you cover up a little," Chen Xing said, glancing at Sima Wei and preparing to apply makeup to mask his deathly pallor.

Sima Wei closed and shaded all the windows in the room. Just as Chen Xing was about to approach with some powder, Sima Wei suddenly grabbed his wrist.

"Exorcist, save me," Sima Wei said in a barely audible whisper.

Chen Xing's eyes went wide and he almost dropped the rouge plate. Suddenly, he realized something, and he looked up at the huge ceiling beam overhead, hearing the pitter-patter of rain hitting the tiles.

"Shi Hai dispatched the jackdaws to watch our every move," Sima Wei whispered. "I must take you to Huanmo Palace. I have no other choice."

"You...you...Sima Wei?"

"There's no time for explanations. Can you use the Heart Lamp to sever Shi Hai's control over me?"

"I don't know," Chen Xing mumbled, reeling. "You were Prince Yin of Chu when you were alive, right? Hold on, you've been dead for nearly a hundred years. Why haven't you entered samsara?"

*Crack!* There was another explosion of thunder, and a flash of white light seeped through a sliver in the window cover.

Sima Wei stood up and paced the room, his voice betraying a hint of confusion. "I don't know who I am anymore," he muttered. "I only remember fragments from my past life, memories from different people. Most of them belong to Sima Wei, but I...I...I just know I'm different from them."

"Them? How many of the Eight Princes have been revived?" Chen Xing had already encountered Sima Lun in Chang'an and Sima Yue in the north, making Sima Wei the third drought fiend king he had encountered.

"Six. Shi Hai wants to capture you and use resentment to refine the Heart Lamp artifact within you. He intends to turn it into the eye of the Ten Thousand Spirits Array as a sacrifice to the Demon God."

"What is this Ten Thousand Spirits Array?"

"There are seven in total," Sima Wei explained. "I've overheard bits and pieces from their conversations. Each array is powered by magical artifacts that absorb resentment. When all seven are activated, the Demon God will be reborn. Shi Hai revived the Eight Princes to guard the arrays for him."

Chen Xing went quiet.

"The Yin Yang Mirror and Zheng Drum are part of Shi Hai's plans, and you already possess both of them. As for the Ten Thousand Spirits Arrays, all I know is that one of them is in Chang'an."

Chen Xing jumped to his next question. "What about the other magical artifacts?"

Sima Wei shook his head. Evidently, not even he had much inside information.

"Where is Shi Hai hiding?" Chen Xing tried. Again, Sima Wei shook his head. "What can I do for you?"

"Can you kill him? If you kill him, I'll be liberated."

Chen Xing didn't even know what kind of yao Shi Hai was, let alone where he was hiding. Killing him would be easier said than done. "Shi Hai asked you to take me back to the Central Plains, so wouldn't he have arranged for a meeting place?"

Sima Wei glanced up at the ceiling. "The jackdaws are always watching me. Once we enter the Central Plains, Shi Hai will send someone to meet us."

Chen Xing raised his hand. He needed a moment to think. Ten Thousand Spirits Array, Shi Hai, Demon God, magical artifacts... His mind was swirling.

"We are now far from Shi Hai, and his control over me has weakened with distance," Sima Wei said. "You need to find a way to free me."

"And then what? What do you plan to do once you're free?"

"I don't know," Sima Wei murmured. "I just don't want to be enslaved by him anymore."

His words cut straight to the core of the matter. In that instant, Chen Xing understood everything.

"I... I can try," Chen Xing said, "but I'm not sure if I can do it. Without the support of the Spiritual Qi of the Heavens and Earth, the Heart Lamp's powers are limited."

Up on the roof, the jackdaws cawed.

"He's getting suspicious." Sima Wei got up and pulled the windows open. Torrential rain soaked the windowsill, and they both stopped talking. The rain was getting heavier and heavier, creating shining white curtains of water everywhere.

Chen Xing moved to look out the window, but Sima Wei waved him back, staying in the shadows himself. The jackdaws were perched on the eaves, watching them.

"Let me go," Chen Xing mouthed to Sima Wei.

Sima Wei didn't reply. The look he gave Chen Xing was opaque; what he was thinking was anyone's guess.

Somewhere outside, in the beating of rain, Chen Xing could faintly hear the sound of weapons clashing. He closed his eyes, contemplating how the pieces of this puzzle were connected, when suddenly the Heart Lamp flickered in the darkness.

Sima Wei was watching Chen Xing in silence, and a thought crossed Chen Xing's mind: Should he seize this opportunity? He had never tried injecting the Heart Lamp's power into a drought fiend king, or even a regular living corpse. Would it dispel the resentment within them? And if it did, would the effect be to cut off Shi Hai's control over and surveillance of them, or would it simply reduce their bodies to ashes?

A ball of gentle light appeared in Chen Xing's hand, and he raised it slightly. Sima Wei immediately turned to face him, putting his hand to his weapon as if instinctively afraid of the light. He managed to control himself, however, and he did not draw his sword against Chen Xing.

Chen Xing took a deep breath, and then—

—a loud crash echoed as Xiang Shu burst through the wall from the neighboring room, sword and all!

"Duck!" Xiang Shu shouted. "Heart Lamp!"

Outside, the jackdaws screeched frantically. Sima Wei drew his sword.

Chen Xing withdrew his Heart Lamp and ducked just in time; Xiang Shu's sword swept past Chen Xing's back, aiming straight for Sima Wei. The blow struck Sima Wei, unarmored, directly in the chest, and it caved in his torso with a muffled thud. He went tumbling and flailing out the window and crashed through the roof of a nearby house, where debris cascaded down around him.

Chen Xing looked up to meet Xiang Shu's gaze. Xiang Shu was dressed in hunting gear, looking wild and drenched, his eyes bloodshot from exhaustion. He'd been chasing them for nearly ten days. Without checking the window, he grabbed Chen Xing with his left arm, retreated, and with a powerful jump off the bed, smashed through the roof and leaped out!

Torrential rain bucketed down as if a hole had opened up in the sky. Chen Xing was immediately soaked, and his feet kept slipping as Xiang Shu pulled him along. The jackdaws unfurled their wings and took off, but they were sluggish in the downpour. All around them, Chen Xing heard the sounds of crossbows—Goryeo had sent warriors to provide cover for their escape.

"When did you arrive?!" Chen Xing shouted.

"Just now!" Xiang Shu shouted back. As Chen Xing turned around, he saw a gray shadow fly swiftly over from the neighboring house's ruined roof, brandishing a long knife. In his gray robe, Sima Wei surged forward with such force that he kicked the tiles beneath him up and sent them spinning.

Xiang Shu pulled Chen Xing close, and together they slid down from the edge of the inn's roof. A deluge of arrows rained down around them, blocking Sima Wei's path.

"Watch out for the crows," Chen Xing said.

"Can you run?!" Xiang Shu shouted.

"I can! I can!"

Even soaked to the skin, Chen Xing was overjoyed: *You came! I knew you would!* As he grasped Xiang Shu's hand, all his worries vanished, and he hurried to keep up with him in the rain.

Xiang Shu glanced back at the approaching Sima Wei and realized that ordinary archers were no match for him. They needed to draw him to a less crowded area.

"I can't run anymore!" Chen Xing gasped. "I think it'd be better to just carry me!"

Xiang Shu shot him a disbelieving look.

Sima Wei let out a fierce shout as he slid down from the rooftop, gripping his sword tightly with both hands. He took a shortcut through the alley, but more Goguryeo warriors rushed in, blocking the alleyway. "Run! Hurry!" one of them shouted to Xiang Shu and Chen Xing. Chen Xing was touched.

Xiang Shu had saved Chen Xing, so he didn't bother to continue fighting Sima Wei. He dashed out of the alley with Chen Xing in tow, and a large group of cavalrymen appeared in front of them. Chen Xing gasped, thinking they were enemies, but the armor-clad leader pointed to the left, showing them an escape route. The cavalrymen then brandished their weapons and prepared to charge into the alley.

"How did you know I was captured?" Chen Xing asked Xiang Shu. "I thought you wouldn't come!"

"You're going to be the death of me!" yelled Xiang Shu, wiping water off his face, but a booming thunderclap drowned out his last few words.

Chen Xing smiled. "What?" he said. "What did you say?"

"My throat hurts! I'm not talking to you!"

They raced across the long street under rain that came down on them like a waterfall. Suddenly, the view opened up to reveal a flat dock that stretched for several miles. A ship was just lifting anchor, unfurling its sails and trying to force its way out to sea through the storm.

Xiang Shu looked back.

"Who was that just now?" Chen Xing asked. "You know him?"

"The king of Goguryeo," Xiang Shu answered casually, shouldering his sword and lifting Chen Xing into his arms in one fluid motion.

Dragging his soaked robe, Sima Wei leaped through the alley toward the dock, bursting forth like a water balloon and splashing gleaming droplets everywhere. Each surge of speed created a powerful gust of wind, and each time he landed on a brick wall, it crumbled with a thunderous crash and sent debris flying in all directions. He swung his sword and shot toward Xiang Shu and Chen Xing.

Xiang Shu made a few quick strides with Chen Xing in his arms, and he stepped onto a wooden crate on the dock. The ship was about thirty feet away, but with a mighty leap that smashed the crate beneath Xiang Shu's feet, they soared toward it!

The very second they left the ground, Sima Wei swung down with incredible force, and the shockwave from his strike sent bricks flying. But Xiang Shu was flying through the air with Chen Xing, and Sima Wei didn't manage to hit them. Xiang Shu and Chen Xing somersaulted in midair and tumbled onto the deck, sliding nearly ten feet and startling the ship's crew, who all pulled back to stare at them.

Dazed and seeing stars, Chen Xing struggled to rise. Xiang Shu had to prop himself on his sword just to sit up. He gasped for breath, his entire body drenched from head to toe. Back at the dock, Sima Wei leaped onto the highest roof, watching them sail away.

Xiang Shu slowly got to his feet. Chen Xing, huffing, slipped on the deck as he went to the ship's side and looked back at Sima Wei. "He finally stopped chasing us," he panted.

The Goguryeo warriors had surrounded the building where Sima Wei was perched. He stood ramrod straight, grasping the hilt of his sword with his left hand, and swept his right arm across, summoning a fierce wind and a surge of resentment that shot skyward.

The large ship was nearly fifty paces away from Sima Wei. The crew aimed their formidable crossbows at him, but Sima Wei remained unfazed. The resentment swirling around his sword formed a crescent-shaped black arc. It gathered immense, terrifying power as he swung his sword in a circle, preparing to unleash a devastating strike that could cleave the ship in two.

Another bolt of lightning flashed across the sky, illuminating the terrified expressions of everyone at and beyond the dock. Xiang Shu raised his sword. "Give me all of your mana," he said in a deep voice.

"No, no, no! We'll die! Don't mess around! This ship will fall apart!" If Sima Wei struck with his sword, Xiang Shu would struggle to withstand the force—and worse, the raging waves would either destroy or capsize the ship! "Don't do anything reckless! Sui Xing, save me, anything will do—"

Sima Wei lifted his long sword into the air, but just as he was about to unleash a devastating strike, a flash of lightning lit up the sky.

*Boom!* Thunder roared as the bolt of lightning struck straight down, drawn by the high point created by Sima Wei's raised sword. In an instant, the entire building shattered under him, and Sima Wei was thrown backward, his body charred black by the electric shock. The resentment he'd gathered exploded outward and disappeared without a trace.

"Ah, just in time!" Chen Xing murmured. "Perfect! Didn't I tell you not to do anything reckless? Now look, you just got struck by lightning."

With that, the last of his strength abandoned him, and he slid down from the ship's railing until he was sitting on the deck.

**47**

AN HOUR later, Xiang Shu and Chen Xing were like two people who had just been fished out of the water. The captain said a lot of things, gesticulating wildly, and Chen Xing nodded continuously. Xiang Shu sat on the ground beside the captain's cabin, leaning against a wooden wall as he listened with his eyes closed.

They were on a trading ship heading south from Goguryeo toward Jiangnan. Along the way, they would make a stop at Shangyu and then head north, passing by Jiankang and Jiaozhou before eventually returning to Pyongyang. Departing, the ship was full of ginseng, leather goods, and other such items, and it would bring back tea, silk, and porcelain from the south when it returned to Pyongyang. The captain was a Han, and in all his long life, he'd never seen a monster like Sima Wei.

After grilling the captain with questions, Chen Xing rambled incoherently about some folk legends; he said that he was an exorcist while Xiang Shu was his protector, and that the two of them were companions who went around capturing yao for the people's sake. They'd met that yao on Mount Paektu and then been chased all the way here, blah blah blah. Fortunately, he was able to please the heavens during a critical situation and summon a divine lightning bolt from above...

Xiang Shu couldn't bear to listen to any more of this. "Save your energy. Aren't you tired?!"

As Chen Xing spoke, he took out the money he'd gotten from pawning Sima Wei's helmet and handed it to the captain. "That's basically what happened. Here's some money for the boat as a humble gesture of our goodwill. Please let us ride on your ship."

The captain quickly refused. "You're exterminating evil on behalf of the people; I won't accept it! I can't accept it! If it isn't too much trouble, please stay on my boat for a few days."

What people at sea feared most were storms and the yao of the legends. With an exorcist on board who could summon divine lightning, their journey was sure to be smooth sailing. The captain couldn't have been happier, and he promptly arranged a clean room for the two of them to rest in.

The ship was carrying a lot of goods, and there were also several Pyongyang scholars on board who were heading south to study. The captain gave Xiang Shu and Chen Xing the best room he had available, with windows and only one bed. He even got people to prepare a stove for the two of them to warm themselves with. Chen Xing was more than satisfied.

The captain explained that this was their first southward voyage of the year, which meant a lot to him. Even in a storm, they had to set sail. The wind and waves were rougher today, sure, but they would be fine once they left the shadow of the rainstorm and reached the open sea.

Chen Xing had been soaking in the rain for half a day, and both his outer robes and inner wear were thoroughly drenched. He was sneezing incessantly when he entered the cabin.

"How did you know I was captured?" he asked Chen Xing.

"I didn't know you were captured," Xiang Shu said indifferently.

Chen Xing frowned. "Then why did you—"

"I thought you'd run off by yourself again. I came after you so that I could give you a good smack!"

Chen Xing was dumbfounded. Xiang Shu bolted the door to lock it, then started taking his clothes off while motioning to Chen Xing.

"Take it off." Xiang Shu stared at Chen Xing as if he didn't know him. "What are you doing just standing there?"

Chen Xing was suddenly feeling a little shy. He took off his clothes and threw them to Xiang Shu, then dove into the bed stark naked and covered himself with the blanket. Xiang Shu didn't try to hide from him; he just stripped naked too and then wrapped a towel around his waist. He rolled up the clothes, placed them in a basket, and pushed them out the door. He placed some money inside and instructed the crew to wash, starch, and dry them and send them back tomorrow.

With their clothes gone, the two of them were left to face each other openly in the room for the rest of the day.

"Xiang Shu?" Chen Xing asked.

Xiang Shu was finishing up his bath in the adjacent compartment. Once he was done, he motioned for Chen Xing to go wash up too.

In the compartment, Chen Xing cheered. "There's hot water?! This is great!"

When Chen Xing came out, he saw that the captain had sent over some hot food—fish and shrimp stewed in a bowl with a little soy sauce and meat—and a vat of shaojiu. Apparently, the captain had ordered it in the mess hall for them. Xiang Shu was just sitting there, crotch covered with a cloth, and pouring a drink for himself.

Once he'd had his fill of food and drink, Chen Xing finally started to feel better.

The time came to get into bed, and he shrank into the inner side; for some reason, his heart was pounding wildly. It was neither the first time he'd been naked in front of Xiang Shu nor the first time they'd shared a bed, but for some reason, this time he was embarrassed. Xiang Shu, not yet in bed, glanced at Chen Xing, looking as if he might be sharing a bit of Chen Xing's hesitance.

"Ready to sleep?" Chen Xing moved back toward the wall again. "Come rest for a while."

Even if everything went smoothly, it would take at least half a month for the ship to reach Shangyu on its way to Jiangnan. For all that time, he and Xiang Shu would have to share a room. Wait, but... in Chi Le Chuan, they had eaten and lived in the same place too. Why did Chen Xing feel weird about it now when he hadn't back then? Was it because now they had to sleep in the same bed?

For some reason, the mood in the room was becoming a little strange.

Xiang Shu removed the cloth and got into bed, under the same blanket as Chen Xing. Chen Xing accidentally touched Xiang Shu's skin and brushed against him slightly. Xiang Shu was scorching hot. Chen Xing's heart pounded, and he pulled back a little. Seeming to sense the awkwardness, Xiang Shu lay down slowly and tried his best to keep them from touching again.

But the bed was small and very narrow, and the ship swayed slightly in the rough water. Under the blanket, Chen Xing did his best to stay pressed up against the wall, while Xiang Shu braced one foot against the footboard to stabilize himself so as not to crush him.

Covertly, Chen Xing changed his posture to hide his body's reaction to the proximity. Right here, right now, between the burning heat of their bodies under the blanket and the fleeting sensation of their naked bodies having touched, Chen Xing's imagination was running wild. He decided to start a conversation to distract himself. "I..."

"What?" Naturally, Xiang Shu's voice sounded a little awkward.

Chen Xing turned his head and looked at Xiang Shu, whose eyes were open and staring at the ceiling. "You must be tired."

"I'm alright."

The ship swayed gently in the waves. The windows didn't close very tightly, and a cold wind was leaking into the cabin. It was early spring and the ice floes were only starting to melt, so the weather was frigid. Chen Xing shrank under the blanket, shivering.

He remembered then. After their reunion, everything had seemed so natural to him that he'd forgotten to ask Xiang Shu about Karakorum and Chi Le Chuan. "When are you going back?"

Xiang Shu didn't reply.

*It's my fault again,* Chen Xing thought. *I made you rush thousands of miles here just to save me. Once the ship heads south, you won't know when you can go back again.*

"Did you...tell your tribesmen?" he tried.

"What?" Xiang Shu asked coolly.

"About coming to save me."

"No."

"What about Xiao Shan?"

"I sent him back. But I don't know whether the Xiongnu can handle him."

"You'll be heading to the south with me, then?"

Xiang Shu turned his body slightly and adjusted his posture. "It depends."

Chen Xing fell silent for a moment. "I didn't mean it when I said all that to the captain earlier," he said. "Don't worry about it."

Xiang Shu shot Chen Xing a confused glance, which only deepened when he realized what Chen Xing meant—that Chen Xing was worried he had angered Xiang Shu by introducing Xiang Shu as his protector.

"And thank you." Chen Xing smiled. "I don't know what you think of me, but I really thought you wouldn't come find me this time."

"Why? Is that how you see me?"

Chen Xing rushed to explain. "You're *the* Great Chanyu. You have your responsibilities, so I couldn't have blamed you for going back. Xiang Shu, what I want to say is, if you don't mind..."

Xiang Shu frowned a little as Chen Xing mustered up the courage to finally say what was on his mind. Yes, Xiang Shu had rejected him once, but they were on more familiar terms now. And he and Xiang Shu shared a goal, so...

"I promise...it won't take too long," Chen Xing said with slight apprehension. "Would you...accompany me for a bit longer? I won't say anything about you being a protector or whatnot. I just know that, relying on myself alone, I probably won't be able to..."

"Ever since I was a child," Xiang Shu said, suddenly turning his head away from Chen Xing, "I knew that, one day, I would become the Great Chanyu of the Sixteen Hu."

Chen Xing stared at Xiang Shu, transfixed. His nose bridge, lips, and the contours of his profile were all exquisite, but not pretty in the way that came from cosmetics. Instead, he had a kind of masculine allure.

Xiang Shu's brow furrowed a little. "After my father passed away, I shouldered the burden of the Great Chanyu. My tribesmen's affairs were my affairs, and their struggles were my struggles."

"Yes, that's why I know that you'll have to return someday. Even if you're willing to help me, I can't hog—"

"Then one day," Xiang Shu continued, "you came to find me and told me that you needed a protector, and that I was that protector. And so my burden expanded from being responsible for Chi Le Chuan to being responsible for the whole world."

"I don't want it either," Chen Xing said helplessly, "but—"

"But through all of this, no one ever asked me what *I* wanted to do."

Chen Xing couldn't respond.

"Never," Xiang Shu said seriously. "They never asked me, 'Shulü Kong, are you willing to become the Great Chanyu?' Nor did you ever ask me if I was willing to be your protector."

Xiang Shu frowned again and turned his head sideways to look at Chen Xing. He seemed to be trying to find an answer in Chen Xing's expression. Perhaps he found one, because his furrowed brow relaxed, and he raised one gentle eyebrow at Chen Xing.

"I understand now, Xiang Shu." Chen Xing suddenly smiled. "So that's what it was. You thought I didn't respect you. That's my fault. At the time...I really wasn't thinking much about that."

"I'm different from you. You want to be an exorcist—"

It was Chen Xing's turn to interrupt. "Of course I don't. If I could choose, I think...I wouldn't become an exorcist so readily. I admit, in the beginning, I didn't think about whether I was respecting your wishes, but I'd like to explain myself too. I'm the same; there are a lot of things that I do because I have no other choice."

"Then why do you want to become an exorcist now?" Xiang Shu asked, sounding puzzled. "Can't you be your own person?"

"I do. I want to be myself. I often ask, 'Why me?'" Chen Xing recalled the first time he'd tried to control the Yin Yang Mirror, the voice he heard in his heart then. "But when he was alive, my father often said, 'Only a few people in this world can do whatever they wish.' In this life, those who can follow their hearts and do what they wish are blessed, but a significant portion of the population lives in accordance with the Mandate of Heaven. That includes the burdens they must bear. It's unfair, yes, but from another perspective...aren't these the expectations that the heavens have for each and every one of us?"

"Expectations?" Xiang Shu said disapprovingly. "It's mere resignation."

At last, Chen Xing understood why Xiang Shu had refused to be his protector when they first met. It came as a relief. "We're just resigning ourselves to the will of the heavens, so to speak."

The ship swayed with the waves. The rain seemed to have stopped, and now they could only hear waves crashing against the ship, one after another. For a while, Chen Xing and Xiang Shu lay quietly beside each other, not speaking.

"What do you want to do, then?" Chen Xing asked eventually. He felt like he had a new understanding of Xiang Shu, and their conversation had become peaceful; it was a peace that came from deep within their hearts. Having shed the trappings of the outside world, they looked at each other as equals, eager to understand.

"Sometimes, I want my mother and my father to come back to life. So that we could live outside the Great Wall just like before." When Chen Xing glanced at him, Xiang Shu's eyes were closed. "But things don't always happen the way you want. They're dead, and so is my anda. Everyone's gone... It's just like the banquet we hold during the Autumn Close Festival. Everyone finishes drinking and says goodbye, then goes where they should go. What I want is simple to say but impossible to achieve: I just want this banquet to never end."

Xiang Shu lay there for a while, lost in thought about the day he bid farewell to his tribesmen in Karakorum. He didn't tell Chen Xing anything else.

To an outsider, their conversation may have appeared inconsequential, but for Chen Xing, it seemed to mark the beginning of another stage of his life—his life that was rapidly running out. It was like their relationship was a ship that had escaped the storm and finally sailed onto calm and tranquil waters.

As the ship they were actually on rocked in the waves, he sang softly. "Those who knew me said I was sorrowful at heart. Those who did not know me said I was pursuing something. O distant, azure heavens, by whose hand was this brought about?"

"What about you?" Xiang Shu asked, and Chen Xing hesitated.

"Perhaps...I want to explore the Divine Land? Go to places I've read about in books but never had the chance to visit." As he spoke, the future Chen Xing imagined seemed to become clearer. "After I've visited all the mountains, rivers, and seas, I'll return to Jiangnan and find a picturesque place to stay. I'll plant wisteria flowers in my yard, and when the flowers bloom"—he smiled sadly—"I'll read books under the trellises. Do you like that? If it ever becomes possible, you're welcome to come visit my house. It would be okay if you wanted to stay too, instead of leaving again. If it's possible, yes... As long as it's possible."

Chen Xing raised his hand, emitting the faint light of the Heart Lamp from his palm. Under the blanket, he pressed it gently against Xiang Shu's bare chest. The Heart Lamp's strength seemed to resonate with Xiang Shu's strong, steady heartbeat, and a bright light penetrated through the blanket.

"Xiang Shu," he said, "I'd like to ask you this once more, properly this time."

Xiang Shu was still staring at Chen Xing.

"Before the future comes, will you join me for a while? I need you. I know now that you don't want your life to be dictated by responsibility. I just want to ask: If you had the chance to choose again, would you..."

"I'll consider it," Xiang Shu said.

Chen Xing smiled. He knew that meant that Xiang Shu agreed.

The storm receded, and strong winds set the ship off at full sail through the silver-white seas. A bright moon illuminated the world outside.

In the tranquility, Chen Xing whispered to Xiang Shu. "Sometimes, I feel like all this 'responsibility' just means that there's someone out there who needs you. Whether it's the Divine Land, the earth, the common people, or all living things, it's the sort of need that will never offer any repayment, but we'll still do whatever we can to fulfill those expectations, just like any other person would if they had someone who needed them. That's a pretty good feeling, right?"

Xiang Shu didn't reply. Chen Xing curled up under the blanket, and after a long while, he assumed that Xiang Shu had fallen asleep. But then Xiang Shu asked him, "Are you cold?"

"Nope," Chen Xing said, although the blanket on his side was slightly damp and he kept shivering.

"Come closer."

Chen Xing shifted over toward Xiang Shu's side and instantly felt warmer. Then a wave hit and the ship tilted a little, pushing Chen Xing into Xiang Shu's embrace. Xiang Shu withdrew his feet from the footboard and wrapped his arms around Chen Xing.

Chen Xing's breathing sped up; he was pressed against Xiang Shu now, held in his arms. He held his lower body away so as not to make things awkward for the both of them, but waves kept crashing, and each time, they pushed him toward Xiang Shu. Chen Xing raised his hand, wanting to stabilize his body, but he didn't have anything to brace it against. After a while, he just put it on Xiang Shu's shoulder and hugged him around his neck. The two of them were now stuck to each other.

"I understand," Xiang Shu said at last.

Chen Xing didn't hear him; he'd dropped off to sleep. Xiang Shu's body was warm, and in his sleep, he just wanted to burrow closer to him. But all night, Xiang Shu squirmed around restlessly, fidgety, as if Chen Xing was tormenting him. He kept waking up. Eventually, though, he stopped caring; he let go of his reservations and embraced Chen Xing.

The next morning, when Chen Xing woke up, he saw that his clothes were folded neatly next to the pillow and he was covered with a new blanket. He blinked, confused. Yes, the blanket had definitely been changed; the bed looked obviously different than it had the previous day.

"Xiang Shu?" Chen Xing called. "Xiang Shu? Where is he?"

After he had breakfast, Chen Xing found Xiang Shu on the deck. Xiang Shu had changed into his clothes and was sitting with the captain, having tea. A sea breeze blew across the deck, and the sun shone bright in the sky.

"Why did the blanket—"

"I don't know!" Xiang Shu snapped.

"Wow!"

Chen Xing stood before the mast and faced the vast sea. Xiang Shu nodded to the captain, then brought Chen Xing back to the cabin with him. He threw a bundle at Chen Xing for him to look at, then left again.

Inside were the two magical artifacts that Xiang Shu had brought along with him from Karakorum—the Yin Yang Mirror and the Zheng Drum—as well as the Four Ruler's Seals, the items that the Akele king had given them as payment for medical services. Seeing the seals made Chen Xing rather upset; he missed their owner. He inspected them and carefully tucked them away, then looked at another bundle that Xiang Shu had packed in a hurry. This one contained a Qiang flute and a long, narrow, unlocked box. He opened up the box to find two pieces of sheepskin scrolls that were rolled up together and tied with what appeared to be a woolen rope. The scrolls seemed old, suffused with a light purple color.

*Is this the Great Chanyu's Purple Scroll? The one Fu Jian yearned for?* Chen Xing looked the scroll over, thinking about the interpretation of the words "Purple Scroll of Golden Conferment," and decided that it probably wasn't the famed Purple Scroll, since the sheepskin didn't have blood on it. Still, he restrained his curiosity and elected not to rummage through Xiang Shu's belongings. He closed the box and put it back just as Xiang Shu returned.

"What do we do when we reach Shangyu?" Xiang Shu asked.

"We go to Jiankang and find my shifu's friend. Do you remember the two other pictures in Zhang Liu's book?"

Xiang Shu took something out and showed it to Chen Xing. Back in Chi Le Chuan, he had re-drawn all three pictures.

There were many capable people in the south. After the large-scale southward migration, a great many ancient texts were preserved. Many exorcist families had, of course, abandoned the profession after the Silence of All Magic and become either scholars or farmers, but they still retained a bit of knowledge about the past. Chen Xing's first priority was to warn Xie An;[15] then he would gather the former exorcists to discuss countermeasures and search for the whereabouts of the Dinghai Pearl.

Xiang Shu saw Chen Xing writing another letter, as he had been doing for the past few days in the cabin. "What are you writing?"

"Visitation cards. I'll get someone to deliver them to the post station so they can send them to Jiankang. My father used to have lots of students, all of whom were my seniors, and after the southward migration, they all submitted to the Great Jin. We might be able to seek refuge with them for the time being. At least that way, we'll have a place to stay in the city."

"Right, I forgot your father was a great scholar. Naturally, when you return to the south, you'll resume your glory as the scion of a prestigious family."

Chen Xing heard the ridicule in his tone and retorted, "No, no, you flatter me; compared to the prestige of the Great Chanyu, this is nothing! What else can we do? We've spent all the money we have. Do you want to go cold and hungry after we get off the ship?"

"There must be a few more Yuwen Xins waiting in Jiankang."

"You...!" Chen Xing really wanted to throw his brush.

Chen Xing really didn't have the heart to keep writing anymore after that little exchange, but he forced himself to write down his itinerary, seal the cards, and pay the little bit of money he had left to get someone to deliver them ashore and take them to the Ministry of Personnel in Jiankang.

---

15  Xie An is a real historical figure who served as prime minister in the Eastern Jin Empire in the fourth century AD. He was highly acclaimed for his leadership during the empire's conflict with the Qin.

If a letter had been received, then logically, a post station employee should have come to deliver a reply, but along their journey, no one approached him. Well, people changed, he thought; he had to accept fate. He would think of a way to get some money once they reached Jiankang.

As the ship sailed south, the weather gradually warmed up. The spring skies were clear, and people became lazier as they approached Jiangnan. Chen Xing just slept in the cabin all day, tossing and turning in bed. Sometimes, Xiang Shu played chess with the captain on deck; other times, he disembarked to buy books when they docked and then read them on the journey to kill time.

Nearly ten days later, the ship sailed smoothly into the Yangtze River and headed along the canal toward Jiankang. The next morning, they reached Jiankang City, half a day ahead of schedule. Chen Xing was still in bed. From outside, he heard the faint sounds of music, followed by the shouting of the ship's crew.

"Coming! Coming!" a boatman said.

Chen Xing turned over. *I thought we weren't getting there until tonight? We reached Jiankang so soon?*

Xiang Shu pushed the door open and entered the room, having already packed his things. He studied Chen Xing impatiently. Chen Xing sat up, wild-haired, and scratched his head as he looked at Xiang Shu.

"Someone here to pick you up at the dock," Xiang Shu said.

Chen Xing perked up. "Who? Who came to pick me up?" He ran out onto the deck.

The ship had arrived at the dock, where it was greeted by peach blossoms and willow trees; the entire city was lush with gorgeous flowers. Thousands of vermilion eaves and tiles shone with a clean luster.

Mount Zhong towered overhead with the grandeur of a coiling dragon, crouching stone tigers standing ready at its base, and a misty drizzle fell over the Huai River, which was thousands of miles long. In the distance stood the Taichu and Zhaoming Palaces, reflected in the mirror of the Xuanwu Lake like celestial palaces enveloped in mist.

Jiangkang City—the greatest capital in the world. After countless trials and hardships, millions of people now called the city home. This was the fluorishing center of Han culture, and of civilization in the Divine Land.

Some distance away, nearly fifty scholars were lined up, each holding an umbrella. Somewhere high above, as the music played, a gentleman dressed in a robe with wide sleeves walked over as if he were riding the wind.

"Upon my leaving, wept the willow," someone sang on the bank. "Upon my return, swept the rain and snow..."

The hair at the man's temples was frosty white; he looked to be about forty years old. He wore the black muslin of an official over a snow-white scholar's robe. His face was fair as jade, and when he smiled it was like being bathed in a spring breeze. His manners were refined, and he wore wooden clogs, fox teeth around his neck, and a jade plaque that dangled from his waist, swaying with his confident gait. He held a jade flute, and his belt fluttered in the wind.

"A friend has come from afar," Xie An announced loudly. "Would you like to have a meal? Xiao-Shidi, this way, please."

THE STORY CONTINUES IN
*Dinghai Fusheng Records*
VOLUME 3

# CHARACTER GUIDE & GLOSSARY

# Characters

**CHEN XING 陈星:** The last exorcist, tasked by his shifu with a quest to restore magic to the world before catastrophe strikes. He has uncommonly good luck, but it will run out in four years, when he is twenty years old.

**XIANG SHU 项述:** Also known as Shulü Kong (述律空), Xiang Shu is the man Chen Xing's heart lamp has designated his Protector Martial God, but he wants nothing to do with it.

## THE ANCIENT CHI LE COVENANT

**CHE LUOFENG 车罗风:** Xiang Shu's sworn brother, the leader of the Rouran tribe.

**KING AKELE:** Leader of the Akele tribe. Lost his son in battle against the Rouran.

**YOUDUO 由多:** King Akele's son. He and Zhou Zhen killed each other in battle.

**ZHOU ZHEN 周甄:** A deceased Rouran warrior who was Che Luofeng's lover in life.

**XIANG YUYAN 项语嫣:** Xiang Shu's deceased mother, a Han woman who came to live at Chi Le Chuan twenty-two years ago.

## GREAT QIN

**FENG QIANJUN 冯千钧:** A skilled swordsman who accompanies Chen Xing and Xiang Shu.

**FENG QIANYI 冯千镒:** Feng Qianjun's older brother. Their family owns Xifeng Bank.

**FU JIAN 符坚:** The Emperor of Qin and the leader of the Five Hu.

**TUOBA YAN 拓跋焱:** The young commander of the imperial guards. Very fond of Chen Xing.

## OTHER

**XIAO SHAN 肖山:** A young boy raised by wolves who Lu Ying entrusted to Chen Xing's care.

**LU YING 陆影:** A once-powerful yao, the Deer God who guards Carosha.

**SIMA YUE 司馬越:** One of the eight princes who died during the War of the Eight Princes, now resurrected as a drought fiend.

**SIMA WEI 司马玮:** Another prince resurrected as a drought fiend; Sima Wei seems to have a will of his own, unlike the other undead generals.

**KJERA 克耶拉:** The mysterious man who transformed Xiang Shu's father into a living corpse.

**CHIYOU 蚩尤:** The Demon God and God of War. His blood is what causes mortals to transform into the living dead.

# Name Guide

## Diminutives, Nicknames, and Name Tags:

**A-:** Friendly diminutive. Always a prefix. Usually for monosyllabic names, or one syllable out of a two-syllable name.

**DOUBLING:** Doubling a syllable of a person's name can be a nickname, e.g., "Mangmang"; it has childish or cutesy connotations.

**DA-:** A prefix meaning big/older.

**XIAO-:** A diminutive meaning "little." Always a prefix.

**-ER:** An affectionate diminutive added to names, literally "son" or "child." Always a suffix. Can sometimes be a fixed part of a person's name, rather than just an affectionate suffix.


**DI/DIDI:** Younger brother or a younger male friend.

**GE/GEGE/DAGE:** Older brother or an older male friend.

**JIE/JIEJIE:** Older sister or an older female friend.

**SHIFU:** Master; teacher.

**SHIXIONG:** Older martial brother. Usually implies that they studied under the same shifu.

**SHIDI:** Younger martial brother. Usually implies that they studied under the same shifu.

**DAREN:** Similar to "milord," a way of respectfully addressing someone who is either an aristocrat or a government official of medium or higher rank.

**XIANDI:** A respectful term of address for a younger man the speaker isn't particularly close to. It is archaic in modern Chinese.

# PRONUNCIATION GUIDE

Mandarin Chinese is the official state language of mainland China, and pinyin is the official system of romanization in which it is written. As Mandarin is a tonal language, pinyin uses diacritical marks (e.g., ā, á, ǎ, à) to indicate these tonal inflections. Most words use one of four tones, though some are a neutral tone. Furthermore, regional variance can change the way native Chinese speakers pronounce the same word. For those reasons and more, please consider the guide below a simplified introduction to pronunciation.

More resources are available at sevenseasdanmei.com

## NOTE ON SPELLING

Romanized Mandarin Chinese words with identical spelling in pinyin—and even pronunciation—may well have different meanings. These words are more easily differentiated in written Chinese, which uses logographic characters.

## GENERAL CONSONANTS

Some Mandarin Chinese consonants sound very similar, such as z/c/s and zh/ch/sh. Audio samples will provide the best opportunity to learn the difference between them.

X: somewhere between the **sh** in **sh**eep and **s** in **s**ilk

Q: a very aspirated **ch** as in **ch**arm

C: **ts** as in pan**ts**

Z: **z** as in **z**oom

S: **s** as in **s**ilk

CH: **ch** as in **ch**arm

ZH: **dg** as in do**dg**e

SH: **sh** as in **sh**ave

G: hard **g** as in **g**raphic

## GENERAL VOWELS

The pronunciation of a vowel may depend on its preceding consonant. For example, the "i" in "shi" is distinct from the "i" in "di." Vowel pronunciation may also change depending on where the vowel appears in a word, for example the "i" in "shi" versus the "i" in "ting." Finally, compound vowels are often—though not always—pronounced as conjoined but separate vowels. You'll find a few of the trickier compounds below.

IU: as in **yo**

IE: **ye** as in **ye**s

UO: **war** as in **war**m

# Glossary

**SUI XING:** An archaic name for the planet Jupiter.

**YAO:** Supernatural beings, ghosts, and spirits—similar to the term "yokai" in Japanese.

**MARA:** A demon from Buddhist mythology associated with darkness and death. In addition to death and destruction, Mara traditionally represents obstruction to enlightenment.

**HU PEOPLE:** Hu is a historical term for non-Han people, sometimes translated as "barbarians." It is often associated specifically with horseback riders from the steppes to the north and west of the Central Plains.

**THREE IMMORTAL SOULS AND SEVEN MORTAL FORMS:** Hun (魂) and po (魄) are two types of souls in Chinese philosophy and religion. Hun are immortal souls that represent the spirit and intellect, and leave the body after death. Po are corporeal souls or mortal forms that remain with the body of the deceased. Different traditions claim there are different numbers of each, but Daoism commonly features three hun and seven po.

**TIMEKEEPING:** For much of Chinese history, time was measured in two-hour increments, starting at 11:00 p.m. The hours in this system are zi, chou, yin, mao, chen, si, wu, wei, shen, you, xu, and hai.

# Timeline of Historical Events

**QIN DYNASTY (221–206 BCE):** The first official dynasty of China that scholars can agree upon. Everything before this (the Three Emperors and Five Sovereigns, the Xia, Shang, and Zhou dynasties) is considered mytho-historical. Qin Shihuang was the first emperor, and the dynasty only lasted through his son before it fell.

**CHU-HAN CONTENTION (206–202 BCE):** Technically composed of two parts—the Eighteen Kingdoms, during which warlords fought for the right to rule, and the Chu-Han period, during which the Chu and Han kingdoms, led by Xiang Yu and Liu Bang respectively, fought. Liu Bang won the decisive Battle of Gaixia in 202 BCE, thus ending the conflict.

**HAN DYNASTY (202 BCE–220 CE):** Established by Liu Bang. It was considered a golden age, and the "Han" name was passed down to the people, the language, and the culture that stemmed from it.

**THREE KINGDOMS (220–280 CE):** A period of conflict where three main kingdoms—Wei (ruled by the Cao family), Wu (ruled by the Sun family), and Shu (ruled by the Liu family)—fought for the right to rule. The conflict technically began with the end of the Han dynasty, with many warlords fighting for the upper hand, but eventually settled into these three factions.

**WESTERN JIN DYNASTY (266–316 CE):** Ruled by the Sima dynasty, who ended the Three Kingdoms era in 280 CE after officially conquering Eastern Wu.

**WAR OF THE EIGHT PRINCES (291–306 CE):** A war fought between eight princes of the Western Jin dynasty, all with the family name Sima, over who would be the regent during the reign of Emperor Hui. The aftermath led to the era of the Sixteen Kingdoms in the north and the reign of the Eastern Jin dynasty in the south.

**UPRISING OF THE FIVE HU (304–316 CE):** This took place in conjunction with the War of the Eight Princes. The combination of all this fighting eventually led to the downfall of the Western Jin dynasty.

**SIXTEEN KINGDOMS/STATES (304–439 CE):** An era in the north where sixteen kingdoms, ruled by a quick succession of Hu and Han both, came and went. The term "Sixteen Kingdoms" is often used in conjunction with the Five Hu, due to the significant role that the Hu played during this time. The dominant kingdom during the time period of *Dinghai Fusheng Records* is the Qin state, led by Fu Jian. (Fu Jian's dynasty is known as the Former Qin in historiographical settings to distinguish it from other, later dynasties also named Qin, but at the time it would have simply been referred to as Qin.)

**EASTERN JIN DYNASTY (317–420 CE):** The period *Dinghai Fusheng Records* is set in. During this period, the two main forces were the Eastern Jin Dynasty in the south and the Qin Dynasty in the north.

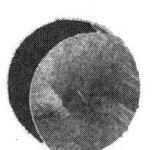